The Tears of Hispaniola

New World Diasporas

Florida A&M University, Tallahassee
Florida Atlantic University, Boca Raton
Florida Gulf Coast University, Ft. Myers
Florida International University, Miami
Florida State University, Tallahassee
University of Central Florida, Orlando
University of Florida, Gainesville
University of North Florida, Jacksonville
University of South Florida, Tampa
University of West Florida, Pensacola

New World Diasporas
Edited by Kevin A. Yelvington

The Tears of Hispaniola

Haitian and Dominican Diaspora Memory

Lucía M. Suárez

University Press of Florida

Gainesville/Tallahassee/Tampa/Boca Raton

Pensacola/Orlando/Miami/Jacksonville/Ft. Myers

A record of cataloging-in-publication data is available from the Library of Congress.
ISBN 0-8130-2926-0
ISBN 0-8130-3052-8 (pbk.)

The University Press of Florida is the scholarly publishing agency for the State University System of Florida, comprising Florida A&M University, Florida Atlantic University, Florida Gulf Coast University, Florida International University, Florida State University, University of Central Florida, University of Florida, University of North Florida, University of South Florida, and University of West Florida.

University Press of Florida
15 Northwest 15th Street
Gainesville, FL 32611-2079
http://www.upf.com

For Blake and Arianna

Contents

Foreword

Migration, diaspora, the circulation in a hypermediated world of recurring images, a sense of cultural fragmentation, of rootlessness longing for and inventing "home"—these are all symptoms of the condition of postmodernity. So, too, are the all-too-real experiences of exile and atrocity, hardship, loss, suffering, and shame. And yet to the burdens of bearing witness to these tragedies through artistic renderings and representations are added the specter of silencing. In the context of evidentiary and ethical relativism—further hallmarks of postmodernity—these imaginings that are revelatory of pain and trauma can simply be ignored or, at best, shouted down, reduced to the status of just a set of self-interested, self-obsessed narratives, dismissed as the stuff of quotidian identity politics.

And yet, as Lucía M. Suárez shows in this book, writers of the Dominican and Haitian diasporas are concerned to challenge this kind of a politics of reception, at the same time as they confront invisibility and interpellate what they construe as salient aspects of "their" past as part of a collective experience to which they are concerned to give voice. Their positionings reverberate as these writers construct a narrated diasporic life by setting, or trying to set, the terms of diasporic discourse with recourse to the past—oftentimes, a past inhabited by images of unspeakable violations that must somehow find a way to be spoken about. How the past is depicted in Caribbean fiction has been a point of focus for Caribbean literary criticism, from C. R. Coulthard's *Raza y color en la literatura antillana* (1958) to Nana Wilson-Tagoe's *Historical Thought and Literary Representation in West Indian Literature* (1998). But it is one of Suárez's main contributions here to place the literary production of diasporic Dominican and Haitian writers under this lens as this corpus has heretofore escaped such a reading. Haunting evocations of the infamous 1937 massacre of Haitians and Dominicans of Haitian descent in the Dominican Republic–Haiti borderlands figure prominently in this corpus, and it is to this theme, among others, that Suárez closely attends. Suárez brings together history, literary, psychoanalytic, and anthropological theory in a concern for the literary imagination's coming to terms with traumas bubbling just under the surfaces of diasporic experiences. For her, *memory* is both the canvas upon which these diasporic writers work and the rubric that drives her own interpretations. Memory can be a positive tool to weave stories of survival and triumph, as well as to expose the banalities of evil and gross criminality, and to try to come to terms with human suffering. But it can also be stifling and limiting, enveloping writer and reader alike in a haze of nostalgia. So, if there is the potential for diasporic writers to use memory to overcome memories, there is the equal potential for them to be prisoners of memory—their own, and of those who would deny them personhood and identity. By invoking a memory analytic, Suárez places herself in a controversial place where there is little agreement as to the utility of memory or even its conceptual status. For instance, in a special issue of *Anthropological Quarterly* (vol. 78, no. 1, Winter 2005) edited by Barbara Rylko-Bauer, entitled "Bringing the Past into the Present: Family Narratives of Holocaust, Exile, and Diaspora," which seeks to mediate on these very themes, there is also an article by David C. Berliner entitled "The Abuses of Memory: Reflections on the Memory Boom in Anthropology" (197–211), where the author questions the imprecise (over)use of memory in the discipline of anthropology. But Suárez intends for memory to be seen as ensconced in a social/cultural (including diasporic) matrix, with the understanding that the politics of recall are overdetermined by sociopolitical contexts. This move offers a bold theoretical-conceptual intervention worthy of the courageous writers who are the subject of this book.

Kevin A. Yelvington
Series Editor

Acknowledgments

This project was begun in the spring of 2001 when I realized that I needed to address the memory of violence and its affect in the Caribbean and its diaspora in a focused, systematic, and urgent manner. Without the strong encouragement, patient readings, and keen commentaries of my friends and colleagues Ruth Behar, Santiago Colás, Jarrod Hayes, Alejandro Herrero-Olaizola, Cristina Moreiras-Menor, Richard Lee Turits, and Michele Wucker, I would not have had the courage to embark on this new work, and later to stick with it. Very special thanks go to them. Thanks also to Ruth Tsoffar, Peggy McCracken and Roger Williams for reading sections of the text at a much earlier stage. Thanks to Jossianna Arroyo, Paulina Alberto, and Jesse Hoffnung-Garskof for their observations later on. I also want to thank Lizabeth Paravisini-Gebert and the anonymous reader for their assiduous evaluation of the manuscript. Their comments aided immensely in revising the book.

In the process of research and writing, many people at conferences, at libraries, and during airplane flights have helped me think through what finally made it to the printed pages here. They are too many to name, but they are gratefully remembered.

Thank you, Merrie Archer of the National Coalition for Haitian Rights, Luz Angela Melo of UNICEF, Évelyne Trouillot of Haiti Solidarité International, Brian Concannon Jr. of BAI, Jean Jonassaint, Guillermo Corsino of the OAS, Raymundo González of the Archivo Nacional, Michele Karshan, the foreign press liaison for the National Palace of Haiti under Aristide, and Sarah Aponte of the Dominican Institute Library at CUNY for informative e-mail correspondence, important contacts, hard-to-get materials, and/or direction with respect to the topics. Thanks are also due to Karla F. C. Holloway for sending me a copy of her book *Passed On: African American Mourning Stories,* which has deeply informed my own thinking.

I have been blessed and honored with generous fellowships that have made the long reading and writing hours possible. At the University of Michigan I received the Rackham Grant and Fellowship Program Award, the Faculty Career Development Award, a research grant from the Office of the Provost and Executive Vice President for Academic Affairs, and an Institute for the Research on Women and Gender Grant. I am particularly grateful to the support, from the beginning of the manuscript writing to the final stages of book production, I have received from Lester Monts.

I received further, critical support for this project thanks to time off arranged by the Department of Romance Languages and Literatures at the University of Michigan, Ann Arbor, and the one-year Woodrow Wilson Faculty Career Enhancement Fellowship.

Cynthia Steele made access to the University of Washington library available. The Richard Hugo House center for writers in Seattle gave me a safe and quiet place to simply sit and write. Thanks for the energy, Tina Hetzel and Frances McCue. Thanks to Cliff Meyer for helping with the finer points of grammar and editing. I am especially grateful to Ann Marlowe, my copyeditor at University Press of Florida, for her expert work. Tom Burnett's help at the Shapiro Library at the University of Michigan is well remembered. The collections and librarians at the Schomburg Center for Research in Black Culture at the New York Public Library made it possible to find the discrepancies of history and the multitudinous stories of Hispaniola.

I remain indebted to WOCAP at the Center for the Education of Women at the University of Michigan for providing emotional and intellectual support. Thank you, Carol Hollenshead, for your knowledge. Being a part of the Autobiography Working Group, IRWG, at the University of Michigan has made all the difference in the ways I've rethought autobiography and testimony. Special thanks go to Sidonie Smith for her frankness and for so generously sharing her own manuscript on testimony and human rights long before its publication.

Many organizations have been extremely generous with their time and resources. Special gratitude goes to Bureau des Avocats Internationaux in Haiti, Dwa Fanm, CARLI (Comité des Avocats pour le Respect des Libertés Individuelles), POHDH (Plateforme des Organizations Haïtiennes des Droits Humains), NCHR (National Coaliton for Haitian Rights), UNICEF (United Nations Children's Fund), Haïti Solidarité Internationale, MUDE (Mujeres en Desarollo Dominicano), PROFAMILIA, CIPAF (Centro de Investigación para la Acción Femenina),and EPICA (Ecumenical Program in Central America and the Caribbean). The work of these mentioned organizations, as well as many others that I have no space to list, is invaluable; I sincerely hope they can continue to be safe havens of information and support despite new waves of violence and political turmoil throughout the island and within the two nations.

Earlier versions of sections of chapters 2 and 4 appeared in *Journal of Haitian Studies*, Fall 2003, vol. 9, no. 2, copyright 2003, and Spring 2005, vol. 11, no. 1, copyright 2005, and is used with permission of the editor. Special thanks go to Claudine Michel for her expert editorial guidance and intellectual support.

The much-loved "nanny time" provided by my mother-in-law, Karin Williams, helped me combine new motherhood with the final writing of this book, and a special acknowledgment is due to her for the mailings of regularly collected newspaper clippings. My parents' intense love has been strengthening. Heartfelt thanks go to Amy Baron, amazing best friend par excellence, for keeping me sane and focused, and to Gabriela Arcila, spiritual sister, for constantly reminding me of the importance of simplicity. My husband, Blake Williams, never let me just put it down, cooked nourishing meals, and believed in me like no one else. Thanks! My lovely daughter, Arianna Lucía Williams, inspires me to keep looking for the good things and ways to mend the bad ones. To her I owe the guiding light that has energized me during the many revisions of this book.

Introduction

The Tears of Hispaniola

It's a wonder I haven't abandoned all my ideals, they seem so absurd and impractical. Yet I cling to them because I still believe, in spite of everything, that people are truly good at heart.

　　It's utterly impossible for me to build my life on a foundation of chaos, suffering, and death. I see the world being slowly transformed into a wilderness, I hear the approaching thunder that, one day, will destroy us too, I feel the suffering of millions. And yet, when I look up at the sky, I somehow feel that everything will change for the better, that this cruelty too shall end, that peace and tranquility will return once more.

—Anne Frank, July 15, 1944

The island of Hispaniola is extremely important in the history of the New World: for example, Haiti was the first free black nation in the Americas. Yet today's Haiti and Dominican Republic have been destroyed by the politics of colonial and postcolonial manipulations, class demarcations, natural disasters, and suffocating dictatorships. The resulting strife has prompted mass migration to lands believed to hold promise of a respite from violence and human degradation.

Twentieth-century migration, in particular, followed periods of repressive dictatorship, in Haiti by the Duvaliers—François "Papa Doc" (1957–71) and Jean-Claude "Baby Doc" (1971–86)—and in the Dominican Republic by Rafael Leonidas Trujillo (1930–61). An earlier peak of Haitian migration to the United States occurred during the U.S. occupation of Haiti (1915–34). Other Dominican migrations were incited by the 1965 civil war and by keen economic hardship experienced from the mid-1980s through the mid-1990s.

In his study of diasporic citizenship, Michel Laguerre notes that tens of thousands of Haitians left their island between 1957, when François Duvalier began his regime, and 1996, when Jean-Bertrand Aristide completed his coup-interrupted first term as president. In the United States, they resettled in cities such as New York, Miami, Chicago, Boston, Los Angeles,

Washington, and New Orleans. The first to leave during the 1950s were escaping political persecution and state violence. Many of these people belonged to the Haitian elite and—unlike recent *balseros*—migrated by airplane. After Castro came to power in Havana, he halted Haitian labor on Cuban sugar plantations in order to end exploitation of neighbors and create more jobs for Cubans; this left huge numbers of Haitians desperate. They too flocked to the United States seeking work. Then the U.S. Civil Rights Act of 1964 encouraged migration by those who dreamed of enjoying broader human rights than the ones they felt were available in their country. In 1971, when Jean-Claude Duvalier had power transferred to him, rural and urban Haitians boarded boats and arrived in large numbers on the Florida shores (Laguerre, *Diasporic Citizenship*, 75–76). While Laguerre's study is focused on migration to the United States, it is noteworthy that many members of the intellectual elite and political opposition chose to go to Canada and wrote about Haiti in French. This information shows that Haitian diaspora communities are composed of a wide array of people who have come from different classes, and have come to their host nations with varying needs and expectations.[1]

In recent investigations of Dominican migration, Ramona Hernández observes that numerous studies between 1970 and 1982 characterized "post-1965 Dominican migrants as predominantly rural, poorly educated, poor and mostly unskilled and jobless" (23). She continues her exposition by examining the work of other researchers (Ugalde, Bean, and Cárdenas), pointing out that most Dominican migrants were from the urban middle-class sector (23). Research completed by the Harvard Immigration Project likewise suggests that migrations from the Dominican Republic included a wide range of classes. Notwithstanding, the two main reasons for migration were, as with Haitian migration, escaping persecution during a brutal dictatorship and seeking economic relief. The Dominican diaspora has become a new and important force in the overall picture of American demographics.[2] The diaspora unity of the inhabitants of Hispaniola, despite the influx of migrants, has remained understudied by scholars in the field.

No study has compared the migration and assimilation patterns of Haitians and Dominicans, despite the similarities in their journey and experience. While I do not directly address this sociological gap in the present book, I show that scholars would benefit from examining the diasporic literary production of the two nations comparatively, exposing the multiple functions of history and memory in Hispaniola's long and fascinating legacy. Hispaniola's diasporic citizens are making a distinctive impact on the ethnic, racial, and religious landscape of the United States. Furthermore, they are challenging mainstream U.S. prejudices from a politically informed position, integrated into their host nation and faithful to their native lands. In this study I show how Haitian and Dominican authors imagine attempts to balance the need to insert themselves into American reality with the desire to remain connected to their native lands and aware of the special role that memory plays in these imagined attempts.

The process of reframing Haitian and Dominican lives in the United States is defined by the act of remembering national culture, history, stories, and traditions within the context of the new homeland. The new frame of reference is shaped somewhat by separate national memories, but particularly by experiences shared across different Caribbean communities. In the diaspora, different national Caribbean realities merge to structure new Pan-Caribbean dialogues.

Caribbean Memories

Previous works exploring Caribbean memory have focused on the way complex and contradictory memories looking back to the Caribbean inform a broken identity in the diaspora. The sociologist Juan Flores, former director of the Center for Puerto Rican Studies at Hunter College, has addressed the uses and misuses of memory and identity construction in his studies of the way that Nuyoricans restore the past according to present needs, maintaining a deeper sense of Puerto Rican identity in the barrio than do relatives on the island. In an essay, "Broken English: Languages of the Trans-Colony," he recounts how Puerto Ricans did not become part of the U.S. national memory until literature giving space to Puerto Rican memory began to appear. He refers to *La Memoria Rota*, by the Puerto Rican literary critic Arcadio Díaz-Quiñones, to propose that broken memory is at the root of all identifications. As Flores notes, "Historical memory is an active, creative force, not just a receptacle for storing the dead weight of times gone by. . . . And the process of memory is open, without closure or conclusion: the struggle to (re)establish continuities and to tell the 'whole' story only uncovers new breaks and new exclusions" (338). Memory, broken because it can never be recovered entirely, entails looking backward to configure the present in some way.

Other uses of memory, like the Cuban-American one, signal the distresses inherent in divided political positioning. Tainted by Cuban exiles' ossification of the past and refusal to accept the present, Cuban-American memory is often politically motivated, with all of its emotional force dedicated to toppling Castro and to the goal of return. It is complicated, or rather balanced, by the realities of a struggling Communist Cuba and by a passionate, humanitarian element to the Cuban diaspora. Cristina García's 1992 novel *Dreaming in Cuban* also serves as a wonderful example of the divisions and tears experienced by Cuban families. The protagonist, a rebellious daughter who wants to learn about her family history, turns out to be the bridge between her revolutionary grandmother (an ardent Castro supporter), her militantly anti-Castro mother, and another relative who retreats into the magical world of the Afro-Cuban Santeria religion.

Some Cuban-American literature tries to reconstruct memories by creating bridges between Cuban-Americans and Cubans. For example, in Ruth Behar's 1994 edited volume *Bridges to Cuba*, memory invokes nostalgia, hope, and creativity. It is fundamental to new conversations, connections, and explorations memorializing the quiet lives lived on both sides of the ocean that separates the Caribbean Cuba and the United States Cuba. In a different vein, Reinaldo Arenas's work decries the repression he experienced in Cuba for his homosexuality. His work highlights the pain of ostracism and imprisonment. It embodies, through fiction and autobiography, a scream so deep that it resonates long after readers put down his books. He screams in pain and in defiance. Until his death—and indeed *with* his death—he repelled Cuba's repressive regime.[3] Conversely, Zoé Valdés's novels show a version of life in Cuba that potentially could be used in an argument against such extreme sanctions as the U.S. embargo, which hurts the people and does nothing to the government. Memories thus refocus our attention on political blunders and individual models of survival and resistance. Creative writing in the Cuban diaspora serves as a venue for public discourse, political denunciation, and a call for change.

In his 2003 study *Voicing Memory: History and Subjectivity in French Caribbean Literature* Nick Nesbitt posits:

> It is here, in the haunting of the present by the past, in which subjects are enchained to their memories, that freedom might be recovered. To write of those who have been stripped of freedom and life itself does not yet free or redeem their premature disappearance but at least denies that their disappearance was absolute. The gift they left behind in others as they passed from this world can then express itself freely as the trace of life that animates our own encounters with the past. (212)

In essence, Nesbitt's exposition of memory is messianic. Memory gives people agency; memory gives history freedom from the dictates of the history writers. I add, one of memory's greatest tasks is to fight the invisibility that comes from silenced stories and buried violations. But a more sustained reflection of memory obliges us to recognize that memory can also be confining. It can be stagnant, unproductive, and detrimentally repetitive. As I show, the memory of violence, if repeated unconsciously and accepted without question in the present, should not be condoned. Memory should not be the excuse for failing to deal with the present *in* the present.

Numerous studies of immigration show that displaced populations often mythologize and ossify the culture and habits of the country left behind. I find it to be a common thread for many Caribbean communities that the notion of home in the Caribbean (for elder generations) and the adoption of the Caribbean as a defining identifier (for the younger generations) generates an intranational sense of responsibility to the Caribbean. Many children of the Caribbean "return" to the island of their childhood, or to the island of their parents, in search of an abandoned world, seeking to match the emotional family memories to the geographic place. But this is not possible. The island that was left long ago has, like any place in the world, changed dramatically. Some countries, like Haiti, have suffered extreme political corruption and decay. Others, like the Dominican Republic, have become tourist centers that gloss over their deep poverty. Yet others, such as Guadeloupe, Martinique, and Puerto Rico, are in a constant renegotiation of postcolonial "colonial status" with the metropolis, here France and the United States respectively. These new images and struggles often demand new attention. Caribbean intellectuals and writers are thus confronted with the shifting framework of history and experience.

Haitian and Dominican Caribbean diaspora memory has not received the kind of attention other Caribbean diasporas, such as the Puerto Rican and Cuban ones, have received. Despite groundbreaking work by pioneers such as Eugenio Matibag and Michele Wucker, I remain astounded by the relative paucity of comparative studies of Haitian and Dominican experiences. With this study, I aim to remedy that. I look to Hispaniola and suggest that this is a literature that lays bare the tears of pain and exposes the traumatic tears between families, homelands, and memories.

Addressing human rights issues, my book makes the case for the central rethinking of memory as a meditation on what was left behind, what exists today, and the ensuing negotiations between life on the island and life in the diaspora. I examine some of the horrible pasts that haunt many of the people of Hispaniola's diaspora to show how Haitians and Dominicans engage in a unique kind of memory departing from traumatic experiences and to further point to the importance of investigating the literary production of these neighboring countries from a comparative point of view.[4]

My critical study exposes the dual nature inherent to Haitian and Dominican memory. I point to a duality that has guaranteed the survival of religions, traditions, and communities, and I examine the process of reinterpretation that is often necessary for this survival and ensuing resistance. Joan Dayan offers a cogent example of this duality in Haitian history. In her 1995 book *Haiti, History, and the Gods*, she tells how Dessalines came to have at least two meanings for Haitians. The great leader Dessalines was killed in an ambush, his body torn to pieces and later buried in a meagerly marked grave. But Dessalines is also the only Haitian leader to have been transformed into a *lwa*, or god, by the Haitian people. He is, then, both dead (killed as a historical human being) and living (consecrated as a god). Dayan also tells of a song that honors Dessalines in which a line is repeated: "Dessalines, Dessalines démembré." This line is important because *démembré* in Kreyòl means dismembered, battered, and beaten. But ethnographers such as Alfred Métraux, Odette Mennesson-Rigaud, and Lorimer Denis all claim that it refers to his power. Thus, Dessalines is both beaten and powerful (Dayan 31). Dayan concludes:

> The history told by these traditions defies our notions of *identity* and *contradiction*. A person or thing can be two or more things simultaneously. A word can be double, two-sided, and duplicitous. In this broadening and multiplying of a word's meaning, repeated in rituals of devotion and vengeance, we begin to see that what becomes more and more vague also becomes more distinct: it may mean *this*, but *that* too. (33)

This duality of meaning is also reflected in the Haitian *vodou* concept of the *marassa*. *Marassa* is defined as spirit twins, or child spirits. They are inseparable, conflicted, and in solidarity. Could we not interpret the two nations of Hispaniola as a *marassa*? Could solidarity not be developing in the diaspora as stories and migration link the two countries' experiences, memories, and incessant returns?

It is with these questions in mind that I offer the linking metaphor of tears. *Tear* performs a double duty, being a noun and a verb, defining an emotional condition and a heartbreaking act. As Dayan proposes, a word—

she mentions *démembré*—can be two-sided. A word can make a concept nebulous, and it can also make it concise; it can mean this and it can mean that. The tear on the face symbolizes grief and exasperation. To tear with the hands is an action that could signal desperation and/or violence. The act of tearing oneself from a homeland ridden with poverty and corruption is very real. I have no doubt that tears are shed upon arrival in the new country, from pure exhaustion and from fear of what the future may hold. I perceive tears as a complex metaphor that discloses depression, disillusion, exasperation, and powerlessness; tears also signal the sociocultural, political mechanisms that tear apart individual lives, families, communities, and nations. For the fiction writers and the memoirist that I study in this book, the duality unveiled by tears—in history, in memory, in text—is crucial for their inventions and their lives.

I propose in this book that, while both Haiti and the Dominican Republic have suffered the violations of dictatorship and continue to struggle with poverty and general violence, these are remembered, or forgotten, differently for numerous reasons. In contrast to a Haitian tradition of disclosure of misery and violence, the politics of silence—or rather denial—have been dominant in Dominican memory. For example, Haiti has produced a truth commission that reviewed the blatant atrocities committed during the 1991–94 period of military dictatorship. In addition, Haitian writers, who cannot ignore the strife their country experiences, have constantly produced work exposing the tragedy of Haitian life. In contrast, the Dominican Republic has continuously rejected any investigation into covert human rights infringements during the Balaguer years. Historical compilations such as Bernardo Vega's extensive work on Dominican history and politics, and René Fortunato's 1991 documentary film *El poder del jefe*, do offer insight into the complexity of Dominican politics. Still, the missing voice of women, Haitian Dominicans, and homosexuals glares blatantly at any researcher seeking a more complex interhistory of Dominican lives.

Notably, the effects of violence was the subject of only two Dominican texts, *Over* (1939) by Ramón Marrero Aristy and *El masacre se pasa a pie* (1973) by Freddy Prestol Castillo. In general, it would seem that Dominican literature has traditionally ignored the violence and strife the country continues to experience. Instead it has focused on romantic, myth-forming stories. This is substantiated by the position taken by authors like Julia Alvarez. For example, at a book tour presentation at Duke University in 1998, Alvarez stated flatly that she was not interested in reviewing violence through her work—even though her story of the Mirabal sisters, for example, departs from a violent act. Her intention in writing about them was not, she tells us, to look at the violence but rather to honor their brave lifework. Recently the works of Nelly Rosario and Viriato Sención have pointed to violence in Dominican culture. Junot Díaz confronts violence, in the United States and on the island, head-on. As I show in my book, it is at this pivotal moment of exposure that a new literary tradition is born.

In particular, I have chosen to demonstrate the persistent trauma caused by violence in Haitian and Dominican experience. The effects of this violence, I argue, are exposed in a detailed fashion by the characters in the novels and the narrator in the autobiography. Through a close investigation of losses, memory, and violence, I suggest that we consider the impossibility of mourning that surfaces from the stories. Consequently, I propose that the process of writing, for the authors, and reading, for us, actualizes the possibility of mourning.

Memorialization

When I started the research and writing of this book, I set out to find the ways in which literature intervenes constructively against a landscape of death, loss, and violence, which the island of Hispaniola and its diaspora have inherited. As a critic, reader, and human rights advocate, I intended my first readings of the texts and analyses of the characters to expand on what I believed to be a foundational message offered by Hispaniola's diaspora literature: if violence and its memory cannot be halted, it must be challenged. Importantly, I have discovered that this literature also offers a significant overview of myths, fantasies, and realities that imposes a need for memory. However, when memory is unattainable, the real need lies in the process of "memorialization," giving literary voice to the lost and/or reframed points of history and to the ever-present scars of violence. The literature produced by the Haitian and Dominican diaspora is thus a monument to Hispaniola's tears—those tears shed because of human suffering, and the geographic and/or physical tears imposed by national borders and migrations.

Stories of terror, dictatorships, and calls for democracy populate our television screens and our imaginations. At issue, for me, is not the general display of horrors but the ways those horrors manifest themselves in the present for different diaspora groups. I have strategically chosen to explore these concerns via specific texts—*The Farming of Bones* (1998) and *Breath, Eyes, Memory* (1994) by Edwidge Danticat, *Drown* (1996) by Junot Díaz, *Restavec: From Haitian Slave Child to Middle-Class American* (1998) by Jean-Robert Cadet, and *Geographies of Home* (1999) by Loida Maritza Pérez—that are particularly focused on violence.[5] As my analyses in this book show, the issues at hand—erasure of subaltern histories, rape, child slavery, family violence and sexism, invisibility of particular groups—cannot be exposed with a simple textual reading.

In order to analyze the function of memory, I have purposefully brought together literature whose authors expose the ways violence, past and present, bleeds into people's lives. I propose that these particular memories underscore both a deep need for a space of mourning and an equally urgent need to engage in constructive sociopolitical action. My methodological approach undertakes sustained readings of specific texts for an emphatically focused examination of the affects and effects of the memory of violence exposed through diaspora literature.

The texts of the Haitian and Dominican diaspora serve as points of deep meditation that I suggest make many linkages and must be read intertextually and transhistorically. I propose that the texts of autobiography and fiction offer us alternative modes of memory. They expose the tears of suffering, the multiple ways violence tears at nations, communities, and people; the texts also advocate the possibility of life freed of violence. The literature of the diaspora unveils the continuing effect of human rights infringements on survivors and their offspring, long after they have emigrated. Arguably, violence's greatest legacy is the dark lacuna it leaves us with.

Therefore my readings, focused on Haiti and the Dominican Republic, propose that autobiography and fiction create a space through which the struggles of present-pasts are addressed. Some diaspora literature also points to how Caribbean enclaves in the United States experience and/or reproduce the systemic dysfunctional conditions they have escaped such as racism, sexism, and violence. With the presence of so much violence, stories of survival and narrative restructuring of horrors may be the only route to reconciliation and reconstruction of personal and national memory and integrity. Perhaps the novels and autobiographies of the diaspora are monuments to personhood; perhaps they highlight human hope and resilience; ideally they fight for human rights and envision citizenship for all of the people of the world. But, in effect, diaspora literature divulges the limitations of memory as well as the need for memory.

Hispaniola's Memory

Haiti has a long tradition of what some critics, following Joan Dayan, refer to as literature of misery, through which the ills of Haitian society and a cry for justice are detailed. Literary theorist Jean Jonassaint has traced a national tradition of Haitian literature of "tragedy" via the works of Alexis, Cinéas, Hibbert, Lespès, Marcelin, Roumain, Thoby-Marcelin, Chauvet, Depestre, Frankétienne, and others. Of note are the works of earlier Haitian diaspora writers, exiled for political reasons in Canada. For example, Gérard Étienne's *Cri pour ne pas mourir de honte* (1982) interpolates the extreme pain caused by the Duvalier reign of terror poetically and poignantly.

Some critics make a distinction between a Haitian national literature, written in French, and Haitian-American literature written in English. More recently, however, Haitian-American literature, like Danticat's, is included within the context of Haitian national literature. This points to yet another duality. Haitian authors writing from other countries belong to both their new countries and their native land. Furthermore, even if their works represent Haitian issues, their stories are globally African-Caribbean stories in the Americas, inclusively. Their diasporic, and thus global, condition is demarcated by the fact that many Haitian authors do not stay in one city or country. For example, Danny Laferrière, who had been based in Canada, was most recently living in Florida, while traveling a lot, especially to France. Edwidge Danticat, who was raised in Brooklyn, lives in Florida as of this writing. Does this mean that there is a new diaspora in Florida? Florida has had a large and very well organized Haitian community for years. But I believe that the authors' choices to move reflects a more complicated, and further unrooted, diaspora situation. Consequently, diaspora literature does not expose one diaspora but rather multiple and multiplying diasporas in constantly shifting conversation with different local and global communities, geographies, and languages. In this context, Haitian diaspora literature intersects with many literary canons including Haitian national literature, U.S. immigrant literature, African-American literature, and Caribbean literature.

Similarly, Dominican-American literature should be contextualized within several literary canons, most notably Latino/a literatures, Spanish-Caribbean literature, and also Latin American literature. Studies of Dominican literature have, until recently, maintained a distinction between

Dominican literature and Latino/a-Dominican literature. Doris Sommer's study of patriarchal rhetoric, for example, focused exclusively on novels written in Spanish by authors exclusively based on the island. However, Daisy Cocco de Filippis includes writers from both the island and the diaspora in her 2000 study *Documents of Dissidence: Selected Writings by Dominican Women*. This underscores the intertextual, interhistorical, and intergeographic nature of the literatures I am working with.

A central theme that has thus arisen for me is: What memories are most salient in the comparative diaspora production of Hispaniola? Haitian and Dominican Caribbean diaspora literature, written in English in the United States, plays a fundamental role in challenging the long history of violence and human disenfranchisement that haunts Caribbean memory and reality.[6] Hispaniola's diaspora writers, I put forth, are pioneers in the manner in which they address traumatic events in new ways that seek to transform them. Memory does not belong only to the past, even if it is disclosed in the process of looking backward. The task of remembering is a political one. Diaspora literature, I insist, refuses to let the violence of the past be buried. It tells the stories of those who might have been and perhaps indeed did exist. Readers are reminded of the pain of violence and, as I interpret it, are asked to dream of possibility, to change the tears of oppression and powerlessness into a deep body—an ocean—of (re)constructive human rights work. While physical monuments have not yet been erected to commemorate the abuse and/or death of thousands, enacted during different repressive regimes, different military occupations, and/or from continuing violence throughout the Caribbean, Haitian and Dominican Caribbean, diaspora writing offers a venue for rethinking the ways to remember and memorialize Caribbean transatlantic experience and history.[7]

Human rights groups have cited both countries for practices such as deep government corruption, child slavery, and violence against women. Haiti draws a considerable amount of bad press on these issues, while the Dominican Republic receives less international attention for its human rights infringements. Both countries suffer from poverty and child slavery. The Dominican Republic has a growing problem with sex tourism, which is in sharp contrast to the high-end tourism known to most U.S. and European visitors. Still, there are formidable people working for solutions. Bringing important human rights infringements out of the shadows of shame into a public forum for discussion, and possible redress, is a first step toward finding resolutions that may change the dire circumstances of the poorest people on the island. Through the voices of Hispaniola's diaspora writers, the divisive rhetoric about the island's people and continuing human rights crimes is being challenged.

Despite a repeated rhetoric of national differences on the island, both diaspora communities are marked most by memories of surviving extreme violence brought on by brutal dictatorships, cold war policies, and increasing poverty and public desperation in their homelands. In addition, in the diaspora, individuals encounter the paradoxes of democracy. While "democracy" was blatantly crushed in their countries, its advantages are not automatically available in the United States, in part because classism and racism often preclude opportunities for many darker-skinned immigrants. These transferred communities find themselves caught between the struggle for a new life in a new place and the need to help family and friends back home. They begin to uncover different ways to view their citizenship status—how they are documented and which community they belong to, both here (the United States) and there (the island)—and to review the artificial antagonism that has been set up between Haiti and the Dominican Republic by a few ruling elite.

It is my contention that diaspora literature offers a critical location to meditate on Haitian and Dominican pasts and to confront Hispaniola's intersecting, diaspora presents. A number of Haitian and Dominican diaspora texts lay bare the experiences of memory, trauma, and pain as central themes that shape Haitian and Dominican (island and diaspora) individual and community identities. Joan Dayan, Myriam Chancy, and Jean Jonassaint, for example, have provided us with excellent studies, interrogating one theme via various texts. My work complements the existing body of scholarship by offering a detailed, systematic study of the deep pain and complexity of memory experienced by Haitian and Dominican diaspora communities as private histories are revealed in individual texts and read alongside other textual guardians of memory such as historical accounts and social documents.

Danticat and Vega: Two Points of View

The epistolary correspondence between Haitian-African-American creative writer Edwidge Danticat and historian Bernardo Vega reveals the deep complexity of memory and the varying modes employed to memorialize the past. The correspondence, published on the Web page of the Dominican newsmagazine *Hoy*,[8] refers to the two ways they interpreted and wrote about the history of the massacre of Haitians on the Dominican border in 1937. The introduction to the correspondence informs us that Danticat and Vega met at a conference in 1998 at the University of Georgia, during which time Danticat was finishing her novel *The Farming of Bones*. Vega later sent her a copy of the French version of his book about the massacre, *Trujillo et Haiti*, volume 1. In their cordial correspondence, Vega thanks Danticat for having cited him in her novel. Novelists are not, after all, obligated to name any sources. He continues, however, to express consternation about her representation of the Dominican people in her novel. He notes that one comes away from her story with the impression that civil society approved and participated in such a horrible genocide. He underlines the fact that it was a military order issued by Trujillo and executed by his army. Vega writes that many Dominicans were terrified and hid during the massacre. Others, despite their fear, hid Haitians in their homes, saving their lives. Consequently, Vega concludes, Danticat is inaccurate and misleading in her novel when she describes a scene in which the Dominicans spit on Haitians and force them to pronounce the word *perejil* (a Spanish word that will reveal a Kreyòl or French accent). The scene renders the Dominicans not only complicit in the massacre but also active in it. To this contention, Danticat responds that she emphasizes in her talks that Trujillo's orders led to the actions by the nation's army. However, she adds, some of the archived testimonies she read make it difficult for her to believe that no friends or relatives of the soldiers participated in the killings. Furthermore, the soldiers wore civilian clothes and used machetes for their killings, never a gun. This made the massacre appear to be the result of a local uprising. Danticat points to the comparable situation in Haiti in which the Tonton Macoutes existed and functioned by following Duvalier's orders and with the express help of some in the civilian population.[9] Some civilians, she asserts, must have been involved in the massacre.

Danticat tells Vega, with all due respect, that she does not mean to misrepresent Dominican history. However, she cannot forget that the only time in her life that she witnessed her great-uncle cry was when the word *perejil* was used by Dominicans to slander José Francisco Peña Gómez during his candidacy for president. His opponents claimed that he was an infiltrated Haitian and would ask him to say the word in order to ridicule him. Danticat's great-uncle confessed that he had been a cane cutter and that he had been subjected to that test of language and national belonging.[10] He requested that she not use his name in her book, because the memory brought him shame and horror. Other than at that moment, he never ever mentioned his tribulation with *perejil* and ostracism in the Dominican Republic in all his eighty-nine years.

From a "historical" perspective, both Danticat's novel and her uncle's memory bring many problems to the fore.

The reframing of the past via a novel is resisted and/or rejected when historians point to specifics. For example, historian Richard Turits argues that those killed at the border were not cane cutters but rather small subsistence farmers, as the northern border areas are mountainous and not suited to cane plantations (161). Furthermore, many of those killed in the 1937 massacre were ethnic Haitians, since most were Dominican born and had lived in the Dominican Republic for generations (148–49).

The *corte*, as the massacre is called, played a very large role in dividing peoples in the frontier region, which was otherwise quite tranquil. Indeed, both Freddy Prestol Castillo in his novel/testimony *El masacre se pasa a pie* and Doris Sommer in her 1983 critical study *One Master for Another: Populism as Patriarchal Rhetoric in Dominican Novels* must admit, despite their own philosophies, that prior to the massacre, the border had not really been pronounced. The people were not divided. With respect to Prestol Castillo's text, Sommer observes:

> And his objections to the traditional subsistence farmers on the frontier, who are unpatriotic to be sure and thus retard the national interests, are tempered by the narrator's appreciation for the decency of their life style. They are productive on communal lands, as they respect each other, the land and their animals. (184)

That is, despite Freddy Prestol Castillo's proclaimed belief that the two nations would be better off clearly divided, his text admits that the people on the frontier were not divided at all. In fact, they got along very well. Sommer's study intends to recontextualize Prestol Castillo into another kind of division between land and patriarch (father-figure, dictator, patriarch). But in this particular instance she fails to make a convincing argument, I believe, because the division between Haitians (ethnic or newly arrived) and Dominicans on the border, like the division between the land and the patriarch, is artificially constructed for those in the frontier region, who before the massacre were not affected by divisive discourse or Trujillo's later manipulations.

The peace that had existed in the pre-1937 frontier is best described by newer studies. Addressing the emphasis on the pronunciation of *perejil*, which played a distinctive role in dividing the two nations, even if imaginarily at first, Turits notes that it is both calculated and performative:

> by acting as if this [pronunciation] test was clear and efficacious, the killers imputed to their victims radical cultural difference that served to rationalize the violence and ethnicize images of the nation. Thus violence in the Haitian massacre and the discourse within which it took place were themselves performances that helped constitute notions of inherent and transhistorical difference between Haitians and Dominicans. (165)

In linguistic terms, the pronunciation of *perejil* as a litmus test of national belonging is emphatically artificial. For example, third-generation Haitians can speak exactly like those around them. Furthermore, Dominicans do not pronounce r's and other consonants clearly. This is exemplified by Prestol Castillo's phonetic reproduction of Dominican language in his text. One of the characters screams "Saigentooooo" for *sargento*.[11]

Regardless of how we would like to review history, the three explications (Prestol Castillo's, Sommer's, and Turits's) highlight the ways that memories of the frontier and its people have been manipulated in an attempt to render a coherent, if not rational, story of what happened in 1937 and why it happened.

In my estimation, what is clear is that a terrible horror destroyed the peace that existed among the people of the frontier. No doubt, different people were affected by the incident differently. Therefore I suggest that, when we analyze Danticat's novel, we keep the inaccuracies of memory and socially constructed histories in mind. It could be argued, in agreement with Vega, that she misrepresents history. Turits reminds us that there were no plantations in Dajabón. Yet we could ask: Were the farms remembered as plantations? It could be argued that her uncle did not cut cane in the northern frontier region but somewhere else. Perhaps, even, he did cut cane, but his experience took place long after the massacre. Dominicans might have used the test of *perejil* to humiliate him, following a tradition established by the massacre. These are the historical conundrums, I believe, that frustrate the memory of the massacre. A further frustration is propelled by the fact that both Haitians and Dominicans don't really want to remember this buried, bloody episode. It is thus very difficult to recover details.

The correspondence between Danticat and Vega demonstrates the distinction between narrative and history. As Shoshana Felman argues,

"What we call history we usually conceive of as a discipline of inquiry and as a mode of knowledge. What we call narrative we usually conceive of as a mode of discourse and as a literary genre" (Felman and Laub, 93). Following Barbara Hernstein Smith's argument, Felman informs us that the occurrence of the event is history and that the telling of that occurrence is narrative. This neat distinction is immediately subverted when Felman records Hegel's position: "The term history . . . unites the objective and the subjective side, and denotes . . . not less what *happened* than the *narration of what happened*" (93). In other words, the distinction between history and narrative is not as evident as we may want it to be. However, if we follow Felman's essay on to the point of her analysis, we do come away with an important issue. When reading Camus's *The Plague*, she argues,

> Since we can literally witness only that which is within the reach of the conceptual frame of reference we inhabit, the Holocaust is testified to by *The Plague* as an event whose specificity resides, precisely, in the fact that *it cannot, historically, be witnessed*. . . . It is precisely because history as holocaust proceeds from a *failure to imagine*, that it takes an *imaginative* medium like the plague to gain an insight into its historical *reality*, as well as into the attested historicity of its unimaginability. (104–5)

The point is that the literary text, a novel, has significant, symbolic importance precisely because a traumatic event can no longer be witnessed. The novel conceptualizes the horrors without claiming firsthand experience. Similarly, the possible details of the horrors and the aftermath of the 1937 massacre reside precisely in Danticat's novel *The Farming of Bones*. It cannot be denied that that massacre was followed by other massacres, less notorious but equally debilitating. It also became both the reason and the excuse for later divisions and violence acted against newly arrived Haitians and ethnic Haitians in the Dominican Republic.

The horror that Danticat writes about can neither be witnessed nor proved. However, she does witness the effect that the 1937 massacre has had on the Haitian and Dominican people. Danticat's story addresses the memory and pain of violence that she has witnessed at critical times, such as seeing the tears shed by her great-uncle and hearing his confession. I contend that the creative writer, writing a memorial fiction, is perhaps obligated to present the misinformation of memory in contrast to the exact accounts offered by history, in this case to honor a deceased uncle. Danticat represents the pain of history and how that inflicts memory; in contrast,

Vega is obligated by profession to script history. Danticat's stories are personal, complex, even contradictory, while Vega's writing still believes in an objective rendering of the past that is nonetheless riddled with inconsistencies.

At issue is how the past is built on stories of tears that both divide and unify Haitians and Dominicans. Danticat's great-uncle suffered a severe trauma, and we will never know the effects on his internal, psychological life. Vega's writing of history details the past, but Danticat's writing of fiction memorializes that past by bringing it into the present, complicating the possible meanings of what happened, and exposing the multiple aspects of how the happenings affected different people. In particular, her novels underscore how the pain of the past continues to affect, consciously or unconsciously, the present.[12] I suggest that we have something to gain by deemphasizing the issue of historical accuracy and emphasizing instead the effects and affects of historical experiences of violence on individual memory, community building and destruction, and nationalism. What pain (*dolor/douleur/deuil*) has been grafted onto the lives and memories of these nations and their people?

The writings of Danticat, Díaz, Cadet, and Pérez that I am examining direct our gaze to the impossibility of mourning for individuals. The horrors of violence leave the victims and survivors, like Danticat's great-uncle, in various states of suspension—a repeated suspended past, as in trauma, and/or a suspended and undisclosed past, when forgetting/erasing the terrible incident. Fiction and testimony, I propose, are fundamental political acts of resistance that create a narrative space for these experiences of horror, and thus bring to the narrative the memory and the experience of that horror. Arguably, the narratives that I scrutinize take charge of trauma, exposing the ways trauma manifests itself (via the characters) and offering a demythification of that haunting present-past (via my critical intervention, using the text as the key to escaping what I call the prison-house of memory).

Remembering Horror

Let us for a moment consider the implications of two critical points about trauma and post-traumatic stress syndrome as proposed by English professor and literary critic Cathy Caruth and by psychologist Judith Herman, who are two leading researchers of trauma.[13] In the introduction to her 1995 text *Trauma: Explorations in Memory* Caruth underscores the literality and nonsymbolic nature of traumatic dreams and flashbacks, whereby a cure is resisted. Trauma, she posits, is constituted by literality and insistent return, "the delay or incompletion of knowing, or even in seeing, an overwhelming occurrence that then remains, in its insistent return, absolutely *true* to the event" (5). Caruth proposes that since the "truth" of the traumatic experience shapes the pathology or symptoms, it is not a pathology of falsehood or displacement of meaning, but rather it is a symptom of history. She explains, "The traumatized, we might say, carry within them, or they become themselves the symptom of, a history that they cannot entirely possess" (5).

Herman remarks, "In avoiding any situations reminiscent of the past trauma, or any initiative that might involve future planning and risk, traumatized people deprive themselves of those new opportunities for successful coping that might mitigate the effect of the traumatic experience"; constrictive symptoms, initially intended to defend the sufferer (survivor, victim, witness) from an overwhelming emotional state, in fact "narrow and deplete the quality of life and ultimately perpetuate the effects of the traumatic event" (47).

According to these considerations of trauma and its effects, temporality is a central concern. The victims/survivors of horrible events either reify the past horror into a continuing, conscious or unconscious, present state of repeated violence and fear, or they bury the horror and remain haunted in less visible but equally debilitating ways. Comparably, the effects of migration in many cases create a system of memory based on a frozen image of a past reality, of a country that has since the time of migration changed considerably. If that frozen memory is further informed by violence, the trauma becomes very difficult to define. In particular, diaspora citizens often hold on to memories of the homeland that are myths, filled with gaps of information and provable history. The present is the essential moment for all considerations of trauma, and the literary representation of the traumatic experience highlights this. The past cannot be reproduced, but the effects of the past can be reconstructed. With *The Tears of Hispaniola*, I ask that we examine traumatic history in diaspora communities from three perspectives: a reading of the characters, an analysis of the function of the text, and my critical intervention weaving histories, characters, and textual studies.

A Haitian Story and a Dominican Story

The experience of history is manifold and often in direct opposition to the writings of history. Arguably, the impossibility of knowledge of the past addressed by Caruth and Herman is at the root of the problem with history. Furthermore, history is always limited in many ways by the ideal of truthful accounting. I suggest that we look to the genre of fiction to supplement history, and thus achieve a more complete picture of the insidiousness of violence and the legacy of trauma. Because literature brings the past to the present, it memorializes that past and demolishes the simplicity that trauma theories are limited by.

For example, the work of literary critic, novelist, and artist Myriam Chancy is informed by her motherland, Haiti, almost exclusively, despite the years spent in the United States and her present residence in Canada. In 1997 her study *Framing Silence: Revolutionary Novels by Haitian Women* became the first critical book to forge a distinctive space for the hitherto silenced voices of Haitian women, thus reframing their memories. With this autobiographical and critical text Chancy tells us:

> The creation of identity in the face of imperialist and colonial oppression begins with the transmutation of the personal into the creative, into modes of self-empowerment that in and of themselves create a theory of self-definition. . . . Haitian women writers have . . . created a vision of Haitian women in fictional form that corresponds to a feminized reading of the history of our country. . . . This reflects a political strategy used not only to create a sense of extra-textual intimacy, but also to create a space within the parameters of the genre that redefines national identity in terms of the personal. (6)

It is of particular interest for my argument that Chancy begins her text with a story she has made up and refers to it throughout her study to signal the way fiction informs, and therefore recasts, history. Chancy tells the story of a little girl she names Solange, who had the fortune to live with parents who allowed her to sit in the Piazza in front of the Palais, where electricity and light were available. There the little girl did her homework, reading about Haitian history, unaware that she herself would soon become part of the lesser-told history when killed. Solange's story, Chancy tells us, is inspired by Paul Farmer's account of the real death of Roseline Vaval, who at age eleven was killed by the army in the town of Petit Goâve: "Her death became symbolic of the repression perpetuated by the army under General Prosper Avril, from 1988 to 1990, through the same dictatorial means established so thoroughly by the Duvalier patri-archs" (4). Chancy's story of Solange becomes symbolic of the many little girls who have been killed or maimed but never acknowledged. Chancy rewrites the story of Solange throughout her study to remind herself "and the reader of the connection between history and storytelling, between Haitian women's lives and the ways in which narrative enables Haitian women writers to preserve those lives" (5). With writing, Chancy ac-knowledges, she inserts herself into academic language and international history. Her writing enables the voices of Haiti to be recovered from the abyss of ignorance. Solange could be any girl reading by the lamppost be-cause there is no electricity in her house. Solange could be any girl who cannot even get a book or find the time to sit, doing chores, experiencing abuse, and being obliterated from the possibility of memory. Chancy muses:

> Solange is not real: she exists in my unconscious. Solange is too real: she exists in your mind and in your heart. Solange is the sun in the midst of despair: she exists. Solange is dignity personified: she is our moral conscious. (166)

I would argue that this kind of literary nexus is fundamental to under-standing the point of origin of diaspora literature: Solange could be Chancy, writing the memories to honor the dead and give way to the liv-ing. It is not a coincidence that, in her conclusion, Chancy reveals her own tears, for tears are a key element of diaspora solidarity:

> Haitian women writers have endeavored to testify to both the tri-umphs and sufferings of their class, but they have done so at great personal risk and in the face of unrelenting persecution. . . . Trinh's words ["Writing in the feminine. And on a colored sky"], like the lyrics of Sade's song ["Sade sings of a colored sky, a blue sky turned red by the force of her emotions. We know that the sky is a mirror for the blue of the world's oceans; similarly, it is a canvas on which we project our feelings and emotions—shaking our fists when it tears into rain"], fall on my ears like rainfall, like tear drops. (171–72)

Chancy tells us that, despite the blue skies, the true contours of women's lives in the Third World and in the Haitian African diaspora are red. From reading all of her works, I understand that Chancy's tears are from pain (caused by the knowledge of continuing violence and violations) and defiance (she will tell stories and work against violence despite the risks she too runs).

I agree with Chancy that stories present the world with a complex groundwork for memory. This is especially true for cultures whose primary access to history is oral. It is necessary to underscore how stories are instrumental to the formation of knowledge when "facts" have been manipulated or simply obliterated. But this work cannot be accomplished in a vacuum. Furthermore, one analysis of a select group of writers and their works calls for further exploration of other texts as these writers enter a dialogue exposing the unspoken and traumatic, creating a venue for multiple memories and strategies of survival.

Fiction produces possibility precisely because it does not follow rules of representation. By extension, it may capture more of the nuances of unknowable history. For example, Julia Alvarez's 1994 novel *In the Time of the Butterflies* represents a bold attempt to recuperate the stories of women from the oblivion of mythification. Tellingly, she attempts to do this through storytelling:

> what you will find here are the Mirabals of my creation, made up but, I hope, true to the spirit of the real Mirabals. In addition, though I had researched the facts of the regime, and events pertaining to Trujillo's thirty-one-year despotism, I sometimes took liberties—by changing dates, by reconstructing events, and by collapsing characters or incidents. For I wanted to immerse my readers in an epoch in the life of the Dominican Republic that I believe can only finally be understood by fiction, only finally be redeemed by the imagination. A novel is not, after all, a historical document, but a way to travel through the human heart. (324)

Writing about the Mirabal sisters honors the work they did against the Trujillo dictatorship. But after reading and teaching the text numerous times over the years, I cannot help but wonder whether the liberties Alvarez took in changing the "facts" of Trujillo's despotism served to soften the extreme cruelty suffered under his reign.[14] Perhaps her effort to honor the sisters and reach the human heart necessitated that she avoid detailing the violence experienced by women during this period. I wonder if Alvarez's literary liberties do not reflect a deeper incision of pain, such as traumatic silence. I believe that Alvarez feels a certain level of fear in visiting the horrors of the country's past, and that the silenced horrors remain silent precisely because of the extent of the "unknowns" of the circumstances she barely remembers. This Dominican-American author exemplifies the effects of the unknown, developed in the theory of trauma by Caruth. While Alvarez retells the story of the Mirabal sisters—national heroines of mythic (and therefore unknowable) proportions in the Dominican Republic—she underscores the impossibility of recuperating the true violence enacted against these women. They died when the car they were in drove over a cliff. Supposedly this was set up. The husbands, who were in jail as political prisoners, had been transferred to a distant prison, and the sisters were then informed they could visit. No witness or document exists to disclose the deaths. Some speculate that the sisters were first molested, then killed, then put in the car and rolled over. Others believe that the car was forced to drive over the cliff. The trauma for Alvarez may be that she cannot access the truth of the sisters' lives and death. In contrast to the undeniable violence experienced during the 1991 coup d'état, Dominicans witness the double violence of the initial, insidious violation and the ensuing amnesia—because it has been so effectively reframed and thus erased—of that violation. In that space of selective amnesia, symbolic of the unknown, Dominicans must fight a double trauma. There is the initial murder and then inaccessibility of accurate information about the murder. Alvarez tries to recuperate the Mirabal sisters from mythification, only to mythify them further, blurring further the violence of Trujillo's dictatorship. Still the violated memory cries; it must be remembered. In order for violence to be battled in the present, its long historical trajectory must be exposed, reprimanded, and changed. This, it seems, is the legacy diaspora writers from the Dominican Republic have inherited.

Autobiographical Memory

While most of my book draws its argument from fiction, I have found it to be of critical importance that I also examine a personal testimony, because this informs Hispaniola's diaspora memory in a very pressing manner. In chapter 4, I examine Jean-Robert Cadet's autobiography to situate Cadet's life-storytelling as a mode of memory that gives testimony to a particular personal past that—since the restavèk practice is still strong in Haiti—can be witnessed in the present.

Cadet's autobiography, offered as a testimony against an inhuman practice, was written, he tells us, with the goal of denunciation in order to change the "crime." In the process of telling, Cadet is caught up in several struggles: truth, motive, and personal pain, which not only cannot be escaped but is further aggravated by the political-theoretical debate around testimony itself. On a personal level, psychiatrist Dori Laub tells us, the process of testimony is "essentially a ceaseless struggle" (Felman and Laub 75). Laub explains:

> The imperative to tell and to be heard can become itself an all-consuming life task. . . . There are never enough words or the right words, there is never enough time or the right time, and never enough listening or the right listening to articulate the story that cannot be fully captured in *thought, memory, and speech* (78).

This constant retelling of a life experience is a form of trauma that traps its victim in a nightmare past, despite the initial goal of telling to heal. We will see in these pages that the text itself, by its very repetition of abuse, discloses this trap of traumatic memory.

On a theoretical level, Cadet's case is critical to a study of Caribbean memory in the present precisely because it comes up against a devastating impasse: the violence he denounces is part of his past, but it is also a very strong part of many children's continuing present. He is not denouncing a crime that comes in the shape of a psychological ghost; rather, he is exposing an ongoing horror that continues to be relegated to the backdrop of Haitian problems because many others seem so much more dire. He offers us a historical truth not of the past but of the present.

The truth of his autobiographical account has been questioned; indeed, the truth of autobiography and testimony has been at the center of many heated debates. In recent years such concerns have been raised especially with respect to the testimony offered by Nobel Peace Prize recipient Rigoberta Menchú. In her defense John Beverley has presented a convincing argument:

> If there is no one universal standard for truth, then claims about truth are contextual: they have to do with how people construct different understandings of the world and historical memory from the same set of facts in situations of radical social inequality, exploitation, and repression. (77)

His point is that there is no specified "level of social facticity that can guarantee the truth" of any representation because "the facts of memory are not essences prior to representation, but rather themselves the consequence of struggles to represent and over representation" (79). Following this position, Cadet's testimony displays his struggles with the memory of the violence done to him; the facts he reveals are, ultimately, modes of memory that disclose violence against children.

His narrated life, with the goal of attaining human rights for children in Haiti and in the diaspora, is also frustrated by the nature of today's markets. In an important new study on the subject, Kay Schaffer and Sidonie Smith contend: "Life narratives have become salable properties in today's markets. They gain their audiences through the global forces of commodification that convert narratives into property of publishing and media houses" (23). Schaffer and Smith point out that once a testimony (narrated life) becomes a commodity, it can have the effect the author initially intended—for Cadet, to get people sufficiently incensed that they become politically active to stop such abuse—or it can have an opposite effect, with stories of horror abounding to the point that people either take them as normal or ignore them altogether. In the latter case, the survivor-victim's quest for reparation and social action through testimony becomes inefficient.

Nonetheless, an autobiography such as Cadet's is invaluable for my purposes. I am specifically interested in the ways that Hispaniola's diaspora is afflicted by memories of past and present violence and human rights infringements. Autobiographical memory intersects fiction and history and complicates the process of memory as memorial. Cadet's autobiography allows him to mourn his own past, but further asks us to move beyond the tears that tear at his fellow sufferer's lives. His autobiography is, arguably, a testimony of the present, written to change the future, from a new geography, and in a different language. His revelations lead me to ask: How do the memories and testimonies of past-presents and present-pasts create a unique community in search of a space for their *dolor/douleur/deuil*?

In *The Tears of Hispaniola* I ask that we focus on the effects of different forms of violence on individual lives and on inter-/intranational memory. How are new inter-American, Pan-Caribbean diasporas imagined? And what role do their stories play in a global culture of growing misery and violence?

1

Meanings of Memory

A Literary Intervention to Confront Persistent Violence

Images of death can haunt us for years. African-Haitian-American writer Edwidge Danticat remembers how, as a child, she was deeply affected by television news coverage of lifeless black bodies washing onto the Florida shores (Trescott). I remain deeply moved by crime and war images presented by television news. The effect is similar to how most of us in the United States felt after seeing the repeated video images of the World Trade Center collapse on September 11, 2001, including shots of desperate people jumping to their deaths. I find it difficult to imagine not being haunted by the presence of death and violence in the world. However, psychological studies (Elsass; Hayner; Herman; Leys) suggest that people have different ways of responding to and healing from traumatic experiences. Studies prompted by news coverage of the World Trade Center's demise argue that people who witness a mass tragedy, even via a television screen, newspapers, or stories, can enter a variety of emotional states, such as apathy, depression, futility, and helplessness. Some people experience, however temporarily, a kind of awakening to the fundamental values by which they want to live their lives. These images, whether or not we were eyewitnesses, will not fade. Their forceful persistence has led me to wonder: What happens when the mind cannot abandon images of death and violence? What determines how deeply these images damage the psyche? How do individuals and societies heal from the psychological pain produced by violence? What role does storytelling play in the production of memory? And more specifically, what is the function of memory?

In this chapter I propose that memory—shaped by multiple, often contradictory narratives including history, historiography, rituals (*vodou*), traditions, and fiction—underscores the double-sided and duplicitous nature of any form of recall. On the one hand, many national narratives have served to erase the experiences of peasants, poor city-dwellers, and non-elite, reducing them to a nondescript, homogenous, and disenfranchised group regularly ignored and/or violated by the empowered—France during colonial rule, the United States during occupations, dictators. On the other hand, as Joan Dayan has described in "Rituals of History," the opening section of *Haiti, History, and the Gods*, counter-acts such as *vodou* safeguard memories and histories that defy Western notions of identity and empower the otherwise disenfranchised. She says:

> A person or thing can be two or more things simultaneously. A word can be double, two-sided, and duplicitous. In this broadening and multiplying of a word's meaning, repeated in rituals of devotion and vengeance, we begin to see that what becomes more and more vague also becomes more distinct: it may mean *this*, but *that* too. (33)

Given the duality of meaning that colors Haitian histories and memory, I would like to propose an analysis of Haitian survival and resistance through fiction. Following Dayan's assertion about meaning, fiction may be just an imaginary story, or it may be a history freed of the limits of historical evidence. When historical sources run up against their lacks and limitations, imagination is critical. At stake is the way in which fiction functions as memory.

Pierre Nora's essay "Between Memory and History" argues for "sites of memory" ("lieux de mémoire"). These sites, he tells us, are developed in lieu of real memory. That is, we are left with sites of memory in the absence of real environments of memory. These real environments of memory are defined as the traditional spaces where families remained in the same location. Traditions and stories were passed on in the very place where they were experienced. In a new global culture, defined by migration and translation, these places have changed dramatically; in many cases the places no longer exist. New venues of memory must be invented. Nora thus proposes three new sites of memory: material memory (such as monuments and literature), symbolic memory (what the production of this material memory symbolizes), and functional memory (the role this constructed memory, symbolic of a lost place and space, plays).

I would add that these sites of memory are themselves complicated by the functions of memory per se. While memory can honor and reinvent the past, it can also limit the possibilities of present and future for those imprisoned by a past that has imprinted itself traumatically in the psyche of the bearer.

To exemplify this, I conclude this chapter, which explores modes of memory through histories and fiction, with a systematic study of Edwidge Danticat's novel *The Farming of Bones*. The text exposes, among other things, the fundamental absence of human rights in Haiti, the traumatic incision that violence leaves on its victims and survivors, and the dire need for mourning and healing.

Rooted in an already established tradition of what Joan Dayan calls "writing misery" (79), *The Farming of Bones* offers a new interpretation of misery. My reading of the novel suggests that the Haitian and Dominican governments should be held accountable for the exploitation to which they continue to subject the dispossessed of history. Setting a Haitian memory in Dominican soil, Danticat signals the fact that the rhetorical national division inculcated into the people's imagination is an elitist governmental ploy that blurs the real divisions between the landholding elites and the masses.

The Farming of Bones, which received an American Book Award in 1999, imagines the names of those whose deaths went undocumented, and uncovers the masks of pain this denied history creates. The text paints a complex chiaroscuro (light/dark, remembered/forgotten) of life. Despite its function as a site of memory and a memorial against forgetting, the novel is informed by a persistent tension between memory and the ineluctable elusiveness of the past.

The novel also focuses on what might have been and makes the case that each and every life is precious. Through the character Amabelle, a basic problem with memory is shown: with so much imaginative energy focused on evoking a past as present, no energy is left to forge a future or engage in a present. Danticat's story puts into evidence the binary dynamics of memory and forgetting. How can one remember violence and still heal from it?

For example, with Sebastien, Danticat both imaginatively evokes the memory of those who died in the 1937 Dominican border massacre and highlights the impossibility of bringing the dead back. This is shown in the novel's introduction, wherein he is given a name and is described in the shadows of the flicker of a candle in a small room, in the darkness of night, and later in absence when his body has disappeared and his death remains unconfirmed. The text informs us, "His name is Sebastien Onius" (1). Later we read what I believe is the author's message, "Men with names never truly die. It is only the nameless and faceless who vanish like smoke into the early morning air" (282). His words in the night soothe her nightmares and fears; they show how a person like him, full of life and hope, can be celebrated. He is described not only with a name but also with a body that harbors a complex history of Haitian agricultural labor in the Dominican Republic. Amabelle says: "His back and shoulders became firm and rigid as he was concocting a new life for me" (55). She thinks: "Before Sebastien, all my dreams had been of the past: of the old country, of places and people I might never see again" (32). His existence represents the possibility of the present. Sebastien's calloused hands and scarred body are depicted in such a way that we understand the strength of his being. In sharp contrast, his later disappearance underscores the fragility of being. His absence highlights the horrors of not knowing what has happened, of waiting for answers without ever getting them, and of knowing that one more unspeakable execution has transpired without the possibility of mourning or vindication. Through the character of Sebastien we can reflect on the meaning of the massacre and the effects of violent deaths. Perhaps the novel asks us to mourn the deaths of those we never knew, who may have never been documented, and whose families may have never known the truth of their loved ones' deaths. *The Farming of Bones* is more than a site of memory. It is a memorial to the dead and the dispossessed of Hispaniola.

The people of Hispaniola, shaped by histories of violence—of the colonial period, the Haitian revolution, dictatorships, natural disasters, and military occupations—encounter new histories of violence as they migrate to Canada and the United States, seeking better lives. Fiction, like Myriam Chancy's *The Spirit of Haiti* (2004), highlights this with scenes that link memories of lynching in the South to memories of violence in Haiti. For example, one scene demonstrates the persistence of racial violence as one of the characters, an African American in the late-twentieth-century United States, is being brutally beaten until his friend, a newly arrived Haitian, comes to save him. Both men must run for their lives. As they run, the protagonist feels dead bodies hanging about him, and Billie Holiday's song "Strange Fruit" is recalled. Chancy's point is poignant: racial violence exists today and will affect an African American as much as a Caribbean immigrant American. Memory eerily exists in the present through a continuing violence that begs for address. Karla Holloway's book *Passed On: African American Mourning Stories* offers a singular reading of text as memorial. It is her memorial to her son Bem Kayin Holloway (1977–99), who was shot to death as he tried to escape his maximum-security prison. She pacifies her grief as she thinks that, after years of violence, he has finally found his freedom. She is left with the difficult task of mourning. In a project that investigates the myths, rituals, and economics of burial and mourning, Holloway presents the ways that death and dying are interpreted and dealt with in the African-American community. These are facts of life, harsh ones that come too often and too early because of poverty and racist violence. How do people survive these realities without becoming embittered? How do survivors find the will to live on? One of her answers comes in her fifth chapter, "The Promise of Hope in a Season of Despair: A Funeral Sermon by Maurice O. Wallace, Ph.D.," from her son's funeral. The following words help us think and understand the passage from mourning to healing and continuing into a fruitful life.

The lament of Israel, in the ears of Isaiah, is no strange lament to us, centuries and centuries removed from Isaiah's writing. Theirs was the bitter cry of near-hopeless captivity in Babylon and the shrill objection to exile so familiar to us, of late.

The exiled Jews Isaiah sought to console were, like so many detained and dispossessed, geographically displaced. But more deeply than that, they experienced a loss of the structured, reliable world of sense and coherent meaning that was existentially home. In its place the vexed persistence of failed hopes, anger, wistful sadness, and forlorn resignation would come to hold forth, and despair would have its dominion.

For us who know little firsthand of the violence of exile or extradition, perhaps the condition of despair is more resonant. From an ecclesiastical point of view, I submit, it is the defining pathology of our day, and quite possibly the greatest threat to our spiritual strivings, to our unique capacity, that is, as people of faith, to be buoyant and keep singing in the strange, disorienting places of life.

So much despair and confusion. So much angst and hopelessness.
. . .

Well, the answer may be simpler than we know. I urge you that if Babylon be your lot, and storm clouds gather menacingly overhead; if you *must* sit down at river's edge and weep with the willows, well then you must. But whatever else the pressures of life have you do, never, never hang up your harp. It is the sign and symbol of your dignity and endurance, your capacity to last still longer and conjure a song in the midst of your storm. (189–90)

It is uncanny for me to read this sermon and remember that the last scene in Danticat's novel takes place at a river's edge, as Amabelle, the bearer of memories—memories of her parents' death at that river, and of the escape from the massacre again through that river—visits it one last time.

Danticat does not hang up her harp. Her writing is her harp, her song, for the dead and to the dispossessed and against the violence of Haitian and Dominican reality and its memory in the diaspora. While her writing encourages hope and resistance, it is rooted in horrible human tragedy. And she has confessed to experiencing a sense of futility because of this undeniable part of her own, and by extension Caribbean, history. During a New York appearance to promote *The Farming of Bones*, Danticat started crying as she read the words she had read so many times before. She later told a reporter, "I was crying because I felt I am so inadequate as opposed to what happened. No matter what you write, it is never going to equal the pain of one person. I was just overwhelmed by the actuality. . . . Often I feel very sad writing about something and I write through that sadness, or because it makes me sad" (Trescott). Not far into her twenties, Edwidge Danticat was consciously illuminating the critical sociopolitical issues of Haiti by imagining the lives of Haitians, giving them names, describing their bodies, and reinterpreting their place in Haitian histories. Her texts journey into a memory of misery, a misery that is exacerbated by a long list of continuing atrocities.

Danticat has taken on the role of witness—to the experiences of those who survived terror as well as those who did not—and consequently is, herself, a survivor of tragic stories. Danticat's work as a writer gives meaning to the memories of violence. Literary critic Renée Shea asked the author, "So is that what you do in your work—you bear witness?" Danticat replied, "I try. . . . But I do it more for my own salvation and emotional survival than anything else" (21). Her novels serve as a monument against silenced tragedies and also as a vehicle to recovery for individuals. Danticat's characters help us learn about the brutal experiences both of nameless, silenced victims and of survivors who retain vivid memories of atrocities visited upon them or their families and friends.

Within the context of American literature, Danticat's work is a foundational part of a recent wave of literary production from writers in diasporic communities whose members have never abandoned their land of origin, emotionally, psychologically, or politically. In the transnational setting, Danticat can be considered one of the newer authors to join an established network of Haitian writers, in particular those writing in Canada in

French, such as Gérard Étienne, and African-American literary scholars, such as Karla Holloway. At issue for all of these writers are the dimensions of loss, the task of mourning, and ethical negotiations between past and present, place of origin (Africa, the Caribbean) and host country. As Danticat herself posits:

> It used to be that an immigrant was one who assimilated quickly and disappeared joyfully into America's melting pot. These days immigrants are transnational global ambassadors for both the country they live in and the one they've moved from. Even as they pay taxes and contribute to the economic structure in the United States, they also build schools and clinics and support businesses in the countries of their birth, helping to rebuild the fabric that forced their own migration and possibly slowing down the exodus of others. (Foreword xi)

Her literature looks to the future by creating a narrative space for multiple histories and memories, giving Haitians the possibility of nuanced representation and value in a prejudiced world that often denigrates them. This narrative space, written in the diaspora, is drawn from the varied raw materials of a collective memory, and informed by family stories, political manipulations, and news media information. Danticat's work allows people, alone in the settings of their new urban lives, to confront violence, recognize its existence, and celebrate their own strength and capacity to survive the memory of violence and its unrelenting presence. This narrative space allows healing (etymologically related to "whole") to occur by reuniting disembodied memories with forgotten bodies. Her literature looks at the past but, more important, creates a vision for the future, both in the realm of literature, understood as a pragmatic act, and in the realm of politics, through work with human rights groups such as the National Coalition for Haitian Rights. Danticat's literature, through stories of human survival, creates the space for mourning, a space essential to overcoming the weight of tragedy and loss.

Depersonification and Personhood: Citizenship and Democracy

The near absolute political, legal, and military power of a string of leaders in Haiti and the Dominican Republic has played a critical role in the way each individual counts as a person or not. For example, in *Le Problème des Noirs et la Révolution de 1789*, Samuel Mack-Kit studies the Code Noir to suggest that we should learn from the repeated history of authoritarian leaders such as Louis XIV and Napoleon Bonaparte (36–37). Their abuse of sovereign powers is comparable to contemporary dictators' disregard for the citizenry. Mack-Kit's study highlights how leaders dehumanize people.

In the sixteenth and seventeenth centuries, European colonizers arrived in the Caribbean, decided the natives were less than human, and enslaved them. The Spaniards declared the Indians to be little men, with scant human traits and without culture (Seed 17–18). The Spaniards subjected the Indians to abuses that reached the level of genocide. The natives died in droves from disease, overwork, and, in some cases, collective suicide to escape enslavement. Fray Bartolomé de las Casas's pioneering work *Brevísima relación de la destrucción de las Indias*, written in 1542 and published in 1552 in Seville, argued that the Indians should be treated like people of reason ("gente de razón"). Unfortunately, rules applying to the rights of indigenous populations have always been deficient, and the slave trade with Africa resulted in part from reforms springing from las Casas's work.[1] Spain changed its laws concerning Indian rights according to its needs. For example, in the colony of Santo Domingo, marriage between Indians and Spaniards was permitted in order to guarantee population of the lands. At another point, authorities denied citizenship to the mixed-blood children, thus disempowering rebellious or even potentially rebellious Spaniards and *criollos* who challenged the Spanish crown.

The Middle Passage—which in many ways foreshadowed the present situation of Haitians who try to flee by boat to Florida--was an act against humanity. Human beings were kidnapped in Africa, then chained, packed, and shipped. African bodies were tossed into the seas when the "cargo" was dead or very ill. After England began to enforce the abolition of slavery in 1834 and France declared its abolition in 1848, slave ships would dump their human cargo rather than be caught smuggling.[2] Economics drove the African slave trade and slavery in the colonies. Africans were conveniently denied personhood so that their labor could be used for the profit of the landowners and the "mother countries." The slaves were abused without consideration of European legal codes, prompting intellectuals of the time to put forth varying views on the human value of these bodies kidnapped and sold for labor.

The French Revolution in 1789, the Declaration of the Rights of Man, and the pioneering work of the Amis des Noirs, free coloreds in Paris, pushed the contradictions inherent in the slave system to erupt, and set the stage for the war of independence (1802–4) in Haiti. Historian David Patrick Geggus informs us:

> At the same time, the autumn of 1789, free colored property-own-ers in Saint Domingue also gathered to demand equal rights with whites. Some also seem to have called for the freeing of mixed-race slaves, and those in Paris spoke of an eventual, though distant, aboli-tion of slavery. In general, however, free people of color acted like the slave-owners they usually were and were careful not to have their cause confused with that of the black masses. (10)

Fears were running high for the stability of the slave regime and new hos-tilities were forming, in particular between the whites and a new black landholding class. Geggus points out that "the National Assembly had maintained an ambiguous silence on the color question"; still, on "May 15, 1791, free coloreds born of free parents were declared equal to whites in their political rights" (11). In 1794 slavery was abolished throughout the French Empire. In 1802 this freedom was brutally rescinded in Guadeloupe and Martinique. Saint-Domingue avoided the same fate by defeating the French. The fight for human rights and freedom was limited by color and still shaped by colonial economic interests dependent on the sugar planta-tions. French intentions were uncertain, and the entire Atlantic region looked on in fear for the stability of its own territories.

Freedom as ideology was one thing, but in practice it was fraught with problems. Historian Laurent Dubois points out the tensions:

> The enslaved revolutionaries challenged the racialized colonial sys-tem of the day, deploying the language of Republican rights and the promise of individual liberty against a social order based on the de-nial of their humanity. In winning back the natural rights of the En-lightenment claimed as a birthright to all people, however, the for-merly enslaved laid bare a profound tension within the ideology of rights they had made their own. The right to individual freedom they had gained was, inevitably, a strike against the property rights claimed by their former masters. The 1789 Declaration of the Rights of Man and Citizen defended both the natural right to freedom and the right to private property. . . . Colonial authorities—charged with overseeing abolition while continuing plantation production—nego-tiated this conflict by combining emancipation with new forms of labor coercion and racial exclusion. The result was a "Republican rac-

ism" that excluded the former slaves from full equality and justified the continued exploitation of their labor, arguing their incapacity to live as free and independent citizens. (3)

During a time when the rights of man were being defended in France, the slaves in the colonies were being treated with extreme cruelty. This new Republican racism Dubois describes is in effect to date. The irrefutable links between the two sides of Hispaniola were grafted during the period of the Haitian war of independence. The stranglehold of Republican racism precludes a real democracy—a sociopolitical system that would grant access to citizenship and civil rights to all—in both Haiti and the Dominican Republic.

The issue, central to contemporary debates on human rights, addressed who counted as a "man"—or, rather, a citizen. It was convenient for some to believe that Africans did not have souls and therefore were not human, could not be converted to Catholicism, and could be treated like animals. France's Code Noir, drawn up in 1685 by Louis XIV "le Roi Soleil," was one of several sets of laws on the treatment of African slaves in the colonies. The Code Noir, which was intended to set up rules for manumission, clarified the rights of the owners. For example, Article 44 equated slaves with furniture and forbid any free "men" to have children with slaves. The slaves were not allowed to testify in civil or criminal matters unless it was absolutely necessary, and only to the benefit of the whites (*Code Noir* 307).[3] Any slave who hurt his/her mistress, master, or slave-owning family member would be punished by death (309). The "rights" herein are clearly the rights of ownership, outlawing human contact, sympathy, and love between master and slave. The slaves had to revolt against the slave-owning hierarchy to fight for their rights.

The fight for freedom—abolition of slavery, independence of Haiti—was brutal throughout. "Battle casualties were heavy, and from the beginning the war was marked by frightful atrocities on both sides" (Geggus 25). Dessalines declared Saint Domingue independent on January 1, 1804, and renamed the new country by its aboriginal Amerindian name of Haïti. Many called themselves Incas during the wars of independence, revenging the extermination of the Arawaks in the sixteenth century. Geggus sees this renaming as strategic: "While anchoring the new state to the American past, the country's new name meant above all a symbolic break with Europe. All whites were henceforth forbidden to own land in Haiti" (27).[4]

The triumphant Haitian revolution had positive repercussions throughout the Atlantic. For example, slavery was extinguished on the Spanish side in 1822, upon annexation. But Haitian sovereignty was aggressively challenged. In particular, the United States denied Haiti's status as a free and independent black country. The abiding fear of slave-owning nations was that slaves on other islands and in the United States would revolt. In the southern United States, policies were reinforced to maintain slavery. France did not recognize Haitian sovereignty until the new country agreed to pay for the losses the French incurred in consequence of the island's independence. That cost of 150 million francs (later reduced to 60 million) was the beginning of an international debt from which, along with worsening corruption, Haiti has never been able to recover.[5] In order to maintain the slave-driven Atlantic economy, the United States and France refused to recognize Haitian sovereignty or that Haitian political leaders were human beings worthy of being included in international policy dialogues. The United States finally recognized Haiti as an independent nation on June 5, 1862, when President Lincoln signed a bill, known as the *amende honorable*, for appointment of commissioners to Haiti and Liberia.

Even though sovereignty was not officially recognized until 1862, it is clear that the revolutionary leaders, including Jean-Jacques Dessalines, Toussaint L'Ouverture, and Henri Christophe, were brilliant and powerful forces that had to be contended with on an equal footing in a ferocious war in which inherited brutality and atrocity—the violence of the colonists, the aberrations of the slaveholders—pointed the path to a future in which continued uprisings would unleash periods of rape and pillaging. Again, the story is double-edged. While France, England, and Spain refused Haiti recognition, they were also terrified of what the Haitian revolution represented. They could not deny its importance. The clock could not be turned back. "Haiti," Dayan remarks, "was conceived as earth blooded with the purifying spirit of liberation" (33). This liberation, I would add, is marked by the double nature of triumph and failure. For example, Dessalines, a cruel leader known for the command "Koupe tèt, boule kay" (cut heads, burn houses), was met with a death stunning in its extreme violence. It underscored the dissatisfaction felt among different factions in Haiti over his rule. He was killed in an ambush laid by mulattoes and blacks, with the express consent of other leaders including General Alexandre Pétion and General Christophe. He was shot, dismembered, and dragged from Pont-Rouge, where he was murdered, to Port-au-Prince. Dayan tells us:

> By the time the body reached Port-au-Prince, after the two-mile journey, it could not be recognized. The head was shattered, the feet, hands, and ears cut off. In some accounts, Dessalines was stoned and

hacked to pieces by the crowd, and his remains—variously described as "scraps," "shapeless remains," "remnants," or "relics"—were thrown to the crowd. (17)

This account is particularly important in the context of my analysis for two reasons. One, it emphasizes the violence with which detested leaders can be removed. And two, it leads us to a more nuanced conversation on memory. Memory can birth gods, and through rituals such as *vodou*, new memories subvert the suffocating laws of the powerful. Rituals of history become rituals of memory and thus intervene in the ways certain people and events are monumentalized and/or demonized. Joan Dayan offers an example that illustrates this narrative transition in her own "Rituals of History" section, which has exerted great weight on my thoughts here. The Jean-Jacques Dessalines of "history" was dismembered by an angry crowd that believed it was relieving itself of a despotic leader. But another, mythified Dessalines comes back full force through "ritual"—in *vodou* he is transformed into a *lwa* (god)—as an emblem of hope and revenge. This situation too is double-natured, as Dessalines is mythically invested with power by those who remained on the margins, but he is also resurrected from obscurity by the elite who use him to placate the masses dissatisfied with the existing government. For example, to mark the centennial of the Haitian nation, the repressive regime of Louis Borno under U.S. occupation in 1915–34 relocated Dessalines' remains, which were marked by a "brick tomb with the inscription in Creole: 'Ce-git Dessalines, / Mort à 48 ans' (Here lies Dessalines, / Dead at 48 years old)" (Dayan 27–28). Dayan observes that it was easier for the literate elite and the repressive government to build a monument to Dessalines and create a state cult with a national anthem, the "Dessalinienne," than to address the real issues of the people's continuing poverty. But the people had already restored Dessalines' power. After all, he had been transformed into a *lwa* many years earlier. Dayan concludes:

Not simply master or tyrant, but also slave and supplicant, Dessalines and the religious rituals associated with him keep the ambiguities of power intact. . . . Gods held in the mind and embodied in ceremony reenact what historians often forget: the compulsion to serve, the potency and virtue of atrocity. The very suppressions, inarticulateness, and ruptures in ritual might say something about the ambivalences of *the* revolution: it was not so liberating as mythologizers or ideologues make it out to be, and the dispossessed, who continue to suffer and remember, know this. (28–29)

The twentieth century offers no relief to the dispossessed—those without legal national status and those living in such poverty that they are not able to take part in the political life of their country—and the incongruities between state-sponsored history and popular memories persist.[6] Given this panorama, we can more easily understand Sténio Vincent's initial passivity in the face of the 1937 massacre. It follows suit in a long tradition of conflicting, and often contradictory, negotiations between the masses and the interests of the economic elite. In the preface to his 1957 book about Vincent, Milo Rigaud laments that never did a man detest the Haitians or humiliate them with such pleasure as did this dictator. He continues, "car il est entendu que la liberté et la vie d'un citoyen haitien ne sont pas choses sacrées pour la plupart de nos chefs d'Etat" (1) [it is understood that liberty and the life of a Haitian citizen are not sacred things for most of our heads of state]. In fact, throughout Vincent's presidency he made arrangements with Trujillo to send colonies of workers to the Dominican sugar plantations. Few, if any, of these contract workers were massacred during Trujillo's rule. The exploited Haitians working in the cane fields were not mentioned in Trujillo's anti-Haitian rhetoric. Rigaud informs us that Trujillo paid Vincent to have them sent over. Sugar companies employed cane workers with both Vincent's and Trujillo's agreement. Vincent's sugarcane labor negotiations made him a pimp of sorts. His people, as Rigaud so emphatically records, counted only if he could make money from them. Their individual lives were meaningless.

Over the years, various Haitian and Dominican leaders have gone to great lengths to deny the people a sense of citizenship, dignity, and responsibility. Some people do not even have birth certificates to prove their existence; some people stay in the shadows to avoid violence. The people are repeatedly discouraged. Time after time, the workers and the poor come out of their makeshift homes to support a newly emerged father figure who claims to be ready to lead the nation into an economically stable, more modern future. The people's hopes are then crushed by quintessential patriarchs, such as Duvalier and Trujillo, who enrich themselves while failing to deliver on grandiose promises of improved education, work, and living conditions. This is exemplified by Duvalier père, who was first a country doctor and later became a major participant in the highly successful campaign against malaria and yaws. In 1938 he had founded Les Griots (from an African word meaning "storytellers"), which officially recognized the importance of the *vodou* religion in Haitian culture and set aside a space of acceptance for Haiti's large black population. Despite all of this seemingly humanitarian and humanistic work, Duvalier betrayed his people. Clément Barbot, who was later shot for having divulged Duvalierian secrets, said, "Duvalier wanted $200 million from the U.S. He did not want money for public works or any benefit to the Haitian people" (Gingras 120). Gingras writes, "Barbot estimated that Duvalier himself amasses $400,000 the first couple of years and [is later] worth well over $1.5 million salted away in a Swiss bank. [Barbot stated that Duvalier] 'is not a Communist, a democrat or anything else—he is an opportunist. Often he said to me: let the people eat cassava'" (120). Anyone who dared to complain was killed.

When the people realize they have been tricked and cannot revolt against the deceit, they become either desperate or numb. State repression reminds them that they cannot speak; the people cannot express their needs because they know they will be punished for treason. This is psychological violence. As the psychologist Peter Elsass puts it, "Physical violence aims at destroying objects and people; mental violence aims at destroying identities" (157). He explains, "There are very strong forces in a large group, and if the group articulates an inexpedient matrix, it will dissolve. Intelligence gets transformed into power and coercion, and leadership becomes hierarchy and the worship of authority" (177). By disciplining a country through fear, dictators negate citizenship. Leaders that use tactics of physical and psychological terror become stronger vehicles of authority, insisting on worship and breaking down the identity and desires of individuals. In essence, the person is crushed under the power of an omnipotent leader (and his advisors and henchmen) who denies him/her individual rights, and consequently the status of being a person, a citizen of his/her own country.

In her essay "Citizenship Revisited: Solidarity, Responsibility, and Rights," Elizabeth Jelin suggests that it is difficult for a country to transition into democracy when the populace has never experienced it, or cannot recall the time when it did exist, as in Argentina after military rule. She argues:

> The transition to democracy has involved the reconstruction of state institutions and the transformation of the institutions of civil society. It implies dismantling antidemocratic forms of exercising power, which may be authoritarian, corporatist, and/or purely coercive in nature. It also entails a change in the rules governing the distribution

of power, the recognition and legal sanction of rights, and the legiti-
mation of social actors. . . . The challenge of democratization lies in
the capacity to combine formal institutional changes with the expan-
sion of democratic practices and strengthening of a culture of citizenship . . . aiming to reconsider the relationship between individual
subjects and collective rights. (102)

Jelin addresses the discrepancy between the "legal definition of rights and
the understanding and practices of the assumed subjects of rights" and
focuses on the "process of individual and collective subjectivity" (101). Her
observations, centered on Chile and Argentina, can be applied aptly to Haitian circumstances. Haitians must become active participants, and therefore citizens, of their country despite being marginalized by the authorities.

Marcel Mauss's essay "A Category of the Human Mind: The Notion of
the Person" offers a historical overview of the evolution of the concept of
the person. Mauss talks about the "role" (*personnage*) that an individual
plays in a sacred drama, just like the role each plays in the family and in the
larger community. He traces the *personne* to the Roman Senate, where
the persons were *patres* represented by the images of their ancestors. A
"person" had a prominent ancestral name; it was equivalent to bearing a
title and affiliation with a privileged group, such as the religious *collegia*,
and conferred on the individual the protection of the laws of the state. The
slave, he tells us, was completely excluded from this category with the
single perfunctory sentence "Servus non habet persona." Mauss continues
his study by noting that the classical Greek and Latin moralists (200 BC–
AD 400) added concepts of conscience, responsibility, and rights used in
Roman law to structure the "moral person." When the Christians discovered the religious power of the moral person as a metaphysical entity, they
introduced the concept we still use today. He points to von Carolsfeld quoting Galatians 3:28: "You are, with respect to the one, neither Jew nor
Greek, slave nor freeman, male nor female, for you are all one person, in
Christ Jesus" (19). The question of the "person," and who/what counts as
a person, has a long philosophical and religious history. Mauss quotes
Cassiodorus as saying, in his commentary on Psalm 7, "Persona—substan-
tia rationalis individua" or "The person is a rational substance, indivisible
and individual" (20). The Renaissance and Descartes ("Cogito ergo sum")
addressed the specific role of the soul, its immortality, by way of the thinking, rational mind (21). And Kant "made of the individual consciousness,
the sacred character of the human person, the condition for Practical Rea-

son" (22). In his essay "The Person," Charles Taylor writes: "The general notion of a person includes not only self-awareness but holding values" (266).

These meditations on the person are Western, referring particularly to those who are "citizens" within European contexts. Yet, as Mauss mentions, slaves were not included in such a category. Enslaved Africans brought to the Americas suffered extreme cruelty calculated to strip them of any possibility of humanity, and were consequently not seen as human. They were brutally beaten, separated from their own groups, renamed according to their masters' fancies, and forced to lose memories of family and origins through overwork and malnourishment.[7]

Even though Haiti is the first free black nation in the Americas, independence does not equate with democracy. This is a plight with which Haiti continues to struggle. Democracy requires a "culture of citizenship" (Jelin, *Citizenship*, 102), wherein people have individual rights and engage in building a community. Lack of basics such as food and medical resources produces a desperate society, always both anxious and hopeful, ready to fight and change. Leaders such as François Duvalier begin by doing good work among the people, but soon suffer from megalomania and fears of persecution. They later cater to corrupt, powerful families who do not want to see a more even distribution of wealth. Despite initial promises, the country is unable to move from authoritarian rule toward democracy.

Truth, Lies, and Contradictory Documents

In Haiti, and in the Haitian diaspora, literature plays an important historical role because the documentation of historical events is imprecise and politicized.[8] Novels and other sources documenting the massacre of 1937, for example, provide contradictory or varying information about the number of people murdered. One source adduced by Bernardo Vega, a letter from a Franklyn B. Atwood, states that almost all of the estimated 17,000 Haitians in the northeast region of the Dominican Republic escaped back to their own country (*Trujillo y Haití*, 344). Yet upon further investigation it is discovered that in 1937 Trujillo ordered his men to kill Haitians with machetes to make the genocide of an unwanted group appear to be an internal conflict among the peasants. Estimates of the number of dead range from 1,000 to 35,000 (Sagás 46). Misinformation, as well as manipulated information, has led to conflicting accounts such as (1) the problem was local and had nothing to do with Trujillo; (2) most of the Haitians were able to escape over the border, so very few were killed; and (3) some Dominicans did not want the Haitians in Dominican territory. Vega points out that many of the accounts of the massacre were written a decade or more after the killings; the problem is

> that the narratives of that tragedy that have survived are so rare and fragmented and they come principally from foreign journalists who had been in the country for that reason (Quentin Reynolds), Haitian authors (Price-Mars, 1953), Dominican exiles (Luis F. Mejía, 1976), or Dominicans who were witnesses of the occurrences but who published their commentaries only twenty-four years after the massacre (Freddy Prestol Castillo and Rufino Martínez mainly), or who forty-six years later interviewed witnesses of the period (Juan Manuel García, 1983).[9]

The passage of so many years puts the details of these accounts in doubt. Vega uncovered information censored in the Dominican Republic and found unpublished materials produced right after the event. The censoring and the gap between event and memory suggest that many of the stories of the massacre are inaccurate.

Scholars and historians disagree not only on the details of the 1937 massacre but on its rationale. A central question is whether the massacre was propelled by anti-Haitianism or, rather, created a wave of anti-Haitianism that did not exist before, at least not with such vitriol. Many scholars argue that elite Dominicans had had strong anti-Haitian sentiments for decades, but that anti-Haitianism became a broad-based discourse only in the decades after the massacre and in response to Haitian migrant laborers. In recent years Ernesto Sagás has put forth the idea that the massacre formed part of Trujillo's plot to eliminate Haitians from the Dominican Republic. He argues that carefully contemplated anti-Haitianism was the reason. This narrative of hatred against Haitians has become very popular in the Dominican Republic over the years. But Turits contends that the genocide propelled Trujillo's official anti-Haitian ideology. Ethnic Haitians on the frontier prior to 1937 were not, for the most part, migrant laborers (Turits 598). Turits's study examines the weakness of national and racial divisions on the northern frontier before the massacre. He claims that frontier communities were mostly bilingual and they "remained indifferent and even hostile to urban visions of Dominican nationality" (4). Small farmers of Haitian descent in the frontier region had lived there for generations and often intermarried with Dominicans. Dominican intellectuals and elites, however, imagined clear distinctions and opposition between Haitians and Dominicans. According to Turits, Haitians on the frontier were a largely strategic concern for Trujillo. By creating a sharply divided Dominican border region, the state could control the political and economic activities that occurred there. In particular, illegal trade would be halted and the movement of people and goods could be registered and taxed more effectively. Turits concludes that Trujillo adopted a clear anti-Haitian position only *after* the massacre.[10]

The Dominican Republic fashioned its national image to discriminate against the Haitians. Dominican politicians depicted themselves and their country as Catholic Hispanics in contrast to Haitians, who were denigrated as *vodou* worshippers and "Africans." Rafael Trujillo—who had a half-Haitian grandmother, Ercina Chevalier—designed, and imposed, himself as a savior who would save his people in the Dominican Republic from the Haitians. He institutionalized anti-Haitianism, manipulating myths of nationhood, and, according to Sagás (68), aggressively excluded poor black Haitians—and a number of poor Dominican blacks—from the national image and from basic livelihood.[11]

A question that fuels much contention about this period is: Was the violence aimed at the Haitians because Trujillo hated them or because it represented a concise national rhetoric that allowed him to consolidate power?

As I have mentioned, at least two interconnected responses have been proposed: Sagás insists that anti-Haitianism was at the root of the massacre, and Turits argues that the vituperative national anti-Haitian discourse was largely strategic for Trujillo himself. Trujillo, Turits reminds us, "sought to dominate the national economy, impose new taxes and fees on external trade, and promote local industry and import-substitution programs via high tariffs" (15). By destroying the camaraderie among ethnic Haitians and Dominicans that existed on the frontier and across the border, he could better divide the two countries politically and control the Dominican territory and people. Turits points to some especially interesting details of Trujillo's manipulation of both intersubjective discourse and power, noting that before "the massacre, Trujillo presented himself not as an eliminationist, anti-Haitian tyrant but rather as a ruler granting state protection and assistance (namely, free land access)" (20). Turits quotes from an interview with a Haitian refugee, "He [Trujillo] said all people are the same. There are no differences between one another. . . . He told everybody . . . that Dominicans and Haitians have the same blood. . . . each citizen must farm productively" (20). This statement suggests that Haitians and Dominicans have many things in common, including ethnic and racial lineage and work goals. So, what was the meaning of the massacre of Haitians in 1937?

Perhaps the meaning of the massacre will remain an enigma in Haitian-Dominican history, blurred by conflicting narratives. Still, different accounts of the horror can inform us of the meaning the memory of the massacre holds for different people. For example, in 1973 Dominican lawyer Freddy Prestol Castillo (1913–81) published *El masacre se pasa a pie*, which offers an interesting, problematic, and nonetheless important document of the massacre.[12] While at first he qualified it as a novel, its blunt style and its content matter insinuated that it was a testimony. The change in genre classification may have been due to the strong criticism his work received from literary critics deploring his writing style. Eventually Prestol Castillo called it "simply my book" (Sommer 161).[13] Also, in a 1983 study of his book, Doris Sommer unquestioningly classifies it as a testimony in the "Latin American tradition of *testimonios*" (161). At the time, the argument was that he was a subjective witness of an atrocity that was being rewritten by the government in order to bury the real horror of the massacre. In Sommer's view,

> The book is the honest account that he dared not give publicly until 1973, although it was allegedly and very probably written during the events of 1937. Prestol's long silence is complicated by the fact that he may have given other accounts much earlier. After all, he had been sent to Dajabón, site of the worst atrocities, as a federal magistrate in service to Trujillo's government. (163)

I give emphasis to the last part of Sommer's contextualization of *el masacre*: Prestol Castillo's account was written while he was working for Trujillo. It is highly suspect, because he is compromised on many levels. His elite background as the son of a sugar oligarch, his education at private schools in the capital that looked down on small towns, and his position as a rural judge employed by Trujillo may have made him more complicit in the massacre than he would like to admit. Sommer correctly juxtaposes the value of the text as historical document with the inescapable human emotion of guilt that seems to afflict the author:

> Much of its value as a historical document and its appeal for the reader comes from the self-reflexivity of Prestol's finger pointing; in

several ways the work is an expression of a tortured conscience in an effort to purge some of the pain. Guilty at least of silent complicity, like the other witnesses to the massacre, the author testifies to his impotence against the dictatorship. (162)

Of note is the way this book was received when it was published—it sold 20,000 copies shortly after publication, in contrast to other books, which sell about 1,000 copies, usually at the author's expense (Sommer 162)—and what it reveals of the memory of such a horror for Dominicans. The success of this text suggests that the Dominicans do not necessarily turn their backs on the horrors of their history. The way the massacre is described, however, also implies complicity, before and/or after the massacre, with the nation-building rhetoric inculcated in the popular sector by the elite and the government.

Prestol Castillo's story offers an important point of view for our considerations of how the horrors were implemented and later rationalized. He begins his text with a memory of a schoolteacher he had as a child in the capital. The teacher would point derisively to the frontier region. Prestol Castillo's narrative skips on to his present position in that small town the teacher once pointed to on a map. His description of a working-class bar frequented by ethnic Haitians and Dominicans is filled with awe and admiration. The Haitians have been there for generations and have achieved high levels of livelihood. Daniel, Prestol Castillo tells us, was exemplary of an entire "pueblo Negro" (black population):

> Un clan de pastores y cultivadores nómadas que finalmente habían asentado en las lejanas y olvidadas tierras de la frontera de la República Dominicana, frente a la República de Haití. Estos negros habían llegado hasta los hatos de los patrones rústicos dominicanos asentados en Dajabón y aldeas aledañas y finalmente se habían injertado en la vida de aquellos señores holgazanes que vivían de los cultivos de los negros de Haití. (30)

That is, Haitians had settled in the forgotten land of the frontier and turned it into a productive area from which they could ascend to a position of comfort and hire other, perhaps newly arrived, Haitians to work for them. Prestol Castillo mentions the case of García's horses that were raised by the Haitian Toussaint. While the testimony continues to try to define difference between the ethnic Haitians and the Dominicans, in the first pages of analysis and memory Prestol Castillo must admit that there are peace and interrelated living and work conditions that defy his urban-informed binary understanding of life on the frontier.

His narrative, however, changes as the massacre begins to take place, and he seems to be a silent and inactive observer. The absurdity of the massacre becomes painfully apparent in the conversations, screams, and orders that ensue. The rest of *El masacre se pasa a pie* reads like a horrible stream-of-consciousness memory of fragments of conversations, orders, fearful comments, and impotent observations by the author. In many ways, I propose, it seems that the text tries to make sense of an irrational horror. That irrational horror is described via fragments of interactions between people who are inebriated actors screaming accusations they will later have to believe. Let me single out one of the many exhaustively repeated examples:

El Capitán hablaba tambaleándose, ebrio. Dentro de la embriaguez hacía un esfuerzo y entre la tiniebla de su mente aparecía una luz roja, como de sol sangriento. . . .—Acabo de recibí unaj óidene seriaj. El Gobierno ordena el degüello de cuanto "mañese" jallemo. No repete edá ni pinta. Quémelos jata vivos. Ey! . . . Saigentoo! . . .

En un momento recordó que su abuelo había nacido en Haití! Y entonces sorbió casi medio frasco de ron. Sus labios temblaban todavía, y miraba la gran sabana como un idiota. (28)

Freddy Prestol Castillo writes the words he remembers uttered by a soldier who is too drunk to be coherent, as he repeats the commands he must follow: to kill. At one moment he remembers that his grandfather was born in Haiti and he looks onto the savannah dumbstruck. Prestol Castillo's account goes on to mention Anta Suriel, *la negra reina*, the black queen, who does not know whether her beloved Haitian boyfriend is alive or dead. Reading these lines, we are led to glimpse the complicated nature of the massacre, as everyone was interconnected in some way or other.

Yet Prestol Castillo's story quickly begins to change its tone. Only three pages later he "copies" the words of a Haitian who speaks French (Kreyòl?) words such as *bon dieu*; he begs for his life and offers to pay. As he seeks mercy, the slayer/soldier retorts, "¡Cállate, negro el Diablo!" (32). The soldier orders, "—Muchachos! Pa'lante! . . . Pa'acabá con estos negros" (33). This moment cuts a deep separation between the two. One is a black Haitian begging for mercy. The other is a Dominican who hates this man in front of him. The former, who is brutally stabbed to death, is one of "estos negros" and thus must be killed. Soon the account begins to show the reasons Dominicans have to eliminate "Haitians": the "Haitians," say the Dominicans, are stealing their cattle and ruining their lives—"me han acabao!" (36).

As I read Freddy Prestol Castillo's account, I am in disbelief that people could have acted in such simplistic terms. Did the Dominicans really need to believe that their neighbors and friends, and in many cases family, of Haitian descent were at the root of their own miseries? Arguably, Prestol Castillo's account points to the fear that was felt under the great dictator. Even though some people did save Haitian lives at great risk to their own, his account leads us to believe that the violence had more to do with this fear for their own lives than with any desire to divide the frontier. Dominicans had to act under the influence of alcohol and had to slander the Haitians and believe their words in order to proceed with the genocide. Still, a city man like Freddy Prestol Castillo came to the dusty country with preconceived prejudices, and I can't imagine that they were easily erased even if he witnessed peaceable living conditions among the people—ethnic Haitians, newly arrived Haitians, and border Dominicans. His 1943 story *Paisajes y meditaciones de una frontera*, which was dedicated to Trujillo, sheds some light on his unannounced mission in the frontier region. The author describes the Dominican side with romantic images that are more reminiscent of some paradise that the Dominican nation must recuperate than the true land that lay before his eyes. I am inclined to believe that this earlier text was intended to establish the need to set up a rigid border and to claim the Dominican side as solely Dominican.

Interestingly, in the process of dividing the frontier region and setting up a Dominican nation stripped of ethnic Haitians, the tapestry of the Dominican and Haitian people—their intertwined histories and their growing free-will exchanges—was butchered into inexistence.[14] Individual stories of kinship and friendship have consequently vanished from the official histories of both nations. It is at this point in history, and in contrast to a testimony like Prestol Castillo's, that fiction such as Danticat's plays a critical role in recuperating the human dimension of the people of Hispaniola. Freddy Prestol Castillo's story reveals a man haunted by the genocide, plagued by guilt, and somehow torn between the need to be Dominican (and therefore anti-Haitian) and to be honest (and therefore give an account that would reveal the peace that had once reigned in the frontier region). In contrast, Edwidge Danticat imagines the intricacies of human relationships.

History and Literature

With so much contradiction marring the historical accounts of the 1937 massacre, it is difficult to understand all of the elements that led to the slaughter and the changes experienced by Haitians and Dominicans in the aftermath of the genocide. It is in this space of confusion that fiction brings its weight to bear on the consideration of the past. That is, because fiction is free to make things up, it can offer a concreteness of vision that presents rounded characters to whom things happen and who do things, that eludes others engaged in the construction of national historical records. On the one hand, history asks and tries to answer: How many? Why? Today's critics and writers are especially aware of the unreliability of the historical record. History—past events that are known, and to some extent agreed upon, whether or not they are documented—can be forgotten and/or re-told. The historical record—that body of information such as government documents and media reports that one community or another recognizes as giving a valid picture of history—can be manipulated, often telling a monolithic story documented by the literate and empowered in further-ance of their vested interests.

Fiction imagines the effects of the past, giving greater depth, and new form, to the questions tackled by history and complicated by compromised testimonials. Fiction can evoke the affects experienced by the individuals in the shadows of official histories and the frenzied drumbeats of collective rituals. Most important, fiction points up the still strong political and eco-nomic ties between Haiti and the Dominican Republic, which sustain a coterie of noncitizens, in both countries, within their divisive national rhetoric. Danticat portrays this through her text. As Haitian descendants living in the Dominican Republic take their children to the one-room schoolhouse founded by Father Romain and Father Vargas, they voice their complaints:

> "I pushed my son out of my body here, in this country," one woman said.... "My mother too pushed me out of her body here. Not me, not my son, not one of us has ever seen the other side of the border. Still they won't put our birth papers in our palms so my son can have knowledge placed into his head by a proper educator in a proper school."
>
> "To them we are always foreigners, even if our granmèmès' gran-mèmès were born in this country," a man responded in Kreyòl. . . .

"This makes it easier for them to push us out when they want to."
(69)

Fiction can also recontextualize time. From the details offered by historians, it could be argued that ethnic Haitian residents were eliminated by the massacre and that new Haitian migrants were cast as foreigners that could be pushed out at any time strategically and most rigorously after the massacre. Thus the above scene, by which Danticat tries to make sense of the massacre, exposes present-day attitudes and experiences via an imaginary historical past. In other words, the scene portrays a presentism, by which contemporary behavior is explained with a possible past.

Danticat's text tries to make sense of the senseless violence of the past and the continuing elimination of Haitians on Dominican soil. Her characters represent those who have lived all of their lives in the Dominican Republic, yet are denied citizenship. Her story attempts to re-member the past in order to understand the present; ironically it exposes how complicated that task actually is. After the massacre, the family members are invited to speak to the authorities, tell their stories, and receive a sort of reparation. One of Danticat's characters reports to the crowd:

> "No, he did not give me money," she said. . . . "He writes your name in the book and he says he will take your story to President Sténio Vincent so you can get your money. . . . Then he lets you talk and lets you cry and he asks you if you have papers to show that all these people died." (233–34)

With this scene, Danticat shows how the poor people were set up to feel their inferiority and their marginal existence: their stories would not be heard by the president. Nor would they receive any compensation for their cruel and extreme losses. By bringing up the question of papers, knowing that no such papers existed, the authorities were mocking the stories the surviving family members presented, in essence claiming these human beings didn't exist and effectively obliterating them from the picture of Dominican and Haitian national discourse.

Bearing this obliteration in mind, I suggest that Danticat's work responds to a disappointment and frustration with history and the historical record felt by individuals from postcolonial nations. Fiction fruitfully supplements the historical record as presented through conventional media. For example, through the protagonist, Amabelle, Danticat creatively calls forth the history of those without names, providing the possibility of acknowledging unspeakable horrors and mourning denied deaths. The

carefully crafted character Amabelle has a bounty of grammatical, historical, and literary intertextuality. The name *Amabelle* can mean *âme belle*,
beautiful soul, or *à ma belle*, to my beauty; it recalls *ama* (chatelaine) and
reminds one of *amable*, *likable* in Spanish. It can also be read as an amal-
gam of Spanish (from *amar*, to love) and French (*belle*, beautiful, or a
beauty). Her name reflects the interlinguistic nature of border culture,
where languages (Kreyòl, French, and Spanish) merge, introducing new
modes of communication. The Spanish *ama* combined with the French
belle can be interpreted as a command: to love beauty. Amabelle highlights
the interdependent histories shared by Haiti and the Dominican Republic,
thus rejecting imposed, binary national memory crafted by brutal dictators such as Duvalier and Trujillo.

Her family name, Désir, evokes Désiré of Jacques Stephen Alexis's
novel *General Sun, My Brother* (*Compère Général Soleil*, 1955). In *General Sun*, Désiré is born months before the massacre to Hilarion and
Claire-Heureuse, who in Haiti face the loss of their house and police
threats for being Communist sympathizers.[15] They evade these problems
by joining a friend on a Dominican sugar plantation. Alexis, in accordance
with his political beliefs, focuses on love and the economic conditions of
life in Haiti. He writes:

> In this country, where not a single rural section, not a single neigh-
> borhood escapes the taste of ashes and unbearable misery, love falls
> quickly from heaven and ends up on the hard soil of life. For Hilarion
> and Claire-Heureuse, love gradually became meals eaten without
> meat while smiling and speaking in an unconcerned manner about
> the rough day at work. Love was a pair of mended trousers that
> looked whole. Love learned to go to bed without supper, chatting
> about everything and nothing, with a mouthful of the salty taste of
> tears, and finally, a quick little sentence just before going to sleep.
> (130)

Hilarion and Claire-Heureuse are depicted as hard-working, humble
people who, despite their best efforts to construct a simple honest life, are
trampled by political injustices. Désiré is their hope and their future, but
the infant dies shortly after a violent encounter with search dogs. As the
novel ends, Hilarion meets his own death. His last words to Claire-
Heureuse encompass Alexis's own belief in struggle for the future:

> I have to say that there were also small pleasures—the beginning of
> adolescence, illusions of love and pleasures with no future, bitter-

sweet pleasures, empty moments of lust, and the emptiness of the
mornings that followed. But friendship and love changed me.... You
must give birth to another Hilarion, other Désirés, and only you can
create them. You have to go forward to other mornings of love. ...
You know ... why men leave their native lands, why sickness ravages
our people, and how little girls become whores. (289)

By giving Amabelle the family name *Désir*, Danticat is answering
Hilarion's request and aligning herself with Alexis' politics of hope despite
the odds. Danticat gives birth, through fiction, to another Désiré. With
Amabelle Désir, Danticat affirms desire—of life, of possibility, of good
things—which is a creative power, a tactic of resistance and survival, in the
face of difficulty. She also pays homage to Alexis, who had been stoned to
death for his socialist views. His dreams of a better Haiti did not die with
him.

This leads to the second interpretation of Désir. In Danticat's novel, it
means the desire for love and a better life. Amabelle, the bearer of a name
about love and beauty, is, as Alexis foreshadowed, a witness to death and
loss of love. Later in the text Amabelle thinks, "This past is more like flesh
than air; our stories testimonials like the ones never heard by the justice of
the peace or the Generalissimo himself" (281). Amabelle is the testimony
and, therefore, a guardian of her history.

The past, for Amabelle, is palpable like a body; her reflections defy erasure and add imagination, memory, and possibility to contested Haitian
history. As Elsass says, "Physical violence aims at destroying objects and
people; mental violence aims at destroying identities" (Elsass 157). There
can be no doubt of the extent to which Haitian lives have been annihilated.
Haitian scholar Michel-Rolph Trouillot likens the erasure of human lives
in Haiti to the erasure of Jewish identity in the concentration camps: "the
literature on slavery in the Americas and on the Holocaust suggests that
there may be structural similarities in global silences or, at the very least,
that erasure and banalization are not unique to the Haitian Revolution"
(96). His argument is structured around the power gained by the victors
when they silence the stories of those who have been eliminated, berated,
or, at the very least, marginalized.

With Amabelle and Sebastien, Danticat creates a story that follows in
an established tradition of fictions of misery. With respect to the importance of the heritage of Guinea preserved in *vodou*, Joan Dayan says of this
literature: "The novels of Jacques Roumain, Jacques-Stephan Alexis, and

Marie Chauvet examine the causes and effects of a misery unalleviated and brutal. These writers historicize the Haitian majority by attending to the one thing that remains in a landscape of loss" (79). In this landscape of loss, and beyond the parameters of the gods (many, like Danny LaFerrière, have humorously mentioned that the gods stay in Haiti and do not migrate with them to colder places in North America), Danticat underscores the continued losses Haitians and Dominicans still experience.

These losses are experienced most painfully in death. While searching for Sebastien, Amabelle finds only his fading memory and testaments of his abandoned past at his mother's house in Haiti. She is confronted with how little the Haitian government will do to help her and others like her. She waits in a long government-organized line to tell her story, but the wait becomes futile when the authorities decide they can do no more and tell everyone to go home. The genocidal events, which were once flagrantly visible in the shape of corpses floating along the Massacre River, wounded bodies in the makeshift camps, and people crying into the night, begin to fade when the corpses stop floating, the dead are buried, the camps empty and close down, and the bodily wounds and bruises engage some semblance of healing. Amabelle can never walk straight again, and her features are forever distorted from the blows she survived, but her body barely exposes the psychological effects that surviving a denied massacre have on her and others.

Psychological wounds are always the hardest to describe, or even pinpoint, in any accurate way. Memory plays tricks on survivors, either torturing them with the horrors they have lived or relieving them of those horrors through glimpses of happier past moments. This stands out clearly in the scene where a survivor tells of waking up in a burial pit after the massacre and recalling his wedding night.

> "Waking up among the dead, I started screaming," the man from the cadaver pit went on. "And then I thought of my woman and our first night together, and in spite of all the corpses, I smiled."
>
> The people around him smiled, too, at the beauty of such an innocent moment, when a young woman wakes up in her new man's bed for the first time and forgets how she came to be there. (211)

The beauty of waking up in a bridal bed is contrasted starkly to the terror of waking up amid corpses. Time is expected to heal the survivors' emotions. But just as their bodies heal haphazardly, their emotions never recover from such brutality. Although Amabelle, unwillingly sensing the reality of Sebastien's death, enters a daily rhythm of work with his mother, she cannot engage with life. She spends much of her time alone, cannot begin another love relationship and, despite logical thought, continues to wait for news of Sebastien. His disappearance, without confirmation of how or what happened, tortures her. She cannot bury his body and make peace with his soul. She cannot see him and help him heal; instead, she is left with the memory of their conversations in the dark, their dreams of return to Haiti as a couple, and the systematic, even celebrated, elimination of Haitians on the border.[16] Given the effect memory has on Amabelle, it becomes a trap. Amabelle's clinging to what few memories she has does not allow her to heal. Here, again, the binary contradiction between memory as healing and memory as debilitating is made evident.

While thousands of people were murdered or uprooted from their humble lives on the Dominican border, letters exchanged between the two presidents, Trujillo and Vincent, were congenial, even amicable (Cuello). Vincent did not seem to be outraged by the elimination of his countrymen. Meanwhile, Trujillo's orders inspired growing nationalism, shaped by eliminating "difference." He looked to European fascists such as Hitler to inspire his own national discourse. In 1936 the national paper *Listín Diario* printed translated sections of Hitler's *Mein Kampf*, in which overt racial intolerance was admired and encouraged. Conversely, he also welcomed Jews at a price of five hundred dollars per person. They were relegated mostly to a dairy farm in Sosua, on the north central coast of the Cibao region near Puerto Plata.

Trujillo also adopted traditional forms of leadership. He wore a suit reminiscent of Napoleon's. And, after the massacre, he challenged Haiti to war in an indirect and outmoded manner. In the *Diario la Marina* he stated that he had thrown down the gauntlet ("lancé le gant") against a people without honor.[17] His choice of words to describe his actions is interesting. He does not say that he had people murdered; instead, he refers to the medieval practice of throwing the glove down in order to challenge an opponent. Here the opponent would have been the Haitians, and his challenge, presumably, would have been to their right of livelihood on the border. According to the *Diario la Marina*, he intended to end the humiliation that Dominicans experienced when they were subjected to inferior people like the Haitians.

Sténio Vincent's lack of initial reaction was rooted in self-interest. Practically speaking, having thousands of starving Haitians returned to his portion of the island only meant more misery and the greater possibility of another revolution. Nonetheless, international pressures forced Trujillo to offer a sum of money to the surviving families. The money was not paid in full, and very few people saw any remuneration or apology for the deaths incurred. In essence, the corruption that existed in the higher political arena erased the dimensions of the massacre, stealing from the people the history of the crime committed and an official space of mourning. The message that the presidents gave was clear: human life was worth very little.

The Farming of Bones speaks to these ruthless historical abominations. The novel imaginatively evokes a situation in which memory is both urgently needed and absolutely nonfunctional. If memory can be stolen from the masses by corrupt, powerful leaders, it can be returned to the people through literature. Danticat's work is complicated by the imperfection of history. The service she performs as a socially and politically aware writer is located in the stark, uncompromising way she lays out the condition of traumatic pasts, traumatized memory, and the dysfunctional aspect of memory. Part of the story she underlines is that terrible things have happened, nobody acknowledges them, or, worse, everybody knows but nobody does anything to change the circumstances. Instead, repeated amnesties give criminals impunity. The survivors cling to their past grievances and are consequently trapped by that moment. The past is no longer a past but a present that imprisons them in pain and fear. Paralyzed, the victims/survivors cannot ignite the imaginative engines that might otherwise propel them into possible new futures. For example, while waiting for Sebastien one night, Amabelle remarks, "When you have so few remembrances, you cling to them tightly and repeat them over and over in your mind so time will not erase them" (45). She closes her eyes and remembers her own past, her parents' house, and the Citadelle from a further past that loomed over that house. Her recall is double. She remembers her deceased family in order to ease her discomfort about the disappeared Sebastien's precarious situation. She also remembers the Citadelle, which links her subjective present to her historical past. La Citadelle Laferrière, which was constructed to protect the area from a French invasion, is a massive fortress balanced on top of the 900m Pic la Ferrière. It overlooks Cap Haïtien and represents Haitian grandeur. It also is tied to another cruel leader, the poet Henri Christophe. "To prove his men's loyalty, Henri Christophe once ordered troops to march off the edge of the Citadelle; they fell to their deaths below" (Wucker 14). Violence is at the root of a history Amabelle clings to.

Bodies in Literature: Citizenship in Life

Diaspora Haitians, geographically removed from the island's misery but continually aware of the effects of relentless violence—historical, economic, natural—become active participants in Haitian politics and Haitian support groups. Organizations such as the National Coalition for Haitian Rights are doing groundbreaking work educating Haitians, Haitian Americans, and others about the possibilities of democracy in Haiti. Authors such as Danticat, whose creative work is grounded in political activism, facilitate participation in politics both in Haiti and in the United States. Danticat's stories illustrate individuals who give form to memory and context to citizenship. Danticat creates human characters who are complex in motivation, thought, emotion, and deed, and thus describes the effects violence has on people. She nuances the way survivors/victims deal with violence, and the ways in which memory does and does not work for them. In one of numerous interviews with Renée Shea, Danticat tells how Amabelle is "modeled on a real story" told by Albert Hicks, who covered the massacre for *Colliers Magazine*. In his later book *Blood in the Streets*, Hicks reported that an officer had his maid slaughtered at the dinner table in order to show his compliance the night that Trujillo ordered the massacre. Danticat was inspired by this maid, but wanted to change the story and make her survive (Shea 14).

With her stories, Danticat pays homage to the maid and, in general, to those that have been forgotten by history. Other characters in *The Farming of Bones*, such as Joël and his father, Kongo, as well as the priest, Father Romain, are *men with names* (albeit names and people invented by the author) *who will never truly die* (282), at least not in the memory of those who have read the novel. By exposure to these characters, the reader is invited to reflect on how terrible some aspects of Haitian history have been. The reader, in shock and disgust, can ignore the message or can be motivated to do something for Haiti, with a better understanding of the sociocultural and historical mechanisms that drive it.[18] Danticat's characters defy obliteration from memory and Haitian history. Even Joël, the first character to be killed—in the night by a racing car before the massacre begins—is immortalized. Kongo keeps his son's memory alive by creating

Joël's likeness in a mask he gives to Amabelle to carry back to Haiti. Joël has a mask that recalls his name. This mask plays an important role in linking him to his ancestral past, underscoring the resilience of Africa despite the repression experienced in the Dominican Republic. Like the ancient masks of the Roman Senate, Joël's mask situates him within the drama of his people, symbolizing him as a moral, hardworking person affiliated with a community and with the long history linking the Dominican Republic, Haiti, and Africa.

Father Romain, who after the massacre loses his memory, believes that "remembering—though sometimes painful—can make you strong" (73). He, like Sebastien, takes great heart from the fact that they have common roots in one Haitian village. "This was how people left imprints of themselves in each other's memory so that if you left first and went back to the common village, you could carry, if not a letter, a piece of treasured clothing, some message to their loved ones that their place was still among the living" (73). Being among the living is synonymous with working, being alive, belonging to some collective. But Joël is killed, Kongo goes off into the night, Sebastien is disappeared, and Father Romain is tortured so brutally that the only way he regains a grasp on life is by forgetting, giving up the priesthood, marrying, and having a family. Amabelle will survive to witness the destruction of the world she knew and any meaning she might have given it. When she hears about Trujillo's plan—whispers that a mass murder to eliminate the Haitians is under way—she can't believe it. It seems so absurd. She has a job; she, like Sebastien, contributes to the structure of the town. Stealing meaning from her life is equivalent to stealing her life. In the aftermath of the massacre, little semblance of civilization remains for a survivor such as Amabelle, who must struggle to cope and again find meaning in the world.

Of the survivors of the concentration camps in Nazi Germany, Peter Elsass has written that "the camps eliminated the possibility of there being a higher meaning of life. The survivor became, in a sense, the person who had lived through the crisis of civilization and suffered its breakdown" (188). Psychiatrist Victor Frankl, who was a survivor of the camps, wrote that people gave up living when they found no more meaning in their lives (Elsass 187). Bruno Bettelheim theorized that by "keeping individual and spiritual morality high, they could combat personality dissolution and [retain] hope" (Bettelheim in Elsass 188). Elsass points out, however, that many people survived in the camps by cooperating with the guards or by stealing from weaker inmates. In either case, survival was contingent upon

finding meaning to life or upon a complete subversion of the social contract of correct human conduct. Arguably, survival was achieved only via
extreme responses. Amabelle's character exposes survival in a middle-
place, survival in a state of emotional paralysis.

Amabelle, as a survivor in and through literature, embodies the possibility of Haitian history and memory. While the massacre stole the place of
many in this world, Danticat's writing resituates them within it. It is not
only Danticat's personal pain that is addressed through characters such as
Amabelle, but also the pain of dehumanization that we all experience
through such unaddressed violence. Violence cannot simply vanish into
thin air. For this reason, Amabelle returns at the end of the novel to visit
Señora Valencia, with whom she had grown up, serving her, even bringing
her children into the world. Amabelle notices that everything has changed.
Even the stream is gone; houses have been built over it. Later when Señora
Valencia takes her to a waterfall, it looks different, smaller, than she had
remembered. The terrain has been cleared and built up. There is no rem-
nant of nights of massacres, of *el corte*—which means the actual cutting or
severance of something, and was used by Dominicans to refer to that brutal harvest of 1937 when humans, not sugarcane crops, were felled. There
is no monument to recall the tragedy of senseless murders, only new architecture to underscore the Generalissimo's project of national improve-
ment.

The absence of revenge or mourning for such a tragedy effectively
erased the memory of those who had been massacred. Shame and silence
took the place of outrage and contestation. Michele Wucker states, "The
Haitians have become invisible in order to survive" (86). But their invisibility (silence) has not helped them survive; instead, they subsist in a culture of violence and trauma that has received limited redress. Literature
can be a strong antidote to this silence, this violence, and its consequent
trauma. What can we do when we witness people being massacred in other
countries, in other languages? If the massacres end, then we immediately
hope to forget the tragedies and move on to a calmer future.

But as Sylvie's and Señora Valencia's characters suggest, violence leaves
a terrible imprint that cannot be erased with new buildings and squares.
Sylvie, a Haitian who must have been saved from the massacre by Señora
Valencia, stays to the side, lowers her eyes, and remains silent. Señora
Valencia does not recognize Amabelle and has very little to say when she
realizes who she is. The awkwardness of the scene reveals the deep pain of
the past and underscores Señora Valencia's inability to deal with it. Still,

that she saved the life of another Haitian girl, even though her husband was a Trujillista military man who was supposedly leading the massacre, also reveals great courage on her part. The three characters embody the effects of the massacre on both Haitians and Dominicans. Amabelle cannot heal from her wounds, Señora Valencia cannot address the memory of such extreme violence, and Sylvie lives in perpetual fear and with many questions.

When they go to the waterfall, Sylvie shakes with anxiety and asks, "Why parsley?" (303) The question refers to how some of Trujillo's henchmen asked people to say the word *perejil*, Spanish for "parsley." If they could correctly pronounce the *r*, they were spared, considered native Dominicans. Sylvie cannot forget this image of people screaming "perejil, pesil, pe—" She is unconvinced by the señora's response. Her character, subservient and briefly presented at the end of the novel, signals the profound effects of violence. It cannot be healed without redress. Sylvie represents the trauma of an entire generation. Her character highlights the presence of the past in the Dominican Republic despite the new terrain and many unaddressed emotional and physical wounds.

The changed geography does not erase the pain and the terror of the massacre. *The Farming of Bones* is thus a monument that does not exist in any border town. It is an international, literary monument to life, resistance, and survival.

Textual Memorials

To conclude this chapter, let me return to the inspiring words spoken by Dr. Maurice O. Wallace in his funeral sermon for Bem:

> Don't hang up your harp, even in the darkest day.
> Don't hang up your harp, it may be all you have, but it may be all you need.
> Don't hang up your harp, lied on, cheated, talked about, mistreated.
> Don't hang up your harp, 'buked, scorned, talked about sure as you born.
> Don't hang up your harp. (Holloway 190)

These words of survival and resistance are critical in our considerations of the meanings of memories in the face of violence. Different acts of violence, and the ensuing memories, are meant to break people and communities down. Danticat shows the ways that memory can be a prison house.

She also offers us a story that we can link to other texts. One that flares to mind is the Declaration on the Rights of Man, later edited and renamed the Universal Declaration of Human Rights. It calls for respect and honor:

> All human beings are born free and equal in dignity and rights. They are endowed with reason and conscience and should act towards one another in a spirit of brotherhood. . . . No one shall be held in slavery or servitude . . . [or] subjected to torture or to cruel, inhuman or degrading treatment or punishment. Everyone has the right to recognition everywhere as a person before the law[,] . . . the right to an effective [judicial] remedy[,] . . . [freedom from] arbitrary arrest, detention or exile[,] . . . a fair and public hearing by an independent and impartial tribunal[,] . . . the right to be presumed innocent until proved guilty[,] . . . [freedom from] arbitrary interference with his privacy, family, home or correspondence[,] . . . freedom of movement and residence[,] . . . the right to seek and enjoy in other countries asylum[,] . . . the right to a nationality[,] . . . the right to marry and to found a family[,] . . . the right to own property[,] . . . freedom of thought, conscience and religion[,] . . . of opinion and expression[,] . . . of peaceful assembly and association[,] . . . the right to take part in the government of his country[,] . . . [and] the right of equal access to public service in his country.

Drafted in 1945 during the San Francisco conference on the United Nations and finally put into effect in 1966, this declaration represents an international call against violence such as the Nazi genocide of Jews during World War II. Reminiscent of documents such as the French Declaration of the Rights of Man, it too is failing to enforce respect for human lives. Political theorists have noted that the problems with an international treaty are rooted in the way different cultures define sovereignty, turning to "traditions" as a way to evade laws that would, for example, grant citizenship to women. When nations enter war, the old adage "All is fair in love and war" seems to permit greater violence to occur. The parameters of respect for human rights are severely obscured by the need to win, through force, brutality, and sometimes complete obliteration of the enemy. At that point, all suffering is part of the battlefield; all rights are but a notion. Haiti's colonial and other leaders—including the Lavalas government of Aristide, blamed for recent atrocities—have disenfranchised the people in order to give power to a select few.[19]

Danticat's literature honors the people and remembers the gods and goddesses. For example, *The Farming of Bones* is dedicated to Metrès Dlo, the female spirit of the river to whom Amabelle dedicates and tells the story. It also honors the powerful female spirit Erzulie. Erzulie is, I believe, invoked by the very exposition of the text. An important figure in Haitian *vodou*, she is "the dream impaled eternally upon the cosmic cross-roads where the world of men and the world of divinity meet, and it is through her pierced heart that 'man ascends and the gods descend'" (Deren 145). According to Maya Deren, who received a Guggenheim award to do research in Haiti, Erzulie is the goddess of love and impossible perfection. Since this perfection does not exist, she instead witnesses the failures of man and must weep. Her "wound is perpetual" (145). Similarly, the wound and pain of Haitian history and the Haitian people is perpetual. Danticat's stories underscore this, but also add a dimension of hope to that dismal picture. She does not put her harp down and sings through her fiction.

In "Nineteen Thirty-Seven," a short story from Danticat's 1995 collection *Krik? Krak!*, the protagonist carries a crying Madonna every time she visits her mother in prison. The mother and daughter of this story are survivors of the 1937 massacre, when the elder saw her own mother chopped up by the Generalissimo's soldiers. Her loss and pain were assuaged ever so slightly by her own daughter's survival. She had flown and escaped the massacre. In Haiti she was accused of being a loup-garou, a witch who could get out of her skin and fly at night. She was imprisoned for this and, on her death, burned so that she would not haunt little children. Throughout the story, she asks if the Madonna has cried and at one point breaks down in sobs herself. Her daughter watches silently. The tears of the Madonna and of her mother embody the perpetual pain experienced by someone who has survived the injustices of murderous soldiers and ignorant policemen. Erzulie is represented by the Madonna, recalled by the mother, and honored silently by the daughter.[20]

Danticat's intimate stories of the dead, and the potential survivors, of the 1937 massacre creates a narrative space for mourning losses, recognizing the pain those losses have cut into people's lives, and envisioning life with dignity despite the experience of those horrors and despite the knowledge that human beings are not only capable of committing atrocities but continue to commit them. On a constructive note, however, novels such as Danticat's may help economic refugees change their status to political refugees (and prompt changes in U.S. immigration policies toward

Haitians). The global lesson of *The Farming of Bones* is to emphasize the potential of human beings and the need to continue fighting for human rights. Danticat's literature speaks to a future where memory is not abolished and the beauty of people like Sebastien and Amabelle is recognized. Through fiction, different versions of life in Haiti and the Dominican Republic are shaped from the darkness of silence. Fiction serves as a site of memory. This memory functions as a memorial that permits the recognition of trauma, creates a space for mourning losses, and inspires survival— letting go and moving on. As a memorial, *The Farming of Bones* traces the horror of the massacre and scripts a memory of human possibility.

What Happens When Memory Hurts?

The Haunting of Rape

Haiti is a country where most aggressors act with impunity,[1] live among their victims, and often feel proud of their actions. Yet violations must be exposed and addressed, however distant justice might seem. Rape, one of a number of commonly deployed acts of violence in Haiti, has been receiving legal and community attention over the last fourteen years. For example, the document "Rape in Haiti: A Weapon of Terror," a 1994 report by Human Rights Watch and the National Coalition for Haitian Refugees (now called the National Coalition for Haitian Rights), sheds some light on the cultural, historical, and political circumstances of rape. It specifically studies sexual abuse under General Raoul Cédras's regime, but also exposes long-term, tacit policies around rape. The report reveals at least nine cases of politically motivated violations. It also cites a United Nations/Organization of American States Civilian Mission report that documented sixty-six rapes of a political nature between January and May 1994 (11). It references the victims' hesitation to testify and their experience that any appeal to the judicial system is futile. "Victims of rape by state agents or their auxiliaries fear that lodging a complaint will only further endanger their and their family's lives" (3). One victim told the docent that she never reported her rape to the police. "She feared for [her] life going there" (10–11). Another woman reported witnessing the rape of a woman in a car by at least two uniformed policemen. Her reaction was not uncommon. "I did not report what happened to the police: What would have been the use? They were the ones responsible. I can't even imagine what eventually happened to that woman" (11). Another woman who was interviewed says simply, "This happened to lots of girls. It just seems to be a common problem and . . . that is what the paramilitary thugs do at night" (12). Unfortunately, the report did not study rape without political motivation, which receives little if no attention in recent human rights/political studies.

In Haiti, honor continues to be one of the most valuable possessions a woman, and her family, can maintain.[2] Therefore, rape explicitly threatens the reputation of the victim and her family. Many victims avoid going public—or reporting the crime to police or military officials, who often are "authorized" rapists—in an attempt to preserve their moral standing within the community. Victims (as they prefer to call themselves in Haiti) and survivors (as many women prefer to call themselves in the United States) suffer long-term consequences from rape, whether it is part of state terror or an isolated incident of abuse. The repercussions of rape are manifold. Disregard of women in law and society characterizes Haiti's history and continues to permeate its culture, despite the recent activism of groups such as Enfofanm (Information for and about women), Dwa Fanm (women's rights), and Fanm Yo La (Women, We Are Here), SOFA (Solidarité Fanm Ayisyen, translated as Haitian Women's Solidarity Group) and Kay Fanm (Women's House), and despite global attention to women's rights at meetings including the Fourth International Conference on Women in Beijing in 1995. State repression, random rape, and denied memories of crimes have long-term emotional and psychological effects. Rape in Haiti is real, and victims are underserved. There are few places for women to get aid, and even those Haitian rape victims who later migrate to other countries sometimes isolate themselves from their new surroundings—and services and support—out of fear and shame.

Rape and its repercussions belittle women, making them feel they have no rights, only haunting memories. What happens to survivors? How do they deal with the violence that has been inflicted on their bodies, their families, and their communities? How can isolated incidents on a faraway island be reviewed within the larger context of violations of women internationally? Does historical and legal documentation offer adequate information about tragedies faced by women in Haiti and its diaspora? Can fiction's disclosure of violence create a still-needed space for public testimony and for personal possibility, such as recovery from trauma and discovery of meaning in life?

Attempting Address

There are many obstacles to understanding rape's full impact on individuals in a society. Often, survivors are accused of being either victims who recall the violence for personal gain or seductresses who are responsible in some way for the violations. Internationally, rape has received embarrassingly little attention. In the United States, less than one rape in ten is reported to the police; conviction of the offender occurs in only one case out of a hundred.[3] Some reports state that a woman is raped every five minutes in the United States, yet we live in a "society where violence against women is supported and condoned, excused and rationalized, the testimony of survivors of sexual abuse is silenced, ignored, distorted, and drowned out by the thundering voices of the patriarchs" (Tal 197). Elsewhere it may be worse. In Brazil, Title IV of the Penal Code states that "rape is a crime against custom and not a crime against persons" (Caldeira 204). Legally, the personal dimensions of rape are thus trivialized. It could be said that the most commonly underreported abuses are those suffered by women, especially sexual abuse and rape (Hayner 77). Repeatedly, and internationally, the right of women to a life safe from personal violation is a contested one.

The history of women's rights as individuals in Haiti is fraught with neglect, even though Haiti was one of the original members of the United Nations taking part in the December 10, 1948, Universal Declaration of Human Rights. International human rights conventions have addressed women's status in print and in theory: In 1949 the International Declaration of Human Rights outlawed prostitution and exploitation. In 1954 the United Nations adopted the Convention on the Political Rights of Women. The UN's Convention on the Elimination of All Forms of Discrimination against Women (CEDAW), agreed upon in December 1979 and ratified by Haiti on September 3, 1981, outlines concern with, and proposes policy for, women's safety and citizenship. Haiti engaged in further discussions about women's rights at the Inter-American Convention on the Prevention, Punishment, and Eradication of Violence Against Women, the Fourth International Conference on Women in Beijing in 1995 (the Haitian delegation was led by Dr. Lise-Marie Dejean, named in 1994 as the first head of the country's Ministry of Women's Affairs and Women's Rights), and the Belém do Pará Convention in 1996. Haiti also ratified the International Convention on the Elimination of All Forms of Racial Discrimination in 1972 and the International Covenant on Civil and Political Rights in 1991—a quarter century after signing the document. Human rights specialist Ann Fuller notes:

> Ratification, however, is but one step, and in Haiti's case, it has had little practical or even formal significance. With regard to the

CEDAW, under both dictatorship and democracy, Haiti has ignored its commitment to make implementation-progress reports to the Committee on the Elimination of Discrimination Against Women. Neither the initial report due in 1982, nor follow-up reports in 1986, 1990, 1994, and 1998 have been submitted. (2)

Conventions and agreements organized and written with the specific goal of implementing, or at least initiating, social change for women's rights can do nothing without the support of the government and a general change of attitude toward women's rights. Violence continues to afflict Haitian women because the problem has yet to be addressed—not only rhetorically and theoretically but also socially—by aggressive government involvement and local, community, and family programming. Furthermore, the rape of women, often in view of their families, has been deployed as a political tactic of terror by several repressive regimes, including those of the Duvaliers (1957–86) and the brutal "de facto" regime (1991–94). Policy proposals aimed at the noble goal of improving women's lives and their safety are severely challenged by a tradition of psychological, social, and political violence against women. One Haitian man told me that other social ills are so dire that rape is relegated to the back burner, considered the manifestation of anger, desperation, and/or a man's right.[4] Violence against a wife, for example, is considered a private matter, not to be addressed by the state or national law. Women, consequently, live under attack. Nonetheless, all attempts to disclose violence against women, including reports, policy proposals, and literature, are fundamental steps toward understanding this violence, fighting it, and ultimately introducing and implementing long-term changes to improve women's living conditions.

The "Rape in Haiti: A Weapon of Terror" report concluded that "documenting rape by police and soldiers is especially difficult, given the climate of fear and repression under which most women's rights activists operate, as well as the rape victims' fear of reprisal, which has long prevented them from reporting rape" (7). During times of war and repressive military regimes, gang rapes, ethnic cleansing rapes, rape during torture procedures, and rape before execution destroy any sense of community and humanity, stealing meaning from individuals and making women feel guilty and shamed within their communities and families. Yet their suffering and stories have rarely formed part of the larger psychological mechanisms of justice and reconciliation. At issue is the question "What good will my testimony do?" Most women believe that their testimonies will amount to nothing more than ghost stories that no one will believe—or, worse, that they will be accused of inviting the violence acted against their bodies. They have a point. For example, members of FAVILEK (Fanm Viktim Leve Kanpe, or Women Victims Get Up and Stand Up) were victims of the widespread and well-documented sex crimes against women during the Haitian coup d'état and military rule between 1991 and 1994. These women are still fighting for financial reparations. In an interview, one of the members coldly asked, "What do we keep telling our story for, if we do not get any help?"[5] The women of FAVILEK are frustrated because they have told their stories to many human rights groups, journalists, and local women's groups, and yet not a single case has made it to a court of law. This is what they continue to fight for.

Truth Commissions and Memory

The past century has witnessed a plethora of repressive governments—dictatorships, military regimes, de facto leadership—that have played truth against lies (or the "official" truth) in publicly denying human rights violations. Truth became a major playing card in twentieth-century politics. Torture has taken place in the name of truth—getting the "truth" out of people. And commissions have been organized to get to the "truth" of what happened. But truth, like memory, is not so simple. As William James has asked: "How will truth be realized? What, in short, is the truth's cash-value in experiential terms?" (169). The value of truth in experiential terms is critical to understanding our expectations, and the manipulation, of "truth." For example, in her seminal 1985 study *The Body in Pain,* Elaine Scarry analyzes the pain of war and the false goals of torture. Introducing the power and weakness of rhetoric within the framework of war and survival, she concludes that the attainment of information, a form of truth, has nothing to do with torture and violence. In the torture chamber, it is not truth that the torturer seeks, although this is the premise of the torture being enacted. Torture destroys the fiber of the enemy, weakening and/or eliminating opposition. Torture and war, she claims, "unmake the world," and literature serves as a means to reconstruct that unmade world. The stories that are told after any fact aim at constructing a truth that makes sense to the teller. Then the victim/survivor's experience is reframed in a constructive, or destructive, narrative highlighting the effects of the experience (told truthfully) on the present.

James proposes another formulation:

> The truth of an idea is not a stagnant property inherent in it. Truth *happens* to an idea. It *becomes* true, is *made* true by events. Its verity *is* in fact an event, a process: the process namely of its verifying itself, its veri-*fication*. Its validity is the process of its valid-*ation*. (169–70)

Truth is presented as an "idea" that requires verification and validation. Let us translate the idea (a philosophical query) into the act (a socio-political situation), and inquire how an act of violence can be verified and validated. What if an event, a crime such as a rape, is denied by the government and by society at large? Is the "truth" of the victim's experience heeded? Under such circumstances, an entire sector—victims, survivors, their families, other women who are fearful for their well-being—cannot verify or validate its experiences. An objective truth is then pitted against a flawed memory.

The debate over truth versus memory shadows the fight for social and legal justice. Violations against humanity continue. People have been taken away at night, imprisonments have not been properly registered, and corpses have been disposed of without a trace. Family members have been misinformed, or not informed, of their loved ones' whereabouts. Children born in prison have been put up for adoption without authorization.

One way the truth of people's denied experiences has been addressed officially is through truth commissions. For countries such as Argentina, Chile, and El Salvador, truth commissions have played a prominent role in wronged citizens' quest for justice, memory, and reconciliation. While governments were denying atrocities, the commissions disclosed them. The commissions have sought to document past human rights abuses in repressive regimes and to bring about a more peaceful democracy by requiring violators to admit their crimes and by helping victims approach the memory of the horrors. In Argentina, for example, seven thousand statements were taken in nine months for the National Commission on the Disappeared, often called CONADEP for Comisión Nacional sobre la Desaparición de Personas. About fifteen hundred survivors gave testimony about detention camps and torture; 8,960 disappeared persons were documented (Hayner 34). A brief version of the full report, *Nunca más*, was later put out by a private publisher. It was an immediate best seller; copies remain available in bookstores today.

Each Latin American and Caribbean country has its own history of terror and violence. A small number of cases of national human rights violations have received address through truth commissions. In essence, however, these represent mostly failed attempts at justice.[6] According to Juan Méndez, former legal counsel to Human Rights Watch, Argentines today feel that reconciliation has no meaning. "*Reconciliation* in Argentina was understood by victims to mean, 'We are being asked to reconcile with our torturers, and they're being asked to do nothing'" (160). The truth commission may have brought many of the denied atrocities to light, but neither it nor the trials that ensued brought real justice. Real justice, many argue, would have put the perpetrators in prison; victims and survivors would not be obliged to live with, or even accept, their violators in their lives.

Truth commissions in Argentina, Chile, and Uruguay were not "proactive in seeking out, encouraging, or facilitating testimony from women," according to Priscilla Hayner (78).[7] She points out: "Truth commissions in the past have occasionally had information about sexual abuse against women but have chosen not to report it, judging that rape did not fall within their mandate of politically motivated crimes"; in the memorable case of the three American nuns raped and killed in El Salvador in 1980, "the commissioners . . . reported only that the women were abducted and killed" (79). In order for women's testimonials about rape to be taken into account by the truth commissions, the data gatherers must prove that the rape was motivated by political goals and/or ordered by officials. Women are described as wives, sisters, and mothers first; often rape is reported as a secondary or tertiary violation after other abuses acted out against the men and their families.

Limited time and resources render truth commissions less than exhaustive, but their goal is to acknowledge the atrocities that occurred in a previous regime. (It must be noted that, by this standard, the Argentine truth commission did meet with a certain degree of success.) This kind of "truth telling" in some cases leads to healing for victims whose losses and suffering are no longer denied. Hayner argues, "Official acknowledgment can be powerful precisely because official denial has been so pervasive" (27). Conversely, revisitation of painful memories can also lead to retraumatization. This factor helps explain why Cambodia has avoided creation of a truth commission: with former Khmer Rouge members living in many communities, an exploration of the past could be more dangerous than helpful (200). The need for and success of truth commissions is contingent on cultural, political, and social conditions in different countries. They are not exhaustive, and other venues of disclosure have proved to be more useful in gaining international attention and inciting international aid.

Truth commissions were supposed to do at least one of three things: tell the truth, acknowledge wrongdoing, and/or lead to justice. In countries such as Guatemala and Haiti, truth commissions have been less than successful because so many people already knew what was going on and, besides, perpetrators refused to acknowledge their actions.[8] It can be argued that the violations taking place in Guatemala have been most publicly revealed by Rigoberta Menchú's now controversial testimony.[9] Despite arguments against Menchú's testimony, it is a critical testament for Latin America and the Caribbean. Problematic as it has turned out to be, testimony does not have to be about one's personal experience. In abused cultures, testimony can testify against the trauma of abuse, its memory, and its repetition. Even if Menchú did not live everything she wrote about, it is possible that she had been traumatized by witnessing some events, and by hearing of others over the years. Perhaps her testimony is about the memory of more than just herself.

From 1991 to 1994, after the coup d'état, between five and seven thousand people in Haiti were murdered, and many others were tortured in prison or in the streets and in their own homes.[10] The problem, as lawyer and Haiti specialist Brian Concannon points out, is that the commission did not tell the people anything they did not already know.[11] A strong history of impunity meant that none of the violators had to acknowledge wrongdoing or feel remorse.

Haiti's 1994 Truth Commission was organized upon Jean-Bertrand Aristide's return to office, to investigate the crimes committed during the de facto military government that ruled for three years after he was ousted in 1991. It received a mandate "to pay particular attention to 'crimes of a sexual nature against female victims that were committed with political ends'" (Hayner 78). This focus on the political ignored, even trivialized, the serious wider history of sexual abuse of women. Nonetheless, such an investigation was groundbreaking in the context of truth commissions of the previous ten years. At least it gave women—even if only a few—a face within the larger picture of state violence.

The commission collected the testimony of almost "5,500 witnesses, pertaining to some 8,600 victims" (Hayner 66). Although the commission completed its work in 1996, its findings were not made public until one year later. Journalist Catherine Orenstein, who was in Haiti during some of the Truth Commission collection period, says that officials just put the report into a drawer.[12] The main weakness of the report was in its distribution. Concannon told the author that although the UN/OAS International Civilian Mission in Haiti (MICIVIH) made fifty copies available right away, piles were later forgotten at government offices. Also available were audiotapes with Kreyòl translation of parts of the original French report. But people were not especially interested in hearing what they already knew, when reparations and justice did not seem to be in sight. Recently, the National Coalition for Haitian Rights (www.NCHR.org) made an English translation available online.[13]

The massive international news coverage of the violence in Haiti after the 1991 coup d'état, and through 1994, contrasts with coverage of the truth commission report. Concannon suggests that the military period was perhaps the most witnessed and documented in Haiti's history.[14] The military men made a point of showing off their human rights violations. Their reign was about terror and snuffing out democracy; the regime was not going to allow elections or even opposition. All opponents of the regime, as well as supporters of Aristide, were hunted down and many were killed. In numerous cases, when the men were not around, their wives, mothers, sisters, and daughters were raped in front of their families to make a point. Many families went into hiding in the mountains. Many people died, but even now there are no exact numbers. Women who had been hurt or mutilated and were in hiding could not find medical or psychological help.

Little can be done to salve these kinds of wounds. Even in silence, the people remember the Tonton Macoutes of Duvalier, the *zenglendos* (bands of thugs) and *attachés* (civilian auxiliaries of the police and army) of the Cédras regime, and the *chimères* (thugs that allegedly worked for Aristide). Most Haitians know that victims seeking justice from the authorities have encountered dismissal: they are told to come back later, that there are not enough funds to give them much-needed remuneration. The mass amnesty programs and impunity that safeguard the perpetrators of sex crimes against women demoralize and erase the victims. Entrenched government corruption prevents improvements to the judicial system and more effective human rights programs. When rapes by government thugs are denied, women's experiences, suffering, and memories of the traumatic events are further denied. Women live with what I call "injured memories," extremely painful memories of continued injustices, and cannot let go of the past, which becomes their present.[15]

In light of the persistent obliteration of women's stories of violence and the problems involved in testimony, storytelling plays a fundamental role in structuring a memorial space of acknowledgment—these crimes, and many others, have happened and they cannot be denied. The stories manifest themselves in different ways, reconstructing the world from different modalities of memory. As we will see in the following sections, one prominent format is theater performances created by the victims themselves, and another is fiction as testimonial narrative.

Acts against Violence

Because of the social stigma attached to rape, it is not only difficult to recall but also embarrassing to describe. Because it changes everything about the way the victim/survivor sees herself in the world, it can haunt her throughout her life, leaving a broken person sobbing in the night from post-traumatic stress, from fear. As we will see in the course of this chapter, venues have been made available for women to denounce rape. But, as one of the interviewed women in *Calling the Ghosts* said, "I feel as though they just want to interview us if we've been raped. What if we were violated in other ways? And doesn't it entail another violation to be given attention only because we are subjects of rape?"[16] Giving direct attention to rape risks reducing the victim/survivor's experience to rape-centered, ignoring other dimensions of her life. Experience, and how it is interpreted and used, is crucial to the denunciation of rape. Here we stumble across an important category that defies analysis. How is "experience" used to tell a story? How can a writer mediate a story that he/she has not experienced personally? How does one divulge a terrible personal experience in the shape of, for example, autobiography, without essentializing oneself or encountering vituperative criticisms as to the veracity of that experience?

In "Experience," Joan Scott posits that experience makes visible something that would otherwise not be known. She refers to the scene from Samuel Delaney's autobiography in which he enters a bathhouse in 1963 and sees "an undulating mass of naked male bodies, spread wall to wall" (57). Delaney claims that at that moment he recognized a political power in the presence of these bodies. His experience gives space to the otherwise underground existence of a formidable, and active, gay community. The sociocultural invisibility of gays during the 1950s is contrasted by Delaney's personal experience and contested through the writing of his autobiography. Scott tells us, "Writing is reproduction, transmission—the communication of knowledge gained through (visual, visceral) experience" (58). Delaney's memoir provides evidence of a hitherto unknown world. That kind of writing, Scott argues, has propelled the careers of many historians who have made great gains by exposing the lives of those ignored, or negated, by previous historical documentation. She notes that this, too, falls prey to reproducing already existing ideologies. His story as evidence, if taken at face value, generalizes his particular experience by depicting it as transparent and referential, thus ignoring the cultural, political, and social constructs that have led to this kind of experience. She reminds us that "making visible the experience of a different group exposes the existence of repressive mechanisms, but not their inner workings or logic" (59). Conclusively, she insists, experience cannot be seen as the origin of knowledge and the "bedrock of evidence upon which explanation is built" (59). Instead, experience "becomes the origin of our explanation, not the authoritative (because seen or felt) evidence that grounds what is known, but rather that which we seek to explain, that about which knowledge is produced. To think about experience in this way is to historicize it as well as to historicize the identities it produces" (60). Scott invites us to interpret experience from its different and challenging modalities. In this manner the interpretation of experience can be a call to defy foundational histories (or fictions), essentializing explanations, and repeated classifications that condone established hierarchies of power. She closes her essay thus:

> Experience is, in this approach, not the origin of our explanation, but that which we want to explain. This kind of approach does not undercut politics by denying the existence of subjects; it instead interrogates the processes of their creation, and, in so doing, refigures history and the role of the historian, and opens new ways for thinking about change. (69)

It is within this context of experience that I examine the stories and the histories that reveal human disenfranchisement.

In Haiti, women are coming out of hiding, solitude, and silence. For example, the members of the Haitian women's group FAVILEK, all of whom are victims of rape,[17] have gathered to seek reparations for violence committed against them, to reach out to other women, and to tell their stories to their children. The women still suffer the physical and psychological aftereffects of the violence of the de facto regime. The women lament that the violence repeats itself in their nightmares and in their everyday lives. Some cannot afford the removal of bullets still inside their bodies. Some suffer unbearable pain from broken bones and torn muscles.

Others are raising children conceived of rape. Most talk about knowing that the rapists still live among them. Because the rapists' faces often were hidden, they cannot be identified by their victims, who are sure that these men still recognize them. These women need money for adequate medical care and to feed and educate their children. Since they were violated by previous government repression, they feel the present government should help them to become healthy citizens of Haiti and to raise their children as healthy citizens too. But without government reparations, they are left to their own devices.

In the 1990s the women of FAVILEK collaborated with the prominent Haitian writer and film director Rachèle Magloire to produce an original theater piece that would help them and others in the same predicament. *Ochan pou tout fanm yo bliye*, or *Paean to All Forgotten Women*, serves as a testimony of violence and an outcry for effective changes. The play allows the women to be themselves in public, to cry, and to question their experiences. FAVILEK members have found that the play has a powerful effect in the villages of Haiti, where women have broken their silences upon meeting them and seeing their performance. In tears and dread, a growing solidarity between victims is leading to the possibility of healing from acts that remain unspoken but are always present, "ghosts."

A video, *Les Enfants du coup d'état*, presents the making of the play. At one point the camera settles on the face of the son of one of the women. He is the child of a rapist. In the documentary, the child's mother talks about her fear that he might become violent, like his unknown father. A psychologist is shown helping the woman understand that the child will grow up with the values and beliefs his mother shows him. The child, who knows his story, sees the play and is presented in the video as a child who will one day be the bridge between his mother's terror and his own life. Thanks to the intervention of human rights groups, the mother and the child find community and creativity (the play, the video) through which they can tell their stories and use those stories to help each other. By telling their stories, the victims chase the ghosts away and identify the violators as real. The women's memories are their truths and the truths of their communities and families. The government has yet to grant financial reparations to the victims, but women's groups, psychologists, and human rights lawyers are giving them the citizenship they deserve, despite a complex political climate in which the past holds a disputed place. Trauma is not a metaphor for a kind of memory; it is a horrible condition that severs the victims' ability to distinguish between the past and the present, reality and nightmares. These women tell their own real stories to counter the nightmares.

Let us return to Scott's theory of experience. In telling their stories, the FAVILEK group have two goals: gaining legal justice through remuneration that would help their dire financial and health conditions, and finding support and solidarity with each other, through the theater piece, reaching out to other victims and their families. By "reproducing" the experience of rape in the theater piece, they are not reproducing the crime but rather transmitting—that is, representing—a message that concerns their present plight as victims. As Scott warns, presenting the plight of the victims falls prey to existing ideologies. They could be underscoring the power that their perpetrators, living comfortably in the safety of impunity, continue to have over their lives. Let us consider other ways in which the representation of the experience of violence might avoid reproducing an already established hierarchy of victims who remain marginalized by the violence that has been imposed on them.[18]

The theater piece produced by the FAVILEK group is a representation of the pain of rape, an act against violence, and, ultimately, an act of community. As an act of community it performs a critical service in helping these victims find modes of emotional healing. Their work together counters that feeling of aloneness Herman observes: "Traumatized people feel utterly abandoned, utterly alone, cast out of the human and divine systems of care and protection that sustain life" (52).

How can victims and survivors who do not have a clear political machinery to fight, or any form of contact with others (like FAVILEK), cure themselves of that feeling of utter abandonment?

Literature and Memory

In the absence of official recognition of the existence, impact, and repercussions of violence, literature provides an alternative format of disclosure, highlighting the complex nature of the fallout of violence. As Scarry proposed many years ago, stories counter a world that is constantly in the "unmaking" by violence. Arguably fiction, which is not encumbered by the limitations that come with the necessary objectivity of truth, can expose the effects of violence.

Marie Chauvet's *Amour Colère Folie* can be viewed as a pivotal text, which discloses the violence of rape by mercilessly enunciating violence within writing.[19] In her seminal piece "The Discourse of Violence in

Amour Colère Folie," Ronnie Scharfman proposes that Chauvet's trilogy, centered on rape, "functions as an act of resistance to the violence from which it springs, but that it can only resist by repeating, by violating the reader as it proceeds, dragging us in as accomplices and voyeurs to the very heart of darkness, of which it is both the semblance and the conscience. . . . The text does not scandalize the foreign reader. It does worse: it traumatizes" (229–30). In such a context, I believe that Chauvet's work does more than remember the continuing violence against women's bodies. It repeats that violence onto its reading bodies, in and out of Haiti. In other words, by leaving readers deeply disturbed if not emphatically traumatized, Chauvet's literary denunciation of rape repeats violence. While this indeed composes resistance through detailed disclosure of continuing human rights violations, I am not convinced that Chauvet's stories point to a way out of the horrors of rape and its emotional repercussions for individuals, particularly survivors. Instead, the writing itself violates and traumatizes its reading bodies and minds and thus further grafts violence.

In contrast, Edwidge Danticat's novel *Breath, Eyes, Memory* invites us to think beyond the boundaries of politically motivated rape. Without attempting to reproduce the violence it denounces, it reconstructs the ways in which violence affects a family. Thus it represents the complexity of memory and the difficult relationships between memory and trauma and between memory and healing. To show how that may work, I suggest that we consider the stories crafted in *Breath, Eyes, Memory* as a memorial, composed of intimate scenes, that honors the women of Haiti and its diaspora. The text denounces very real violations, highlights the webbings of memory, and imagines futures freed of the grip of violent memories. The experiences depicted in Danticat's novel serve as a composite of the struggles rape imposes on individual lives. Like the work produced by FAVILEK, *Breath, Eyes, Memory* is an act against violence. The text does not allow the crime to be forgotten. Fascinatingly, the characters struggle with remembering and forgetting. A tension between the function of text and the nuances exposed by the characters presents a contrapuntal message that questions the role of memory with respect to healing from violence.

Through the novel we become intimately familiar with the emotional plight of two women: Martine, for whom recovery from violation and reconciliation with life is an incessant struggle in isolation, and her daughter Sophie, who "inherits" her mother's trauma. The emotionally maimed main character, Martine, who was raped as a young girl, leaves Haiti to find a better and safer life. This abrupt and violent move—from innocence to responsibility, from childhood to adulthood, from life in her country with her family to life in the diaspora far from her family—shapes every aspect of Martine's life and her daughter's. The novel offers an intimate view of the lives of two women struggling with severance from an old life and acceptance into a new one. Martine makes a life in New York, dates a nice Haitian immigrant, and raises her child to adulthood. But she cannot let go of the violence from her past: "a man with no face, pounding a life into a helpless young girl" (193).

In the United States, Martine lives outside the real world and in the suppressed memory of the traumatic event. She repeats, "There are ghosts there that I can't face, things that are still very painful for me" (78). The ghosts are not a part of the past; they are monsters in Martine's present that further diminish the person she is, the person she could be. She is a frail human being by the time Sophie, her twelve-year-old daughter, flies to New York from Haiti, where she has been raised by Martine's sister. Martine's "face was long and hollow. Her hair had a blunt cut and she had long spindly legs. She had dark circles under her eyes and, as she smiled, lines of wrinkles tightened her expression. Her fingers were scarred and sunburned" (42).

There is, however, one memory that brings a beam of happiness to Martine's drawn face. Sophie hands her a card she had made many years earlier for Mother's Day. In the card Sophie had copied a poem:

My mother is a daffodil,
limber and strong as one.
My mother is a daffodil,
but in the wind, iron strong. (29)

Daffodils had been Martine's favorite flowers. She loved yellow, dressing and decorating with yellow at every opportunity. She asks Sophie if there are still daffodils in Haiti. Sophie lies (as she was leaving Haiti she remarked how barren the ground had become), replying that there are many. Martine sadly comments that she has not had time to even notice them in the United States. While daffodils may offer a link to recovery from the dark nightmares that haunt her, she cannot see them. She has a bright red outfit hanging in her closet, but she does not dare wear it. The colors of light and passion linger in Martine's background, but not in her present.

The night of her daughter's arrival, after tucking away her poem about daffodils from the past, she surprises young Sophie, who narrates:

Later that night, I heard the same voice screaming as though someone was trying to kill her. I rushed over, but my mother was alone
thrashing against the sheets. . . . When she saw me, she quickly covered her face with her hands and turned away. . . .

"It is the night," she said. "Sometimes, I see horrible visions in my
sleep." (48)

Martine is oppressed by her experience of violation, by illness, and by Haitian tradition, in which women are considered inferior to men and in
which women's honor is based on virginity while men's is based on virility.

When she learns she is pregnant a second time, the hauntings from her
past take on a new life. She cannot face pregnancy again, even though the
circumstances are dramatically different.

Through the victim's story, Danticat reveals how violence is remembered and reproduced and, specifically, how it can be internalized and self-
inflicted. At the end of the novel we are reminded, "There is always a place
where nightmares are passed on through generations like heirlooms.
Where women . . . return to look at their own faces in stagnant bodies of
water" (234). Because the bulk of the novel takes place in the United States,
it exposes how the repercussions of traumatic events in Haiti are psychologically, physically, and cognitively reexperienced in the diaspora—which
represents more than one million Haitians, compared to the eight million
still in their home country.

The narrator, Sophie, laments, "It took me twelve years to piece together my mother's entire story. By then, it was already too late" (61). In
the diaspora, they are far from the world of the Tonton Macoutes, the
dreaded groups of militarized thugs created by the Duvalier dictatorship.
Nonetheless, Martine continues to fear them, and Sophie learns how they
destroyed her family. That history of violence bleeds into their present,
manifesting itself in self-inflicted abuse, such as starvation and even suicide.

Martine is a traumatized self, who cannot find wholeness because of her
never-ending, ever-increasing flashbacks. She is disconnected from reality,
despite her efforts to live in the present. The memory of past violence
shapes her present and leads to a self-imposed isolation.[20] Trauma studies
reiterate that it is impossible to represent the horrors of the traumatic
event in any artistic form without reconstructing that which cannot be
reproduced. Reconstruction means putting the pieces together with the
hope of understanding the violence, working through it, reporting it, or at

least accepting it in order to move on. In contrast, reproduction entails reenacting the exact violence to produce the same effects. Trauma theories inform us that the violent experience is inaccessible to language. Indeed, violence cannot be reconstructed or reproduced without being violence again. That, if one is denouncing violence, must be avoided. But the effects of violence are significant. These point to the violence without being the violent act. The effects of violence, I believe, are more insidious on many levels. The stories of Martine and Sophie lend narrative reality to effects that are difficult to describe. How do these women deal with the violence and its effects? After all, Sophie is a product of that very violence. When Sophie suggests that Martine tell someone, she hints at how she believes that telling the story might somehow alleviate her mother's heavy burden of the rape. Martine responds, "You cannot report a ghost to the police" (199). This response suggests that Martine thinks of telling only if it will bring justice, but she feels that justice is unlikely. The possibility of vindication or of having the life she knew before the rape does not exist for Martine. The memory of the violence is her present, and her nightmares preclude her healing from violence. Her suffering is so deep that she commits suicide. Sophie seeks community and healing. The memory of her mother's rape leads her to find strength in pain. Arguably, these two characters narrate a fundamental experience in trauma and healing as emphasized by Herman: "The core experiences of psychological trauma are disempowerment and disconnection from others. Recovery, therefore, is based upon the empowerment of the survivor and the creation of new connections" (133). Martine, the victim, never finds reconnection. Sophie, a second-generation survivor, starts her healing process through community when she seeks therapy and joins an international group of women all healing from past violence.

Trauma is the mode in which Martine and Sophie experience their present. The two characters embody two critical manifestations of violence through traumatized memory and active memory. Martine, who embodies traumatized memory, is silenced. Her life is displaced via her nightmares and phantasmagoric experiences; she consequently engages new violations (her testing of Sophie) and completes the self-destruction the rape set into motion (her suicide). The suicide functions as an acting-out of an initial violence that she cannot escape. Martine's memory is failed memory because it does not work as a strategy for self-preservation. For survival, she would need to forget the rape. Since she cannot forget the rape, she lives in a space of insurmountable trauma and suffers from melancholia, or possession of the body by sadness. The story of her trauma is reproduced via two routes: acting out against herself, and transmission of the violent experience to her daughter.

Sophie's memory is a mixture of truth and fiction. She must deal with her own memory of her mother's insistent trauma (her mother's truth) and her interpretation of what might have happened (which will be reconfigured through what information she can gather and, inevitably, will contain elements of fiction). Hers is the memory of mourning by which she is left to work through (grieve) her loss (her dead mother). Sophie must engage in active memory (a memory that puts together the pieces she can find) in order to mourn the violence her mother lived, the death of her mother, and the violence and trauma she has inherited. The experience of violence is manifested in different levels of trauma, which in turn produce different memories. All of these experiences and memories must be taken into consideration for a deeper understanding of the effects and affects that violence produces in individuals, families, and interconnected global communities.

Breath, Eyes, Memory plays a number of important roles. It can be viewed as a tool against repression of memory. It underscores the dissociation from women's violent experiences and the denial of such circumstances, informing readers in developed nations and in other diaspora communities of the atrocities that occur under dictatorships and other repressive regimes. The text shows how atrocities become present in the "developed nations" and how no nation or community escapes the emotional and psychological consequences of rape, whether politically motivated or random. It inspires social awareness of the dimensions of a history of violence in Haiti and its diaspora and invites active human rights work to change that history.

Danticat joins with women in Haiti and in the diaspora to create spaces of disclosure of violence through creative means. She tells stories and helps women without support groups to discover solidarity and strength in memory. Writing from the diaspora, the author fills a very important gap, sharing women's stories and giving all women a space for remembering and mourning their violent pasts and seeking ways to heal, through disclosure, solidarity, and the fight for rights.

On one level *Breath, Eyes, Memory* can be read as a text of memory and healing that memorializes the victims of Haiti's human rights violations. On another level, the text, through the characters' skillfully elicited memories of experiences, encourages more complex meditations about memory, and complicates the function of remembering.

Memory has been proposed as a first step toward justice. For example, in her study "The Minefields of Memory," Elizabeth Jelin argues that memory is in the present: "There are, therefore, active and ongoing political struggles about meaning—about the meaning of what went on in the past and also about the meaning of memory itself" (24). In her essay "The Politics of Memory," Jelin explores how memory, truth, and justice are inextricably linked to a struggle for human rights. She posits: "Truth implies governmental recognition of the responsibility that governmental agents had in the crimes and abuses committed" (50). Nonetheless, she recognizes that "there is the factual impossibility of bringing to trial *all* those responsible for violations and compensating *all* the victims" (51). Jelin suggests that memory is an important factor in the recovery of personal dignity and justice:

> Memory can then partially take the place of justice. Because this phase of justice is unfinished, at the societal level there are signs of collective frustration, and at the personal level of the victims and their relatives, there is a sense of irretrievable loss that can never be articulated at the political level and for which no justice is possible. (52)

Jelin concludes: "Those who have suffered directly or through their immediate relatives define themselves as the bearers of pain and memory" (53).

Danticat's novel addresses this pain. It also shows how memory does not always bring justice. In theory, memory can force revenge. If a criminal's actions are forgotten, he/she can escape without punishment, but if the act of violence is remembered officially, then perhaps that perpetrator might be caught and reprimanded, avenging the victim's violation. As Herman has shown, remembering in private can become a great detriment to the sufferer without having any effect on the criminal. When justice is not the final outcome, why tell the story? Perhaps a story is told to help create a community of awareness. Not only does the crime of rape happen, but the effects are annihilating. Fiction tells an important story without implicating sufferers who would never be able tell their pasts succinctly. Fiction tells a story that resembles the truth of an experience without burdening real victims and testifies about stories that cannot be proved. At issue is not the accuracy of these stories but, rather, their pervasiveness.

Rapists in Haiti and elsewhere are rarely brought to justice; victims are rarely vindicated. Survivors' status as citizens is diminished with each violation or knowledge of continued violations. They are left only with inexorable pain.

In Martine's case, violence further afflicts her when other forms of illness and physical change etch themselves onto her body. She struggles with cancer and must have two mastectomies. A new pregnancy brings up the feelings she had during her first pregnancy, the one that resulted from rape. As she senses a new life growing in her body, she cannot escape the images that have been haunting her for years. While Sophie was still a child, Martine had a reason for staying alive. But when the child has become a woman, has married, and has her own daughter, Martine feels abandoned and even more alone. Even though her lover, Marc, seems to be kind and supportive, she does not turn to him for the help she needs. She does not reveal the depth of her horror to him. Her body, without breasts to feed anyone, reflects her feelings about herself. She cannot nurture anyone, not even herself. Through Martine's character, Danticat dramatizes the ways in which a repressive regime and indiscriminate sexual violence continue to dismember the survivors, especially after forced and sudden migration. As we learn about Martine's pathos, we witness how the traumatic event returns again and again through nightmares and flashbacks, becoming a larger part of her present than the real present she lives in. The autobiographical literature of trauma provides an important opportunity for victims to testify to the world about the abuses they suffered and to emphasize that they will not be silenced. Yet there are many women (and men) who cannot find release through writing. In some way or other—theater, truth commissions, private therapy, fiction—rape must be acknowledged for what it is, a crime against an innocent person. Fiction, as space of disclosure, dramatizes the effects of violence and alienating trauma, and proposes an alternative outcome. In *Breath, Eyes, Memory*, Martine is a haunted woman who cannot report a ghost to the police. Even so, the ghosts must be reported, if not to a legal system she does not trust, then to someone she can confide in. Martine is the trapped, traumatized, helpless person Herman describes.

Sophie, I suggest, presents an alternative life story. Sophie must struggle with her mother's memories to come to terms with the person she herself is and can become. She wants to know her mother's story, her aunt's story, and her grandmother's story. She wants to find her own meaning in life and act responsibly in light of the trauma she witnesses and, by extension, experiences. Sophie does not want to be paralyzed by memory the way her mother is; she wants to find resilience in her past and pride in her present. Consequently, she has a journey of discovery of and recovery from her past ahead of her. Yet her mother's suicide adds to Sophie's struggles with her own pathos, hindering her ability to lead a healthy life. Sophie recalls:

> After Joseph and I got married, all through the first year I had suicidal thoughts. Some nights I woke up in a cold sweat wondering if my mother's anxiety was somehow hereditary or if it was something that I had "caught" from living with her. Her nightmares had somehow become my own, so much so that I would wake up some mornings wondering if we hadn't both spent the night dreaming about the same thing: a man with no face, pounding a life into a helpless young girl. (193)

It is through the character of Sophie, whose name means knowledge or wisdom (*sophia* in Greek), that Danticat describes women's migration from Haiti to the United States. Sophie, who was born in Haiti and raised by her aunt Tatie in the poor village of Croix-des-Rosets, finds her childhood shaped by the mystery of her mother. Sophie has a picture of her mother, and regularly hears her voice on cassette recordings, but does not know details of Martine's life in the United States or the reason for her sudden "escape." When Sophie is twelve years old, an airline ticket arrives in the mail: the child is to join her mother in the United States. With this physical journey begins Sophie's growing awareness of the darker side of life. In the cab leaving for the airport in Port-au-Prince, she witnesses some of the political violence that can afflict Haiti:

> Some of the students fell and rolled down the hill. They screamed at the soldiers that they were once again betraying the people. One girl rushed down the hill and grabbed one of the soldiers by the arm. He raised his pistol and pounded it on top of her head. She fell to the ground, her face covered with her own blood. (34)

Tante Atie reminds Sophie that this is the reason for leaving: the violence makes Haiti too dangerous for a little girl. That little girl knows only that she is abandoning her beloved aunt. In her new school in the United States, she discovers a different kind of ostracism: racism. She quickly learns that many of the American children accuse Haitians of having AIDS because television coverage says it affects the four H's: heroin addicts, hemophiliacs, homosexuals, and Haitians. Concurrently, she learns the horrible reason for her mother's sudden departure from Haiti. Furthermore, in the private confines of her own home, which is supposed to be safe, she undergoes the humiliation of "testing."

The Haitian community has leveled much criticism at Danticat's description of a mother's testing for her daughter's virginity. In fact, there have been denials of its existence as a tradition in Haitian culture to guarantee a daughter's honor. In the novel, Martine starts to test her daughter every night when she reaches puberty: Martine puts her finger into Sophie's vagina to ascertain that the hymen is still there. This testing is a pivotal violation in the text, because it is caused not by a stranger but by the only person Sophie is allowed to trust. Despite her own horrible memory of testing, Martine violates her daughter in the name of tradition. This violation sets the pattern for Sophie's own difficulty with her body, her sexuality, and her sense of value in the world, her community, and her family.

During the testing, Martine tells her daughter the story of two inseparable lovers, the Marassas, and adds, "There are secrets you cannot keep" (85). Afterward, Martine covers her daughter's body and leaves the room, her face buried in her hands. The story of the Marassas is about love, and the testing, she implies, is also about love. Yet Martine reveals her shame by covering her face. Sophie experiences the testing as a violation and evidence of her mother's lack of trust, which, according to the text, is transgenerational. In Haiti Sophie learns that her aunt was also tested, and concludes that it made sense that Atie screamed during the tests. Conversely, Sophie remains silent during the testing:

> I mouthed the words to the Virgin Mother's Prayer: *Hail Mary . . .*
> *so full of grace. The Lord is with You . . . You are blessed among*
> *women . . . Holy Mary. Mother of God. Pray for us poor sinners.*

> In my mind, I tried to relive all the pleasant memories I remembered from my life. My special moments with Tante Atie and with Joseph and even with my mother. (84)

Sophie's silence during the testing is comparable to Martine's reluctance to talk about the rape in her own life. Sophie does not fight her mother during the testing; instead, she defies her mother by breaking her own hymen with a pestle from the kitchen. Her defiance is acted out through self-mutilation. With this act, she rejects her mother's overprotection and her culture's repression of women and symbolically precludes violation by a stranger: she has beat him/her to it. The next time her mother tests her, there is no barrier left. With calm anger and resignation, Martine throws Sophie out, telling her to go to "him." Sophie gathers her things and limps from the pain of her self-abuse to an unsuspecting Joseph (her neighbor and friend and, later, her husband). Sophie's departure, like her mother's from Haiti, does not resolve problems. They become worse.

The testing and self-imposed deflowering, like Martine's rape, are the violations that afflict Sophie's life. Sophie has experienced a series of abusive events that ultimately lead to self-abuse and the denial of pleasure. Toward the end of the novel, Danticat reveals that Sophie cannot enjoy sex with her husband. During "lovemaking" she remembers the testing and how she coped with it. She remembers her mother's story of the Marassa doubling, pretends she is elsewhere, and feels a stronger bond to her mother. Without saying so, she joins in her mother's frigidity and denial of life's simple pleasures. She recalls the image of the faceless man who raped her mother; she recalls the tradition of testing that made her feel so bad. After her absence in lovemaking, she goes to the kitchen, eats everything she can find, goes to the bathroom, and empties herself of the food and any possible feeling of plenty.

Sophie's dislike of her body leads her to binge and then vomit. This constitutes another act of self-mutilation in the dark; bulimia is a private disease. Sophie struggles with guilt over how her life has been blessed. She has an understanding husband, but still she cannot enjoy carnal pleasures with him. She has a lovely daughter, but still she rejects her own body, which has grown robust from the pregnancy. Sophie does not know how to embrace happiness, and so she hurts herself. The pattern of the life she has witnessed most intimately, her mother's, is so replete with pain that Sophie has internalized this pain as a way of living. She must reproduce it to feel the comforting sensation of what is familiar. But she has grown up in the United States and understands, at least on a rational level, that this is wrong.

Martine had been anorexic; she starved her body for years, long before she stabbed it. Sophie does not annihilate herself so completely. She is tempted by food and indulges in it—but she immediately feels guilty. How could she eat so much? Quickly she goes to the bathroom and purges herself of the pleasures of eating and satiation. Perhaps this is in a partial contrast to her mother's starvation. Figuratively, Sophie's bulimia evokes her emotional relationship to life. She wants to live fully, even excessively, but she feels she cannot. She has never had an intimate role model of how women can be in the world. What can she do? Is being a wife and mother enough? Can she go to school? What can she do with her life? Martine's memory of the rape, persisting trauma, and self-mutilation deeply impact Sophie's life. Martine hoped Sophie would vindicate the women of the family; she wanted her daughter to study and succeed. Clearly, Sophie wants this too. But living with her mother's history of erasure through rape, migration, and anorexia, she cycles between eating and vomiting, nourishing herself and rejecting nutrients, strengthening and weakening herself. Bulimia for Sophie is about wanting and not wanting, living excessively and depriving herself violently. Her mother was not able to speak of the horrors that isolated her, and Sophie struggles between wanting to tell and wanting to "gag" herself into silence, illness, and thinness. Her discomfort with her physical body suggests that she does not value herself for who and what she is. Her personhood is unclear to her; she is afflicted with severe emotional and psychological distress that results in self-inflicted, physical pain.

While her mother experiences her trauma in isolation, Sophie seeks help. Her New York education and the dreams of her mother and aunt have given her a certain sense of self that she will eventually explore. Her trips to Haiti show her how people change, how circumstances can be confronted. For example, her illiterate aunt learns to read and write. Sophie is a woman of the future who can and will struggle for justice, starting with her own emotional healing. She seeks help through therapy. Her therapist is not a traditional person with rigid office hours; Sophie could not go to someone from whom she would fear judgment. She needs someone who understands her cultural heritage and its manifestations in U.S. culture. Sophie's therapist is a "gorgeous black woman who was an initiated Santeria priestess. She had done two years in the Peace Corps in the Dominican Republic, which showed in the brightly colored prints, noisy bangles, and open sandals she wore" (206).[21] Their sessions take place during walks in the woods by a river. The casual contact between therapist and client allows Sophie to feel safe. She can more easily speak to someone whose work in the Dominican Republic has increased her ability to understand Sophie's Haitian past. The therapist serves as a role model for Sophie. Sophie too can be and is a beautiful woman. She must believe in herself, in what she can accomplish, and how she can love and be loved. Sophie can eat and she can live. If she stops binging, she will finally be a fully realized person, an active member of her family and her communities in the United States and Haiti.

But to heal, she must struggle for years. Binging is the manifestation of contradictory experiences, such as the enormous love Sophie feels from her mother as opposed to the lack of love in Martine's life, and Sophie's wealth of opportunities in the United States in contrast to growing poverty in Haiti. Sophie is pulled by two extreme conditions that leave her wandering emotionally in a miasma of desire and self-punishment.

In seeking a healthier life with the sense that she deserves it, Sophie begins a healing process that will prove to be gradual. She joins a "sexual phobia group" (201) with an Ethiopian college student whose clitoris was cut and labia sewn up when she was a girl, and a Chicana woman who was raped for years by her grandfather. Together they work toward finding a sense of self-acceptance, self-respect, and self-love. They dress in white for their meetings, and repeat affirmations that are meant to drive out the horrible experiences and beliefs that have been inculcated over the years. "We are beautiful women with strong bodies. . . . Because of our distress, we are able to understand when others are in deep pain" (202). The tragedy of abuse and rape is not confined to Sophie or to Haiti and its diaspora. The three women share their plight in a safe, private space, and recognize their responsibility to heal themselves and to help others. They pray, "God grant us the courage to change those things we can, the serenity to accept the things we can't, and the wisdom to know the difference" (202). The serenity prayer, as they begin their affirmations, reminds them that they cannot take the world by storm. Instead they must find peace and the strength to work slowly but with determination toward healthy bodies and minds. Despite injured memories, these women are on the path toward healing from pain and becoming whole persons.

Living with Rape: Considerations toward Healing

When rape is part of the political terror machine, redress becomes part of civilian social responsibility. By contrast, when rape is a personal or random injustice, it is less distinct in legal terms and even less likely to be addressed. As we have seen, redress is elusive, regardless of the circumstances. Through the characters of Martine and Sophie, Danticat reveals the complications of living with the memory and trauma of violations against the body. Danticat's characters also address rape in different sociopolitical eras. Unlike FAVILEK's play, which presents the violations of a highly covered period of political terror, the character Martine exposes the violations and memory of a different political period, that of the Duvaliers, when violations were more covert. In fact, for many years the United States had good relations with the Duvalier governments, despite the regimes' repeated human rights violations. In the name of democracy, the Duvaliers put on an excellent show of arguing that their actions of terror were taken against communism. During this time many violations were overlooked, and the circumstances of a rape like Martine's point to this neglect. She was not raped for political reasons; she was not a communist. The country was neither in the limelight of international attention nor being denounced by human rights groups. She shares with many women the experience of a violation that does not fit into the neat parameters of politics of public outcry.[22] She is a victim in private. She migrates in silence, and she never finds solidarity in any women's groups. Perhaps this is because she is an immigrant, poor, and black. Before the late eighties, insufficient attention was given to rape victims in the United States and even less to rape victims who had migrated with post-traumatic stress symptoms from rape.[23] Danticat's character Martine reveals a global cultural attitude of silence and isolation from a localized Haitian lens.

Haitians only recently developed a culture in which therapy is an acceptable treatment, perhaps as a direct result of psychologists working with victims of the 1991 coup d'état.[24] Therapeutic aid for survivors of trauma is, of course, a recent phenomenon. Research conducted on the survivors of torture after World War II, the Korean War, and the Vietnam War has helped create an important set of emotional and mental support systems for these victims.[25] Groundbreaking research—not conducted in the Haitian community but applicable to it—is being done at the Bellevue/NYU Program for Survivors of Torture, where psychologist Hawthorne E. Smith has been working with the psychology of displacement and isolation experienced by French-speaking African refugees who survived torture. His work has no direct relation to the trauma Martine's character embodies, but it does shed light on the dimensions of refugee trauma, which can be applied to the crisis of isolation Martine experiences. Smith argues: "The multiple losses, social dislocation, feelings of fear, inadequacy, and disempowerment combine with cultural and linguistic barriers to form a difficult psychological reality for people living in exile as refugees" (294). Smith quotes Y. Fishman and J. Ross, suggesting that for some survivors, "Exile is the most painful part of torture" (293).

To stress this point, he describes an exercise he uses when presenting information about torture and refugee trauma to students and mental health professionals. Each audience member jots down on paper the five most precious things in his or her life. Smith then reads aloud some responses—health, marriage, children, material things—and rips the papers to shreds. Smith asks his audience to imagine that all of these things have been violently taken away from them. As audience members ponder the meaning of such sudden and dramatic loss, they get a slight sense of the experiences of torture victims who then also are forced into exile.

Most of Smith's clients at Bellevue cannot even get in touch with their families in Africa, for fear of exposing the remaining members to added trouble from the authorities. According to his records, these survivors have lost not only their material possessions but also their self-esteem, dreams, aspirations, feelings of emotional and physical security, and sense of personal control. Smith's point is that the post-traumatic stress syndrome his clients experience is not just about the trauma of the past but also about the sometimes equally traumatic emotional and cultural challenges of the present. His work is important because it creates an alternative space for these survivors. Smith talks about helping the clients apply for political asylum and creating a new model of psychological therapy in which they meet in groups and, unlike in most traditional therapeutic styles, can have contact outside the sessions. By getting together "on the outside," the survivors can create a community that provides support, solace, and a new sense of belonging and meaning. Smith notes that the progress of his group has reaffirmed his faith that healing is possible, under the right conditions. Community is the critical goal, and Smith's patients are fortunate enough to have access to it.

In contrast to active psychological counseling, how does a text of fiction function in the process of healing from violence? My response is that the narration is a critical tool of exposure. Not only does it relate a story that might have happened but, more important, it shows different responses to violence. While it may seem mundane to the literary elite, it is telling that *Breath, Eyes, Memory* was an Oprah's Book Club selection. Oprah, whom I view as a larger-than-life community-building apparatus, brings texts of endurance and survival into the isolated living rooms of an extensive U.S. public. This public may, and probably does, include the Haitian diaspora. An otherwise private event, rape, becomes a public issue of conversation and address. Judith Herman has noted that "the most common trauma of women remains confined to the sphere of private life, without formal recognition or restitution from the community" (73). While restitution from the Haitian community might not be automatically granted because of Danticat's text, within the parameters of the public sphere to which it has come, the crime of rape and its aftereffects do receive recognition. Fiction, read in private, marketed in public, addresses a deeply painful alienating experience.

Coping with Memories of Violence

Danticat is making a political and personal appeal. She speaks to survivors of abuse, reminding them to breathe and see and remember, to defy the odds of annihilation and instead recover. Perhaps the title should be interpreted as a series of commands: *Breath* = Breathe in, breathe out. Inhale. Exhale. Maintain a supply of oxygen in your body. Stay alive. *Eyes* = See. Observe. Witness. Testify. *Memory* = Remember. Recall. Historicize. Contextualize. Honor. Understand. She speaks to the general public, describing potential consequences of rape.

Remembering one's private and political history is important to keep identity, family, and dignity alive. Memory—which can be manifested as cognition, knowledge, recall, and trauma—can be used to change the social structures that promote violence and post-traumatic stress syndrome. Judith Herman reminds us, "After every atrocity one can expect to hear the same predictable apologies: it never happened; the victim lies; the victim exaggerates; the victim brought it upon herself; and in any case it is time to forget the past and move on" (8). These denials must be challenged aggressively. As I have suggested, one venue to challenge denial is offered by truth commissions, which we should study as a form of memory. We must ask how that memory will be perpetuated so that the denounced crimes never occur again. Truth commissions often fall short of their potential to confirm the abuses of the past. In those cases, literature and theater play an equally critical role in exposing the evils of violence and its repercussions. These function as harbingers of memory, and beg us to analyze the ways in which memory—as truth, testimony, and trauma—shapes our understanding of the human condition.

Through the character of Martine, Danticat leads us to consider how the words *breath, eyes, memory* can also be interpreted to mean something awful:

There is always a place where nightmares are passed on through generations like heirlooms. Where women like cardinal birds return to look at their own faces in stagnant bodies of water.

I come from a place where breath, eyes, and memory are one, a place from which you carry your past like the hair on your head. (234)

While Martine still breathes and can see what is around her, the memory of her past does not let her really breathe or really see. She is so severely hindered by the memory of rape that she wills herself to arrest her breathing. Her memory, in trauma, suffocates her. Trauma does not let its victims move on, and they pass on their own inability to those who witness their pain. The only way to address trauma is to develop new venues of social support. Herman says:

To hold traumatic reality in consciousness requires a social context that affirms and protects the victim and that joins the victim and witness in a common alliance. For the individual victim, this social context is created by relationships with friends, lovers, and family. For the larger society, the social context is created by political movements that give voice to the disempowered.

. . . In the absence of strong political movements for human rights, the active process of bearing witness inevitably gives way to the active process of forgetting. Repression, dissociation, and denial are phenomena of social as well as individual consciousness. (9)

Novels such as *Breath, Eyes, Memory* and theater pieces such as *Paean to All Forgotten Women* bear witness to the act of violence against women. These venues of revelation also create the possibility of social support, which elicit political changes that will respect women.

The women of FAVILEK can count on each other and have reached out to other victims in hiding. Different forms of artistic expression, such as theater pieces and videos, create spaces of solidarity and public action. Similarly, literary characters take on a life of their own and become symbolic venues for the disclosure of violence. Martine evokes victims of the past who had little recourse to human rights action. Sophie, on the other hand, suggests that there is hope for recovery from trauma through community and engagement in a present that allows the trauma of the past to be viewed as the past. An important point in the stories of Martine and Sophie is that trauma begets trauma and that much work must be done to address violence and its repercussions. Violence and trauma impede a life with dignity and deny basic human rights.

The women of FAVILEK, working against real political impediments and dependent on the aid received through centers such as the Bureau des Avocats Internationaux, find themselves trapped by Haitian bureaucracy. In the diaspora, Danticat is relatively free to engage political projects actively.[26] Through her first novel, she asks us to analyze the ways in which rape steals meaning from people's lives and shapes a dysfunctional culture in which people experience psychological pain that can manifest itself in physical self-mutilation. Through the novel, Danticat challenges a long history of violence, machista culture, and the horrors of dictatorships. The fictional exposition of women's experience as a strategy of disclosure shows the insidious effects of rape. The haunting memory of the experience of rape revealed through the text shows to what extent memory can hurt. The first-generation victim Martine cannot escape violence, because her trauma is her present. Conversely, her daughter is shown to start the long process of healing through forgiveness and, to a certain extent, through forgetting. Only in that way can she engage in the present, freed of the haunting of her mother's rape, free to believe that the future can hold good things for her. Disclosing the effects of such a personal and subjective crime as rape, Danticat transforms a very private memory into a public issue. What happens when memory hurts? It can, as in the case of Martine, destroy its victim. It can also, as in the case of Sophie, strengthen its victim, inciting her to play a harp or write a story. Arguably, the violent memories of Haiti's women hurt the author. As Danticat has said, she writes to work through that hurt. Her writing is her music; it is the harp she will not put down. That way she creates community for healing.[27] Danticat's novel is a memorial to Haiti's women, denouncing rape in the past, in the present, and in the future.

Exposing Invisibility

Drown

Dominicans, like many previous immigrants, come to America acting on their hope for a better future. But hope is challenged by the dismal economic reality many minorities in the United States suffer and by a legacy of ingrained prejudices and patterns of abuse against communities of color. When Dominicans come to the United States, they are set aside in the category of "black and Hispanic." Thus they are made invisible by socially constructed, and sometimes binding, mechanisms of disempowerment. Often, when they do gain visibility, it is only to underscore a negative image of the population. Contemporary Dominican diaspora history thus intersects with African Americans' long history of disempowerment and struggles for economic, political, and social justice. Junot Díaz's 1996 collection of short stories, *Drown*, foregrounds a sense of drowning (*ahogo*) in Dominican lives, both in the diaspora and on the island. In this chapter I engage Díaz's short stories to explore the nexuses of invisibility for the Dominican diaspora and the as-yet-unrecognized intersections with African-American literature.

A sociocultural dialectic of invisibility and visibility is part of the struggle experienced by Dominicans in the diaspora as they enter into dialogue with other disempowered groups. I suggest that Díaz is confused, as he tries to find a voice that represents his community, the Dominican diaspora, and represent it in a way that satisfies the expectations of the mainstream U.S. literary agent, publisher, and reader. Diaz's short fiction serves up what could be viewed as stereotypical representations of Dominican diaspora violence. Does his writing respond to a broad-based fascination with stories of ethnic groups on the margins?[1] Do these groups gain visibility only through negative representation? In this chapter I suggest that negative representation is much desired by the mainstream public, affecting the ways that ethnic communities remember themselves and struggle with the impact of violence and its repetition on their lives. The work of Junot Díaz may elucidate the point.

For example, let us look at the way the title has been changed in translations. The Spanish editions do not use a literal translation of *Drown*, which would be *Ahogar(se)*, and therefore would emphasize tragedy. Marketing considerations might have precluded a cover that highlighted the possibility of doom. So the title of the Spanish translation in the United States, released in 1997, is *Negocios*. This title, taken from the final story in the collection, focuses on the protagonist's father, Papi, and his success with women. Papi has two wives, two sons named after him, and several mistresses. The story emphasizes the kind of masculine success that is valued in the traditional Dominican culture of manhood. In contrast, the title in English is taken from another short story, "Drown." This story explores homosexual desire—a topic that, in the Dominican national identity, is drowned out (made invisible?). Another marketing twist is evident in the title of the translation published in 1996 in Spain, *Los Boys*, calling to mind rough boys from the 'hood. A French translation is also titled *Los Boys*.[2] While that title was not used on the U.S. Spanish edition, it reveals a particular and widespread fascination with stereotypical conceptualizations of Dominican marginalization and macho toughness in the ghettoes of the United States.[3]

The title piece in the original English text, "Drown," offers a revealing story about the protagonist's psychological reality, how he views himself, and how he occupies the world in which he lives: "One teacher, whose family had two grammar schools named after it, compared us to the shuttles. A few of you are going to make it. Those are the orbiters. But the majority of you are just going to burn out. Going nowhere" (106). Years later the protagonist recalls, "I could already see myself losing altitude, fading, the earth spread out beneath me, hard and bright" (106). Rather than orbiting the earth, or shining like a star, or standing strong on the earth, he is "drowned out" by the atmosphere. His presence is diminished by the image of a solid and radiating earth that he does not belong to.

The characters in "Drown" struggle with self-respect and self-worth. Their visas have not come close to fulfilling all of the dreams they had at home. They must fight numerous kinds of poverty—not the explicit one of the Dominican countryside, but a more pervasive poverty of spirit. More than a memory, which it does not claim to be, *Drown* is a reminder of the ways people are rendered invisible by historical excuses, by marginal behavior, and by social class.

Colliding Histories and Fictions: Surfacing Invisibilities

Silvio Torres-Saillant and Ramona Hernández, coauthors of *The Dominican Americans* (and, respectively, the former and current directors of the Dominican Studies Institute of the City University of New York), have lamented that Dominicans are not included in many reference publications that claim to account for "all" ethnic groups in American society. In the essay "Forging a Dominican-American Culture: Dominican Invisibility," they contend that Dominicans "have often been left out even of sources dealing specifically with the Hispanic portion of the U.S. population" (102). As evidence of the way that Dominican faces are missing from the U.S. Hispanic/Latino imagination, the authors point to the hefty two-volume *A Comprehensive Bibliography for the Study of American Minorities*. This 1976 work's section titled "From the Islands" consists of "The Puerto Rican-American Experience" and "The Cuban-American Experience," with no mention of Dominican life in the United States. Torres-Saillant and Hernández also cite a 1968 book titled *Spanish-Speaking People in the United States* that made no mention whatsoever of Dominicans, but focused on Mexican Americans, Hispanos of New Mexico, and Puerto Ricans, and erroneously designated Filipinos as Hispanics.

Part of the invisibility they are disclosing has to do with migration history. Many Mexicans became Mexican Americans and Chicanos by default in the nineteenth century when the United States annexed the land where they already lived, but Dominicans did not begin arriving in the United States in significant numbers until shortly after Trujillo's 1961 assassination. The flow increased after the U.S. occupation of the Dominican Republic in 1965, the same year as the Hart-Celler Immigration Reform Act, which reopened the United States to mass immigration, particularly from Latin America. In addition, Balaguer's 1966 election began a period during which the Dominican and U.S. governments saw emigration as a safety valve that could dissipate still-virulent political tensions. Visas became easier to get, creating a growing Dominican community in the United States. In the 1980s the largest wave of migration was prompted by economic crisis and austerity programs in the Dominican Republic, and a sizable Dominican contingent was established in the United States.

It could be argued that the invisibility pointed to by Torres-Saillant and Hernández has roots in two main factors: the small presence of Dominicans in the United States prior to 1965 and the lower economic status of Dominicans from later migrations. Yet sociologists such as Patricia Pessar claim that numerous Dominicans were skilled laborers and educated professionals—middle class—thus receiving more visibility. The two positions, Pessar's and Torres-Saillant and Hernández's, are not mutually exclusive. A recent study of immigrants, led by Carola and Marcelo Suárez-Orozco at the Harvard Immigration Project, reveals that migrations consisted of low-skilled workers as well as of educated and skilled workers (16–35).

This debate as to the socioeconomic reasons of Dominican invisibility was surfaced in the Dominican newspaper *Tiempo de América* in 1996. The paper summarized several stories from the New York–based Spanish-language newspaper *El Díario/La Prensa* that focused on what some Dominican writers see as the "pecado original de analfabetismo," the original sin of illiteracy. This brief newspaper story suggests that Dominicans are given short shrift in the U.S. publishing world because high illiteracy in the country and its diasporic communities has created a culture that shuns reading in general. Literary critic Carlos F. Mieses has argued that migrations from the Dominican Republic have consisted largely of illegal, undereducated peasants whose dominant cultural expression is the *merengue*, which has vulgar content and appeals to base passions and customs such as machismo, sexism, and consumerism.

Torres-Saillant emphatically disagrees with Mieses's theory on Dominican invisibility; as evidence he notes writers including Julia Alvarez, Franklin Gutierrez, and Daisy Cocco de Filippis already bringing Dominican stories to the U.S. imagination. In particular, Torres-Saillant signals Junot Díaz's *Drown* as a success story for Dominican visibility (23). Still, invisibility is a theme encountered by Dominican communities regularly.

Invisibility is a recurring theme, if not a valued quality, in Díaz's work. In an interview with Torres-Saillant and Diógenes Céspedes, he mentions his deep admiration for Ralph Ellison's *Invisible Man*. While Díaz does not treat the theme of invisibility with any of Ellison's political force, it is interesting that the concept resonates, even invisibly, throughout his text. In effect, Díaz's Dominican story intersects with African-American experiences.

In American literature the theme has a formidable literary and sociopolitical precedent in *Invisible Man*. In the prologue to his 1952 masterpiece, Ellison introduces us to the complexity and the power of invisibility. He meditates that it gives him a strength that has not, until that moment, been recognized. Forcefully, the protagonist of the novel presents himself with these words:

> I am an invisible man. No, I am not a spook like those who haunted Edgar Allan Poe; nor am I one of your Hollywood-movie ectoplasms. I am a man of substance, of flesh and bone, fiber and liquids—and I might even be said to possess a mind. I am invisible, understand, simply because people refuse to see me. Like the bodiless heads you see sometimes in circus sideshows, it is as though I have been surrounded by mirrors of hard, distorting glass. When they approach me they see only my surroundings, themselves, or figments of their imagination—indeed, everything and anything except me. (3)

He goes on to argue that it is sometimes advantageous to be invisible, even if it can be unnerving, because that way he is free to do as he pleases. He tells us that he did not become "alive" until he became invisible. To exemplify his position on invisibility, the narrator tells us a story. One dark night he accidentally bumped into a tall blond man who called him an insulting name. Our narrator proceeded to demand an apology that he knew he would not get. In reaction, he yelled and hit the man, bitterly demanding an apology. In barely controlled outrage, our narrator kicked the man, beat him, and prepared to slit his throat with a knife. The man was saved by our narrator's thought, "He lay there, moaning on the asphalt; a man almost killed by a phantom" (5). Our narrator highlights the fact that since the tall blond man did not recognize him as a particular individual, the crime would not have a particular author. Instead it would be attributed to an entire race, a race effectively deprived of citizenship and the expectation of civilized conduct. Our narrator is invisible because of his color—a nebulous blackness. He is an invisible man because he is a socio-historical phantom in the politics of racist white America.

The narrator concedes that he is an "irresponsible bastard" (14). He then informs us that that is correct. Responsibility requires some kind of agreement, a form of recognition between two parties. But if one party is invisible, by choice or by circumstance, then that invisible person is free to do as he/she pleases. Invisibility liberates one from responsibility and consequently from racism. Once this is discovered, invisibility offers the erased person access to resistance and a means to survival. From this perspective, invisibility is a great thing. However, as we read on we realize that invisibility is not necessarily a choice. What one does with one's invisibility, we may conclude, is another matter. Part of the violence in *Invisible Man* results from the anger and frustration inherent in being denied access to rights of citizenship, through education, improved work possibilities, and voting. Ellison also underscores the many ways in which African Americans have been denied civil and basic human rights, rendering invisibility a horrible state in which to exist.

Invisibility, then, must be treated dually. In one instance it can, as in Ellison's prologue, liberate the invisible person from the constraints of responsibility. In another case, however, invisibility must be challenged.

Aware of the pervasiveness of invisibility, Ellison wrote in his 1981 introduction to *Invisible Man*: "the voice of invisibility issued from deep within our complex American underground" (xviii). Arguably, in the context of U.S. demographics, the Dominican diaspora joins this "complex American underground" with its own violent history and invisibility.

Invisibilities

The multiple invisibilities that appear in Diaz's work, I propose, are the result of a series of erasures. One explanation for these erasures can be found in a long history of violence in Dominican history. Violence, as evinced through the stories in *Drown*, serves no purpose other than to destroy the dignity of the abused. Díaz's stories demonstrate exactly how verbal and physical aggression belittles all of the actors—the perpetrators and the victims. In the first story of the collection, "Ysrael," Rafa and Yunior have been sent to the country, far from the city, for the summer. "Ysrael" is not a simple story of two boys in the countryside, emulating some kind of nineteenth-century communion with nature and the higher self. Instead it is a violent exposition of bored boys in an unpromising land. Rafa, who is twelve years old, feels constricted by the rural quiet, while Yunior, who is nine, looks to his brother to learn what he should do when he grows up. The elder puts down his younger brother with racist comments such as "Hey Señor Haitian, Mami found you on the border and only took you in because she felt sorry for *you*" (5). Rafa is insisting that Yunior is a bastard, uncivilized, and African—a derogatory term that underscores self-hatred in the Dominican Republic because of the African ancestry of many Dominicans, as we have seen. Rafa repeats a litany of slurs common to the mythology of superiority of Dominican culture, promulgated by years of government and intellectual propaganda.[4] Con-

sciously or unconsciously, Rafa uses these degrading verbal tools and follows an established pattern by which people cast others in the inferior role,
even if the aggressor and victim are equally poor and dark.

The model Rafa sets up for Yunior, like the model the caudillos and
dictators have historically imposed on their people, is based on disrespect
and violence. Rafa, even at such a young age, is already sexualized and
sadistic. "He'd take the campo girls down to the dams to swim and if he was
lucky they let him put it in their mouths or in their asses" (5). Rafa laughs
at the ignorance of country girls, including one "who believed she
wouldn't get pregnant if she drank a Coca-Cola afterwards" (6). It is clear
he would not care, let alone take responsibility, if a girl did become pregnant.

Studies such as Christian Krohn-Hansen's "Masculinity and the Political among Dominicans: 'The Dominican Tiger'" argue that this kind of
behavior receives respect rather than disapproval. Krohn-Hansen suggests
that "masculinity is a dominant political discourse across the country, and
is produced, reproduced and modified by ordinary people in everyday life"
(110). Masculinity is at the base of a "shared language" for constructions
of power and legitimacy among Dominicans. To support this thesis,
Krohn-Hansen tells the story of a small-town politician who is a
mujeriego, a womanizer. The man claims that his promiscuity is anything
but a hindrance to his career: it aids his political advancement because he
befriends the women's husbands and brothers. This way he has a greater
community of support. This network of men is called *el compadrazgo*, in
which the men bond and further themselves, ignoring the women that
they hurt along the way. It seems that the more women they can lure and
abandon, the more they have proved their manliness. This type of masculinity, involving seduction of women, freedom from entrapment, and advancement of career or social status, makes them *tígueres*, tigers.

Krohn-Hansen summarizes his theory, saying that "specific ideas and
categories which structure discussions of masculinity among Dominicans
correspond to a dominant political discourse—or to a legitimate problematic which helps to structure and give form to particular power relations in
Dominican society" (120). He then argues that ordinary men, repressed by
Trujillo's omnipotent masculinity, forged an imitative masculinity to make
sense of their own "Dominican imagined identity" (126). Krohn-Hansen
offers a persuasive theory. However, I believe that Dominican masculinity—read machismo and sexism—has a longer and more complicated history. This is the complication that Díaz draws out in his texts where the

tiger—the womanizing, abusive, inconsiderate, smooth-talking male—represented by Rafa and Papi is contrasted with a confused Yunior, who reproduces similar scenes of abuse and macho bravado while feeling both depressed and oppressed by it.

Nonetheless, Yunior understands that violence proves the achievement of a desired Dominican masculinity. The most violent of his experiences involves Ysrael, a boy who wears a mask on his deformed face. Yunior and Rafa take a bus to find Ysrael and to abuse him, in a calm, premeditated manner. Rafa approaches Ysrael with a request for help, saying his little brother is sick and they need to be taken to a *colmado*, a grocery store, for a cola. Ysrael, who is a foot taller than Rafa and dressed in clothes from the United States, obligingly leads them. On the way back, Rafa breaks the bottle on Ysrael's head. Once Ysrael is on the ground, Rafa kicks his side and tears off the mask that hides the gruesome evidence of the accident that maimed him in infancy: a pig had eaten his face when his parents weren't paying attention. He has no lips; his tongue is visible through his absent cheek; his ear is only a knob. Rather than inciting pity or sympathy, this image disgusts Rafa, who proceeds to move Ysrael's face from side to side with two fingers, as if he is being careful not to catch a disease. Rafa follows in his father's footsteps, the footsteps of a long lineage of men who engage in cruelty because they can. No one stops them; some onlookers even admire them for taking so much pride in malice.

This continued macho bravado traps all of its actors. In a later story, "No Face," Ysrael is once again being beaten up.

> The others stand over him and he's scared.
> We're going to make you a girl, the fat one says and he can hear the words echoing through the meat of the fat boy's body. (156)

It is not enough for the boys to pick on Ysrael because of his deformity; they must belittle him further by stealing his masculinity, threatening to make him a girl, castrating him emotionally and physically. Being a girl, like being castrated, has no place in the forced hierarchy of masculinity. But Ysrael tells himself, "STRENGTH." He reminds himself that, in the past, he has been able to push the bully and run away; he has survived the other beatings and will survive this one.

In another case, Yunior witnesses his father's forged masculinity, one that plagues his family with sadness. In one story, the father takes his young son to his Puerto Rican lover's house, leaving him to watch TV while they go to the next room. Afterward Papi expects Yunior to defend his own manhood by not telling his mother anything. Yunior must lie because, already, he has been inducted into masculine *compadrazgo*. If he tells, he is precluding his own entry into manhood. Once home, Papi scolds his wife, ignoring her pretty dress, makeup, and perfume. "Fiesta, 1980" is a story that exposes the many ways in which macho bravado defiles women and breaks down solidarity within families.

Yunior calls his father, Ramón de las Casas, "old-fashioned." By this he means that Papi will whip the boys for any misbehavior. Yunior's infractions are usually minor; nonetheless, they are cause for punishment and anger. Virta, in her new clothes and perfume, is overlooked. The only attention she gets is a scolding because she allowed her son to eat when he should not have, before riding in Papi's shiny new green van, which makes him carsick. Papi scolds everyone and loses no time insisting upon an order in the house that he himself violates with his violence against his family. Yunior writes an essay, "My Father the Torturer," which his teacher makes him rewrite because she thinks he is joking. The brief mention of this essay in the story is made shortly after Yunior lets us know that his father is "creative" with his punishment. He uses techniques such as thrusting his finger into his son's cheek to cause sharp and inexplicable pain. This creative punishment is reminiscent of the creative control deployed by Trujillo's secret police. Perhaps the description of Papi bears some resemblance to the actions of the dictator and his thugs.

In another story, "Negocios," we meet Papi before his family joins him in the United States. Responsibility is not Papi's strength. Despite his new clothes, shiny shoes, and new jobs, he does not send his family money. Instead he marries another woman and lives off her kindness and financial stability. Why is it so easy for him to find another woman to marry? Perhaps the new wife feels that she would prefer any man to no man. Perhaps she feels pressure from her family and her community. Her story is not expanded upon, and we are left to guess. What we do note is that Papi does what he wants and no one stops him. The result is that, in essence, Yunior and his family have no father. Later, when Papi leaves the other woman, she and her son also have a broken family. When Yunior visits the second wife at the end, we notice that both he and the woman are sad and distrustful. They have lived through indescribable emotional pain at the hands of one man's incontestable display of masculinity.

All have waited for the affection of "el hombre." Mami waits for Papi; Yunior and Rafa feel abandoned; and Yunior tells us that all he wants is his father's love, even if it is abusive. The new woman too wants Papi's love.

She helps him get his visa by marrying him, and eventually gives him a son, whom he also calls Ramón. Papi now has two "wives" and two sons named after himself. He also continues to have affairs and, worse, to be violent against those who wait for his love to no avail.

According to these vignettes, rather than banding together to forget the macho man, women reproduce sexism as well. The family calls the lovers "sucias," dirty women, and Yunior and Mami call the second wife a "puta," whore. In all instances the women, whose self-sacrifice is absurd to the outsider, are further downtrodden by the way they are categorized even by themselves. That is, they do not get honored for their devotion and love. Instead they are cast as dirty whores. Regardless of how much they do to make Papi's life better and to raise his children and maintain his households on their own, they are hit if they complain and are called derogatory names when they are subservient. The women despise each other, becoming each other's enemies, fighting for the love of one unloving male. In a way, this probably makes the man feel more "hombre," inspiring other men to act accordingly to create their own twisted love triangles.

As they grow up, the boys follow the tradition of male dominance, disrespect, and violence. So we are not surprised to see Yunior hit his girlfriend and make "blood come out of her ear like a worm" (65). All of the characters exhibit hatred toward each other and ultimately toward themselves. Papi, with his new clothes and fancy Volkswagen, is responsible for broken homes, abuse, violence, and broken hearts. Material things do not change violent psychosocial dynamics that destroy people's potential for personhood, the condition in which individual development is nurtured and respected.

These stories demonstrate that violence, pain, trauma, and broken memories are not shaped by political repression only but also by sociocultural traditions. They draw attention to invisible people and taboo subjects, exposing heterosexist repression and its repercussions, which maintain invisibilities.

Dominican Diaspora Literature: Struggling Visibility

Díaz's work has appeared in prestigious U.S. publications such as the *Paris Review* and the *New Yorker*. In addition, he received a six-figure advance for *Drown* and a novel in progress. For Torres-Saillant, Díaz's sudden success demonstrates the triumph of Dominican life and its presence in the United States. Yet it creates a seeming contradiction. At the end of the century Dominicans were still being overlooked in historical and sociological accounts of U.S. Latinos, although in 1996 a young Dominican writer was triumphantly heralded as the pride of U.S. letters. What, then, is the real picture of the Dominican diaspora in the United States? Is its main issue invisibility or visibility?

The Dominican diaspora is a growing and strong force that is exposing its own struggles with memory, trauma, pain, and emotional, national, and transnational definitions of individuality and personhood. The founding in February 1994 of the City University of New York's Dominican Studies Institute, the first and only university-based research institution dedicated to the Dominican diaspora, proves this point. Its primary goal, says its Web site, is "to further the understanding of the history, culture, socioeconomic, and political position of Dominicans in the United States." The outstanding academics that created the Council of Dominican Educators are Luis Álvarez, Ana García-Reyes, Franklin Gutiérrez, Ramona Hernández, Fausto de la Rosa, Nelsón Reynoso, Anthony Stevens-Acevedo, and Silvio Torres-Saillant. Their work and the resulting institution confirm Dominicans not only in the U.S. imagination but specifically in the intellectual history of the United States.

The first piece of Dominican diaspora literature to hit mainstream audiences and lay bare the struggles of assimilation and definition was Julia Alvarez's *How the García Girls Lost Their Accents* (1991). Viriato Sención's *Los que falsificaron la firma de Dios* (1992) captivated Dominicans and was later translated into English as *They Forged the Signature of God* (1995). It sold tens of thousands of copies in Spanish, a phenomenon that many critics offered as proof that a reading tradition existed in the country. These works disclose a hushed Dominican history of fear, terror, painful memories and a need for recovery from often unrecognized or denied emotional trauma and from a long history of cultural and economic violence.

Within diaspora literature, Díaz is often cited alongside Alvarez, even though their personal backgrounds and writing styles are vastly different. They embody two kinds of migratory experiences. Alvarez's work reflects sociological factors studied by Sherri Grasmuck and Patricia Pessar, who have written that "many Dominicans sought refuge abroad because they had witnessed the murder of compatriots with whom they shared political sympathies" (43). They provided compelling evidence that "Dominican emigration between the 1960s and early 1980s has been overwhelmingly an urban, middle-stratum phenomenon" (13).

In contrast to Alvarez's predominantly middle-class stories, which are marked by the memory of terror during the Trujillo dictatorship, Díaz's stories describe the margins. His world is one where poverty adds to an already established disenfranchising culture of machismo, homophobia, racism, and violence. At first glance, his work is less obviously colored by the country's history of dictatorship and government corruption.[5] Yet it is nevertheless rooted strongly in Dominican national identity and sharply influenced by the expectations of migration. Díaz contrasts dehumanization, self-deprecation, and invisibility with the possibility, however remote, of achievement, escape, visibility, and survival. Written in a stark style, his stories describe a complex version of Dominican diaspora life. In effect, Díaz utilizes bareness and simplicity to convey the unspeakable, often denied, complexities of life for young people in the Dominican diaspora.

Class, a central theme in Díaz's fiction, is examined sociologically by Ramona Hernández in her 2002 study *The Mobility of Workers under Advanced Capitalism*, which cites extensive evidence that Dominican migrations have not necessarily improved the lives of emigrés. "Poor at home," Hernández remarks, "they continue to be poor in the receiving country. Many had no jobs at home, and after leaving, many remain jobless" (14). Hernández supports her thesis, which challenges previous literature such as Patricia Pessar's *Visa for a Dream*, by drawing a historical overview of migration from the Dominican Republic to the United States. In the 1930s and throughout his many years in power, Trujillo encouraged reproduction and discouraged emigration. This way, he believed, the nation would become bigger and stronger. This way, the Dominican Republic could supply more low-paid, unskilled laborers to meet the demands of the island's U.S. caretakers—and eventually to wrest control of customs from the Americans, once the Dominicans had repaid the foreign debts that had prompted the U.S. occupation of 1916–24. By the time Balaguer took office in 1966, the need for low-cost labor had decreased. Official policy now promoted birth control and migration out of the country. "Emigration provided a pipeline through which the country could systematically eliminate unwanted and unneeded surplus laborers whom the new system of production was unable to absorb" (Hernández 8). In other words, migration helped Balaguer to rid himself of people—including dissidents potentially interested in toppling his forced presidency—who would have created greater economic and political problems on the island. The migrations from the Dominican Republic during this period encompassed large groups with little or no education, who were escaping in desperation, often only to find more misery in the United States.[6]

Hernández's study proposes that post-1965 migrations from developing nations to the United States reflected a shift to surplus unskilled labor that the host country did not really need (5). She argues that migration from the Dominican Republic was encouraged during Balaguer's first presidency by de facto policies that facilitated departure. This was further encouraged by the United States, which did not want to see the Dominican Republic destabilized and thus vulnerable to a communist or socialist takeover (8–9). Hernández also argues that people do not necessarily benefit when they migrate to a richer country (13). "The precarious conditions of most Dominicans suggest either that the host country did not need workers when Dominicans arrived, or that it did not specifically need the labor of Dominicans" (5).

Drown translates this demographic and economic information into vignettes. In the fourth story, "Aguantando" ("putting up with" or "enduring"), the narrator recalls: "I can't remember how many times I crouched over our latrine, my teeth clenched, watching long gray parasites slide out from between my legs" (71). This vivid image of a young child sitting in an outhouse in the Dominican countryside excreting living creatures underscores some of the ways poverty is monstrous. Since hygiene and medical care are limited, the children have an annual bout of worms. The family barely has money for food. In order for Mami, the mother, to buy the Verminox to kill the parasites, the children have to skip meals. The worms have power over these frail bodies because there is no medicine to kill them. But the worms could kill the children, draining the last bit of nourishment from their bodies or choking them to death as they reversed peristalsis and squirmed into the children's throats.

Yunior tells about the depth of despair and embarrassment brought on by the family's financial circumstances. They live south of the National Cemetery in a wood-frame house. The father left for the United States shortly before Yunior's fourth birthday, promising to send money. The family waited, but he broke his promise. Instead, Virta (Mami) works endless hours for exploitative pay at a chocolate factory. Yunior and his brother, Rafa, spend long hours by themselves or under the negligent eye of the aged grandfather. For Virta, poverty is synonymous with overwork; for the boys, poverty is synonymous with too much time to get into trouble. For all, poverty limits opportunities. The boys' lives are devoid of constructive and educational activities. Learning and productivity are squelched by the very lack of structure in which the boys live.

In the same story, a messenger with news from Papi shows up, telling Virta to get ready to leave for the United States. The grandfather, whose cane-cutter's hands grip the handrails of his rocker, is outraged. Despite the broken promises and an absence of more than five years, Papi invites the family to the United States. He promises that their lives will be better. How could it be worse? Well, Papi breaks yet another promise, and Mami almost loses her mind. The boys are sent to relatives' houses, and Mami is gone for five weeks. The story does not tell us where she has gone, but we are informed that she has lost weight and gotten darker. With the additional evidence of the heavy calluses on her hands, we are led to understand that she went to cut cane in the fields under the heavy sun. Without her husband's financial help, and with two sons and an aging father to support, Virta takes on the job Dominicans most despise. And still things get worse: "On Saturday a late hurricane passed close to the Capital and the next day folks were talking about how high the waves were down by the Malecón. Some children had been lost, swept out to sea and Abuelo shook his head when he heard the news. You'd think the sea would be sick of us by now, he said" (85).

Eventually the family moves to the United States. Virta finds a job as a house cleaner, and the boys go to bad schools where the teachers and counselors have little faith in their assimilation and advancement. Díaz draws us into a world where dreams of success go unfulfilled. *Drown* serves as a metaphor for the opposite of floating, of making it across an imaginary body of water between poverty (the Dominican Republic) and promise (the United States). The word *drown* means "die through submersion in and inhalation of water" or "make inaudible by being louder"; it is used in the phrase "drown one's sorrows: forget one's problems by getting drunk" (*Oxford American Dictionary*). Díaz's stories convey a sense that the characters are submerged in circumstances that drown them out. The silence of Yunior's mother, the sexual escapades of Rafa, and the dope-selling of Yunior himself all reflect their need to "drown out" their situations of boredom, lack of opportunities, and poverty.

Díaz's book invites the reader to contemplate the ways in which poverty and machismo erase human potential. On an at-face-value reading, some could argue that it also reinforces beliefs that the Dominican diaspora is plagued by crime, violence, and base moral behavior. This dichotomy, like that proposed by invisibility/visibility, shapes an important and painful struggle for the Dominican diaspora community. Specifically, this di-chotomy complicates the role of the writer who mediates experience for his community, but might fall into the trap of elaborating preconceived images of Dominican stories of life in the 'hood. Highlighting these kinds of stories creates a problematic visibility whereby Dominicans enter main-stream U.S. narratives only to advance the profile of violence and despair in the community. In such a light, I could argue that Díaz is exacerbating the situation of the Dominican diaspora community by confirming this profile of violence and despair. Yet, were he to fail to be true to the stories he believes need to be told, he would also do a disservice to his community and to his art.

In sum, the *Drown* stories emphasize disempowered selves and dehu-manizing circumstances. Díaz does not describe female characters with depth or narrative development. His exclusively male, heterosexist per-spective voids female agency of any kind. This male visibility contrasts with multiple invisibilities—gender, sexual orientation, race. In "Drown," it is difficult for Yunior to develop self-worth. Neither can he believe in a dream of success. To the contrary, he notices the false promises that sur-round him. For example, an army recruiter drives around the barrio look-ing for eligible young men, to invite them into a career that will help them get out of poverty. Contrasting images underscore the fallacy that under-lies the dream of success. Yunior must be in good shape, because he can run three miles with ease. The recruiter tries to stop him several times. Out-wardly, at least, Yunior must give the appearance of potential. The re-cruiter asks him if he has discipline and loyalty. Yunior immediately re-sponds that he is not army material. The officer tells him that he used to think that of himself, too. He goes on to enumerate what he believes are material signs of success: a house, a car, a gun, a wife. He has all of that. Yunior listens and thinks:

> He's a southerner, red-haired, his drawl so out of place that the people around here laugh just hearing him. I take to the bushes when I see his car on the road. These days my guts feel loose and cold and I want to be away from here. He won't have to show me his Desert Eagle or flash the photos of skinny Filipino girls sucking dick. He'll only have to smile and name the places and I'll listen. (100–101)

Yunior does not believe in the success the officer is trying to lure him with. Besides seeing an overweight man, Yunior also sees a dishonest man. The recruiter's success is measured in possessions that Yunior does not value; it is based on exploitation Yunior has witnessed personally, from the perspective of the exploited. The officer's lure could include a skinny Filipino at his beck and call. But Yunior notes the desperation of the image and the violence in this recruiter's pride. The girl is young, no doubt underage. She is skinny, probably malnourished. Perhaps she even has worms from lack of potable water. Still, the recruiter holds her picture as a sign of what can be attained. Yunior knows the price. The exotic places are all poor and reminiscent of his childhood home. They have all been invaded or occupied by U.S. troops. The troops, Yunior might remember, have trampled on the people putting up with (*aguantando*) the extreme heat of the islands and the inescapable despair of poverty. Yunior does not abandon his material poverty to engage in more deprivation of body and soul. He does not allow himself to drown in false promises.

In one scene he jumps a fence to illegally swim, after hours, in the neighborhood pool. Yunior swims underwater for as long as he can. This offers an image of total submersion that contrasts with the concept of drowning. I believe that this depiction is distinct from the image, suggested by the title, of drowning; specifically, it holds symbolic significance. Swimming underwater, Yunior cannot hear or see any of the problems that make waves above. He has strong lungs that he trusts, regardless of his low self-esteem in other areas. Swimming underwater allows him some peace of mind and gives him a sense of freedom in movement he does not experience when weighed down by gravity out of the water. Underwater, he is temporarily invisible to his neighborhood friends; thus he escapes, very briefly, his stifling barrio existence. Once above, he sees the younger siblings of the friends he always played with at the pool. Despite himself, he must come out of that submerged state, analyze his life, and perhaps do something with it or drown in the very limitations he claims to feel oppressed by—dirty streets, drugs, kids with no clear future.

Yunior's image of himself is contrasted with that of his friend Beto, who tells him, "You can't be anywhere forever" (107). Beto, who initiates him into homosexual pleasures, has explored the world beyond his barrio. Beto has gone to nightclubs, visited other areas of the city, and, more important, is leaving everything behind to go to college. He looks at the dirt and crime around him with disgust and emphasizes his relief at abandoning all of that. Yunior stays behind, worried he will end up "abnormal" (104) because of his intimacies with Beto, and sells dope to the children in the neighborhood. Yunior drinks with some friends to drown out his existential feelings, the experienced pleasures of homosexual intimacy, and his sense of worthlessness.

Yet implicit in Diaz's work is a criticism of the very traits that his writing embodies; it is as if he has made their operation so clear that alert readers cannot help but judge the characters harshly in the unsparing spotlight that Díaz has trained on them—and, by implication, on those who mislead his male characters so badly.

I cannot read Díaz's stories at face value. Instead I suggest that they serve as a springboard for a complex meditation on a long trajectory of violence and its reproduction.

Violent Histories: Empowered Leaders

Violence, as we have seen, is an act against a community and/or person. It is intended to destroy the victim's sense of self and security while giving power to the perpetrator. Many forms of violence—physical and psychological, organized and random, economic and political—consolidate to create miserable conditions. Over the years, violent acts have affirmed a male-dominated hierarchy, devaluing women and homosexuals. In totalitarian regimes (extreme left as well as extreme right), violence has been used to eliminate "unwanteds" such as handicapped persons, political dissidents, and ethnically, racially, and sexually different groups. The violence produced and reproduced in Hispanic Caribbean culture is fashioned on macho bravado, based on caudillismo (rule by tyranny, despotism), and originates in the European "discovery" and colonization of the Americas.

Let us recall the colonial violations experienced by Latin American and Caribbean islands such as the Dominican Republic. After the Middle Ages, Spain, France, and England were beginning to categorize themselves as civilized empires, yet their men, after "discovering the Americas," were acting in uncivilized ways in the name of God and country (euphemisms for fame and riches), killing people whose languages they did not speak and raping women whose faces they would never remember. As Eduardo Galeano explained in 1971 in *Las venas abiertas de América Latina*, power was synonymous with having the greatest strength and the least guilt. In his 1956 examination of Mexican power dynamics, Eric R. Wolf observed that "we confront a society riven by group conflicts for economic and political control" (1067). His study of Indian villages and the Indian peoples shows how the crown manipulated the local estate owners, the *hacenderos*, to create power conflicts between the nation and its numerous communities, particularly Indian and Negro slaves. Wolf comments:

> Alongside the Indian villages and the entrepreneurial communities located near haciendas, mines, or mills there developed loosely-structured settlements of casual farmers and workers, middlemen and "lumpenproletariats" who had no legal place in the colonial order. Colonial records tended to ignore them except when they came into overt conflict with the law. Their symbol in Mexican literature is *El Periquillo Sarniento*, the man who lives by his wits.... "Conceived in violence and without joy, born into the world in sorrow." (1068) (Fernando Benítez 1947: 47)

In the nineteenth century, the Dominican writer Manuel de J. Galván wrote the seminal story of Enriquillo, an Indian who had been educated according to Spanish codes of conduct and who later rebelled against the Spanish to defend the indigenous populations. He was honored with the title of *caudillo soberano* because of what Galván described as his superior intelligence and morality. Galván's novel *Enriquillo* is but the first of a series of self-imaginings constructed by Dominican intellectuals to create a history of Indian and Spanish heritage, negating African influences on the culture and the peoples. The character Enriquillo also serves as an example of masculine leadership. He is a *cacique*, a chief, and later honored with the title of caudillo. The latter honor is granted precisely because of his ability to show strength, through violence, against Spanish rule.

In *La isla imaginada*, the historian Pedro San Miguel indicates that the island of Hispaniola has been imagined and imaged by different leaders, caudillos and dictators, erasing the histories of the subaltern. He contends that in the nineteenth century the history of the Dominican Republic was valorized only if it represented the interests of the bourgeoisie. Academic circles, with their critiques and questions, were disqualified as presenting ideologies, fictions, or an inaccurate philosophy of history. This debate over "real history" barely veiled the power and control gained by the dominant version of history, which negated the voice and experience of the exploited. The mission of historiography was to trace the avatars of the nation. In societies in which authoritarian regimes and dictatorships emerged, the link between historiography and power was all the more visible.[7]

The "historical facts," and in particular the historical discrepancies, inform us that men have violently battled for centuries to control Saint

Domingue, the island of Hispaniola, including during the wars between Spain and France and, later, the imposed unification with Haiti. Both Henri Christophe and Dessalines were known for their brutal violence. Later, in 1822, Haitian president Jean-Pierre Boyer marched into Santo Domingo and a turbulent unification began. His despotic rule lasted until 1844, when Santo Domingo gained independence. The new country eventually came under the rule of the first caudillos, Santana and Báez, whose governments did not prove to be more peaceful or constructive. With respect to caudillo politics and political volatility between 1865 and 1879, the historian Frank Moya Pons explains: "Dominican politics had always been based on personalism and *caudillismo* because the population was primarily rural and illiterate, and their loyalty was only possible through a system of personal connections" (220). The Santana and Báez governments were followed in 1886–99 by the dictatorship of Ulises Heureaux, "el General Lilís."

Installed in 1930, the dictator Rafael Trujillo did not come to power and stay there by worrying about the rights of Dominicans. His narrative of national progress ignored his people. Fifty percent of those people, women, to him were commodities to be conveniently designated, glorified, or forsaken: he made his wife and daughter rich, kept his prized lovers well, and discarded his one-nighters to the amnesia of history, their honor lost to the great "benefactor."

A great part of the Trujillo mythology revolves around his macho bravado (in hushed lore, it is said that he eliminated the husbands of some of the women he seduced, precisely to seduce them), crimes, and misdemeanors (ordering murders to rid the country of opposition, funneling federal money into his private bank accounts). Bernardo Vega has analyzed the oral myths, the biographies, and the court papers safely housed at the National Archives in Washington, D.C., to explain the ways Trujillo not only challenged the law but also broke it to his advantage. In the introduction to *Trujillo ante una corte marcial por violación y extorsión en 1920* Vega wonders what would have happened if Trujillo had been convicted of the crimes, including rape and robbery and extortion, with which he was charged before he came to power. Would he have been sentenced to death? Would he have been discharged from the army and, therefore, had a blighted career?

What is important to an understanding of Trujillo's Machiavellian (in)sensibilities is that in 1920, during U.S. occupation, the twenty-eight-year-old Trujillo was charged with rape, among other crimes, but got away with these exploitations of human lives. Different versions of the story were constructed, and the incidents were quickly relegated to whispers that could not be proved. Vega informs us that, although the story became oral history, no one officially documented the crime until 1972, eleven years after the dictator's death (9). The victim never received justice. Her story was mostly buried and ignored. Some brief articles addressed the incident, Vega says. For example, the Dominican historian Félix Servio Ducoudray interviewed the rape victim and published some articles. It seems that the rape was regarded as a private matter, of lesser importance than other misdemeanors. At issue was not Trujillo's violations of a woman in the community but rather his ability to get away with his infringements of the law. In 1946 Albert Hicks wrote in *Blood in the Streets* that Trujillo had once been sentenced to a six-month prison term for falsification of legal documents. Years later Trujillo's biographer Robert Crassweller would tell his readers that in 1916 Trujillo belonged to a gang called the 44, which had a bad reputation for robbery and assault at bodegas and storage compounds (Vega 14). All of these details point to a man who manipulated the system and to a system that did not give rape due criminal punishment. Rape was situated in the same category as petty thefts and gang membership. Trujillo proved his prowess with women and his dominion over even the law imposed by the U.S. Marine Corps.

The first charge of rape was dropped, supposedly because it implicated the Marine Corps. They were relocating the country people to other less desirable regions in order to make space for new enterprises. A cunning Trujillo was able to have charges either dismissed or not made at all because of his ability to point a finger. Vega writes that, according to U.S. archives, most of the Marines wanted to be located in Europe for the Great War. Those who were left in the *zona gavillera del este* in the Dominican Republic were mostly interested in drinking rum and finding prostitutes. Who was to say who were prostitutes and who were innocent abducted girls if the men responsible for law and order practiced the most extreme debauchery? Trujillo took advantage of the general disorder and violence to advance his own causes. In the Caribbean, Trujillo mastered sexism and violence, like leaders before him, to attain power. Power and violence in Dominican politics continues to be synonymous with success and manhood. But those with the power have systematically ignored the welfare of the country's citizens. A particularly striking recent example of the long history of *caudillista* trickery occurred in 1986, when Joaquín Balaguer became president with the intention of staying in power for the rest of his life (Moya Pons 423). In a successful campaign to destroy the credibility and political popularity of his predecessor, Salvador Jorge Blanco, Balaguer "produced" allegations against him. Anyone who tried to defend Blanco was imprisoned without trial or went into exile. Balaguer did not keep any of his electoral campaign promises, running the country "against all free-market principles" (427). He eliminated all foreign currencies, including the dollar, from the country and imprisoned without trial anyone who kept dollars. The Dominican national currency plummeted in value over the next few years, leading to an "economic dictatorship" (427) and desperation among the people. Amid widespread economic crisis in the mid-1980s, Dominicans resorted to abandoning the country, escaping to Puerto Rico and the mainland United States. Circumstances were so dire that people were risking their lives at sea. Interdictions by the U.S. Coast Guard rose from 76 people in 1983 to 1,246 in 1990. If the leader could not help the people, they would help themselves by finding alternative life and work options regardless of the costs.

The present is tainted by some of the habits of the past and tarnished by new histories of abuse, violence, and disempowerment. But with history and nation "imagined," as San Miguel suggests, we need to resort to fiction to figure out what may lie in the missing parts of Dominican and Dominican diaspora experiences. We can see the impact of historical and political forces in Díaz's fiction, which is full of brutality. In Díaz's text, women are derided, homosexuals assaulted, and Haitians belittled. Without recognizing the past, much less scrutinizing it, people continue to behave according to bad habits that they cannot understand. The present, then, is fraught with continuing violence, violations, silence, and fears. Omnipresent in Díaz's work, violence begets violence. Each hostile act makes the actors feel the briefness of the triumph, for another event will force them to prove themselves again or be defeated. I propose that the stories themselves embody violence by their description of invisible people and their relentlessly violent expositions.

"Other" Invisibilities

Díaz illustrates different versions of invisibility in *Drown*. Ysrael, aka No Face, and Virta cultivate invisibility in order to survive different kinds of prejudice, which erase them from active membership in their societies. Ysrael's and Virta's invisibility is a necessary response to Rafa's and Papi's relentless macho bravado. Their invisibility adumbrates the ways in which sociohistorical violence continues to disempower entire groups of people and how these disempowered people berate themselves, precluding the possibility of escape from their predicaments.

In the penultimate story, "No Face," Ysrael tells himself he "has the power of INVISIBILITY and no one can touch him," yet he knows "So many wish him to fall. So many wish him gone" (155). No one wants to see his eaten face or the mask that covers the deformity the neighbors speculate about. His masked face signals the fragility of our bodies and our lives. This fragility reminds those who see him that we are insignificant and powerless. For some perverse reason, one that the author does not elaborate, this marker of fragility invites others to show their own power through violent acts. History is riddled with intolerance of abnormality and difference. Hitler proposed eliminating all homosexuals, political dissidents, and Jews. Fidel Castro during the seventies proposed to eradicate, via prisons and labor camps, all of Cuba's political dissidents and homosexuals.

Why does Ysrael's abnormality so incite his peers' cruelty? Perhaps it is so they do not have to contend with their own fragility and their fears of their own powerlessness. When Ysrael helps a cat in the street, a motorist yells, "Hey No Face! . . . You haven't started eating cats, have you?" Another chimes in, "He'll be eating kids next" (155). Some boys come to beat him up, threatening that they will make him a girl. When a female shopkeeper comes to his defense, we learn that she has received no respect since the day her husband left her for a Haitian. One marginalized person trying to help another marginalized person gets further erased from humanitarian consideration and humanity.

Soon Ysrael, like Ellison's invisible man, learns to be invisible to his neighbors. He can thereby escape their daily mistreatment. He is free to cultivate his inner dream: to get to the United States, where he will find the doctors who will reconstruct his face. Ysrael exercises every morning, visits a priest who teaches him reading and writing for two hours a day, and accomplishes his daily tasks in the shadows of his angry and scared neighbors. But, like the invisible man, he too feels anger and exhibits an edge of violence. After he is beaten up, he tells himself to be a man. In another incident, he bends the bars of his neighbor's gate to show the hostile cleaning lady that he is not to be messed with. Looking for some kind of strength, he buys a Kaliman comic with a superhero who "takes no shit and wears a turban. If his face were covered he'd be perfect" (155).

Invisibility, it seems, gives Ysrael the time to cultivate himself so as to confront his neighbors with his personal success. Although invisibility liberates Ysrael from abuse, it also precludes his membership in his community. We are then left to wonder if the neighbors did not succeed in getting rid of him. Invisibility is synonymous with the invisible person's exclusion from membership in his/her community and from political action in the national arena.

Virta's invisibility is twofold, but also traditional. Her character lacks any depth or development. Yunior observes that the Spanish-language television news is "drama for her, violence for me" (95). She does not recognize the extent of the violence to which she has been exposed. It seems like part of a life within which she must live. Unconsciously, her silence is her only form of survival. Just as she "disappeared" in the Dominican Republic to work in the cane fields to provide for her children, in the United States she becomes a house cleaner to forge her family's future. She is silenced by the parameters of traditional sexism.

In "Fiesta, 1980" Díaz writes that Papi "told her to shut up, what did she know about anything anyway?" (35). Yunior tells us that "Papi's voice was loud and argumentative; you didn't have to be anywhere near him to catch his drift. And Mami, you had to put cups to your ears to hear hers" (33). In the title story, "Drown," the narrator notes: "She's so quiet that most of the time I'm startled to find her in the apartment. . . . She has discovered the secret to silence: pouring café without a splash, walking between rooms as if gliding on a cushion of felt, crying without a sound" (94). He calls her a shadow warrior. She fights for her children's livelihood silently.

While Yunior credits her silence with the strength of a warrior, that silence is traditional in sexist cultures. She is silent, and she is her family's backbone, working at whatever job she can to provide for her children. She sacrifices everything, putting all of her hope and expectations in her children's future. She does not fight the husband who has mistreated her; she does not go to court to demand alimony or child support. She cleans, cooks, and works silently, demanding nothing.

In another story, she is seen whispering long distance to the long-gone husband who now lives in Miami with another woman. He lies to Virta, telling her that he will abandon his girlfriend in Florida if she comes to live with him. Yunior angrily grabs the phone from his mother and hangs it up. He reminds her that the father lies and describes him as "a sad guy who calls her and begs for money" (101). Despite Virta's strength in keeping the household together against all odds, her character is weak. She wastes her life waiting for the only man she ever loved, and now she lets her son censure her behavior. In the end, her character is limited and pitiful.

These expositions of the self-sacrificed mother figure are extraordinarily traditional. The stories consequently demonstrate a lack of understanding in Díaz's interpretation of women—an inability to explore women's invisibility and denied personhood within Dominican culture and to recognize the incredible achievements many Dominican women make against all odds—that actually reproduces sexism in the culture. In other words, I point out Virta's invisibility in the text from my vantage point as a critic to underscore how Díaz himself reproduces female invisibility by not elaborating on the potential of characters like Virta. I find it difficult to see Díaz's collection as representative of the Dominican diaspora, as has been suggested by numerous book reviews and advertising blurbs, because a number of the characters are flat and do not give voice (and visibility) to the complexities of the Dominican people and their multiple realities, which encompass Dominican traditions and universalist sexist codes of conduct, and which intersect with other, ongoing problems present in the United States. The stories inscribe already traditional roles for disenfranchised groups such as women.

But let me complicate my discomfort with Díaz's flat expositions of traditionally repressed groups. Could it be that, by repeating traditional "invisibilities" so glaringly, he might be exposing their ill effects via exaggeration? For example, his exposition of homosexual desire, brief as it is, could be interpreted as a challenge to Dominican machismo, which denies and rejects any homosexual presence.[8] In the scene of the title story, "Drown," where Yunior has a first sexual encounter with his friend Beto, he cannot allow himself to admit that he actually enjoyed it. Instead he recoils into hiding. "Mostly I stayed in the basement, terrified that I would end up abnormal, a fucking pato" (104). In the next scene, Beto has just performed fellatio on Yunior. When Yunior fears that someone is entering the room, he gets scared, pulls up his pants, and runs away. Rather than thinking about his friendship with Beto, or the pleasure he derived in the moment, he avoids Beto. Weeks later, when Beto goes off to college, Yunior sees him and decides to cut contact with his friend; he throws away, without even looking at it, the book he receives as a parting gift. This scene is critical. Perhaps he is afraid that the book might address issues of sexuality; he prefers to remain ignorant of its content. More broadly, he is ignoring how much he claims to want to abandon the world he lives in; ignoring also that Beto is not trapped by the macho codes of conduct or the stringent homophobic parameters of his ethnic neighborhood. Beto repeats that no one can stay in one place forever. He takes charge of his life by living it on his terms, without fear. But Yunior cannot do likewise. Instead he is trapped by the fear of being different, of being beaten, of having done to him what he and his brother have done to others. His understanding of social conduct is warped by violence and shadowed by fear and depression. By abandoning Beto's friendship, he is also limiting his ability to see and understand alternative ways of experiencing life, thus trapping himself further in violent, heterosexist behavior. His behavior has been molded by a legacy of maleness inscribed by the Catholic Church and varying country leaders.

For example, in the early 1950s Trujillo created two concentration camps for "middle-class intellectual and/or political male dissidents suspected of being, or known to be, homosexual or bisexual" (Moya and García 125). More recently, the first Gay Pride Parade in Santo Domingo, held on July 1, 2001, led to widely publicized violence, with one man shot to death and many injured. "Coming out"—identifying oneself as gay— was synonymous with being attacked. Coming out also exposed people's fears of difference (named illness by some) and signaled the undeniable presence of homosexuals in Dominican society. Some studies have addressed the issue of bisexuality in Dominican culture and the potential health hazards that the practice poses, in particular the spread of AIDS. In general, however, people ignore or actively try to silence such speculation. Bisexuality and homoeroticism continue to be invisible in mainstream representations of Dominican culture.

The growing number of AIDS and HIV-positive cases among Haitian and Haitian-Dominican sugarcane workers between 1983 and 1986 constituted a further reason to marginalize nonheterosexual behavior and poorer sectors of society.[9] In their study, Moya and García argue that many men do practice bisexual behavior (overt heterosexuality and covert homosexuality), perhaps to hide their homosexual preferences in light of strong homophobia in the society. They conclude that the pressures of masculinity also lead to profound feelings of guilt and self-loathing for these men.

The Gay Pride Parade in Santo Domingo in June 2001 sheds some sociocultural light on Yunior's behavior. The parade, which had originally been scheduled by the OPC (Oficina de Patrimonio Cultural, or Office of Cultural Affairs) to take place in one of the more prominent squares of the city, the Plaza de España, was moved over to the Avenida del Puerto, a less controversial venue, on short notice. Many parade participants viewed this move as a calculated impediment to the planned events. They felt that the city was backpedaling on its original support, according to a story in *El Nacional*, "Ratifican llamado a marcha de gays." The newspaper article commented that Dominican society was not used to dissident expression and noted that the change of place also represented a change in space. The original demonstration site was a large two-way street, and the new site was a narrower area. The article asked why homosexuals were not allowed to be included in "la humanidad," reflecting that whether they are accepted or not, they are present, and they have the same modes of living as other people, working, suffering from colds, and experiencing the same crises and celebrations as the rest of humanity. The debates on social acceptance of homosexuality were covered in numerous newspapers, with many people claiming that they suffered from discrimination by the police and at their work, while a few noted that they felt loved and accepted by friends and family and in their work environments. A determining factor, perhaps, is the type of work and the families' and friends' individual levels of political commitment to diversity and tolerance in Dominican society.[10] Nonetheless, Leonora Ramírez S. observed in the *Hoy* section of the Spanish newspaper *El País* that a strong wall exists against discussion and integration of the presence of homosexuals in the culture. They remain on the margins, made invisible by fears and ignorance.

The parade met with scandal, as at the end someone was shot. Exact details were never made public. Apparently a report was made to the Agencia Española de Prensa (Spanish Press Agency) that a man had been murdered shortly after the Gay Pride Parade, implying that the violence was directly related to the event. In *El Expreso* Leonardo Sánchez, the director of the lesbian and gay collective Amigos Siempre Amigos, complained that those were only rumors and the murder had nothing to do with the parade. A heated debate ensued, with some arguing that there was no link and others insisting that there was. In the end, the dead man and the cause of his death became invisible in the midst of the debate over the link. For some, the most important thing was to erase the memory of the violence in order to salvage the country's first step toward free and liberating expression of self. Others seemed to feel that underscoring the link would prove that such parades only lead to more violence that should be avoided.

The gay and lesbian communities' invisibility to date bares a quiet violence, brutal nonetheless. Similarly, the continued invisibility of women's role as backbone of family and culture in a panoramic Dominican (and Dominican diaspora) image points to the violations women endure in silence, as many, exemplified by the Díaz character Virta, are kept isolated by lack of recognition and whore/Madonna social dynamics.

Challenging the Binaries

Reading between the lines and into the complicated history of Dominican silences and violence, I propose that Díaz's expositions of poverty, sexism, and violence are the initial steps toward a more sophisticated treatment of the numerous degrees of invisibility and visibility in Dominican and Dominican diaspora culture and memory.

Considering a long history of violence that is driven by masculinity as a code of conduct and "honor"—which, in reality, dishonors women and the other subordinate groups that it keeps in a disempowered state—stories like Díaz's underscore how little attention is given to the pain of invisibility. The violence against women and "others" exposed in these stories highlights the psychological damage inflicted on boys and girls, who as adults reproduce the same violence. Machismo in this text does not follow the codes of gallantry by which women should be protected and for which families must be provided. Instead, machismo is described as a perverse power play that punishes differences and destroys individual potential for personhood and respectful membership in the family and the community.

Inadvertently perhaps, Díaz is showing how the Dominican diaspora community suffers from a deep denial of pain caused by the trauma of repressive regimes and caudillo culture. I believe that his stories force us to see violence and therefore recognize its impact on different lives in the Dominican Republic and elsewhere. Díaz's work effectively jogs the memory of its Dominican readers, exposing how limited and painful memory is and how traumatic migratory culture can be.

The *Boston Globe* covered Díaz's apparent struggles with writer's block. After an impressive debut and an immediate contract for an unwritten book, Díaz finds himself admitting, "I don't know what's happened. It's as if my writing has fallen off the cliff. I'm not rehabilitated yet" (Jones E1). The newspaper article mentions that Ralph Ellison had a similarly brilliant beginning and a painfully long hiatus between works. This is important, because the silences Díaz struggles with, no doubt, embody the very problems of invisibility and visibility he must explore to keep writing both from the gut and from the interstices of the silences and tragedies experienced by Dominicans on the island and in the diaspora. In his interview with Vanessa E. Jones of the *Globe*, he talks about a possible next project, which is

> a sci-fi Latin American history novel that he labels "kooky." Begun before Sept. 11, 2001, the story takes place 20 years after a military dictatorship seizes control following a catastrophe that demolishes New York City. A young Dominican woman returns from exile to interview survivors of the kidnapping and torture that occurred under the new regime. (E3)

It is extremely revealing that, after *Drown*, Díaz would consider the topics of dictatorship, torture, and survival through the genre of science fiction. Perhaps he is getting closer to exploring some of his historical past and its effects on his psychological present. The next book may, after all, point explicitly to the pain of memory.

In brief, the complexities of the human condition, which may be drowned out by songs (such as fast meringues) and heavy silences, cannot be ignored for long. But it takes an enormous amount of courage to challenge the comfortable binaries set up by the academy and politics, and it takes memory to disclose the complexities of the identifiers of Dominican and Dominican diaspora cultures.

Modes of Memory

The Restavèk Condition and Jean-Robert Cadet's Story

Restavèk is a Kreyòl word[1] derived from a seemingly inoffensive French phrase, *rester avec*, to stay with. Yet restavèk refers to an abusive practice in Haiti in which children of impoverished families are sent away to become domestic workers in other households, which often badly mistreat them.

In this chapter I revisit the many ways in which the restavèk condition has been studied and explicated in Haiti and in the United States. I offer a sustained analysis of Jean-Robert Cadet's 1998 autobiography, *Restavec: From Haitian Slave Child to Middle-Class American*, to propose that autobiography and testimony function as modes of memory that reconfigure the process of self-formation and human rights work. Furthermore, I describe the transhistoric, transnational, and transliterary connections Cadet's text engages in the ongoing fight for civil and human rights.

Restavèk: In Reality and in Representation

The restavèk condition is at the center of many heated debates in the Haitian and Haitian diaspora communities. Its existence is disputed, and its role in society is both condemned and condoned. Consequently, controversial literature and representation of the condition has been produced. One of the first reports about Haitian children serving as domestic labor was Élie Louis Vernet's *La Domesticité chez nous*, published in 1935. Living conditions in the countryside were still bearable then, and the tradition of children in domestic service in the city was considered a minor problem. At the time, and until recently, the restavèks' plight was a neglected topic. Many adults are still convinced that they are helping the children, no matter how terrible the treatment. Until the 1960s some restavèks lived with well-off families, but no longer. The Reverend Miguel Jean-Baptiste, a social worker who directs the Maurice Sixto school for restavèks, points this out in Karen Kramer's 2001 documentary *Children of Shadows*: "You won't find restavèks among the bourgeois. They have money and pay maids. It is a poor child who goes to live with another poor person."

The condition of restavèks in Haiti has been severely aggravated by an acute economic crisis. The economist Arnold Antonin laments, "The situation of the restavèk is a manifestation of the general misery the country experiences" (Kramer). In the last twenty years the continual decline of Haiti's rural economy has spurred a mass exodus to Port-au-Prince. Rural families dream of a better life there, unaware of the misery that awaits them. Since entire families can rarely pick up and move, they often send a child to the city, hoping that he or she will be the link to their future relocation. In many cases, families will send their most responsible daughter to stay with "relatives" in the city. They come from the most degrading situations in rural areas, where there are no schools and poor facilities for health and hygiene. These children are promised education and food in exchange for work. Often the promises are empty. By law, the children who work as domestic helpers must be at least twelve years old, but many are as young as three or four, and very few receive education or food for their hard labor.[2] In 2001 their numbers were estimated by Haïti Solidarité Internationale (HSI) at 300,000. Three-quarters of the restavèks were female.

Child domestic labor represents a major impediment in the struggle for human rights in Haiti.[3] According to the HSI study *Les Fondements de la pratique de la domesticité des enfants en Haïti*, the word *restavèk* has a pejorative connotation used to isolate and devalue the children. The official term for them is *enfants en domesticité*, children in a domestic situation. In many cases, the children feel so humiliated that they cannot see themselves as laborers, but rather identify with the concept of slavery. An international children's rights advocate, Claudette François, notes that restavèks' work is not shameful, but their conditions are. The restavèks might see themselves as domestic laborers instead of slaves if they were well fed, clothed, and educated and had working hours appropriate to their capacity as children. Furthermore, if the families and the community treated them with respect instead of with violence, slurs, and threats of expulsion, the children would not identify with the destitute emotional and psychological condition implied by the label *restavèk*.

The number of restavèks is hard to calculate, since the practice is considered an unofficial exchange between families. Some restavèks are blood relatives, but often the family in the country euphemistically call the family in the city their relatives. The HSI study estimates that in 1946–60 as many as 60,000 to 80,000 children were live-in domestic laborers. During the 1970s—the period known as Jean-Claudisme—the number grew to 100,000, and as of 2001 it was thought to be 300,000 or more. This situation received very brief political attention in 1934 under Sténio Vincent's presidency. Conversely, opportunities for education were diminished in 1930–35 with the Law of Dantes Bellegarde, which abolished the baccalaureate in public schools. Children in public schools, who would have included the domestic workers, no longer had access to a complete education.

A 1947 law prescribes conditions to be met by employing families with one or more children in "domestic service." Domestic service was viewed as a legal part of Haitian culture, the laws protecting the adults more than the children. Until the 1960s, child domestic labor was informal, and the treatment of these children was vastly inconsistent. The Code du Travail (Work Code) of 1960 recognizes the category of children in domestic service. Domestic child laborers finally were seen as workers who must receive certain treatment. They could not be less than fifteen years old; if they did not receive a salary, they must be educated, clothed, and fed. Until the 1970s, families with live-ins saw themselves as benevolent hosts, having ready servants at their disposal and helping these children leave their poor families. Some interviews show that a number of the children, now adults, would agree with this assessment. Well-off families were able to offer better conditions. Some children were treated as part of the host family and became reasonably well employed adults. Other restavèks, after becoming adults, helped siblings or other relatives relocate out of the impoverished countryside to the city.

Greater legal attention was not given to the issue until 1987, with the drafting of the Haitian Constitution. Article 261 states that the law must ensure the protection of all children, who have the right to love, understanding, and the moral and material care of their parents. The UN Convention on the Rights of the Child, adopted in 1989 and ratified by Haiti in 1995, recognizes in Article 32 the right of children to be protected from economic exploitation and from work demands that impede their education or their physical, mental, spiritual, moral, or social development. This article asks that each signatory state take legislative and other measures to establish a minimum employment age, regulation of working conditions and hours, and punishment for violators. However, implementation is be-

coming more difficult in Haiti, because resources must be devoted to helping the many impoverished people meet basic food, shelter, and other
needs. Elite and bourgeois families now favor adult maids and servants, so
domestic child labor is more common among people who live in a desperate squalor of their own. The children then are forced to endure this misery.

Until very recently, children in domestic service rarely had access to
school. Port-au-Prince has witnessed a proliferation of night schools that
may help children who work all day. In May 2002, President Jean-Bertrand
Aristide addressed the United Nations Special Session on Children. A
press release distributed by Aristide spokesperson Michelle Karshan at the
time described ways in which Aristide has given children attention. In the
1980s, when he was still a priest, he founded the Lafanmi Selavi Center for
Street Children. These children are given exposure on radio and television
programs, for example on Tele Timoun.[4] There they can discuss their circumstances and hope for better understanding from the community.
Aristide set up a special fund to help children develop their artistic talents
and a scholarship fund for gifted children. Aristide also promised to give
special attention to the 160,000 children left orphaned because of AIDS.

Many critics argue that Aristide's plans help only a select few and ignore the large numbers of children in domestic service and/or on the
streets. Indeed, it seems that there is a huge gap separating the laws, ratifi-
cations, and discussions concerning children's rights from any actual im-
provement in their living conditions. In a 2001 letter to Aristide, former
National Coalition for Haitian Rights executive director Jocelyn McCalla
warned, "Your government can either join its predecessors or make a real
break with the past by ensuring that every child born in Haiti is legally
registered at birth, and records are maintained properly" (NCHR news
release, 12 June 2001). The release also stated that NCHR "contends that
millions of Haitians are stateless by virtue of being denied citizenship because of willful government negligence and incompetence."

One private school, the Foyer Maurice Sixto, has been doing groundbreaking work to alleviate the desperate conditions of children in domestic
service. The school was founded in 1990, with the help of Terre des
Hommes Suisse and the support of UNICEF, by the Reverend Miguel
Jean-Baptiste, who had studied in Fribourg, Switzerland, under the tute-
lage of the American psychologist Abraham Maslow. Jean-Baptiste contends that children have five psychological and physical developmental

needs that must be met in order for them to grow up to be active adults participating in their communities: the need for (1) survival, comprising nutrition, rest, freedom from pain; (2) protection from abuse, whether physical, psychological, or sexual; (3) belonging, being accepted as part of a group; (4) validation (domestic children are often belittled); and (5) self-realization through education and job training. The school encourages the children to be creative and to feel a sense of community among themselves. It also holds special meetings with families to make them sensitive to the live-ins' special needs. According to the school's philosophy, a new focus on education may help change the tradition of child domestic service in Haiti.

If until recently these children were denied recognition as human beings and active members of the Haitian nation, coverage and interviews now legitimize them and make them a part of the Haitian national image. One of the first stories in Haiti to give critical public attention to the restavèk is *Ti Saintanise*, directed in 1971 by comedian Maurice Sixto. The story has since been performed, recorded, and distributed in cassette format in Kreyòl. It is set in the household of a professor who devotes himself to teaching the public about human rights. But when this important professional returns to his house in the evening, he is met by a little girl restavèk, Ti Saintanise, whom he treats with scorn and disrespect. Despite his public rhetoric on human rights, in his private life he follows the codes of the traditional abusive, disrespectful male. International awareness of the situation has come through the work of UNICEF, which has published accounts by J. P. Slavin of little children such as Celine (not her real name) in "Restavèk: Four-year-old Servants in Haiti." As the restavèk children get more media and literary coverage, they leave the shadows of inhumanity and enter the realm of citizenship.

Historically, most Haitian literature was written by the bourgeoisie, and it has trivialized the existence of children in domestic service. For example, author Fernand Hibbert describes a boy domestic servant in his tale "Orphise" as immoral. Paulette Poujol Oriol, on the other hand, creates a character, Madan Marye, who has no common sense and is so ignorant that she is silly. René Depestre, in his poem "Face à la nuit," describes a child domestic laborer as immoral. Even though she has been raped, she is considered responsible and guilty for what has been done to her. She is thrown out of the house, and later she must resort to prostitution to survive. Her character, echoed in other texts such as Justin Lhérisson's *Zoune chez sa ninnaine,* falls from servitude to abuse and thence to the streets, where her lot in life cannot escape prostitution and further abuse and moral incrimination.

More recently, new methods of representation including film have been used to expose the restavèk situation. *They Call Me Dog: A Film about the Cinderellas of Haiti* is a docudrama that exposes restavèks' dire living conditions through the experiences of a character named Asmithe, and suggests that the children can be helped by understanding adults and two new UNICEF-funded school programs. Asmithe has been given away by her mother to a woman in town who puts her to work in rags and denies her schooling, while her own daughter gets new clothes and goes to private school. Asmithe wants to send her mother a letter but can neither write nor remember her address. The family she stays with does not have this information. When Asmithe runs away, seeking help from her brother, she learns that he has been taken to the police station, accused of stealing money at a cockfight. Asmithe arrives at the station in time to see her brother's bloody and bruised corpse taken away. She returns to the cemetery where he had been staying and cries herself to sleep. Many restavèks would return to their grown-ups or surrender to street crime or even death at this point. But Asmithe's story has a happy ending. She is taken to a home where she will have to earn her keep but will be treated kindly and have the opportunity to spend two hours daily at a special school for children like herself. Her life has indeed changed from rags to riches, the riches of human potential. She becomes a Cinderella because of the possibility of schooling through a program that teaches her value in society and a system in which her potential is cultivated. In effect, the docudrama is an advertisement for the possibility of addressing the restavèk situation in Haiti.

Karen Kramer's film *Children of Shadows* observes, "This is the story of a form of slavery in the modern world." Kramer interviews children who cry and look desolate as they answer questions for the camera. She films the back alleys these children walk every day, and shows the dismal living conditions of the families they work for. She asks the children what they want to be when they grow up. One boy says a mechanic. Some years later, in a follow-up interview, he has changed his mind and wants to become a professor. His desire is in sharp contrast to his condition as a household servant with no, or little, time to study. In another interview, Vanya, who is seven years old and does all of the cooking and housework, feels betrayed by her parents, who could not have imagined how much worse her life is in the city. Her body language reveals a child in deep suffering; she does not look directly at the camera, and she cannot contain her tears.

This child's hopeless tears raised many questions for me. In particular, what was the director of this documentary doing to help her? Filming a child's destitution, to sell it in video format as an educational tool, does nothing to help the child. It is painful to know that in a follow-up interview years later, her condition has not changed and her body language seems even more pained. The Reverend Miguel Jean-Baptiste notes in the film, "No one talks about the sexual abuse the children experience. They are guinea pigs for the young males of the house." Vanya is not asked about this, nor does she describe the ways her life is downtrodden in her grown-up's house. What is happening to this little girl? And why does the filmmaker do nothing other than film her?[5]

I suggest that the restavèk condition should not be represented as yet another case study of the poor in developing nations. For this reason Jean-Robert Cadet's story, the first to offer the powerful evidence of a first-person perspective, is very important. Cadet's autobiography completely shifts these images of children in domestic service. Not only does he tell his own story, but he also contradicts previous literature that judged and dismissed people with his type of childhood. His story serves as an example of will, moral dignity, and human possibility. His fight for memory and for the abolition of child slavery, both in Haiti and as it illegally exists in the United States,[6] is a call to arms for civil and human rights that intersects a long historical and literary tradition in the United States.

Remembering Abuse

Restavec is the coming-of-age testimony of a man who escapes a situation of destitution and domestic servitude in the poorest country in the American hemisphere, has a successful military career in the United States, and later encounters further struggles of alienation and depersonification through racism in Florida. In an afterword to his autobiography, Cadet concludes:

> I felt like the silent victim of a rape. . . .
>
>   Restavec slavery is wrong. It is the worst crime imaginable, because the victims are incapable of resisting their adult predators. It is a crime against nature as well, because the child's very rights to life— to belong, to grow, to smile, to love, to feel, to learn, and to be a child— are denied, by those whose ancestors were slaves themselves.

For Cadet, nightmares ensure that his past remains a vivid part of his present. In the book's foreword, his American-born wife, Cynthia Nassano Cadet, writes: "I lie beside him now each night as he sleeps. And when that sleep is fitful—when I hear his laboring breath, his muffled cry, or feel his arms tremble and his legs thrash about—I know that the reality from decades ago is upon us again." He struggles daily with self-esteem and the slow, growing awareness that his case is not an isolated one. His text, both personal and political, is a cry that makes us feel his experiences and the traumatic incisions they have left on his person. With his story, since published in Kreyòl (University of Texas Press, 2000) and French (Éditions du Seuil, 2002), he fights to gain international attention for the restavèk situation and hopes to see the "crime" abolished.

The pages of his story are laden with detailed memories of degrading personal experiences. For example, the woman who agreed to raise him, his "mother/aunt" Florence,[7] calls him a "shithead bedwetter" (9), "extrait caca" (essence of shit), a "son of a whore" (7), and "motherless son of a bitch" (49). She insists that he will "never be anything but a shoeshine boy" (66). Florence threatens to take back her family name, which she has given him, and give him the generic surname for children without legitimate parents, Joseph. She beats him with the spike heels of her shoes, chairs, a rigoise (a whip made out of cowhide), and a martinet (four-strip leather whip). He is ordered to sleep on the floor in a corner or under the kitchen table (but only after completing all of his chores), and is obligated to wake up before everyone else. The significance of these experiences does not escape Cadet, who is called Bobby in his youth. His body suffers from material discomforts and pain, his emotions are ignored, and his self-esteem is erased. The child is repeatedly erased, and a slave, presumably without a future, is shaped. Pain becomes the central signifier of his life, one that "unmakes" him.

Further experiences of unmaking include his first memory of law and order. He tells the story of another restavèk, René, who steals two dollars from his "grown-up" (the person in whose house he lives) and buys food, which he shares with Bobby. The theft is discovered, and René is severely whipped. Bobby, terrified for his own life, never confesses to eating with René, who does not reveal his friend's role. René is forced to kneel on hot rocks until he faints, at which point he is taken to the police. When the police bring René back to the house, his "nose was bleeding, his eyes were swollen shut, and his lips resembled two pieces of raw cow's liver" (15). That night René disappears, his fate a mystery. His friend's exit underscores the fragility of Bobby's own life and the power his grown-up has. Afterward, whenever someone threatens to send Bobby to the police, he fears for his life, understanding that he could be similarly "disappeared" without prompting any judicial, political, or social retaliation.

The place—or, rather, nonplace—in society of these enslaved children is further dramatized when a little girl, Anita, comes to the house as another restavèk. She sleeps on the floor under the dining room table, eats worm-ridden mangoes for dinner, and remains silent regardless of what she witnesses. One week she falls ill. When she does not get better, she disappears. Bobby asks a cook what happened to her. He is informed that because she was ill, she was returned to her mother: if she could not work, she was not needed. Bobby never contemplates whether the story of return is true, but we know that Anita may have died or been sent to another "aunt."

The inhuman treatment Bobby experiences in the private space of the house is paralleled by political violence in the national arena and a history of human disenfranchisement. During the Duvalier years, citizens were aware that protest or insurrection would result in immediate death, imprisonment, and/or torture. During these dictatorships, corpses would be left to rot in full view of passers-by. These swollen bodies bore a message that escaped no one: behave or be eliminated. The authorities had impunity. Bobby recounts a conversation during Christmas and New Year's festivities. Florence's cook asks if Bobby saw "the dead Kamokins [communists or communist sympathizers] on the roadside near the airport" (37). She explains that they had been shot by the secret police, the Tonton Macoutes, and their bodies were dumped near the airport to be a very visible warning. Those who dared to sympathize with the communists, or become one, would surely meet the same fate. Their bodies would lie swollen on the roadside like run-over dogs. Later Bobby listens to the cooks' conversation. They are telling another horrific story. The driver of a tap-tap (a colorful bus driven in Haiti) accidentally splashes mud on a black car with official license plates. When he gets out to apologize and clean the mess, the terrified driver is shot in the head by a Macoute. As a silent witness to abuse and death, Bobby learns that life is precarious. "I already knew that the most effective way to commit suicide was to stand in the middle of the street and shout 'A bas [down with] Duvalier!'" (37).

Restavèks were further belittled by Haiti's tradition of corporal punishment (dating to the colonial period and slavery), beatings with the *rigoise*, and name-calling—"crétin," idiot, or, conversely, "petit blanc," little white one, used to indicate a child's superiority to others in the classroom. When

Bobby attends school (Florence allows him to go if and when he has completed his household duties), he witnesses the whipping of five students in front of the blackboard. The philosophy is that unless the children are terrified, they will not do their work. When they do not do their work correctly, they must be punished or they will become lazy and ungrateful. Cadet remembers:

> During eighth-grade recess, I would watch Maître Jean-Charles with his rigoise standing behind a student at the blackboard. For every mistake the student made, Maître Jean-Charles would strike him on his back as he shouted, "Crétin! Cochon marron! [Idiot! Wild pig!]" A student who arrived late to class would receive twenty lashes in the palms of his hands. (77)[8]

Cadet's early years, as we have seen, are filled with experiences meant to erase his individuality and sense of initiative. When Florence is about to permanently depart for New York City, he shudders to think what might happen to him. He has observed other restavèk children being abandoned when they were no longer needed. The children would then become street wanderers. In this context, it is worth holding on to life as a servant.

When he and Florence live with another family for a while, he befriends the son, Olivier. They are the same age. Olivier defies his family's hierarchy of power, prestige, and money, meeting secretly with Bobby and sharing games and treats as any two boys would under normal circumstances. This results in terrible trouble for Bobby. He is told, "You don't know your place" (58), and is reminded that he is merely staying with the family and is not a part of it. To prove the point, his face is dunked in a toilet filled with excrement. The adults insist that the excrement is better than he is because it knows that it must stay at the bottom of the toilet, it does not rise. Bobby should learn from this metaphor. He must submit to staying at the bottom, far away from the family. Florence chimes in that he must learn his place as an inferior being. In Bobby's adult years, the memory of these experiences will crop up constantly, never letting him live in a present free from the incessant abuse of his past.

We learn from the repetition of scenes of psychological pain in the text that our narrator is haunted by his deprivation of emotional nurturing. He is terrified of abandonment and repeats throughout his autobiography that he first wants Florence's love and later his biological father's acceptance and approval. But Bobby's life is loveless for many years. In addition, there is the disintegration of life in Haiti in general. When Bobby goes back to the countryside, he encounters terrifyingly inhuman images. He returns to the house of Grannie Alcée, Florence's mother, where he had developed fond memories of the old woman cooking and everybody rejoicing in the simple pleasures of the country. What he sees four years later is reminiscent of a plagued Macondo in Gabriel García Marquez's novel *One Hundred Years of Solitude*. The house he remembered so dearly has fallen apart. The kitchen roof has a big hole in it, the water well is in ruins, the chicken coop empty, dusty, and smelly. Aggressive flies buzz around the back door, in and out of the house. To Bobby's horror, "Grannie Alcée was lying in her mahogany bed, staring at the ceiling. Her eyes were deep in their sockets and her face looked like a giant dried prune with a hole in the middle of it. Her white hair clung to her head like Spanish moss dangling from a dead branch" (62). When he calls out Grannie's name, she answers, "Gertrude?" (63). The demise of the family is tied to Grannie's son Léon's involvement in a political killing, for which he was promised a good government job. But it turns out that Léon chose the wrong political side. He was killed and his family isolated for his actions. The stress of losing a son and the state terror brought upon her family may be the reasons for Grannie's stroke. The story underscores how the government would obliterate any opposition and, in this case, leave a poor country family decimated.

This scene serves as a metaphor for the rapid economic decline that began in the Haitian countryside in the 1960s and has culminated in abject despair in recent years. Bobby's life in the city is better. Although he is abused while at Florence's house, he has access to some food and shelter. Had he stayed in the countryside, Bobby might have been subjected to a living death, to such extreme neglect that he would not have even had the energy to defend his right to life. Bobby cannot stand the sight of this kind of human deprivation and, since he has no means to alleviate it, he runs away from Grannie's house, the flies, the darkness, and the impending death.

The constant ostracism for being illegitimate, and its resulting absence of love, form the violation of human spirit from which Bobby suffers most acutely. However, as he grows up, it is also the condition that gives him the impetus to strive for self-improvement. That is, Florence's abuse is nothing compared to his father's indifference. Ironically, his biological background is something that others note with an element of pride: his mother was beautiful and his father is a successful white man called Blanc Philippe. He strives to emulate his father. He does not have to identify with Florence, who is described as a wicked, dependent woman. The author tells how Florence prostitutes herself to pay her bills and how she is more concerned with what her middle- and upper middle-class neighbors and friends think about her than with how she is mistreating the child left in her care. Here Cadet offers a critique of the hypocrisy of social standards. He is also setting up a distinction between Florence's abuse, which is physical and direct, and his father's abuse, which is indirect via emotional neglect. Could the distinction extend to another parameter? Could it be that Bobby forgives his father because he is white, and all white is good, and further criticizes Florence because she is black?

When Florence goes to the United States to be with her son, Blanc Philippe decides to pay to send Bobby to continue living with her. When Bobby is taken to get his passport picture and papers arranged, he hopes, finally, to be recognized as the biological son of Philippe. But when a clerk questions father and son for passport information, the result is disillusioning:

> "What is your mother's name?" he asked. Suddenly I thought about the name Henrilia Brutus. I was about to say it, but Philippe answered "Florence Cadet."
>
> "What is your father's name?" I looked up at Philippe, hoping he would at least acknowledge me by saying his own name. He looked at the clerk and said, "inconnu," meaning "unknown." The clerk glanced at Philippe and me for a few seconds as if he knew that I was standing beside my father. A sinking feeling came over me. I was dead inside. (96)

I cannot help but signal the similarities between the relationship of the white father to Bobby and the relationship of plantation owners to their illegal offspring. I will elaborate on this link later in this chapter.

Bobby's story takes an extremely unusual turn when he is sent off to be with Florence in the United States: most restavèks in Haiti never leave the country.[9] The restavèk condition thus migrates from the far-off land of Haiti into the United States. Since laws and social codes are different in the two countries, the family does not know what to do. They do not want problems with the authorities and therefore comply with U.S. laws, putting Bobby in high school. There he fends for himself. Yet Denis, Florence's son, insists that Bobby find work. Bobby must lie about his age, find work, continue school, resume his duties as the cleaner in the house, and pay to stay with the family. While he is not mistreated as badly as he was in Haiti, he is still subjected to humiliation and threats. Finally he is kicked out of the house. Whereas teenagers thrust into the streets in Haiti face early death or a life of begging, in New York Bobby has more options. Cadet's irrefutable will to survive and escape danger guides his life. In school he gets help from his teacher, Mr. Rabinowitz. In town his friend's father gives him a contact for a housemate. Through his own sacrifice and perseverance, he finishes high school and enters the United States Army.

Bobby recognizes the advantages he has had: Florence allowed him to attend school after his chores were done, and Blanc Philippe sent him to the United States to be with Florence. Leaving Haiti presented many opportunities to the ambitious young man. His horrible restavèk days could be archived as the past. Nonetheless, they haunt him; as the repeated, and graphic, images of his memory of abuse attest, Cadet is severely marked by traumatic memory. The abuse in his childhood has shaped a very scared and angry man. He has a difficult time making friends, and trusts very few people. He confesses that during shooting practice and other drills in the army, he often imagines Florence as the target. Although he buys her Mother's Day cards, he never sends them. Cadet's loveless upbringing causes him to feel inferior to others and painfully ashamed of himself.

In stark contrast to this loveless life full of abuse that Cadet's written memory recalls, the author insists in both the beginning and the end of the book that his autobiography is grounded in love. He tells us that when he became a father he realized that he had been blessed with the opportunity to give love. Suddenly, I suppose, he was faced with a responsibility that neither his own father nor his caregiver, Florence, ever fulfilled. I suggest that when Cadet is confronted with the responsibility to give love and nurturance to an innocent life he has engendered, he is incited to seek venues that will help him heal from the abuse he suffered. But how can one engage in the long and arduous process of healing after a life full of such bitter degradation? I believe that life and literature intersect; Cadet discovers the possibility of remaking himself through the writing process.[10] Cadet's writing activates a symbolic process of giving birth. By telling his story, he bears witness to his desire for goodness. His story testifies against a practice that must be abolished and thus contributes to the protection of future generations of children. This new experience with love and emotional nurturance underscores the importance of writing his story, giving value to his family history and his struggles, so that Cadet's child will be able to understand his roots. Furthermore, through the text, Cadet imposes paternity on Blanc Philippe. His unassumed role as Cadet's father is in writing; more important, the effect of his neglect on Cadet's person is publicly condemned. Cadet's child can have access to a complete family narrative. After becoming a father, and through the act of writing, Cadet becomes an activist against the restavèk situation. He thus consciously engages with a significant sociopolitical battle against human degradation—even though it is at the price of revealing his most debilitating, traumatic memories. Emphatically, the act of autobiography is his process, which validates his haunting memory of abuse and underscores the importance of human rights activism.

A Tradition of Autobiography: Cadet's Contribution

The function and origin of autobiography are multiple. James Olney remarks that "we have a sufficient demonstration of the rich variousness of autobiography and clear evidence of the stubborn reluctance of autobiography to submit to prescriptive definitions or restrictive generic bounds. . . . the performances of Wright, Valéry, and Yeats at least hint at how various are the different *bioi* that may inform autobiographies by way of as many different exercises of memory" (267). Olney proposes that Richard Wright based his autobiography on creative memory, Paul Valéry abandoned memory, and William Butler Yeats transformed memory beyond recognition. Before arriving at these three formulations of memory in autobiography, Olney presents us with a long, reflective essay that explores the meaning of *ta onta*, existing things, and examines the usage of *bioi*. According to Plato and Heraclitus, he tells us, *ta onta* specifies not only things that exist but, in particular, a present that is opposed to the past and future. The importance of *ta onta* in his study of autobiography is related to both truth, which Olney says is always in the process of being represented by the present moment's needs, and memory, which is also shaped by the present. He elaborates on the significance of memory with respect to a life story with the following consideration:

> If *bios* in the sense of "lifetime" is seen not simply as a span of years—set, complete, and finished: a simple case of "was"—but as a *process* ever moving towards the ineluctable present of "is" and if memory can be taken as a backward projection of "is" that gathers up into its own creative image all that "was becoming," then the autobiography of memory, having become a vital and intensely creative mode, attains to a certain philosophical dignity. The key is to view *bios* as a process the whole of which the autobiographer is in a posi-

tion to see, recall, and compose; and it is up to the autobiographer to cut it where he will so that the process will be complete and unified. (240)

Thus autobiography depends on memory, which is consciously shaped by the autobiographer with reference to the present; meaning is attained through the exercise of memory. Let us apply this to Cadet's autobiography. The sum of Cadet's narrative reveals a man whose experience of abuse is so present that his memory exists in a traumatic register. Yet, as I have shown, he tells us that his writing is about love. How does he create a space of love with memories of such horrible experiences? I suggest that the process of memory through writing an autobiography helps Cadet attain meaning. This meaning through writing is attained on at least two levels. One, Cadet inserts his otherwise obliterated life into a meaningful political fight. His literary intervention gives meaning to his life by creating a life's work. Two, his literary product, the autobiography, grafts him into an established and important tradition of writing selves.

Cadet's autobiography, exposes the restavèk condition, recalling conventions of nineteenth-century autobiography in American literature. That is, Cadet, writing in the United States about a condition of slavery in Haiti, is engaging with an established tradition that entails interlacing gyres of history, memory, and social action. Haitian memory clearly includes the African diaspora in Haiti and the Haitian diaspora in the United States. Specifically, Cadet's memories dialogue with an established African-American literary tradition, becoming a new voice in African-Haitian-American literary representation.

Let us take a brief look at African-American autobiography. The late Yale professor of history and African and African-American studies, John W. Blassingame, has claimed that "salvational autobiography"—stories of escape from slavery, in which the author is saved from abuse and injustice—is one of the most American of literary genres. He quotes from "Narratives of Fugitive Slaves," written by the Reverend Ephraim Peabody of the *Christian Examiner*, "AMERICA has the mournful honor of adding a new department to the literature of civilization,—the autobiographies of escaped slaves" (xxxvi). Blassingame contends: "Antebellum black autobiographers consistently asserted that the chief reason for portraying their lives was the need to bear witness against slavery, to wake their fellow Americans to its evil, and to cheer on those who labored in the cause of human freedom (xxi). Earlier autobiographies that caused a stir included Indian captivity narratives by blacks such as *A Narrative of the Uncom-*

mon Sufferings and Surprizing Deliverance of Briton Hammon, A Negro Man (1760) and *A Narrative of the Lord's Wonderful Dealings with John Marrant, a Black, Taken Down from His Own Relation* (1785). According to Blassingame, antebellum Americans frowned on novels, favoring the reading of personal accounts of survival. To this day, I would argue, we continue to relish personal accounts of survival and resistance, which are often synonymous with the attainment of the American Dream. This American fascination with stories of self-made success contrasts sharply with Cadet's Haitian background, where the person who can escape poverty is often too embarrassed to recall the misery of the past. With his autobiography, Cadet breaks with this aspect of Haitian culture and reveals his past in order to make a statement, not only for himself but also for fellow Haitians who might be inspired by his story.

In the late eighteenth and early nineteenth centuries, a tradition of autobiography in the United States was firmly established with texts such as Benjamin Franklin's *Autobiography* (1791–98) and the Reverend John Foster's "On a Man's Writing Memoirs of Himself" (1805). According to Blassingame, this twenty-one-page essay "played a primary role in establishing the conventions of English and American autobiography" (xi). Key to all of these writings was the exposition of truth, through which the author would acquire complete knowledge of himself and his personal growth. The writing was considered "authentic" if it was simple and to the point. In effect, the readers and critics of the time insisted on truthful memory.[11] Although memories can be faulty and all autobiographies, especially those of former slaves, were subject to intense scrutiny and rejection, these stories had the primary goal of structuring moral character. The autobiography had a utilitarian social function: to inspire readers to cultivate intellectual development and moral conduct.

For escaped slaves, the autobiography also served as a testimony that would authenticate their life experiences, their voices in later speeches and writings, and the memory of their contribution to U.S. history. Authors such as Frederick Douglass were faced with the challenge of establishing their credibility. As Blassingame points out, this was a highly complicated matter. Douglass's text was introduced by the highly respected antislavery leaders William Lloyd Garrison and Wendell Phillips, who attested to its veracity. Nonetheless, the story encountered resistance. Douglass sent a copy of his autobiography to one of his former owners, Thomas Auld. This fearless act, as Douglass would point out, proved not only the truth of his story but also the challenge it was to represent. As would be expected, this action incited Auld's friends and other supporters of slavery to dispute Douglass, claiming that his text bore "the glaring impress of falsehood on every page" (xxxiii). Douglass's autobiography, regardless of the challenges and scandals it spurred, created an important practice of testimony, advocating freedom.[12]

Autobiography, I suggest, also plays the role of public record. In Douglass's case, he recorded his service to the United States, his thoughts about the rights of the individual, and his belief in the rights of man through his autobiographical writings, which reflect a period of political and social changes and work, as well as his own life story. Douglass's autobiography—written as three distinct texts: *Narrative of the Life of Frederick Douglass*, published in 1845, seven years after his escape from slavery; *My Bondage and My Freedom*, published in 1855 and considered his finest writing by the critics of the time; and *Life and Times of Frederick Douglass*, published in 1892, nine years before his death—expose his flight from, and fight against, slavery. But more important, they recount Douglass's lifework as an important member of the U.S. diplomatic service and an ardent human rights activist. He served as consultant to President Abraham Lincoln and was the assistant secretary of the Santo Domingo Commission of 1871. He was appointed minister resident and consul general to the Republic of Haiti in 1889–91. While Americans had problems with this appointment, Douglass was well received and greatly loved by the Haitian people. This affection was reciprocal, as we learn in his last autobiography (the only one in which he talks about his time in Haiti). He also reflects that he felt the greatest honor during service as Haitian commissioner at the World's Columbian Exposition at Chicago in 1893.

Henry Louis Gates Jr. observes that "the act of writing for the slave constituted an act of creating a public, historical self" (H. Brown xx). It was through the autobiography that (former) slaves would be able to place themselves in history in general and in social consciousness in particular. Frequently, the first text of an ex-slave would be his/her autobiography. Once instated as an entity in social circles, the author could go on to other speaking and writing engagements. In fact, the entry into society of ex-slaves was facilitated by the written testimony of their lives. This is succinctly exemplified by *The Narrative of the Life of Henry Box Brown* (1850), which evokes period mythology, in this case the mythology of resurrection. Brown escaped from slavery in the South to freedom in the North by packing himself in a box and having himself mailed. His escape involved a figurative coming back from the dead—he put himself in a box, reminiscent of a coffin, and then came out into freedom. Some were concerned that he would not arrive alive. While he does meet with wonderful people who are fighting for the freedom of all humanity, he also encounters a deeply coded racism. His rebirth into freedom is fraught with limitations. He may be able to do as he pleases, but only within tacitly imposed parameters. Ultimately, should he stray from those, his freedom would prove artificial. Eventually he had to escape to England for fear of being captured and returned to the South under the Fugitive Slave Act of 1850, which sent hunters to the North to retrieve runaway slaves. Nonetheless, Brown wrote his story of slavery and escape, had a profitable lecture circuit, spoke for the rights of man, his rights, and the abolition of slavery. In the introduction to the recent reissue of Brown's *Narrative*, the late Richard Newman, senior research officer at the W.E.B. DuBois Institute for Afro-American Research at Harvard, describes Brown's feat:

> Once a slave, he becomes free; once a factory worker, he becomes an abolitionist lecturer, writer, and performer; once a nonentity, he becomes somebody. . . . the mythic and passive slave becomes the real and active freeman. . . . Brown's final word and continuing message is that he used confinement to achieve his liberation. (xxxii)

At the time, unfortunately, the success of his experience deflected the focus from the trauma of slavery as well as the long-term psychological effects that enslavement, emancipation, and storytelling-to-survive had on its victims/survivors/escapees. Newman proceeds to outline the protocol adhered to by slave narratives such as the *Narrative . . . of Briton Hammon* and Booker T. Washington's *Up From Slavery* (1901), commenting that these constitute a means for the African-American community to resist, subvert, remember, and document their own experiences from their own point of view.

Autobiographies that are more recent include *Black Boy* by Richard Wright, who, like Bobby, was told, "You'll never amount to anything" (159). Critic Jerry W. Ward Jr. notes in his introduction to the recently restored text that Wright's autobiography traces his "reflective movement from homegrown optimism to tested knowledge" (xiii)—from the dreams of his childhood in the South to his real experiences of further hardship and continued racism in the North. Richard Wright is shaped by both private and public disadvantages. At home, his father abandoned the family when he was a small boy, making survival all the more difficult for him and his sickly mother. In the public sphere, Wright recalls and writes about his early experiences: wanting to learn like the "young Jewish boys and girls receiving instruction in chemistry and medicine that the average black boy or girl could never receive" (304). He informs his readers that he played with other children and learned their lessons, thus circumventing the learning restrictions placed on poor black children in the South. Literacy, migration (a train ride from which he never looked back), and integration into literary society (the Harlem Renaissance, communist groups in Paris) become Wright's keys to his citizenship in the United States and the world. Nonetheless, his lifework also led him to a deeply dark understanding of human conduct and the manipulations of power that continue to strip the struggle for human rights of forward progress. In a November 8, 1960, speech to an audience at the American Church in Paris, Wright accused the American government of creating dissension among literary and social intellectuals, undermining their work toward international human rights, equality, and democracy.

Richard Wright escaped the racism of the South only to see it further practiced in the North. He laments, "Negroes are told in a language they cannot possibly misunderstand that their native land is not their own" (302). Later he recalls working in the basement of a hospital, where he was kept from interaction with white doctors and nurses; responsibilities were divided by race.

> The sharp line of racial division drawn by the hospital authorities came to me the first morning when I walked along an underground corridor and saw two long lines of women. . . . A line of white girls marched past, clad in starched uniforms that gleamed white; their faces were alert, their steps quick, their bodies lean and shapely, their shoulders erect, their faces lit with the light of purpose. And after them came a line of black girls, old, fat, dressed in ragged gingham, walking loosely, carrying tin cans of soap powder, rags, mops, brooms. (303)

Ward notes that the unexpurgated text of Black Boy and American Hunger (the original autobiography manuscript's unused portion, posthumously published in 1977) "provides grounds for the claim that Wright originally wanted less to shape from his life a representative myth of growing up Southern than an American story which speaks to 'the hunger for life that gnaws in us all, to keep alive in our hearts a sense of the inexpressibly human'" (xiii). I am inclined to believe that Wright's autobiography embodies a graphic record of desire, will, disappointment, and a call to continue the struggle for improved human standards of life and moral conditions.

Following a long historical tradition of autobiographical writing, *Restavec: From Haitian Slave Child to Middle-Class American* is a continental "American" contribution to autobiography in the United States. Instead of originating in the South of the United States, however, his migration from Haiti into the United States transgresses national borders and points to the failure of U.S. foreign policy as well as the lamentable effects of the U.S.-led cold war on the Caribbean. Like those before him, through literacy, migration, and literary success Jean-Robert Cadet transforms himself from an abused slave child into a man of letters, engaged in an important fight for human rights and dignity; like those before him, he discovers that there is no such place as a promised land of democracy. Sparing with his words, he observes:

> As a young black man, I found civilian life in the South very harsh. My blackness was an obstacle to obtaining the most basic necessities of life. A part-time job was harder to obtain than decent housing. While I felt like a soldier [Cadet had served in the U.S. Army] who was not properly trained to survive in enemy territory, most white people, it seemed, had been trained all their lives to see me as dumb, dirty, dishonest, devilish, and a threat to their security. I couldn't despise them, because in my black native land and environment I was conditioned to think of whites as intelligent, honest, caring, and godlike. Nonetheless, I avoided their bigotry and concentrated on reaching my goal. (147)

However, compared with those before him, Cadet's codes of racial understanding are much more complicated. In Haiti, a rhetorical national pride in blackness exists. Furthermore, even though Haiti has an entrenched mulatto elite, during François Duvalier's years as leader, blackness was consciously applauded and prioritized over and against the mulatto elite. Cadet came to the United States with a different and more complex set of racial codes. He tells us at one point that a person who is good or smart or wealthy can be addressed as "blanc" even though he is not white. Ironically, although Haiti was the first black nation to win independence, the colonial legacy of rhetorical white superiority pervades Haitian culture. Évelyne Trouillot comments that Haiti is experiencing a new obsession with white skin (67). This contradiction, between a history of African pride and symbolic white prioritization,[13] further complicates Cadet's identity, as he experiences a new series of codes and racism in the American South. Was he not, as in Haiti, "blanc" if he excelled at what he did? No, in the United States he is black even if he has internalized, or privileged, whiteness in Caribbean terms. Caribbean cultural and political identities, based on gradations of color, shade, and class, do not function in the same way in Florida.

Regardless of the racial-social obstacles imposed on Cadet, he resolves to become a "model citizen" and a "moral person," so as to disprove that he would "never be anything more than a shoeshine boy" (66) and to challenge his biological father to recognize his goodness, success, and worth. His need for approval and authority lead him to an outstanding career in the army. He thinks he has finally found a place where he can belong. In the army, Cadet follows instructions and learns new skills that give him a sense of accomplishment. Nonetheless, Cadet's is a haunted and shredded character. His expectations of goodness and honor, shaped by extreme punishment during his childhood, exceed reality. In the army, contrary to his initial expectations of "excellence," he sees that the men in the barracks smoke marijuana and curse. He tells on his barrack mates, getting them in trouble and necessitating his transfer for safety reasons. At the new barracks he encounters the same kind of behavior— cursing, marijuana, extreme disrespect to women. Cadet is confronted with constant contradictions that isolate him from his surroundings and lead to depression.

In Haiti the police and the armed forces were feared. They imposed order through disorder and murder. They would leave the bodies of reported communists on the roadside to warn others and conduct nightly raids on families suspected of antigovernment activities. They had power and were corrupt. In the United States, Cadet believed that the army and, by extension, all law enforcers were beyond reproach, introducing order throughout the world by exemplary moral and social conduct. Reality subverts his beliefs. He seeks the purity of soul and noblesse of character he feels he must attain in order to prove himself a model citizen, but everywhere he turns, he is tragically disappointed.

Cadet repeatedly draws the contrast between his need for love and acceptance and his lack of it. I am obliged here to address a discrepancy between the message of the author—a loveless life until he meets his wife and they have a child—and the message of the text, which the author may not have intended. Cadet's story of survival and success departs from an extraordinary sense of self-love. It is this self-love, which he never talks about, that leads him to seek education, to defend himself against violence, and to write. Perhaps he has focused so intently on the destructive external elements of his life that he is unconscious of an elemental self-love that is necessary for anyone to find the strength and will to survive, move on, and even excel with a life project such as the one Cadet has found, fighting for the rights of Haiti's children.

Let us look at an exceptional example of this self-love I am pointing out. The author confesses that since he does not have any family or lovers to write to him, he starts to write to himself. While this confession is intended to underscore the lovelessness of his life, I believe that it does the contrary. In the army he writes to himself under the name of Josephine Benson. Eventually he invents a mother and two girlfriends. When the others receive letters from their loved ones, he does too. Even if the letters are autoproduced, the imaginary correspondence and the ability to share it with his barrack mates makes him feel less depressed and isolated. Writing, at this point, becomes his solace and his means of insertion into an emotional world that has, until that moment, denied him the love and acceptance of his dreams. His epistolary relationship to himself signals a strong sense of love that creates a new reality. Ironically, this detail eludes him. As he continues his memoir, he seems to be obsessed with his biological father's love, which is perhaps unattainable.

For example, when he leaves the army, he returns to Haiti with gifts in his bag for his father. Cadet assumes that his father will be impressed by his success in the army, his polished look, his muscular body, and his new knowledge. Again, he meets disappointment. Blanc Philippe leaves the house and has no contact with Cadet. Cadet returns to the United States to start a new plan of self-improvement and character building. He goes to college, which proves to be a challenge, not because of the academic material but rather because he is black and encounters racism at every turn. He cannot find an apartment to rent. When he does, his white roommate must keep Cadet a secret from his racist parents. At the college, many people distrust him openly, closing doors to him. Once he is finished with college, he has an even harder time finding a job.

It is at this point that he meets Mrs. Alvina Jefferson in Tampa, Florida. Cadet's memory of Mrs. Jefferson illustrates a personality type that contrasts explicitly with himself. Of notable importance is her resilience through humor. She does not internalize others' prejudice, and therefore she does not have problems with self-esteem. Mrs. Jefferson, Cadet notes, looks like she survived slavery. This is a point of similarity between the two. But the similarity stops there. Rather than seek the acceptance, or love, of those who denigrate and shun her, she has no sympathy for white people and laughs at their intolerance. Her presence in Cadet's life introduces comedy and U.S. slave history (and still flagrant racism) into his understanding of the world he occupies. It also offers an alternative narrative possibility for living. She laughs at the absurdity of her experiences. She recounts a time when a little girl stared at her in the bus. When asked why, the little girl said, "My mother got a dress just like yours, and when I get home I am gonna tell her and she's gonna burn it." Mrs. Jefferson retorted. "I told her to tell her mama that I got a p——y just like hers and she can burn that too" (158). She laughs as she tells her story. Whenever Mrs. Jefferson sees a police car, she tells Cadet, "They must be looking for some niggers to beat" (158).

Cadet observes, "Little by little, my black Haitian soul was being Americanized" (160). He experiences degradation in racism. For example, the police stop him for running a red light and treat him with unnecessary hostility. He is paid less than the normal scale for his job, and visitors to his office do not believe that a black man reads and writes French.

He finally belongs to a group of people, but his struggle for human rights, dignity in life, and respect for his accomplishments were still being negated. Social and racial violence, which affect and depress him, continued to deny him the place in the world he sought. Cadet remembers that "my mission was the same as before: to be accepted and recognized in name by my father, Philippe" (164). Once again, he returns to Haiti with gifts and new reports for Philippe. Once again, Philippe goes away. Philippe's twin sons invite Cadet to go out, but it is a further disappointment. Cadet's half brothers party and do drugs. He leaves them and reports this to Philippe. In the back of his mind, he wants Philippe to recognize how much better he is than his half brothers. He wants his impeccable moral conduct and judgment to be celebrated. But Philippe becomes angry. He does not want to be reminded of how his sons have turned out, and he will never legitimize Cadet.

Cadet tells us that it is his own entry into fatherhood that leads him to recognize his undeniable status as a person, a human being capable of giving and receiving love. He emphasizes that with paternity he became determined to play an active role in the world as a fighter for human rights, against the evils of the restavèk system and a history of discrimination. Cadet closes his autobiography with these words:

> As the baby was being born, the emptiness that I'd always felt in my
> chest was slowly filled. My heart was no longer a stone in the middle
> of a cold and empty cave. After the delivery, the nurse plopped the
> beautiful baby boy in my arms. I looked in his eyes and saw some-
> thing that reminded me of Blanc Philippe. Inside me was an explosion
> of contentment that vibrated all the way up to the shores of my eyes.
> (182)

Blanc Philippe may never have officially recognized Jean-Robert Cadet,
yet his influence could not be denied. Philippe's genes helped shape Cadet
and are visible in his grandchild. But fatherhood presents Cadet with the
opportunity to give what he never received: love, support, and acceptance.
And writing an autobiography provides Cadet a way to fight what he
knows is wrong, childhood slavery, which deprives human beings of the
necessary conditions of love and nurturance.

I would like to add that this transformation from a loveless person into
a person full of love does not happen as abruptly as Cadet insists it does.
His own writing attests to that. While Cadet may point to his fatherhood,
and the acceptance of the responsibility that entails, as the significant
event that brings love into his life, we as readers have a special glimpse of
his self-love. His fight for love, his acts of self-improvement, and his acceptance of romantic love with the woman who later becomes his wife are all
precursors of this final embodiment of love through paternity that moti-
vates him to write (or to write again, if we remember his letter-writing to
himself in the guise of family and girlfriends).

The birth of Cadet's son, like the publication of his autobiography, is
about hope and human possibility. Cadet's message is reminiscent of
Wright's last words in *Black Boy*:

> I would hurl words into this darkness and wait for an echo, and if an
> echo sounded, no matter how faintly, I would send other words to tell,
> to march, to fight, to create a sense of the hunger for life that gnaws
> in us all, to keep alive in our hearts a sense of the inexpressibly hu-
> man. (384)

Against all odds, Cadet has found love through his wife and child. From the
pages of his autobiography, he hurls words into the darkness of human
deprivation, calling for justice against both childhood slavery and racism.

Memory and Cadet's Testimony

Contemporary psychologists—Ulric Neisser, Daniel Albright, and Greg J. Neimeyer, among many—insist that autobiography is less a factual account and more a writer's creation of a past that explains his or her present. Clinical research psychologists such as Geoffrey R. Loftus and Elizabeth F. Loftus suggest that there are different ways of storing and retrieving information. After years of studying test cases, the Loftuses have proposed six kinds of memory: (1) sensory store, (2) short-term store, (3) long-term memory for new material, (4) recognition memory, (5) long-term memory for meaningful material, and (6) semantic memory (85–135). Cadet's autobiography taps into recognition memory and long-term memory for meaningful material.

Recognition memory emphasizes the importance of "both rehearsal and organization" (Loftus 84). This concept recalls Aristotle's exposition on memory: recognition memory depends on observation, memorization, and exacting retrieval. This kind of memory should be accurate, but it is impeded by interference. According to interference theory, "people forget an event because something else they have learned prevents the event from being remembered" (74). Retrieval failure—forgetting—would also detract from recognition memory's dependency value. The act of forgetting, however, holds a very important place in studies of mental sanity. Individuals who cannot forget or work through horrible events could not participate in the present. Yet studies of long-term memory for meaningful material conclude that "a person often remembers only parts of the newly learned material, and he tends to construct other bits and pieces in order to have a coherent story" (118). In clinical studies where people have been given a sentence and then asked to remember that same sentence from a multiple-choice list, test subjects were more likely to remember meaning than exact syntax. It could be argued that Cadet retrieves his life story using both memory styles. He taps into recognition memory when he remembers the exact insults Florence repeated against him, over and over again. But he also relies on long-term memory for meaningful material; in seeking meaning for his life, he necessarily reconstructs it in such a way that it makes sense both to him, many years later, and to his reader who may be uninformed of certain nuances of Haitian culture or African-Caribbean-American experiences.

In "Mind, Text, and Society: Self-Memory in Social Context," Kenneth J. Gergen makes a distinction between the above-described approach to memory (psychological essentialism) and a literary approach to memory (textual memory) in which the "remembered self is a literary achievement" (80). Gergen proposes that personal memories are not personal but rather sociopolitical acts that exist in a "state of intertextuality, borrowing and bending and replying to the cultural conventions of writing about the personal past" (81). According to his argument, memory and forgetting become critical only if we recognize the mind as a locus of knowledge, interpreting knowledge as essential for action (a common good, social action). Arguably, Cadet is a literary achievement and, through that achievement, also a re-membered person. Through writing he redeems his potential and claims his successes. With these memories in writing, he then tackles a severe sociopolitical problem. This process—acts of memory that redefine the speaking subject within a larger and more important sociocultural scenario—is very important in memory studies and to our interpretation of the function of Cadet's autobiography.

In "The 'Remembered Self,'" psychologist Jerome Bruner proposes that "Self is a perpetually rewritten story. . . . remembering reaches far back beyond our own birth, back to the cultural and language forms that specify the defining properties of a Self" (53). Bruner tells several stories that underscore the importance of self-perception on experience, memory of that experience, and telling of that experience. In one story, he quotes Henry James saying that "adventures happen to people who know how to tell it that way" (48), suggesting that we may all experience adventures, but not all of us can recount them as the adventures they might have been at the moment of the experience. In another story, he mentions that studies have shown that girls experience academic failure as their own inadequacy but regard success as good luck; boys experience their failure as bad luck and their success as the result of competence (48). Does Cadet experience his "enslavement" as bad luck? Is that the premise from which he can escape the situation?

In Haiti, three-fourths of the restavèks are girls,[14] but the most prominent story is of a boy. Do boys see themselves with more agency inherently? Several human rights reports comment on girls being more passive and less rebellious. They tend to endure the abuse without reporting it. Cadet points to girls' silenced condition when he describes the restavèk girl who just disappears when she gets sick. In contrast, as a child he is rebellious, stealing licks of ice cream and sneaking the remaining soda when no one is looking. Even though he is constantly beaten and put down, he demonstrates the skills of other survivors in situations of extreme deprivation (such as Primo Levi in the concentration camps). Perhaps because he is a boy, and thus part of the "dominant" gender, his initial perception of his experience is shaped by this position, superior to that of girls.

Cadet's text serves as a unique example of Haitian-American memory. It transects with a long tradition of autobiographical writing and interplays with a new critical praxis of testimony.[15] When considering Cadet's text as testimony, we must review some of the successes and impasses the genre has encountered. In their study *Human Rights and Narrated Lives*, Kay Schaffer and Sid Smith have pointed out: "The post–Cold War decade of the 1990s has been labeled the decade of human rights, the decade in which, Michael Ignatieff claims, 'human rights has become the dominant moral vocabulary in foreign affairs'" (1). They acknowledge both the importance and the limitations of testimony, and show how in the "transits of this multivectored space there are many flows, but also many detours, undercurrents, dams, and blockages" (6). In addition, they probe the multiple ways in which testimonies are used. Ideally, testimonies should incite constructive political action against a crime against humanity. But we are warned:

> They can also produce pleasure out of another's pain, turn subjects of story into spectacle, reduce difference to sameness, and induce exhaustion. While affect offers a potential for change, for becoming, it is impossible to predict how sensations will be channeled into knowledge practice. (9)

At issue, again, are the function and truth of testimony. Like many theorists before them, Schaffer and Smith privilege function over exactitude:

> Since personal storytelling involves acts of remembering, of making meaning out of the past, its "truth" cannot be read as solely or simply factual. There are different registers of truth beyond the factual: psychological, experiential, historical, cultural, communal, and potentially transformative. The present of personal narrating becomes a fulcrum, that point where the pressure of memories of a traumatic past and the hopes for an enabling future are held in balance. As balancing acts, directed back to a past that must be shared and toward a future that must be built collectively, acts of personal narrating can become projects of community-building, organizational tools, and calls to action. (11)

Let us return to Cadet's "act of personal narrating." It is no surprise that his testimony has met with support from human rights groups and literary scholars, as well as challenges from people who say he is not telling the truth. The former hope that a community fighting against child slavery will form and change the situation. The latter offer conflicting arguments as varied as "there is no restavèk problem" and "Cadet is not real because it is impossible to remember the details so accurately" and "it is impossible to escape the destitute conditions of a restavèk." Even those who oppose the restavèk condition want more proof of who and what Cadet is. For example, at a presentation I gave at Duke University in October 2002, Haitian scholar Jean Jonassaint questioned the existence of a Jean-Robert Cadet. Jonassaint said that on his recent trip to Haiti he had unsuccessfully sought people who might have known Cadet as a child. As Jonassaint said this, I wondered if class did not play a role in Cadet's "nonexistence." If Cadet did come from such dire circumstances, who would care to remember him? Perhaps all who might have known him had died, were in the streets peddling, or had migrated, erasing their memories of a miserable past. As if reading my mind, Jonassaint suggested that publishers often rewrite the text of developing-world authors. For example, without giving away the parties, he referred to the story of an African writer who submitted a novel in perfect English. The publishers, interested in the story, had an editor change the language so that it would sound more "authentic," more African. Jonassaint also pointed to a very interesting, if not intriguing, lexical detail: in Haiti, to *faire un Cadet Jacques* or *kadéjak* is to commit a rape.[16]

Could Jean-Robert Cadet mean a Jean-Robert who is the issue of a rape? In *Restavec*, Cadet informs us that all children without a family name are called Robert (similar to being named John Doe). If so, then there is further reason to suspect that the name, if not the person, is an invented one. Robert is any John Doe who has been violated/raped. Or should we believe that the author does not want to disclose his real name? That he did escape nonpersonhood without even a registered birth certificate? That in life as well as in literature he has remade himself despite the social and political rape of his person? Earlier I suggested that life and literature intersected; here, perhaps, it is possible to wonder if autobiography and fiction intersect. Cadet tells us that most names have been changed. Does this not already consist of a breach of truth?

To tell the complete story of one's life, starting in Cadet's case with his arrival at Florence's house at age two, requires some reconstruction that necessarily taps into the imaginary. The latter part of the twentieth century witnessed an explosion of studies challenging the veracity of autobiography and concluding that, indeed, elements of fiction always slip in. After all, who remembers back to the toddler years? Cadet may have received his information from Florence.

In Haitian Kreyòl there is a saying, "Pote mak sonje, bay kou bliye," which means that he who bears the scar remembers, he who gives the blow forgets. It might be unfair to judge the "truth" of Cadet's story, since for some reason or other the author feels a close affinity to the downtrodden of Haiti and offers a narrative that may help improve the condition of restavèks. In addition, there is no doubt that, like Douglass before him, Cadet will be challenged by those who do not want to face the implications of what he exposes. In the United States, many may not want to have knowledge of what happens in other parts of the world because it is, to a certain extent, overwhelming; people might feel bereft because they remain helpless, dealing with their own economic and personal struggles. In particular Haitian Americans, and those of us who have grown to love Haiti and respect it, may find the constant exposition of bleak human degradation embarrassing, since it is too easy to point a finger at the problems of less developed nations without noticing the good things or how many equally bad things take place on U.S. soil. Nonetheless, Cadet has been affected by the degradation of the restavèk system and must reveal it. Like Wright, Cadet describes a reality that is ongoing, and his memory of abuse can be further marked by what he witnesses in the present. If Cadet exists, it is of critical importance that he was an abused child who met with further abuse in the United States. This abuse has left a wound of pain and trauma that he still suffers from today. If the story is made up, we must ask what personal pain led him to engage with the afflictions of a domestic child laborer? Perhaps the messages in his text should be analyzed from a perspective critical, not of him, but of the social injustices he describes. The restavèk system that Cadet claims to have been a part of is not a personal tragedy but, rather, an ongoing human rights violation. Cadet has, after all, gone on tour with his book, further challenging the restavèk system. I suspect that there must be some honest link between his story and his experience.

In order to allay my suspicions a bit, I decided to contact the author. He was kind and efficient with his responses, which in some ways addressed Jonassaint's concerns about the interference of publishers. Indeed, the publisher had a hand in the presentation of the text. Originally, Cadet had called it *Restavec*. His concern was to expose his memories of his experience in this situation, to bring international attention to its ongoing status, and to find ways to work against it. The publisher, however, wanted a subtitle, "From Haitian Slave Child to Middle-Class American." These words ensured that the book would enter the canon of immigrant stories of success. It would affirm that the American Dream is still achieved. As I have noted, however, we never get a real sense of how Cadet becomes a middle-class American or how the American Dream has been achieved. When I asked Cadet how he felt he was a middle-class American, his response was telling. Cadet, who was born in a farming town called Grand Hatte in Petite Rivière de l'Artibonite, now dedicates his time to touring for human rights, in particular against the restavèk system. He does not consider himself to be part of any economic class. He does not want to be pegged with any kind of class description, middle class or otherwise. Instead, he considers one of his fights to be against racism. He fights for justice. For example, in our electronic correspondence he claimed that he was involved in a lawsuit against a high school in Cincinnati that fired him for using a word that the white teacher who has replaced him uses. The word in question was "douche," French for shower, which he had used in a literary context. With this story Cadet affirms what he already has said in the autobiography's story of his friend Mrs. Jefferson in Tampa: racism is alive and well, still destroying people's potential for full participation in predominantly white communities. He does not let himself be broken; he acts on principle, engaging in true citizenship by being an activist. Through direct contact with the author, I have added another dimension to my reading. While publishers have a say in how a text gets presented, they cannot change an author's intentions. Cadet's message with *Restavec* seeks action to end child slavery. In the process, he has encountered other injustices and is also fighting for the right to life in dignity in general. The question still remains, how much of his version is accurate, and does that matter?

If one's story is contingent on culture and language, how are we to read and understand a text that recalls things that happened in another culture and another language? Cadet's memories are not only restructured but also translated. Would it have been more painful for him to write about the first half of his life in Kreyòl and French? Does writing about his experiences in Haiti while he is away from Haiti give him greater poetic license to remember more systematically? How will an English-speaking audience respond to such a text?

I suggest that Cadet writes in English for several reasons. First, his formal education took place in English, in the United States, throughout high school, the military, and college. Perhaps, as is the proven case with most Latino/a writers in the United States, English is the language in which he writes best. In particular, through a second/third language, Cadet can remove himself from the actual pain of the memory. Writing in Kreyòl and/ or French might make the experience too real, too unbearable to confront. Furthermore, it is in English that he finally discovers the possibility of transforming himself from a slave child, the slave child he saw himself as in Haiti, into a citizen, an American citizen. In English, he recalls the encouragement and support of a Jewish teacher, Mr. Rabinowitz. In English, he has confessed his past to his wife, worked in therapy to create a present free of haunting, and built the possibility of a future for his new family.

Perhaps, by writing in English, he has conformed to contemporary conventions of international writing and publication (whether he admits it or not). English texts are distributed better and have a wider audience. But that is the point. When he denounces childhood slavery in the afterword, he engages in a political project calling for human rights attention to a subject that historically has been neglected for reasons we have explored. If he had written in Kreyòl, his audience would have been severely limited. In addition, everyone in Haiti knows about the dire living conditions. But by writing in English, he can take his message to an international audience, and consequently back to Haiti, where it has been translated and, in a limited way, distributed.

Bruner argues that the self is constantly being rewritten. Perhaps, through the process of writing, it is in English that he can put forth his "best self." Kreyòl might be his private language, reminding him of a past of pain, whereas English might be his present language, with which he connects to human rights documents and work. In English he engages a public sphere that discloses abuses that occur in a private sphere; Cadet thus exposes a silenced crime through his public testimony.

In the same decade as the Convention on the Rights of the Child, Cadet's writing comes at a timely and important moment in the history of human rights in general and of the rights of the child in particular.[17] Cadet's autobiography taps into the memory of his own childhood, and it also reveals the continuing social injustice of child slavery.[18] Traditional Haitian literature was written in the "we" voice. Haitian literature in exile, in the diaspora (what Jonassaint calls *littérature du dehors*), takes on a first-person singular voice as it continues to examine Haitian lives inside and outside the country. This style, influenced by Western traditions of literary representation, allows the author to engage with larger histories of nation, community, and memories.

With *Restavec: From Haitian Slave Child to Middle-Class American*, written in the first-person singular but addressing a (bi)national "we," Cadet is putting forth a clear message denouncing child slavery and constructing the possibility of personhood, citizenship, and active political and social resistance.

Writing to Re-member

With this chapter I have exposed the ways the restavèk condition has been represented. Histories, legal documents, autobiographies, and testimonies, considered as modes of memory, have distinct sociopolitical functions. I have consequently argued that Cadet's autobiography—in dialogue with a foundational tradition of African-American autobiography—is an inspiring example of how Pan-Caribbean diaspora literature denounces violence and fights for human rights.[19]

Cadet taps into his memory to construct the self he can be today, working through where he has come from and how he achieved personhood, for his readers, himself, and his family. Contemporary autobiography studies have dismantled the presumption that autobiography is a true and accurate testimonial of a life lived. Rather, autobiography reveals how a life's experiences are remembered. It could reflect how the author wants to be remembered or the author's psychological truth at that moment. In Cadet's case, the autobiography reveals a person who cannot escape the pain of the violations he experienced in his youth. By writing an autobiography, Cadet has entered the literary world of the remembered self through the written self. His confessions of traumatic memory testify to the wounds of violence; his writing is an example of the process of making the world and the self through literature.

Mapping Home

Inaccessible Memories

Recently, while doing research at the National Archive in Santo Domingo, I explained to the librarian that I wanted to look at Trujillo's letters and speeches from the period immediately following the 1937 massacre. The librarian smiled knowingly and said that many scholars were trying to trace that information. The problem was the missing documents, contradictory documents, and even invented documents that some intellectuals claim were added after the fact. His comment reminded me of an experience I had had at the Schomburg Center for Research in Black Culture in New York City. A librarian gave me a private letter from Trujillo and told me that the organization would be grateful if I learned more about its origin and destination. Easy, I thought at the time.

My visits to the National Archive were challenging, reminiscent of a strange journey into a labyrinth of emptiness in a Borges story. Getting there was far from complicated; buses and cabs are everywhere and the nearby roads are quite good. To enter the archive, I had to pass a guard and a clerk, sitting at an old metal desk, who recorded my name. Unsympathetically austere, the building reflected a Caribbean strain of functional, brutalist architecture reminiscent of some government buildings I had visited in Cuba. The entrance seemed unusually bare; it displayed no poetic words of inspiration from great writers. Nor did I smell the pages of books and learning in the air. The eyes of the employees seemed anxiously fixated on the clock that would strike the time of lunch break and the hour of departure from their boring desk jobs. As the kind librarian and I walked down long corridors and wide concrete and steel staircases, he apologized for the state of the library. With a tone of resignation, he noted that the building was undergoing select renovations. The area with the Trujillo information was the most affected.

Although the Dominican Republic's National Archive could have been a safe haven for the history of the nation, it held an incomplete pile of books that reflected the decayed or lost memories of a nation. None of the books had been safeguarded from the construction work. Instead, they had been knocked to the floor to make room for new walls intended to improve ventilation and access to the shelves. This renovation supposedly would allow for airflow in an area that had been known for its cavelike darkness, dust, humidity, and mosquitoes. Researchers had become very ill from mosquito bites and suffered from allergic and asthma attacks. Now there was some airflow, so I did not need the intense DEET insect repellent I had put on. The room was airy, albeit dusty from construction and many years of enclosure. The librarian and I stepped over mounds of books and papers just to get from one stack to the other. The holdings were only partially indexed, and nothing was in order. The librarian would grab a manuscript, dust it off, and say, "This is from 1938. We must be close." But the next document would be from the twenties and very far from the topic of interest. We spent hours in the stacks and then went to his private bookcases, which included some very helpful but crumbling books. He said he trusted me to take them to be photocopied. I was nervous that opening the books would cause them to crack and start falling apart instantly. The books had become relics long before their time, perhaps because of cheap paper or the intense humidity of the Caribbean.[1]

As I had these books photocopied, I wondered how much of their information was accurate. What were the intentions of the authors? What had *not* been recorded?[2] What remained in the memory of a country that had survived the brutal Trujillo dictatorship and its chaotic aftermath and where brief moments of economic progress had not eradicated deep pockets of poverty? How did this affect the way the diaspora community could remember its past and visualize its present? How did this country's sexism—embodied in horrific form by its highest leaders—and convoluted version of racism color the fragments of history that did persist? And did women's stories, confined to the private space of the house, find any visibility in the country's national imagination?

The jacket art on Loida Maritza Pérez's 1999 debut novel, *Geographies of Home*, bears an uncanny resemblance to the unruly renovation project at the National Archive in Santo Domingo. It depicts a chaotic scene, with stripped walls, scattered chicken feathers, floors covered with flames, and doors that lead to a barren gray. The book's cover evokes a sense of abandonment, decay, and loss that is similar to what I saw in the downstairs area of the Archive. *Geographies of Home,* as the name suggests, at first appears to be tracing the geography of a place the main character, Iliana, wants to define as home; however, it discloses a deeply etched cartography of sexism and violence that to date remains largely invisible in Dominican and Dominican diaspora literature. I propose that although Pérez's novel could represent the gentle musings of a woman's search for home, it instead exposes the invisible (because denied or silently accepted) degrees of violence women experience in the family. Home, whether in the Dominican Republic or the United States, is plagued by a long history of violations against women that precludes the recognition of their very important work in nation building and diasporic memory making. Almost in defiance of the Dominican Republic's buried histories, Pérez creates a character, Iliana, whose story maps the experience of an immigrant family weakened by the myths, sexism, and violence that have dominated Dominican culture and bled into its diaspora.

Geographies of Home is a feminist story that traces the journey of self-discovery and self-empowerment taken by a first-generation Dominican woman whose family is settled in Brooklyn. Iliana, the protagonist, defies her culture's conventions and goes away to college, only to be haunted by those very conventions. Caught in an emotional crisis that leads her to leave school and go back to her family's house, Iliana does not find a home. Instead she learns that

> Everything she had experienced; everything she continued to feel for those whose lives would be inextricably bound with hers; everything she had inherited from her parents and gleaned from her siblings would aid her in her passage through the world. She would leave no memories behind. All of them were her self. All of them were home. (321)

During a summer with her family, Iliana grapples with multiple degrees of violence and its repercussions. The novel serves as a bildungsroman; Iliana's passage into womanhood entails not only self-discovery but also self-affirmation through her final denunciation of a personal, family, and national history that has obliterated women's lives. As a contemporary bildungsroman, *Geographies of Home* does not show Iliana growing up; rather, it shows how the main character develops personal and political consciousness.

With this chapter I argue that women have been dually invisible in Dominican and Dominican diaspora memory. The object of violence, and the subject of silence, women's lives are made invisible on at least two levels. In literature, the presence of women in relation to a long tradition of men's writing is relatively slim. In the private space of the home, the role of women, as backbones of their culture, families, and communities, continues to be subverted through violence. I study Pérez's novel as a critical site that reveals a number of sociocultural dynamics of violence against women.

"The future can hurt if you deny the past"

Geographies of Home is sprinkled with the central motif of finding out about the past in order to derive strength from it, understand the present, and recover a history that will offer a sense of origin to the family. Aurelia, the quiet matriarch, finds herself missing something and is "determined to discover what had caused the loss and to figure out how she had brought herself to the present moment so that she might guide herself into the future" (23). She recalls her last visit to her childhood home, when her mother, Bienvenida, showed her a quilt composed of patches that had belonged to different, now dead, members of the family. Aurelia felt spooked by the remembrances invoked and asked why she was being shown this. Bienvenida, who was preparing for her death, enigmatically responded, "Because the future can hurt if you deny the past. Because I want you to never forget. Because, as the youngest of my children, it is for you to sew me in" (132). Yet Aurelia seems to have forged forgetting over remembering for the greater part of her life.

This motif of remembering is echoed by Iliana, who notes that "hearts relentlessly pumped blood even as brains recoiled from whatever horror was presented. . . . Knowing little of her parents' lives, she wanted to learn of the past of which they rarely spoke. She also wanted to borrow from both the strength she saw reflected in their eyes" (44).

But what does the past entail? What exactly should these women never forget? The answer to those questions is never given to us in the text. Could it have been the history of their ancestors, which included African blood that they denied? Could it have been the political history of their country, which ignored the poor in the countryside as well as the rape and murder of women in the quiet confines of their own homes? Could this past be about the ways that Trujillo silenced a nation that still ignores the human rights of its people, especially its women and children? Could the past they refer to actually be the continued violations committed against women that creeps its way into the present precisely because it was not denounced in the past?

As I mulled over these questions, it struck me that Pérez was probably making me feel something that she, the author, feels: the frustration of lack of information and a history of denial. Denial protects us from painful emotions. In *States of Denial: Knowing about Atrocities and Suffering,* Stanley Cohen outlines the manifestations of denial: accommodation, routinization, tolerance, putting up with it, collusion, and cover-up (51). All of these normalize or numb the effects of violence on people. "The need for an alternative story is especially acute when the manifest interpretation of the acknowledged 'something' is unthinkable. This is the response to the most extreme forms of mass human suffering" (31). The levels of violence that Dominicans have experienced, whether they tell it or not, are high. For example, various texts recount Trujillo's favorite warning tactic. First his secret police would kill a person from one neighborhood. Then they would kill a person in another neighborhood. These corpses would be hung up in conspicuous places for all to see. Families would often be unable to track the bodies of their loved ones because either they were too severely mutilated or they were hung in such a far-off community that (before mass media could resolve such questions) the bodies were never identified. The secret police, who all feared, drove about in little Volkswagens. The secret police would also take people away in the night, usually noisily to make a point.

Many parents wanted to protect their children from these realities. They did not mention the horrors, hoping their children would not suffer the fear. But the parents' fear was palpable. The children watched and revealed no knowledge. Knowledge without acknowledgment is one of the most insidious forms of denial. Over the years, no one has talked about the horrors. In diaspora communities, these fears shape family dynamics, but no one can address the real issues underlying the family fear, myths, and continued self-imposed repression.

Thinking of these issues, I remembered that shortly after a trip I took to the Dominican Republic, the seven-time president Joaquín Balaguer died. Balaguer is an important piece of the puzzle of Dominican history, yet little is known about him. Even his age was uncertain: though the official record put him at nearly ninety-six, his aides had long insisted that he was actually a year older than that, because of an error made when his birth was registered several years late. Balaguer had been Trujillo's puppet president for a brief period, when the United States insisted on democratic elections. After Trujillo was assassinated, Balaguer fled into exile, then won the 1966 election with the support of the Dominican oligarchy and, importantly, of the United States. He remained in office until 1978, when U.S. president Jimmy Carter insisted that the military respect the popular vote that went to the opposition. But Balaguer returned to power eight years later and, in all, served for some two dozen years, 1960–63, 1966–78, and 1986–95. It was said that even in his late nineties, blind and no longer able to stand by himself, he was mulling another run for the presidency. Balaguer's rule was considered by many to have been as cruel as Trujillo's.[3] In fact, Jan Knippers Black, who has written about this, counts more political killings during Balaguer's first presidency (1966–78), *los doce años*, than under Trujillo. In his 1988 memoir, *Memorias de un cortesano de la era de Trujillo*, Balaguer left one page blank. Twenty years after his death, he said, that page would be filled in with the truth about the 1975 murder of the political journalist Orlando Martínez.

This page became the center of attention for many historians, journalists, and human rights advocates. After all, the Dominican Republic has an outstanding history of cover-ups of judicial and human rights violations. The blank page, some speculated, might have been the perfect link between denial of human atrocities and disclosure of the horrors no one will speak of. Unfortunately, Balaguer's death brought with it one more denial. His close aide General Enrique Pérez y Pérez declared that the blank page had been merely a publicity stunt and that Balaguer had left no details behind. Once again the Dominican nation must continue looking forward without knowing the complicated details of its history.

The novel draws out these issues of truth, justice and discrimination, repression, and sexism. Through the story, we are invited to uncover the dark side of the legacy of repression. Like Balaguer's blank page, the people are given hints of the horrors, but like a tourist brochure, they are covered up with the images of pristine beaches, the sounds of sexy *bachattas*, and the challenges of migrations.

Aurelia, the matriarch, laments at the end of the novel:

> She also thought of the many more things she had never revealed to her children or her grandchildren: details of their own and of their family's past which might have helped them better understand themselves as well as the world through which they moved. The silence enveloping these legacies, the half-truths meant to gloss over and protect, the falsehoods uttered for fear of causing pain, and the

inability or unwillingness to speak, now seemed to her to have inflicted greater harm. (298)

Aurelia had wanted to protect her family from the pain that certain knowledge could have caused her children and grandchildren, but she realized
that burying history only made it almost impossible to confront the
present and forge the future. Aurelia had not heeded the advice of her
mother, Bienvenida, that "the future will hurt you worse if you deny the
past" (295). But, in the novel, we get the sense that the past is buried too
deeply to bring up. Perhaps this explains the unanswered question of what
Aurelia and Bienvenida mean when they say they must understand the
past. They would like to unearth the gaps of history. But they witness only
denial, not just of the past but also of the problems in the present.

The most developed characters in Iliana's family—Rebecca, Marina,
and Aurelia—embody different forms of denial. Rebecca denies the depth
of abuse she experiences at her husband's hand. Marina denies herself, her
blackness, her sensuality, and her sexuality. Aurelia denies the extent of
the family problems. Denial is the challenge faced by the Dominican community in the Dominican Republic and in the United States.[4] Unless the
communities confront the forms of repression and terror they have been
and continue to be subjected to, they cannot address the pain caused by the
denial of history, both national and familial (and of the rights of the individual).

Sexism and Human Rights Violations in Dominican History

The Dominican Republic, unlike its neighbor, Haiti, has never confronted
its past. Proposals for a truth commission in the Dominican Republic have
been turned down repeatedly. Despite its shortcomings, a truth commission filed a report in Haiti. In contrast, the Dominican Republic has buried
the horror that pockmarks its history. The U.S. Department of State's 2001
Country Reports on Human Rights Practices in the Dominican Republic
underscores the numerous types of exploitation, despite increased tourism
and the country's much touted "democracy." Several details stood out for
me:

> The authorities rarely prosecuted abusers, and at times members of
> the security forces committed abuses with the tacit acquiescence of
> the civil authorities, leading to a climate of impunity. . . .

The authorities infringed on citizens' privacy rights, and police entered private homes without judicial orders. Members of the President's security force mistreated journalists, and journalists at times practiced self-censorship. . . .

Violence and discrimination against women; prostitution, including child prostitution; abuse of children; discrimination against persons with disabilities; discrimination against and abuse of Haitian migrants and their descendants; and child labor were serious problems. (1)

As I read the full report, I thought about Papito and his intense need to instill fear in Iliana. All along, he claimed it was for her own good. As I read about the human rights conditions in the Dominican Republic, I concluded that Loida Maritza Pérez constructs Papito's character to help us understand the kind of terror people bring with them when they come from such repressive circumstances. Papito lives with this sense that anything horrible can happen and that no one will do anything to help or find justice.

The report also discloses corrupt police practices. For example, the police in the Dominican Republic rarely document citizen killings. Often the only witnesses to the killings are other police officers. Civilians will not step forward to report what they saw. They know that few cases are tried in civilian court and that they will put themselves and their families in danger if they contradict official police stories. Consequently, most cases are resolved in military courts, with the police exonerated and the victims ignored. The report concludes that "there is a lack of meaningful training in human rights as applied to police work" (www.state.gov/?).

The next part of the report leads me to believe that certain people get the least respect. In some 250 deaths at the hands of police, the majority of the victims were characterized by the police as delinquents; the rest were wives, girlfriends, other civilians, or fellow officers. The police act to eliminate crimes; they kill, rather than according their targets a fair trial to prove their innocence. In most cases, the police claim that the deaths resulted from an exchange of gunfire in the course of arrest. The State Department document cites a 1999 report from the Inter-American Commission on Human Rights (IACHR) criticizing the police for committing extrajudicial killings and neglecting to investigate and punish officers responsible for such abuses. Police assert that they killed the "delinquents" in self-defense, but in a number of cases this was demonstrably not the situation. (2)

Human rights do not exist where human life is not valued.

Another group that is consistently denied human value and Dominican citizenship is found in the Haitian and Dominican-Haitian communities in border shantytowns. These groups, as we saw in chapter 1, have been eliminated without the slightest protest. During Trujillo, the lies and the fear contributed to this lack of opposition. But today I wonder if Dominicans have not been induced to really believe that their Haitian neighbors are inferior. Haitians in the Dominican Republic are considered "in transit." Since most Haitian laborers do not have documentation of their birth, they cannot prove how long they have lived on Dominican soil. They cannot ever gain citizenship for themselves or their children. Similarly, any Dominican who exhibits strong African traits is ostracized. In Marina's case, she deprecates herself. Not only can she not accept her own African blood, she dismisses anyone who is black as inferior, evil, and unworthy. She denies herself, her history, and her links to the expansive world of the African diaspora. The myth of the horrible Haitian translates into the denial of Dominican history.

Exclusion is at work in flagrant as well as subtle ways. While women and minorities are not impeded from active political participation, the "percentage of women and minorities in government and politics does not correspond to their percentage of the population" (8). Dominican law prohibits discrimination based on race and sex. However, the law is usually ignored by the private sector. For example, some employers reportedly give pregnancy tests to women before hiring them. A positive test means they will not get the job.

Women and children suffer human rights abuses most regularly. "NGO's estimate that 40 percent of women and children are the subject of domestic violence" (8). While the police remain reluctant to deal with rape cases, many NGOs and the Secretariat of Women are engaging in groundbreaking work against rape. In 1997 the Law against Domestic Violence incited the state to prosecute for rape, incest, and other kinds of domestic violence. "The Government's center in Villa Juana (Santo Domingo) for the legal support and forensic examination of abused women handles over 100 cases per day" (8). This center's success has proved the need for other centers, which are expected to open eventually. However, shelters for battered women have not been set up yet.

Another danger for women and children is human trafficking. According to the report, this continues to be a serious matter, with women between the ages of eighteen and twenty-five at greatest risk. Most women are lured by promises of jobs and better lives. Instead they are forced into prostitution, far from their homes and families, where they cannot escape. To counter this serious problem, the government founded the Interinstitutional Committee for the Protection of Migrant Workers (CIPROM) in 1996. An NGO, the Center for Integral Orientation and Investigation (COIN), has been set up to counsel women planning to take jobs in Europe and the Eastern Caribbean. Still the number of exploited women exceeds the available programs and help. More commonly, very poor women in the interior do not know of these programs. Access to help and guidance is not available to marginalized and undocumented families.

As in Haiti, some families send their children to work in the city. The children are called *palomas*, doves. *Paloma* is a poetic word, unlike *restavèk*, but it describes the same dismal condition of abusive child labor in which the children have no rights to personhood and self-fulfillment. It is highly symbolic that Dominicans call domestic child laborers doves. Torturers also use beautiful words, otherwise associated with harmony and nurturance, to describe horrible acts that destroy human meaning, the human body, and human potential. "In the secret world of torture—where the infliction of pain is so personal—pre-junta meanings of words change and neutral words are retranslated" (Cohen 82–83). For example, in Argentina, during the "dirty war," *asado*, which is a term for a barbecue and reminds one of summer evenings with friends and family, means a bonfire to burn dead bodies. Israeli torturers gave Palestinians the "banana." Bananas are my favorite fruit; they are high in potassium and good for the muscles. Significantly, in the language of torture, they represent being tied in a painful floor position. Cohen argues that "Every torture regime uses the same linguistic technique: something awful that is *being done*, a verb, is transposed into some mundane *thing*, a noun" (83).

The 2001 *Country Reports on Human Rights Practices* in the Dominican Republic underscores the ways in which people are deprived of rights and citizenship in the communities where they live. Because of poverty, gender, and race, many people in the Dominican Republic are officially marginalized and negated. This is the world that many flee; Papito's fears are, to a certain extent, well founded. If so many women and children are lured into prostitution and child slavery, what keeps his family safe from the perils of the outside world? If he knows that the government allows some crimes to be committed with impunity in the Dominican Republic, why would he believe in any institution anywhere? In contrast to women who head families, Papito remains the strongman of his. His experiences in the Dominican Republic lead him to act in ways that continue to negate the rights of his family. I would argue that his form of sexism, and the violence that is portrayed in *Geographies of Home*, responds to a long history of abuse, fear, and repression. Papito wants the best for his family, but he does not know how to make that happen, so he repeats familiar patterns —patterns of violence.

This view of Papito as the benevolent caretaker could lead to dangerous conclusions, which I would like to avoid. I am thinking in particular of how Trujillo excused the brutality he inflicted on citizens by arguing that he was doing it for the benefit of his country. He was eliminating the communists as well as any other kind of unsavory individual. The poor who were seduced by the image of the paternal strongman cried relentlessly upon news of his death. In fact, they were like the children of abusive parents who become dependent on the abuse and eventually believe that everything the parents are doing is for their good. This dependency on abuse repeats itself throughout the generations. To break from this is very difficult, requiring a severe rupture from the familiar. Iliana's character, I suggest, can be examined as a case study in what might happen when one is willing to embark on the long and arduous process of confrontation, examination, and rejection. The resulting rupture, as we will see, demands that the past abuses and repression be recognized for what they are and not excused for any reason.

Dominican Diaspora Women's Literary History

In a 1991 essay, Silvio Torres-Saillant, a literary critic and former director of City University of New York's Dominican Studies Institute, claimed, "Dominican writing remains generally relegated to what has been called 'the periphery of the margins'" (Torres-Saillant and Hernández 120). No doubt, much credit must be given to Torres-Saillant's pioneering work against the position Dominicans held outside even other outsiders. But it is safe to claim that more than a decade later, Dominican diaspora writing has entered the domain of important American literatures "bearing witness to the inexorably traumatic immigrant experience of their people" (120). The stories of the Dominican community are multifaceted, rich, inspiring, as well as heartbreaking. These stories, written by Dominicans or by allies of the Dominican community, trace the trajectory of Dominicans to U.S. residency and citizenship. They describe the process of transformation that individuals, families, and communities experience. Especially, the stories function against the egregious belittling of Dominican integrity.

Among the first journalists to cover one of this community's stories for the mainstream media was a Jewish New Yorker, Barbara Fischkin. Her boss at *Newsday* gave her the assignment in the early eighties. A twelve-part monthly series, "A Chronicle of Hope: The Odyssey of the Almonte Family," began publication on April 27, 1986. Her work on the story of this immigrant family who came to New York in sections—first the father, then his wife and various children—won the 1986 Livingston Award for International Reporting. It has since been published as a book, *Muddy Cup: A Dominican Family Comes of Age in a New America*. This story covers the plights of migration and the hardships of life in the Dominican Republic and in Queens, New York. It also points to the successes that can be attained. One of the four children goes on to graduate school. Another one returns to the Dominican Republic, but lives relatively well with help from her family in the United States.

A Dominican literary scholar and translator at York College, Daisy Cocco de Filippis, has engaged in pioneering work of dissemination with her compilations *Poems of Exile and Other Concerns* (1988), *Stories of Washington Heights and Other Concerns of the World* (1994), *Tertuliando/Hanging Out* (1997), and *Documents of Dissidence: Selected Writings by Dominican Women* (2000).

The growing number of titles from Dominican, and Dominican diaspora, women's literature includes *Los débiles* (1912) by Jesusa Alfau; *Yania Tierra* (1981) by Aída Cartagena Portalatín; *Where Horizons Go: Poems* (1998), *The Shadow I Dress In* (2004), and other titles by Rhina Espaillat; *How the García Girls Lost Their Accents* (1991), *In the Time of the Butterflies* (1994), *The Other Side* (1995), *¡Yo!* (1997), and *In the Name of Salomé* (2000), among the many titles by Julia Alvarez; *Soledad* (2001) by Angie Cruz; and *Song of the Water Saints* (2002) by Nelly Rosario.

A dark, inexplicable violence seems to permeate many of these novels. For example, in *In the Time of the Butterflies*, one of the little girls in the boarding school leaves in the middle of the year. Rumor has it that Trujillo has bought her a big mansion and that she has become one of his many young kept women. The girls whisper their speculations in fear, but the nuns do not allow mention of the incident. In *Soledad*, the dark secrets revolve around the family violence. Why does Manolo beat up Soledad's mother all the time? Why does he come on to his sister-in-law? Why does he molest Soledad in the middle of the night? When he falls to his death from a fifth-story window, Soledad does not believe that it was an accident. Her life is shaped by violence in the home, but also by warnings of the dangers that she could confront outside the apartment in Washington Heights, where neighbors like Toe-knee are drug dealers. The warnings of the dangers of the outside world make no sense in light of the abuse and violence the children witness inside their own home. In many ways, this parallels the warnings of dictators—warnings against communists, against delinquents—when they themselves continue a reign of terror based on violence and egregious, continuing human rights violations.

I believe that many of these texts also expose women's struggles for self-affirmation—social, sexual, political—against a backdrop of illiteracy, machismo, and racism. Thus they stress women's possible paths to personhood: self-acceptance, self-esteem, education, financial independence. Could we talk about a new genre of Dominican diaspora women's bildungsromans? For example, Yolanda in *How the García Girls Lost Their Accents* is transformed from a little immigrant girl into an anglophile English professor in the United States. In *Soledad*, the protagonist also experiences a transformation of beliefs and conduct as she negotiates between Washington Heights' Dominican culture and downtown marginal culture. Likewise, Iliana crosses the boundary between her tightly bound family and the less welcoming world of college and life alone, away from that family.

Defying a long tradition of female erasure and joining in a new tradition of female empowerment, Loida Maritza Pérez concludes her novel with the protagonist's emancipation from her fears.

> The tears, when they fell, streamed so fast that Iliana did not bother to wipe them dry. Each of her reasons for returning home was shadowed by the knowledge that her sister would have preferred for her to stay away and by the sudden realization that she had returned not so much to help as to be embraced. She had wanted, more than anything, to belong. Having spent years plotting how to leave only to discover, when she finally did, that she felt as displaced out in the world as in her parents' house, she had made the decision to return and to re-establish a connection with her family so that, regardless of where she went thereafter, she would have comforting memories of home propping her up and lending her the courage to confront the prejudices she had encountered during eighteen months away. (312)

Dominican diaspora women's literature reflects the economic, emotional, and psychological hardships experienced by Dominican diaspora women and their path to freedom from a past that continues to be shrouded by censorship. This literature features the increasing successes of Dominican women, including sociologists Ramona Hernández of the CUNY Center for Dominican Studies and Ramona Peralta of PROFAMILIA in Santo Domingo, and psychotherapist Carmen Inoa Vázquez, coauthor of *The Maria Paradox*, to add to the poets and novelists mentioned. Literature, as has been discussed throughout this book, presents the private stories of families' and individual's struggles to lead a life of dignity, working with respect and emotional nurturance.

The stories to which we are made privy allow us to better understand the importance of political and social work accomplished by organizations both in New York and in Santo Domingo. These organizations and groups, including the Dominican Women's Development Center, the Dominican Women's Caucus, the Association of Progressive Women, Centro de Investigación para la Acción Femenina (CIPAF), Mujer Dominicana (MUDE), Secretaria del Estado de la Mujer, Colectiva Mujer y Salud, and Asociación Dominicana Pro-Bienestar de la Familia (PROFAMILIA) address issues of rape, family violence, and sexism. Often these organizations and groups do not get enough governmental and private support because their work is not valued as much as it should be. A text such as *Geographies of Home* serves to highlight the conditions that necessitate more attention to violence and the fight against it. Together, social work and literary text participate in the mission of attaining human rights.

Literary Cartography of Sexism

Let us now turn to scenes and characters of Pérez's novel to better understand some of the trials of migration and appraise the shadows of sexism. Although Iliana's parents, Papito and Aurelia, have left the destitute Dominican countryside to find better living conditions in the United States, they bring with them and propagate Dominican superstitions, as Iliana's existential crisis signals, which, along with other socioeconomic factors inherent in U.S. hierarchy of race and class, inhibit their success in America. Their knowledge of legal matters and rights in the Dominican Republic was poor, but they have an even more limited understanding of U.S. social codes and law. The family is informed by their past experiences with a repressive dictatorial regime under which people disappeared or were murdered in the night and where policemen raped girls on the streets with impunity. In their new home in the United States, they respond to many social circumstances, including new threats to their safety such as inner-city violence, with heightened fear and distrust. Painfully aware of how girls can be abused, and steeped in a sexist code of honor where girls must be virgins protected by the authority of their fathers and brothers to the point that they have no voice and can exhibit no desire, Papito tries to ingrain fear in his daughters so they will remain within the safe confines of the family. In many ways, his instinct to protect is well warranted. Rape, as well as other violence against women, is still an underpunished crime throughout the world, destroying the integrity of many women and their families.

In other ways, Papito's protectiveness is excessive. Even if Iliana does not demonstrate signs of sexual activity, he is inclined to err on the side of distrust. For example, when she stays late into the night at her gay male friend's house to get some respite from her schizophrenic sister's abuses, Papito will not consider any excuse. He immediately assumes that Iliana was engaged in sex. Rather than talk with her, he accuses her and abuses her further with anger, threats, basic distrust, and physical punishment. He may intend to "protect" his daughter's "honor," but his actions are enactments of domestic violence. In contrast to other men who abandon their families or cheat on their wives, he is a commendable man. Through his character, however, a feminist critique of men in the family is sketched out. Perhaps the author is nuancing men's roles. On the one hand, he is faithful and involved with his family, and this makes him a good person. But that is not enough. On the other hand, he lacks compassion, communication skills, and understanding. He is still violent, despite the supposed reason behind his outbursts.

Aurelia, who defers to her husband, pardons all of Papito's actions because she sees a tired, hardworking man who supports the household to the best of his ability. She views his blind faith in and involvement with the Adventist church as a way to keep order in the house and keep the children off the streets and out of prison. In the text we are informed:

> He thought back to his conversion from the Catholicism of his youth. What had appealed to him about the Adventist doctrine was its specificity in distinguishing right from wrong. In a country where both had shifted according to a tyrant's whims and little had offered relief or hope, religion had granted him salvation, unmediated access to the divine, and steadfast rules by which to live. These he had offered to his children as buffer against poverty and pain. (149)

Papito sees his adherence to the Adventist church as a way to correct the effects of corruption during Trujillo's rule and as a way to mitigate the suffering caused by the poverty he has lived through and continues to experience. He wants to offer his children some kind of moral structure that will save them from the reality they live, but he does not notice that his strict application of Adventist rules mirrors the conditions he wants to avoid. He, like Aurelia, refuses to acknowledge that such extreme restrictions parallel the repression they once lived with in the Dominican Republic. It is left to Iliana to make this observation as she transitions from Dominican-style family loyalties to an independent life in the United States, where an ideology of the individual—the self-made person, against all odds—prevails.

Pérez presents several scenes that allow us to better understand the complicated issue of sexism in Dominican culture and memory, its intersections in diaspora life, and the new emotional pain that these produce for those caught between assimilation and transculturation, where new forms of abuse and sexism complicate the fight for women's rights. In the first scene, Iliana remembers her father bringing home a scented soap in a strawberry wrapper. He was very happy with his purchase, but quickly became infuriated when Iliana insisted that even though the wrapper had strawberries on it, the soap smelled like cinnamon. He yelled:

> "Muchacha de la porra! Admit it! It smells like strawberries!"
> "Cinnamon," Iliana mumbled.
> "What does it smell like?"
> Iliana defiantly braced herself for another blow. "Cinnamon!"
> The back of Papito's hand again flew toward her face. Determined not to cry or cringe, Iliana held her ground.
> "It smells like cinnamon! Why ask if you don't want to know?"
> Her father unhooked his belt and drew it from the loops around his pants. "Sinvergüenza! I'll teach you to disrespect me!"
> "Cinnamon—" Iliana had shouted, blocking out the sound of the belt whizzing toward her and glaring at her father with all of the contempt she could muster. "Cinnamon, cinnamon—" she had chanted, her legs stinging and welts rising as the leather strap landed repeatedly on her thighs. (8)

Not one of Iliana's thirteen siblings stepped in to help her. Her mother refrained from disrespecting her husband as he whipped their daughter for what he called her insolence.

An earlier formative moment for Iliana occurred when she was three years old and walked a mile beyond her yard to sit at the edge of a river and throw rocks. Her disappearance worried her parents, but once reunited with them, she was beaten by her father. Many years later he reminds Iliana, "You were headstrong even then. I had to teach you a lesson so that you'd learn to be afraid. Without fear, anything could've happened to you. It was my responsibility to teach you about danger and keep you safe" (318). Although parents are expected to keep children "safe," and children must allow themselves to be taken care of, this scene underscores a cultural nuance. If a boy had behaved as Iliana did, his parents would have merely considered him precocious. This example accentuates the very different lessons taught under traditional Dominican values: girls must learn fear, while boys must vanquish it, or at least hide it.

Iliana, the only daughter allowed to go to college, is haunted by such lessons of subjugation. It is as if her life experiences have muted her. Her parents and siblings believe that too much education will destroy her possibilities of marriage (even though it is not clear if they believe she has any romantic possibilities, since she is considered too skinny, too tall, too dark, too flat, and generally too masculine). The family back home has many problems she feels she should try to help out with, and school has turned out to be a big disappointment as she encounters racism, such as the scribbling of "nigger" on her dorm door. So, after eighteen months at a college far from home, Iliana is not sure that she has made the right choice for her life, abandoning the strict traditions followed by most of her sisters, who married young and had children. She briefly lets go of her educational goals and thinks about becoming the kind of woman her family expects: a wife and mother at an early age.

Another highly nuanced and revealing passage in *Geographies of Home* encompasses Papito's memory of his first love, as a young man in the Dominican Republic. The nineteen-year-old Papito has had plenty of experience with women. But then he sees Anabelle, a beautiful and chaste young maiden who lives with her widower father and sisters. His desire grows by the day for the woman he cannot touch, or even speak to, because she is so zealously protected by her father. His friends and neighbors advise him to forget Anabelle and find someone within his reach. Instead Papito cleans and furnishes his little house and dresses more neatly, waiting for the appropriate moment to ask Anabelle's father for permission to court her. One night, with a hurricane threatening to bring down his house, Papito is forced to seek safety in the nearby town. As he struggles to make his way through the wind and rain, he is alarmed to see the woman in whom he has invested his dreams wandering into the danger. It is the choice of a shamefully abused woman, a victim of incest that has left her pregnant with her father's child. Anabelle uses the storm as a God-given opportunity to end her life. Papito feels that he has not been a real man. He did not recognize this horrible situation. He was not able to save her from her father's lust or from the storm. This memory haunts Papito. His manhood was tested by a higher power (nature? God?) and, he believes, he failed to prove himself.

Papito's macho expectation that he was responsible for this woman's honor and safety is one example of how heavily sexism weighs on men and their conduct in Dominican society. In contrast, Iliana's sister Rebecca embodies the effects sexism has on women and their place in society. Rebecca's story, while pointing to her weaknesses, also describes her path to self-erasure, self-hatred, and self-destruction. The first in the family to leave the Dominican Republic, like many women before and after her, Rebecca settles in New York, works in a factory, and sends money to her family on the island.[5] Eventually her parents and all of her sisters and brothers follow her to the United States. We would expect that after her sacrifices, she would receive a special place in the family. She has proved that being alone in New York is not a terrible thing. When she tells us that she was a virgin until she was thirty, she also is defending herself. That is, being alone did not lead to promiscuity. Rebecca follows the codes of honor and conduct her family expected and exceeds those expectations by making the family migration possible. But no one recognizes her accomplishments. No one thanks her. Instead, upon arriving in the United States, Papito resumes his role as the paterfamilias, and she is demoted to obedient daughter. She must listen to him and ask permission for everything she wants to do. She is now expected to find a husband and follow tradition. Much to her embarrassment, her two younger sisters marry before she does, and Rebecca feels the pressure to prove her femininity. She must follow the old rules, including living with the family until she marries. Rebecca spirals into a depressive state no one recognizes or understands. This state manifests itself through acts of self-hatred and denigration.

Her story is a very sad one. Rebecca leaves the family home to live out of wedlock with a man who beats her. When he leaves her, she returns to her family in shame. Soon she finds another man, who promises to marry her. He tells her he has a house. Without seeing the house or getting to know the man, Rebecca marries him. For her, marriage will erase the shame of being left behind by her younger sisters and of living out of wedlock with someone who then abandons her. This man she does not know has a dilapidated house, beats her more viciously than the previous lover did, brings junk and chickens into the home, and has sexual relations with other women both away from her and in front of her. Yet she suffers this abuse in silence. She tells her family that she is happy and that things with her husband, Pasión, are good. On her own, she tries to go to work while he is not in the house. But every time he finds out, he seeks her out, makes a scene, and gets her out of work. Pasión admonishes Rebecca: "I may not always provide you with everything you need, but God knows I do my best. And how do you repay me? By shaming me and going out to get yourself a job. By letting the world think I'm not man enough to take care of you myself" (56).

Pasión does not care about Rebecca. His only concern is what others who adhere to sexist macho roles would think of him, even though there is no evidence in the text that anyone is observing him or that he responds to anyone. Pasión beats Rebecca so badly that she has to wait for the bruises to heal before she goes out in public. The only thing she can think is that she is grateful that he has saved her from spinsterhood. "'Pasión owns a house,' she had boasted to those who had called her 'spoiled goods' for moving in with Samuel and had then gloated with compassion after he threw her out" (55). As an American citizen, Pasión offers the dream of wealth and security; as her husband, he provides her with legitimacy. Pasión, Rebecca believes, saves her from the judgment of her community and family. Consequently, she must help him become a better person. She believes that having children will change Pasión. She bears three. But Rebecca has lost touch with reality. She enters a world of cycles of abuse and neglect. To defend her position, she recalls how she saw people who were assumed dead during Trujillo's reign of terror come back from prison. She considers that a miracle had taken place then—the resurrection of the disappeared—and waits for a miracle to occur to Pasión. Nothing changes Pasión. He is increasingly gone, and the family lives in squalor. Rebecca's bitterness makes her irrational. She will not listen to the children's teachers when they ask her to watch their hygiene. Instead she goes into a tirade, screaming that she will raise her children as she sees fit. The children, in turn, do not eat enough. They begin to act like prisoners, hiding what little food they can get their hands on, in case there is no food the next day. To all this Rebecca's mother, the children's grandmother Aurelia, turns a blind eye.

Aurelia waits for Rebecca to leave Pasión and move back in with her and Papito. She does not call social services or demand that the children be put in her custody while Rebecca gets counseling. By Dominican custom, problems of the house are private matters. Rebecca comes from a culture where a good wife must do everything to keep her husband, where women baby men and forgive them because they are not considered capable of behaving better.[6] Rebecca goes mad, and her mother remains powerless, on the margins till the end, when she gets chickens to pluck and performs *brujería*, witchcraft, to eliminate her son-in-law. The only power to which Aurelia can resort is supernatural. In the realm of the spirits, Aurelia is not restrained by the conventions of macho culture. She thus finds the power to beat Pasión down in a flurry of chicken feathers.

Iliana's mind is populated by memories of punishment at the hands of Papito, as well as stories of his failure to save the honor of a beautiful maiden in the Dominican Republic, Rebecca's self-destruction, and Aurelia's self-sacrifice. These memories prevent her from moving on with her own life. While living in the college dorm, she hears the voices of her dysfunctional past. These voices tell her that she might burn in hell, she is needed at home, and she has abandoned her duty as a daughter by going away to college. This internal psychological conflict is compounded by present threats such as anonymous graffiti on her dorm door calling her a "nigger" and others suggesting that she does not belong. She decides to return, to find a home and family that will give her the strength and pride she needs to tackle the challenges of college and the ostracism of racism.

Where Is the Home? Where Is the Love?

Throughout the story, home does not offer Iliana the support she dreams of. Summer in the family house in Brooklyn does not help her become the daughter/woman she believes she is expected to become. This situation, presented in an early moment in the text, incites me to ponder what the title *Geographies of Home* could mean. Could it refer to the many ways a home can be defined? Or could it point to the numerous routes that lead to home? How do we explain the way the idea of home—which is usually equated with safety—is juxtaposed to the nightmarish happenings we read about throughout the text? The focus on "home," along with the way the scenes play out in the novel, obliges me to consider Freud's work on the *unheimlich*, the uncanny. I propose that we reflect on the home that Iliana returns to as haunted by a history of violence that repeats and reproduces itself in many, often predictable, ways.

Freud tells us that "the uncanny is that class of the frightening which leads back to what is known of old and long familiar" (220). He continues his compelling essay by quoting a series of definitions of *unheimlich*. Those that stand out the most for me are:

> English: . . . Uncomfortable, uneasy, gloomy, dismal, uncanny, ghastly; (of a house) haunted; (of a man) a repulsive fellow.
> Spanish: . . . Sospechoso, de mal agüero, lúgubre, siniestro. (221)

Freud then proceeds to quote definitions of *heimlich*. Of particular note, for my purposes, is

> II. Concealed, kept from sight, so that others do not get to know of or about it, withheld from others. (223)

Finally, Freud concludes:

> What interests us most in this long extract is to find that among its different shades of meaning the word *heimlich* exhibits one which is identical with its opposite, *unheimlich*. What is *heimlich* thus comes to be *unheimlich*. . . . In general we are reminded that the word *heimlich* is not unambiguous, but belongs to two sets of ideas, which, without being contradictory, are yet very different: on the one hand, it means what is familiar and agreeable, and on the other, what is concealed and kept out of sight. (224–25)

In Pérez's text, the uncanny, this eery feeling, is exemplified in numerous instances. At college Iliana hears voices. These voices are both familiar—they are her mother and her father—and haunting, as they do not allow her to be at college without feeling a deep sense of guilt. From the outset we are made aware of how home—family, past, history, Dominican culture—harrows Iliana. Iliana returns to a bedeviled house of familiar scenes and experiences, which are also discomforting. Iliana's home harbors fears, illness, and secrets no one can uncover. The shadows are laden with the repetition of violations that reproduce a colonial, machista, racist past on individual bodies, in the private sphere of the home, and in the extended community space of the church.

For example, Marina's story and its place in the family saga are multi-layered. Her character bears the weight of many social, racial, and gender problems prevalent in repressive regimes as well as in strict religious traditions. Marina is a madwoman in the basement who contrasts sharply to the classic figure of the madwoman in the attic. The original madwoman was carefully crafted in *Jane Eyre* (1847) by Charlotte Brontë. Other madwomen characters were developed in "The Yellow Wallpaper" (1892) by Charlotte Perkins Gilman and *Wide Sargasso Sea* (1966) by Jean Rhys. The madwoman figure has played a prominent role in feminist discussions of the way women have been historically and physically marginalized.

Marina is a dark woman from the Caribbean who cannot fit into the world of white businesspeople in Wall Street, where she works as a secretary and dreams of marrying a rich white man. She tells Iliana, "You know how black men are. . . . They're lazy as shit and undependable" (38). She continues to negate the complete identity of the woman she sees in the mirror. Marina insists, "I'm Hispanic, not black" (38). She has adopted the anti-Haitian and anti-African ideologies crafted and affirmed by Trujillo. She accepts her sister Beatriz's criticism that "No one . . . would ever consider her attractive. Not with her baboon nose and nigger lips" (42). Marina comes to hate herself. She scrubs herself with Brillo pads, leaving her skin wounded, in an attempt to cleanse herself of her dirt, her color. In a basement far away from a racist world, she immolates herself. The cultural history denying the pride of African heritage shapes her askew world, which further denies her self. She is unaware of the fact that "Dominican society is the cradle of blackness in the Americas. . . . A demographic assessment taking account of racial distinctions today would show that blacks and mulattoes make up nearly 90% of the Dominican Republic's close to eight million inhabitants" (Torres-Saillant and Hernández 143). Marina suffers psychological pain to the point of madness. Her body is a map on which we can read how the existence of an important African heritage has been unmade by centuries of racism (in the Dominican Republic and in the United States) and decades of denial (Trujillo, Balaguer, and so on).

Theoretically, Marina's madness suggests the madness provoked by the denial of one's self. Her madness physically obliterates the body that has been historically shunned. Her robust womanhood, the deep color of her skin, and her sensual needs were squelched by Dominican racism and sexism. She was further disembodied when she confronted the same racism and sexism in her host nation, the land that was supposed to offer her freedom. Marina's case is beyond recovery, because she is trapped by her family's protection and lack of understanding. Papito once suggested that she would be cured of her madness if she were married. He continued that she could find a husband in the Dominican Republic, where men are willing to immediately marry a woman who has lived in the United States. Once she had children (he never mentioned regular sex) and the overwhelming responsibilities of taking care of a husband and family, she would not have time to be mad. Aurelia rejected this idea, but followed all other cues from her husband. In strict traditional cultures, women are responsible for keeping the family fiber intact, even at the price of denying an illness as serious as schizophrenia within the family.

Therefore, despite professional recommendations that she be institutionalized, Marina lives at home. Aurelia will not let her leave the house because this would mean that she was unable to take care of her own daughter. The admission would make her look like a bad mother, a failed woman, who could not keep the family together. Letting Marina get the necessary attention would be, she and Papito believe, the beginning of the disintegration of the family. The real disintegration exists in the way rules of family privacy are followed with such vehemence. Aurelia's quiet matriarchal position is briefly exhibited in the scene that follows Marina's attempted suicide and consequent hospitalization. She warns Papito that if Marina dies, it will be his fault because he ignored her to save face with his congregation. Papito seems lost and scared. He does not want Aurelia's wrath. He prays for Marina's recovery and for his wife's return. Both wishes are granted. However, his remorse and repentance prove to be short-lived. The presence of dysfunctional codes of conduct in this family is disturbing, to say the least. Papito resorted to religion to give his children a set of rules and regulations that, he believed, would keep them from prostitution and jail. But the church is not a panacea against evil. The story tells us quite the contrary. The church is one more haven for machismo and repression. In a Sabbath sermon, Pastor Rivera asks the congregation, "But tell me. Can the sanctity of marriage be upheld when men are mercilessly tricked by women?" (105). The listener (or reader) might expect these words to herald an important topic in religion such as adultery. But no. The sermon, pronounced in the holy space of a church pulpit by a respected preacher and titled "The Virtues of Marriage," could be interpreted as a joke if the narrator did not underline its severity. The pastor extemporizes:

> Let me give you an example. A man meets a woman. She has the smoothest skin, the reddest lips. And her hair, Lord, is the softest he's ever touched. It frames her face and makes her look prettier than any

painting he's laid eyes on in his entire life. Then there are her lashes, fluttering like the wings of birds whenever he comes near and making him feel like he's soaring toward heaven. She is beautiful, more beautiful than he had imagined a woman could ever be. (105)

But, the pastor continues, things change on the couple's wedding night. Something goes wrong when the man sees his bride:

> Who is this creature daring to impersonate his wife? Who is this being with a helmet of green and blue plastic things around which strands of its hair are wrapped? And its face! Mercy me! It is pock-marked and creviced like the moon! (106)

The message of the sermon is clear: the pastor is giving men tacit permission to seek beauty where true beauty can be found. In other words, if men have been tricked, they are within their rights to trick their wives and have extramarital affairs. Iliana, in the congregation, imagines that the pastor has tired of his aging wife with her artificial beauty aids, has strayed and got caught, and is now justifying himself by giving his congregation a twisted message. Others laugh, but Iliana is infuriated. This moment in fiction exposes the codes of conduct to which women are subjected.

In his *Memorias* the late Dominican president Joaquín Balaguer adulates one of Trujillo's sisters, known as Doña Japonesa. He describes her as "una mujer dulce, con la voz suave y con el trato de seda"—a sweet woman, with a soft voice, and a silken manner (191). Women are trapped in a long tradition of "softness," synonymous with silence. Beauty, as the pastor points out, is fleeting, and men are always the victims of lies and tricks. Women in Spanish Caribbean culture are expected to dress up. The streets of Caribbean ethnic neighborhoods are filled with women with long, bright red nails (real or not), tight pants that show off their wares, and high heels that may be a man's fetish but only ruin women's backs and feet. Women are expected to wear makeup and pretty dresses, look feminine, and be a subservient pleasure for their *hombres*, their men. A woman is valued highly when she cultivates her femininity.

Pérez exposes the church as one more place that represses individual thought and subjugates women. To that end, she also describes a time when Iliana's schizophrenic sister Marina is thrown out of church. Marina, who is described as very fat, dark, thick-lipped, and wide-nosed—all traits, Pérez tells us, that are ugly by Dominican standards—begins to act as if she were possessed.[7] She sways and screams and makes a commotion akin to a public orgasm. No doubt, in certain kinds of churches, her behavior would have been welcomed as a sign of communion with God. In an Adventist service, however, her conduct is blamed on Satan. Papito, a congregation leader, and his son watch Marina with disdain. The church does not accept such behavior. Marina is shaming the family and has to be eliminated from that "sacred" space. Aurelia is once again silent; she cannot defend her daughter. Others stand by passively as Marina is accused of being possessed by the Devil. After Marina leaves, Papito is relieved that the church space is once again peaceful. Aurelia is worried, but she stands by her man and stays in the church for lunch festivities. No one recognizes the dimensions of Marina's illness, despite her previous suicide attempt and prolonged hospitalization. Marina is a victim of silence and of myth.

The story of *Geographies of Home* is clouded by Trujillo's legacy. Scenes of tacit unholy messages from the pulpit are reminiscent of Trujillo's use of the church to make his own nefarious message known. "Dios y Trujillo" had to be called out at every service. Trujillo was like God. Anyone, priests included, who did not honor his godliness would be punished. For example, the government required that a picture of Trujillo be hung prominently at the entrance of every house. Trujillo manipulated the populace via the church sermons. But the populace is composed of individuals who may find a way out of internalized repression.

Let us look at the sequence of scenes that leads Iliana to demythify the mysterious past—traditions of machismo and racist culture—and allows her to confront it without fear or shame. Throughout the text we see Iliana suffer because she does not fulfill the expectations of womanhood placed on her. There are things she cannot change: she is thinner and taller than her culture's ideal type. And she refuses to change what she could: she pulls her hair back in a low bun and wears long skirts and flowing shirts that do not reveal any of her body parts. She only starts wearing lipstick in college, when her best friend, Ed, points out that it is becoming and that, by Western standards, she is an incredibly attractive woman blessed with height, slimness, high cheekbones, and a natural sway in her walk that models would dream of emulating. Iliana is baffled by the contradictions of the two cultures: she is deemed ugly by one and beautiful by the other. She recalls the pastor's sexist sermon at the Adventist church and has no doubt that he would rebuke her androgynous look. Everyone in her family tells her that she is masculine. Her brother Gabriel asks, in all seriousness, if anyone can tell whether she is a man or a woman, since she wears no makeup and has thick brows.

Marina is convinced that Iliana is actually a man. Later, in the middle of the night, in the middle of one of her dangerous fits of delirium, Marina attacks her. She jumps on Iliana, thrusts her hand up between Iliana's legs, grips, and pulls frantically. Iliana screams in horror. Her brother Tico eventually comes to remove Marina's big body from Iliana's limp limbs. Oddly, Iliana is frozen calm. She goes to the bathroom to clean the blood off. She tells herself that she understands and forgives her sister, that she can survive this horrible violation of her body and this final confirmation of her sister's madness in silence. "This was the litany that buoyed her thoughts. Bodies recovered. Wounds healed. Scars faded and left no mark" (287). Like Rebecca, like Aurelia, Iliana tells herself that women must be strong, withstanding and silencing the most unnatural abuses.

In deep physical pain and emotionally numbed, Iliana goes back to her bed. She eyes her sister and wants to believe that the worst is over. But it is not. Marina attacks Iliana with greater vehemence, groping into Iliana's vagina, determined to pull out a penis. In even greater pain, Iliana lurches upstairs to find some respite from her sister's attacks. The next day she goes looking for Ed in Manhattan. She returns in the early morning with a resolution to not become the martyr and victim of domestic violence and unconditional sexism. But the worst is yet to come.

When Iliana returns, she is attacked one last time, in a predictable manner that, nonetheless, she does not expect. Her father is waiting for her like a possessed demon:

> His arm swung up so fast that she had no opportunity to move out of its reach.
> "Shameless hussy! Whore!"
> Iliana heard the sharp sound of his palm as it landed on her face. Yet she felt no pain, only rage. Rage potent enough to swell her veins and cause one of them to throb rebelliously on her forehead.
> "It's not bad enough one of your sisters has gone and lost her mind and another has crawled back to her husband. No! You have to stay out till all hours of the night like you too have no sense!"
> Papito again lashed out with the strength of his accumulated anger and frustration. Iliana remained where the force of his hand had knocked her against a wall. The words *hussy* and *whore* resounded in her ears, overriding pain and searing a path along her brain. (313)

This scene, albeit in a different context, reminded me of Pasión's beating of Rebecca and screaming that she shamed him. In both cases the men reacted to some artificial law of respect and honor that they determined the women had broken. The men acted within what they believed was their right to punish. Both husband and father believed violence to be within their right of action. The women were supposed to accept this punishment without question. Why not? Generalissimo Trujillo and his band of thugs took the same liberties with women. Violence was imprinted on the Dominican Republic during its colonial history. The conquistadors had also raped, pillaged, killed, and abused in the name of God and honor.

The final scene of macho bravado, when Papito ignores Iliana's suffering and her victimization at her sister's hands, serves as the impetus for Iliana's awakening from guilt and from the grip of sexism. It is at this point in the narrative that Iliana reconsiders her relationship to her family and begins to act out of self-love and self-respect. At this pivotal moment, I suggest, the message of the text should be interpreted as: the past may haunt you if you ignore it, but if it is violent and demeaning, it destroys you when you repeat it. In his considerations of *unheimlich*, Freud adds that "for animism, magic and sorcery, the omnipotence of thoughts, man's attitude to death, involuntary repetition and the castration complex comprise practically all the factors which turn something frightening into something uncanny" (243). The frightening circumstances Iliana returns to when she goes "home" are uncanny precisely because they are involuntarily, and unconsciously, repeated. Machista codes of conduct repeat themselves. And spaces that should encourage love and family solidarity, such as the church, deny women respect, recalling a long complicity between church and repressive governments in the Dominican Republic. Iliana is frightened by the voices she hears at college. She returns "home," which is familiar but insufferable. Her experience at home is veiled by a repeated message that the past will hurt if you ignore it. Initially she sets out to unearth that past, but her experiences and observations lead her to recognize a legacy of sexism, racism, and violence. The mysterious past is, in effect, a dysfunctional present. The *unheimlich* is transformed. Home must be rendered safe or abandoned.

Iliana represents possibility through responsibility. She takes action and escapes from the violence that bleeds into her present life. She does not let herself be broken:

> *No, No. I will not fall or flinch. I will not let you or anyone else ever knock me down again. I may have been molded from your flesh but this body is mine and mine alone. You will not make me be ashamed*

*of it as my sister did. You will not make me recoil from it or renounce
my life as I thought I would do. I will survive all this. I will walk out
of this house erect. I will amount to more than you can ever hope to
be and you will rue the day you saw me leave.* (313)

She leaves the broken home that is no longer haunted in her imagination
but, rather, is simply dysfunctional. Early the next morning she takes her
suitcases and says good-bye to her mother, who awaits her departure in sad
resignation. Even so, Aurelia communicates Papito's position one last time.
If Iliana leaves, Aurelia admonishes, her prideful father will not allow her
to return. Aurelia asks Iliana to forgive her father because he does not
understand his outbursts and reactions. He did not know that Iliana remained a virgin during the eighteen months she lived away. He did not
understand the depth of the violation Iliana experienced at her sister's
hands. He did not understand Iliana's need for support and nurturance. He
only understood old codes of manhood that did not allow women to have
needs or opinions.

Aurelia is a prisoner in her own house, but Iliana has found the confi-
dence to leave. She decides to go back to school in the fall. While she cannot
change her family or her history, she can change herself. Her freedom lies
in self-respect, self-honor, and hard-earned self-esteem. She is not a defeated woman, but rather a person, a citizen in the world, with rights and
goals. Unlike Aurelia, she will not remain silent. Unlike Rebecca, she will
not deprecate herself. Unlike Marina, she will not fall prey to madness.
Iliana will take responsibility for her own life and face challenges with
pride and strength. She is the daughter of the diaspora, distinguishing between old-world myths and present realities.

The message of the text *Geographies of Home* can be interpreted on
many different levels. One significant reading suggests that home is one's
inner self. I propound that the Iliana character delineates a possible trajectory in which self-love is discovered despite, or perhaps because of, a history of self-hatred and violence. But there is a critical twist that necessarily
complicates this contention: "*Heimlich* also has the meaning of that which
is obscure, inaccessible to knowledge" (Freud 226). Iliana never finds the
past that her grandmother mentions; not only is digging it up impossible,
but that past has led to dysfunctional behavior in the present. Iliana's
home—homeland, casa, patria, family—is plagued by uncanny memory
that is buried and irretrievable. The only route to home—the inner self
that exists in the present, freed from the mysteries of the past—is via a
conscious act of letting go. The future must be forged now, and the repeti-

tion of violence cannot be tolerated. The Iliana character serves as a model of the way one can choose to halt the projection of a mysterious past that is nothing other than a trap and/or an excuse to repeat violence.

Defying Erasure, Discovering Human Potential

I am looking forward to the new directors' success in organizing and cleaning up the National Archive. Still, I will never know how much has been lost over the years from the archives. I don't know if we will ever see Balaguer's famous blank page, or if it existed. I do know that writers, such as Loida Maritza Pérez, challenge violence and its repetition. Social change is impossible without knowledge. People who reject their experiences are erased by the very history they deny. However, when there is no way to retrieve a past that has been efficiently recast, trying to unlock the secrets of that past can prove frustrating, at the very least. Pérez's protagonist Iliana faces the challenge of understanding that. Since her story is missing so many pieces, it is only when she stops accepting mysterious evocations of a hidden past as acceptable excuses for violence that she is liberated from the presentness of the past and its ever-present reproduction of violence. The narrator succeeds in making us feel the intense frustration of denied history. That is, we, as readers, are deeply frustrated by the notes of a past that we expect to be revealed within the text, a past that neither the narrator nor we will ever know. This renders Iliana's final departure the more meaningful. It is not her history she rejects; it is the repetition of the violence of the past in the present that she renounces. By not entertaining the repetition of different modes of violence, and by situating the memory of the experience of violence in a real past, she gives herself the promise of a simple present and a possible future.

Since Iliana's family and national history do not offer her a concrete knowledge of herself, she learns to create her own space in the world and her own history. She cultivates her personhood with what she discovers and how she decides to interpret it. This is an act that defies the perfidious unmaking of women and minorities through decades of violence and negations of that violence. In the end, Iliana decides to go back to college. She is not abandoning her family or her roots; instead, she is finding her place in the world as an active and educated citizen who can defy silenced horrors, sexism, and violence in both Dominican and U.S. culture. Pérez's characters elucidate the evils of sexism and violence, and her text serves as a much-needed memorial that honors the strength, struggles, resistance, and successes of Dominican women everywhere.

6

Conclusion

Present Memories

Like a scar
attached to
the aches of
nighttime,
Anne Frank
visits me often.

I know we live in memory, or in the metaphor of memory, or in
memory that does not allow oblivion or in the imagination of
memory.
Marjorie Agosín

Haiti and the Dominican Republic share one island and many migrations.
Unfortunately, they also share the experience of constant economic, political, and natural devastation. In 2004, on the bicentennial of Haitian independence, constitutional president Jean-Bertrand Aristide was escorted out
of office under the protection of the United States military. Opposition
leaders took over a country plagued by disillusion, poverty, and violence.
Next door in the Dominican Republic, newly elected president Leonel
Fernández took office democratically but immediately faced a potential fis-
cal default. In both countries, shameless financial fraud has left the people
with tears of desperation. Their torn-up lives find little respite from dismal
living conditions. This is, of course, not the entire picture. A few live in
relative comfort on both sides of the island. Recent pieces in the *Sun Sen-
tinel* underscore, for example, how Dominicans in the diaspora look forward to returning to their island because they find that life there is simpler, more family-focused, and more leisurely.

Perhaps nothing can symbolize the shared fate and common suffering
of the diverse peoples of Hispaniola than the twin scourges of natural di-

saster and poverty. When hurricanes blow over the Caribbean, they buffet the poor on both sides of the island, without regard for language or national identity. In 2004 some 200 milliliters of rain fell in twenty-four hours on Jimaní, a small border town in the south. This arid area of the Dominican Republic usually registers 600 milliliters per year.[1] On June 7 Tony Pichardo, communications officer for the Jesuit Refugee Service in the Dominican Republic, circulated an article about the devastation caused by unusual rainfall: "The torrid downpours left more than 400 dead, with a further 374 reported missing, 250 wounded, and more than 900 damaged houses, according to one official report" (1). Of interest are the comments proffered by the interviewees in the article. One Alfredo Paredes, a small businessman who lost his entire investment, lamented that the Dominican state ignored these disasters, although they can happen again in other places throughout the country. Paredes's comment reminds me of the schoolteacher that Freddy Prestol Castillo remembered in his novel-testimony. Poor border towns of the Dominican Republic hold limited interest for the urban elite and the government.

Pichardo's informative essay articulates issues that recall some of the problems that seem to repeat themselves throughout the course of Haitian-Dominican frontier history:

> According to human rights NGO the Dominican-Haitian Cultural Center (CCDH) the exact number of people affected by the River Soleil's turbulent waters will never be known by Dominican authorities, simply because the majority are of Haitian descent. Executive director Antonio Poló said: "As most Haitians do not have official papers that define their status, nobody knows who, or even how many people, have died. Their names will never be known." (1)

In legal terms, it seems, Haitians are still undocumented, and therefore do not form part of a very important official history in the Dominican Republic. The frontier regions are, nonetheless, critical areas of history and memory for both Haiti and the Dominican Republic. The response to the recent overflow of the River Soleil highlights the peaceful coexistence between ethnic Haitians, whether resident or migrant, and Dominicans. Pichardo's report points to the selflessness with which Haitians have come across the border to help their neighbors, bringing food and helping to recover the bodies of the dead:

> Jefferson, a 45-year-old Haitian, was one of those who took food to the Dominicans. "We are all brothers" was his sole explanation for

why he helped the survivors. Other compatriots, such as truck drivers who arrived at Jimaní at dawn, were the first to offer aid, according to residents. The truck drivers dived into the water and rescued people to help the town. They returned with water and even offered the food they were carrying. Many Haitians of Fort Parisien have continued to cooperate with Jimaní to mitigate the tragedy. Here solidarity has overcome prejudice. Dominican and Haitian corpses were buried together without distinction. (2)

The report underscores the way that the disaster has affected both sides and the extent of solidarity—"brotherhood"—that it has inspired. Since the two nations share one island, natural disasters affect both peoples, as do political violence and corruption, making them one in their efforts to survive and/or recover from the tragic damage brought upon their already difficult lives.[2]

Repeating a powerful scene in the history of the Dominican border, in 2004 many victims were buried, without names or individual histories, together, in an effort to mitigate contamination to the riverbed caused by rotting corpses. The image of bodies with no names in an unmarked grave recalls the first chapter of this book. Edwidge Danticat imagines the lives of people in the frontier region, giving them names and personal narratives that allow us to envision the simple human lives our neighbors far away might lead. Perhaps it is at this critical intersection between the desperate economic and sociopolitical conditions of the past and the equally desperate conditions of the present that the question of memory arises. Whose memory gets written about? Why specific memories and not others? Why is violence such a fundamental element of Hispaniola's memory?

It is my contention that diaspora writers—who feel as connected to their island of descent as to their new homelands—are haunted by the ongoing strife experienced by the countries that shaped them: Haiti, the Dominican Republic, the United States, and the interrelated, overlapping spaces in these three countries. Confronted with continuing hardships in their homelands, as well as newfound injustices in their new worlds, they are tormented by images of violence, like the bodies of those who did not survive the treacherous escape by boat, washing up on Florida's shores. And they are fixated on experiences of violence originating in the ignoble and manipulative exploitation and interventions of the United States, violence that is, arguably, responsible for the creation of Haitian and Dominican diasporas in the first place. Finally, these authors are inspired by transecting histories of endurance, survival, and resistance in both their native lands and the United States. They remember that the Dominican Republic has one of the oldest feminist movements in the Americas and that the civil rights movement in the United States has informed notions of citizenship throughout the Americas. The authors of these diasporas write stories of pain in an attempt to explain their positions, informed by continuing crises in Hispaniola and by economic/racial assault in their host countries.

Belonging emotionally, and perhaps legally, to two countries, diaspora writers offer unique stories of pain (*dolor/douleur*) that beg for a space of mourning (*duelo/deuil*). But this remembering and mourning are not the extent of their political interventions. The writers of the Haitian and Dominican diaspora confront their own political responsibilities, looking back to the great struggles that their ancestors led—the wars of independence—and engaging in a contemporary fight for human rights. Edwidge Danticat, whose writing life and literary production are committed to two nations and two memories, with multiplying experiences of violence caused by natural disaster, poverty, coups d'état, pillaging, and the like, still hopes that the constructive side of the human heart will prevail.

The tasks of disclosure, mourning, and social activism are international, recognizing a globalized world where struggles for justice are more and more closely interrelated. But the literature of the Haitian and Dominican diaspora is also local—to the islands and to the United States. Often from within the United States, this literature does not allow the particular problems of these tiny nations to be forgotten within the larger framework of global misery.

Hispaniola's diaspora memories expose both the pasts and the presents that haunt a new generation of Haitian and Dominican writers. It is precisely by linking the pain of the past to the injustice of the present that some—Cadet, Danticat, Díaz—become energetically involved with human rights projects. Literature as a vehicle that incites human rights action, I claim, is defined by present memories. In the present, the memories are both reminders of horror and memorials to underscore survival, resistance, and possible recuperation from haunting violations.

Throughout the research and writing of *The Tears of Hispaniola: Haitian and Dominican Diaspora Memory* I have attempted to show the significance of literature as an agent that intervenes in society beyond the strict realm of the aesthetic act. I have been interested in showing how the analyzed texts participate in the world on behalf of causes of personal liberation and social transformation; and I have emphasized the ways in which autobiography and fiction create possible routes toward healing, understanding, and sociopolitical action through the exposition of violence, trauma, and pain. Unfortunately, my initial utopian vision of literature as the rescuer of humanity is restrained by realities such as the market—which is often interested in stories of violence, and which drives what gets published and how it gets sold—the limitations of memory and setbacks to human rights initiatives.

Andreas Huyssen has noted that some historians are uncomfortable with the "surfeit of memory in contemporary culture, raising serious questions about the depth and the effects of our obsessions with memory" (95). These historians are skeptical, he suggests, worrying that the present is held "hostage to the past" but that easy political or commercial renderings of the past are ultimately unsatisfying. Huyssen counters that the imperfections of memory do not undermine its political potential: "memory and amnesia always exist side by and remain part of a political struggle" (95). He concludes that "human rights activism in the world depends very much on the depth and the breadth of memory discourses in the public media" (95).

That is, despite recent scholarly attempts to trivialize memory discourse into a literary fashion of the 1990s, despite certain problems relating literary memory to actual human rights justice, and despite the strategic amnesia that always parallels a focus on memory, Huyssen still believes in the power of memory. And I agree with him. Were I to jump on the bandwagon and say that memory writing is a passing trend of the 1990s—or, worse, that the consideration of memory by the academy has been overdone and picked fully clean—then I would preclude an important critical study of national and personal histories. I would ignore writings that lead to much-needed transcultural and transhistoric communication, denunciation, and revelations for the Caribbean and its diasporas, in a global context.

Ultimately, I have ended up with stories of tears, *lágrimas y rupturas*. The metaphor of tears signals the duality of memory. For example, memory can be liberating but it can be suffocating. Memory can lead to resolutions, but it can be the excuse for repeated violations. Memory is always tainted by forgetting. Like tears, it calls forth both object and action. As object, memory is a memorial; as action, it is the processing of the past. I have proposed that autobiography, fiction, and testimony are sites of memory. Through in-depth textual readings, situated in the conundrums of history and against a backdrop of contemporary human rights considerations, I have examined the functions of memory in Haitian and Dominican diaspora writing. I have suggested that certain literature in the diaspora can be interpreted as a literary memorial to difficult sociocultural losses. These literary memorials incite global conversations about the effects of violence on individuals, communities, and nations. Furthermore, I have argued that the memory of the experience of violence can be both debilitating and empowering. Traumatic memory is crippling; in contrast, active memory can be empowering if, and when, it leads to emotional and/or judicial redress.

By interpreting the characters and stories of specific novels, I hope to have led readers toward a deeper understanding of the complex, and sometimes contradictory, nature of memory for Haitian and Dominican diaspora communities. The past may be static or forgotten, but its interpretation is forever dynamic. Consequently, as I have become engulfed in stories of the Caribbean (from the islands, and on newly formed and sometimes metaphoric islands in the United States), I have come to understand the forces set in motion by the trans-Atlantic African slave trade, which shaped a major, painful, and violent diaspora whose legacy still torments us, and by the colonial mechanisms of dehumanization, plunder, and terror. Indeed, we live in a culture of memory; that memory is critical to how identity is negotiated, how communities are structured, how families function, and how the world responds to different national and international crises. Arguably, migrations from the Caribbean have shaped a new reality for a growing Pan-Caribbean diaspora population in the United States. Our communities, although often distanced from each other by language, are also united by a common history of violence and its memory. I propose that this book serve, like an old iron portal in the Caribbean, as a threshold through which new dialogue and deep meditation can begin and continue.

With *The Tears of Hispaniola* I suggest that we rethink the function of memory through the stories of the Haitian and Dominican diaspora. And I conclude that the future holds hope only if we oppose the insidiousness of violence, and fight for political justice and social change.

Notes

Introduction: The Tears of Hispaniola

1. Of course, this could be said of any immigrant community. I mention it to counter general myths that all Haitians are poor and illiterate. To a certain degree, many Haitian migrations are political as well as economic. The two are not mutually exclusive. For more information on Haitians in the diaspora, see Laguerre's *Diasporic Citizenship*. His detailed research includes numbers of migrants between 1982 and 1995. He notes that the largest number of Haitians went to New York City, and some are not included in official census counts because the census has no accurate way of counting illegal immigration. An earlier study that focuses on Haitians in New York City is Laguerre's *American Odyssey*.

2. "The number of Dominicans admitted under permanent status to the United States rose, from 4,603 in 1962 to 10,683 [in 1963]. . . . This number increased to more than 16,000 during the 1970s and to more than 30,000 during the 1980s. Similarly, since 1983 the number of permanent residencies granted to Dominicans has exceeded the 20,000 per-country limit set by the United States. In 1991 and 1992, the number of Dominicans admitted to the United States grew to more than 40,000 each year" (Hernández 22–23).

3. Reinaldo Arenas incorporated into the autobiographical *Antes que anochezca* his own death and the blame for it as well.

4. Most studies refer to Haiti or the Dominican Republic. Pioneering texts that examine the two nations comparatively include Eugenio Matibag's 2003 political science text *Haitian-Dominican Counterpoint* and Michele Wucker's 1999 sociocultural study *Why the Cocks Fight*. Still, to date the literary production of these two nations' diaspora has not been reviewed comparatively.

5. While working on this book, I came across Florence Bellande-Robertson's *Marassa Concept*, in which she offers an impressive study of *Les Chemins de Loco-Miroir* (1990) by Lilas Desquiron. Reading the pages of her investigation, I felt solidarity: someone else also believes in the power of the novel!

Through her analysis, she probes the depths of Haitian *vodou* rituals comprehensively. Danticat calls her the perfect reader because of the respect with which she has entered the novel, thus offering a poetic text that exposes the conflicts inherent in Haiti's bipolar society. In the following pages I engage a larger project with the same kind of curiosity and respect, and I have taken every care to try to be the "perfect" (and humble) reader of the works I herein explore.

6. Critic Pierre-Raymond Dumas underscores how Haitian diaspora literature focuses on the image of a tortured country, visceral attachments to a native land, and feelings of powerlessness; see *Panorama.*

7. These two nations that occupy the same island have intersecting and diverse histories as well as vastly different perceptions of those accounts and their impact on the present. For example, Haiti has a long history of political involvement and consciousness in nation-forming discourse. Haiti was the first free black nation in the Americas in 1804. But the Dominican Republic has a complicated national history in this respect. The Dominican Republic requested to be recolonized by Spain after the long and treacherous Haitian presence led by President Jean Pierre Boyer. He occupied Spanish Haiti in 1822 and won the Dominican battle of independence in 1844. Since then, the Dominican Republic's national identity has been imagined in contrast to Haiti.

For example, in the twentieth century Trujillo and his successor, Joaquín Balaguer, cultivated an anti-Haitian ideology that affirmed the Dominican nation as Spanish and indigenous in order to further deny its evident African ancestry. This, again, was in direct opposition to Haiti's national image, where African ancestry is celebrated. A strong similarity, however, stands out in how the world identifies these two nations: both continue to undermine the rights of the individual. In effect, the stories that are used to define Haiti and the Dominican Republic are often based on overused clichés that are ultimately ahistorical, facile, grand statements that do not honor the dual and intertwining realities of Hispaniola's people. This creates a tension in memory and representation, which I explore.

8. Found at www.hoy.com.do, accessed 9 June 2004.

9. See Raoul Peck's *L'Homme sur les quais* for an excellent filmic representation of this point. In 1994 Peck was awarded the Nestor Almendros Prize by Human Rights Watch in New York, and in 2001 he received its Lifetime Achievement Award.

10. Turits's account informs us that those killed were mostly small farm workers (161). Does Danticat use literary license to tell her story? Or does the uncle remember it to be in Dajabón when in fact he cut cane somewhere else?

11. Prestol Castillo, 28. See also Jiménez Sabater, *Más datos.*

12. For an excellent study of the present-ification of the past exposed through literature and film, referring to Franco's Spain, see Moreiras Menor, *Cultura Herida.* Huyssen, *Present Pasts,* also makes this point with respect to architecture and national monuments.

13. See also Felman and Laub, *Testimony.*

14. The issue of memory is pivotal here. In conversation with friends both in the Dominican Republic and in Miami, some people actually remember the Trujillo years with pride. They claim that the streets were safer then than they are now and that they miss that.

Chapter 1. Meanings of Memory: A Literary Intervention to Confront Persistent Violence

1. This latter point has been greatly disputed in recent scholarly debates.

2. France first abolished slavery in its possessions during the French Revolution in 1794. Slavery was then restored in 1802 and reabolished in 1848.

3. As stated in the Code Noir, blacks "ne pourront aussi être témoins, tant en matières civiles que criminelles, à moins qu'il ne soient témoins nécessaires et seulement à défaut de Blancs; mais dans aucun cas ils ne pourront servir de témoins pour ou contre leurs maîtres. . . . l'esclave qui aura frappé son maître, sa maîtresse, le mari de la maîtresse, ou leurs enfants avec contusion ou éffusion de sang ou au visage, sera puni de mort."

4. It is interesting that an indigenous past was relevant to both Haitian and Dominican nation formation. Haitians identified with the genocided Arawaks as they fought the injustices of the slave system. Dominicans would presently call upon their indigenous history to recolor their undeniable African inheritance.

5. I should note that Joan Dayan says the indemnity was to be paid to the dispossessed French planters. Other studies, such as Hurbon's, claim that the indemnity was to be paid to France directly. Again, the annals of history have conflicting facts. But this is pertinent to my study insofar as it underscores the greater importance of the events' impact than of their exact details.

6. Globally, most dispossession from lands arguably occurred during the twentieth century.

7. But the will to survive is far greater than human evil. Stripped of personality, the slaves sought spiritual strength to survive their conditions. Rather than forget, the slaves of Saint Domingue forged their own memories through religious practices. *Vodou* allowed the slaves to find community through their practices, finding spirit to survive the burden of the violence of slavery. "The unseen power of voodoo was so terrifying that it succeeded in attacking the very foundation of the slave system" (Hurbon 40). Boukman, one of the first to incite slave revolts in Haiti, had recourse to the power of the *loas*—the semidivine spirits—and presented himself as a god who would lead his people to freedom. Although he was eventually caught and burned to death, the mystery that surrounded his capture led to greater belief in his powers, further empowering the slave rebellion.

8. It is difficult to talk about how important literature is in Haiti because of the high rate of illiteracy. Furthermore, Danticat writes in English, and most Haitians speak Kreyòl. *The Farming of Bones* was published in a translation by Jacques Chabert as *La Récolte douce des larmes* (Paris: Grasset, 1999). Danticat has also given readings of her stories in Haiti. Most educated Haitians know Danticat and many agree that her work is extremely important on a political and social level. Diaspora literature creates new spaces of awareness and communication. Various groups, from schoolchildren to human rights activists in Haiti and abroad, are informed of the tragedies in Haiti and then encouraged to help. Haitians recognize

their situation and appreciate the attention their stories are getting. As such groups gain knowledge of Haitian circumstances through the intimate space of literature, they can take political and social action that may instigate much needed change in the way violence is enacted and ignored under repressive governments as well as under dire conditions exacerbated by poverty.

9. Vega, *Trujillo y Haití*, 326: "En lo relativo a la matanza de haitianos de 1937 . . . es que son tan escasas y fragmentadas las narraciones sobre esa tragedia que han sobrevivido y provienen principalmente de periodistas extranjeros que estuvieron en el país con motivo de ella (Quentin Reynolds), y autores Haitianos (Price-Mars, 1953), de exiliados dominicanos (Luis F. Mejía, 1976), o de dominicanos que fueron testigos de los hechos pero que publicaron sus comentarios tan solo veinticuatro años después de la matanza (Freddy Prestol Castillo y Rufino Martínez principalmente), o que, casi 46 años después, entrevistaron a testigos de la época (Juan Manuel García, 1983)."

10. Interestingly, the massacre did not eliminate Haitians from the Dominican Republic. During the Trujillo regime, the number of Haitian sugar plantation workers actually increased.

11. I believe that it is very important to note the exclusion of poor Dominicans. This further precludes a neat binary representation of Dominicans versus Haitians.

12. Prestol Castillo, "the son of a sugar oligarch residing in the capital," lost his favorable position when his father died and left the family with outstanding debt (Sommer 163). He found himself so poor that he was unable to pay for his diploma at graduation. With the unexpected debt, he was deprived of the privileged life he had expected. He garnered favors until he found a job as federal magistrate in service to Trujillo's government. In an interview with Doris Sommer, he told her that since his "economic and social marginalization made him an early critic of Trujillo," he believed it would be wise to leave the capital, where anti-Trujillo sentiment was rising and where informants were ever present (163). Regardless of the reason for his transfer, he became a rural judge in the far-off town of Dajabón and witnessed *el corte*.

13. See Doris Sommer's "*El masacre se pasa a pie*: A Rhetoric in Search of Referents," in *One Master for Another*, for an argument of why this text is classified as a testimony.

14. The exception was with the growing presence of Haitians who were brought in specifically to work in the cane fields by government and sugarcane industry agreements. They did not, of course, become part of the Dominican national image, as they were kept in isolation on the plantations and were sent back as soon as the harvest was completed.

15. The intertextuality between history and fiction is here further exemplified. Claire Heureuse is the name of Dessalines' wife. Of the many stories about her, one claims that she saved the life of a white man by hiding him under her bed during the brutal slaying, ordered by her husband, of all remaining whites in Saint Domingue.

16. This psychological condition is like the one that family members and loved

ones experienced—and in many cases continue to experience—as a result of the Pinochet dictatorship in Chile and the military regime in Argentina with its tactic of "disappearing" government dissidents during the Dirty Little War.

17. In an unpublished file of clippings from the *Diario la Marina*, in the Kurt Fisher Haitian Collection, archived at the Schomburg Center for Research in Black Culture, New York Public Library.

18. Danticat came to the University of Michigan in April 2004 to read from her new book *The Dew Breaker*. During the question-and-answer session, a woman told Danticat that her reading group did not read the author's works because they were too sad and full of violence. This kind of reader position made me aware of the limits of fiction: people can and will shut out the messages and the images. Despite this, however, I continue to believe that the reach and effects of fiction are very powerful. If not, why else would this woman have been in the audience, asking questions about Haiti and listening to others address ways in which they could help? Danticat's texts play a fundamental role in consciousness-raising.

19. The topic of this chapter is Haiti, but I would like to emphasize that such a study on human rights has universal repercussions. Television news reports about Eastern European nations, as well as war in the Middle East, lend an urgency to this topic that I cannot ignore.

20. Erzulie is a hugely important figure that further underscores the double nature, and the multiple interpretations and usages, of the gods. Joan Dayan informs us that Ezili (Kreyòl spelling), "best known as the elegant lady of love," is also Ezili Freda in mild Rada rites and Ezili-je-wouj or Ezili Mapian in Petwo or Zandò rites. In the two latter instances, she is more savage. Yet another interpretation of her exists: "For some Haitians, the beautiful coquette is linked to the terrifying Marinèt-bwa-chèche, who evolves as another aspect of Ezili. Ezili the gracious mulatto, enraged by too much coercive praise and worn out by too much use, turns into the cunning and cannibal woman of the night, Marinèt, the spirit of the bush" (Dayan 106). These different representations of the same goddess should be borne in mind as we think about Danticat's story showing the mother imprisoned for being a loup-garou. Her guilt cannot be proved. All we see is a quiet woman honoring the tears of the Madonna, tired and yet not vengeful.

Chapter 2. What Happens When Memory Hurts? The Haunting of Rape

1. Impunity is a huge problem in Haiti, so huge that the country's judicial system is largely ineffective. International human rights lawyers consider the Raboteau case, concluded on November 9, 2000, a major triumph. Human rights lawyer Brian Concannon Jr. wrote, "The Raboteau case marked a sharp break with a long tradition of impunity in Haiti" (641). Raboteau, a poor Gonaïves neighborhood of fishermen, salt rakers, and small merchants, was known for its democratic activism. In 1985 this community initiated nationwide protests that led to the departure of Jean-Claude Duvalier. After the 1991 coup d'état, the occupants of Raboteau were terrorized. Young and old men and women, as well as children, were beaten, forced to lie in

sewers, arrested, tortured, and murdered. The violence culminated in 1994; while the international community increased pressure on the regime, the regime increased pressure on the Haitian people. In 1996 the Haitian government–funded Bureau des Avocats Internationaux (BAI) started working on the Raboteau case. BAI's Concannon wrote that "the Raboteau massacre trial reflected broader improvements in Haiti's justice system since 1994" (643). Some of the justice achieved included incarcerations and remuneration to the victims. Sixteen of the twenty-two defendants were found guilty of serious crimes. Twelve were convicted of premeditated murder and received lifetime prison terms. Victims were awarded the equivalent of $140 million in damages (646).

Lovinsky Pierre-Antoine, psychologist and founder of the largest victims' group in Haiti, Fondation 30 Septembre or Fondasyon Trant Septanm, reported that the trial had been "fair and balanced for victims and accused alike" (646). He hopes it will serve as the model for future cases and an improved justice system. While the Raboteau case represents a huge breakthrough for human rights activists and sends a hopeful message about the future of Haiti's judicial system, it remains an anomaly.

2. I have followed attentively the discussion addressing this issue in May-June 2004 on the Corbett list (see chapter 6, note 1). Indeed, virginity is not the only marker of honor among many women in Haiti and throughout the world. However, there is a long tradition in conservative cultures where at least the idea of purity continues to hold tremendous importance. When virginity is lost willfully, this aspect might be ignored. When it has been robbed, the violence of the act, combined with the silence of the crime, I believe, does lend value to a tradition by which virginity is equated with honor. This is unfortunate, as it is after a crime that a person needs the most support. Again, not ignoring the Corbett discussion, honor is defined and lived up to differently under different circumstances.

3. It was not until 1971 that the first public speak-out against rape was organized (Herman 29). The speak-out was not a mainstream event, as it was coordinated by the New York Radical Feminists, radical being a key definer.

4. First of all, the economy is, as Aristide has stated, in misery beyond poverty.

5. Interview with author, Haiti, summer 2002. Names will not be disclosed, by members' request.

6. I believe, though, that a certain degree of justice has been attained in other instances such as South Africa.

7. The most prominent truth commissions took place in Argentina, Chile, El Salvador, Guatemala, and South Africa. Other commissions of lesser prominence were convened in Bolivia, Burundi, Chad, Ecuador, Germany, Haiti, Nepal, Nigeria, Sierra Leone, Sri Lanka, Uganda (1974 and 1986), Uruguay, and Zimbabwe.

8. The commission that was organized in Oslo in June 1994 (and finally started work in 1997) was called in Guatemala the Commission to Clarify Past Human Rights Violations and Acts of Violence That Have Caused the Guatemalan People to Suffer (Hayner 45). This commission followed two other projects that gathered data and testimonials, the Recovery of Historical Memory Project of the Catholic

Church's Human Rights Office and the Centro Internacional para Investigaciones en Derechos Humanos (the International Center for Investigations of Human Rights). The commission had fewer limitations than these earlier investigations. The report was released in February 1999 in "an emotional ceremony attended by thousands of persons in the National Theater in Guatemala City" (Hayner 48). The report exposed

> "extreme cruelty ... such as the killing of defenseless children, often by beating them against walls or throwing them alive into pits where the corpses of adults were later thrown; the amputation of limbs; the impaling of victims; the killings of persons by covering them in petrol and burning them alive ..." and noted that a "climate of terror" permeated the country as a result of these atrocities.... the "vast majority of the victims of acts committed by the State were not combatants in guerrilla groups, but civilians." In addition to rape, killings, and disappearances, the commission described the military's scorched-earth operations in which civilians, suspected of providing support to the armed guerillas, were targeted indiscriminately, and whole villages were burned to the ground. (48)

The report, in no uncertain terms, pointed to the "racism, structural injustice, and the 'anti-democratic nature of the institutions'" in power in Guatemala (48).

9. Rigoberta Menchú's 1982 testimony *Me llamo Rigoberta Menchú y así me nació la conciencia*, which has been published in more than twenty languages, brought international attention to the racism and violence enacted against the Maya populations of the country years earlier. Writing/telling her story was not a personal project but, more important, an international human rights pilgrimage. Her testimony bears witness to more than just the crimes against her and her family and her community; it bears witness to the risks involved in telling a story—accurate, recalled, flawed, metonymized—that haunts a survivor and/or a witness of repressive violence.

Menchú received the 1992 Nobel Peace Prize. This great honor has been accompanied by scrutiny of her words. Did all of the events she described happen to her and her family? Or did she use poetic license to represent the atrocities imposed on the Maya communities through her family as a representative focal point? Some critics have suggested that the text, written by Elisabeth Burgos-Debray from recorded interviews with Menchú, may have been translated with Burgos-Debray's own political agenda. Perhaps even Menchú's political agenda and affiliations inspired her to color her testimony. In *Rigoberta Menchú and the Story of All Poor Guatemalans* (1999), anthropologist David Stoll confronted Menchú's text, arguing that many of the details and stories Menchú tells are not true. Disclosing violations against Maya groups has come at a harsh price: the constructive political changes initiated by her work have been called into question. In extreme cases Menchú has been dismissed as a liar. In 2001 Arturo Arias gathered a series of essays to address these discrepancies in *The Rigoberta Menchú Controversy*. In her defense Victor D. Montejo argues, "For those who lived those moments of despair and massacres, this is an effort on the part of the unconscious mind to ensure that one's voice is effectively heard—that the voice elicits a strong commitment and solidarity from those who may respond immediately to human rights abuses" (in Arias, 372). Stoll responds that the problem lies in her having framed her work as a testimony. Testimony, he insists, must tell the "truth" without consolidating experiences for dramatic or literary effect. Had Menchú called it fiction, however, she and her very important political agenda might not have received such attention or support. Her voice would have been muffled because it is generally accepted that fiction is not truth, and it therefore does not merit attention.

10. The coup took place at about the same time as the Rwanda genocide.

11. Interview of Concannon by author, Haiti, summer 2002.

12. Informal phone conversation between the author and Catherine Orenstein, June 2002.

13. See www.haiti.org/truth/table.htm.

14. Interview of Concannon by author, Haiti, summer 2002.

15. Despite all of their flaws, truth commissions have incited important changes in many countries, even as many government officials and the ruling elite hold on to old patterns of human abuse. In some nations, the commissions have forced perpetrators to admit their crimes, confirming the truth of the victims' experiences. In Haiti, the truth commission has served as a tool to bring some perpetrators to justice. Thanks to the commission, Haiti has convicted more people of military crimes (albeit many in absentia) than any other country. As of 2003, few had been put in jail, although lawyers hope to change this, as unlikely as it may seem. Truth commissions, local and diaspora social programs, nongovernmental organizations, and human rights groups, as well as literature, all function to counter the dismal Haitian reality and thus aim to make memories of violence a horror of the past rather than a present reality of reinforced injured memories.

16. Jacobson and Jelincić, *Calling the Ghosts*.

17. These women have chosen to empower themselves by calling themselves "victims" rather than survivors. After all, they live among their violators, who have not been punished yet.

18. Since the coup took place at about the same time as the Rwanda genocide, we might view violence in Haiti as part of a severe global problem. Claudine Michel has noted:

> To date, in all regions of the world (though this may be worse in some countries than others) women and children do not enjoy the same rights and privileges as men. Also, gender-specific violations, such as rape, sexual intimidation, and sex trafficking, as well as genital mutilation and female infanticide continue to exist . . . and recent mass rapes, which have taken place in Bosnia-Herzegovina with the intended purpose of "ethnic cleansing." Abuses faced by the Somalian, Peruvian, or Haitian women may be less documented, but are nonetheless as real and devastating. The systematic abuse of these women and mass rape leads to what Adrien Wing called "spirit

injury," a combination of physical and psychological effects, which affect not only the individual victim but society as a whole. Patricia Williams refers to the same phenomenon as "spirit murdering." (19)

19. Marie Chauvet, born in Port-au-Prince in 1919, was the daughter of one mulatto bourgeois highly placed in the Haitian government and was married to another. An accomplished writer who won the Prix de l'Alliance Française and the Grand Prix France-Antilles, she died in relative isolation and poverty in New York City. Her book *Amour, Colère, et Folie* was, until recently, of great interest to an underground Haitian/Haitianist community, giving it cult status. Madeleine Cottenet-Hage, Ronnie Scharfman, and Joan Dayan I would argue are responsible for introducing Chauvet's literature and life to a larger audience; see Scharfman 245n4.

20. Martine's behavior can be explained clinically. According to the DSM IV— the Diagnostic and Statistical Manual used by mental-health professionals to clarify the symptoms and experiences of their patients—one of the most typical symptoms of trauma in PTSD is "re-experiencing of the event in recollections or dreams or in a dis-associative state [where there is] a numbing of general responsiveness, diminished interest in previously enjoyed activities; estrangement; reduced ability to feel emotions (especially those associated with intimacy, tenderness, and sexuality)" (Diagnostic and Statistical Manual, 463–65).

21. While Santeria is not the *vodou* of Haiti, it is an important African-Caribbean religion that shares many aspects with *vodou*. This Santeria connection may be Danticat's way of claiming a larger history of African-Caribbean resistance and survival manifested in multiple diasporas.

22. For example, Emmanuel "Toto" Constant, who is alleged to have directed his paramilitary group, FRAPH (Front for the Advancement of the Haitian People), to rape, torture, and murder thousands of people in the wake of the 1991 coup, was found in the summer of 2000 living peacefully selling real estate in Queens, New York.

23. Women's support organizations have gained strength in recent years both in Haiti and the United States. In Brooklyn, New York, for example, the group Dwa Fanm (Haitians Against Violence at Home Project, and Restavèk Project, in Brooklyn, New York, DwaFanm.org) has been working for women's and girls' rights since 1999, organizing activities and reaching out to women who would otherwise remain isolated like Martine.

24. In an interview with the author in Haiti in the summer of 2002, Haitian psychologist Lovinsky Pierre-Antoine noted that during his work in Montreal he had mostly African, not Haitian, patients. At that time this kind of work was new, and little information was available about who would benefit from it or even seek it. Since the period of the Duvalier dictatorships, Montreal had been a major harbor for Haitian refugees, and Pierre-Antoine had initially expected to have some Haitian clients. However, he lamented, he met none in a formal counseling situation.

25. For example, see Peter Elsass's work on survivors of torture.

26. I say "relatively" because I have no doubt that, in moments of political unrest in Haiti, she considers her words before acting out too critically for fear of jeopardizing the lives of the family she has still living in Haiti.

27. At her reading in Ann Arbor, Michigan, in April 2004 Danticat mentioned that she writes to work through the sad things.

Chapter 3. Exposing Invisibility: *Drown*

1. These are contrasted by the 1996 film *Nueba Yol*, directed by Ángel Muñiz, in which the protagonist encounters abuse and exploitative working conditions in New York City and returns to his island at the end.

2. The French *Los Boys*, published in 2000 by La Flèche, was preceded in 1998 by a Plon edition of the same Rémy Lambrechts translation, titled *Comment sortir une latina, une black, une blonde ou une métisse* after the story "How to Date a Browngirl, Blackgirl, Whitegirl, or Halfie."

3. In contrast to the marketing of tiger-type success suggested by the title *Negocios*, Díaz remarks, "I think that if you're poor in the United States, chances are you are going to be poor for a very long time. It is very much the same way in Santo Domingo. People say there are lots of opportunities here. And when a country is very big, some weird permutations happen" (Torres-Saillant and Céspedes 893). In other words, migration is not the panacea it is often touted to be. His stories show that many of the same problems are experienced both in the Dominican Republic and in marginal, poor communities in the United States. Díaz remembers that his native village, Villa Juana, was very poor and lacked running water and electricity until the late eighties. In contrast, most Dominicans in New Jersey and New York can count on electricity and running water. Poverty is a matter of degree. Still, people have to *aguantar*, put up with, different levels of poverty and resist being made invisible by it.

4. Ernesto Sagás claims that Trujillo's reign was the zenith of anti-haitianismo, which is the "manifestation of the long-term evolution of racial prejudices, the selective interpretation of historical facts, and the creation of a nationalist Dominican false consciousness" (21).

5. This is not to say that dictatorship and governmental corruption are unrelated to the conditions Díaz writes about. However, Díaz creates characters symbolizing the numerous people who are not explicitly aware of the impact of corruption and dictatorships on their lives.

6. At the same time, the 1965 Hart-Celler Act in the United States "made family reunification a priority for gaining entry into the United States," as Carola and Marcelo Suárez-Orozco note in "Rethinking Immigration" (56). They add that this act, which also recruited people with needed skills, caused an unprecedented wave of diverse migrations. They argue that prior to the Hart-Celler Act, migrations were predominantly Canadian and European. The most-educated immigrants came from the Jewish communities escaping Nazism. However, since 1965 the United States has experienced a shift in which migrations come mostly from Latin America, the

Caribbean, and Asia. According to the authors' long-term study at the Harvard Immigration Project, immigrants today are "overrepresented in the category of people with doctorates just as they are overrepresented in the category of people without high school diplomas" (56). Their study points to the diversity of immigrant experience caused by original class and educational background as well as political and economic opportunities proffered by the United States to different ethnic and national groups.

7. Pedro San Miguel's original words were: "La misión de la historiografía fue, en primera instancia, trazar los avatares de la nación. Mas ese proyecto se redujo, en la mayoría de los casos, a una suerte de 'biografía del Estado,' sucedáneo en las narraciones históricas del colectivo nacional. En las sociedades en que emergieron regimenes politicos autoritarios o abiertamente dictatoriales, fue mucho más patente la relación entre la historiografía y el poder" (19).

8. A cover story in the Dominican magazine *Rumbo* titled "El precio de la diferencia: Del armario al mundo" (30 October 2000) notes that an abysm separates the closet and the rest of the world (49). The article also spotlights an activist group, Amigos Siempre Amigos, working against the silence and taboos faced by the homosexual population. This well-documented and thoughtful story follows others presented by *Rumbo*, such as "Homosexuales unidos en el nombre de Dios" (26 June 1995) and "Lesbianas en RD: Un mundo desconocido pero real" (18 February 1994). Of particular interest is another story, "La burocracia que recibió Leonel: La dramática situación de Peña" (16 September 1996), which disclosed Luis Villalona Pérez's request for a visa to stay in the United States. He claimed that the discrimination he received in the Dominican Republic for his open homosexuality jeopardized his physical safety. This was discounted by a number of Dominicans, who claimed that he was exaggerating and that people accepted him. At about the same time that Díaz was publishing *Drown*, these issues were taking center stage in the Dominican Republic, making way for the visibility of a shunned sexual preference that does not comply with national heterosexist formulations of Dominican identity.

9. Capellán, cited in Moya and García 122. Because of the population studied, the nationalist Dominican discourse segregating Haitians and Haitian Dominicans from the rest of the Dominican national imaginary is further enforced, with the added fear of AIDS.

10. "Pero lo cierto es que las discusiones sobre los derechos de los homosexuales de la República Dominicana apenas afloran públicamente, debido quizás a las murallas morales que impone la sociedad dominicana" ("En RD muralla moral impide debatir sobre homosexualidad," *Hoy*, 2 July 2001).

Chapter 4. Modes of Memory: The Restavèk Condition and Jean-Robert Cadet's Story

1. Cadet's book, written and initially published in English, spells the word *restavec*. In the Haitian national language, Kreyòl, and in the Haïti Solidarité

Internationale document *Les Fondements de la pratique de la domesticité des enfants en Haïti* the word is spelled "restavèk." In this chapter I will use the Kreyòl word when discussing the issue and the Cadet spelling when referring specifically to his text.

2. Karen Kramer's 2001 documentary video *Children of the Shadows*.

3. Consequently, human rights organizations, social work groups, researchers, filmmakers, and writers are devoting resources to raising awareness of this growing phenomenon, through films such as Frode Pederson's *They Call Me Dog*, funded and distributed by UNICEF, and through studies including Archer and McCalla, *Restavèk No More*; Haïti Solidarité Internationale, *Fondements de la pratique*; E. Trouillot, *Restituer L'Enfance*; H. Trouillot, *Condition des nègres domestiques*; and UNICEF Haïti, *Enfants d'Haïti en situation particulèrement difficile*.

4. Tele Timoun is a government-owned, pro–Fanmi Lavalas television station that has as its mission the broadcast of children's programming. However, observers say it is primarily used to broadcast pro-Aristide propaganda.

5. I tried to contact the filmmaker to screen the film. She told me I had to buy it and had no time to meet with me to discuss the film, its effects on Haitian children, or the reception/action it is receiving in the United States. Sadly, I wonder if this film isn't more about exposure for the filmmaker than about real human rights activism and human healing.

6. Tim Padgett's *Time* article "Of Haitian Bondage" (5 March 2001) discloses a growing use of restavèks in the United States. He mentions that it is especially difficult for authorities to find these children because they do not run to the police, fearing that the U.S. legal system will be as brutal to them as Haiti's; also, the children do not want their "grown-ups/aunts" to face reprisal. It is interesting that the children interviewed in Haiti were more forthcoming with their information. In the United States they feel greater shame and isolation. Since the 1990s, Haitian-American activists and social workers such as Romer have brought the matter to the authorities and the public. Attorney Philippe Brutus, Florida's first Haitian American state legislator, told Padgett, "We are not going to let traditions like *restavèk* flourish here because we know now that America is the great equalizer among us." Jean-Bertrand Aristide called the practice "one of the cancers in our social body in Haiti that keep democracy from growing."

7. In Haiti, these women can be referred to as "mother" (rarely), "aunt" (most commonly), "godmother" (sometimes), or "grown-up" or "adult" to show the status of overseer. Regardless of the title, they are rarely related to the child and are often abusive.

8. It is sad to make the connection, but in a country that is renowned for being the first to abolish slavery, these stories are shamefully reminiscent of the humiliation slaves were subjected to.

9. News reports such as Carolyn Salazar's piece in the *Miami Herald*, "One in Ten Children in Haiti Is Enslaved" (13 April 2002), signal a new, and illegal, trend of Haitians bringing their restavèks to the United States without changing their harsh

treatment. Although this phenomenon has received attention from social workers, many of these children are kept clandestinely.

10. And anyone who writes understands what a slow and challenging process this is.

11. Today that would be called psychological essentialism. According to psychological essentialists, memory is "fundamentally a mental process, or more formally, the mental capacity of retaining and reviving impressions, or of recalling or recognizing previous experiences" (Gergen 78). A self-memory, according to psychological essentialism, would include exact details such as names, places, dates, and activities. It would not engage subjective observations that could, and arguably do, change with retelling and an individual's different life stages.

12. Sadly, Douglass's work did not extend to women's rights. Abolitionist discourse of the period tended to focus mostly on men's rights. This is also notable in Henry Box Brown's life history. It seems that he could have bought his wife out of slavery but never did.

13. When Cadet was in Haiti, his biological father, Blanc Philippe, was always referred to as a good man, both because he had money and because he was white. Cadet's memory of his father is rather binary. He does not recognize that his father is, after all, not such a good man. Reminiscent of slave owners, Philippe has numerous affairs with women who work in his factories, leading to illegitimate children he neither claims nor raises. Later scenes in Cadet's autobiography show an angry Philippe who, regardless of Cadet's successes and gifts, will not grant legitimacy, or even love, to him.

14. Girls are highlighted, for example, in the 1996 UNICEF docudrama *They Call Me Dog* (see Pederson).

15. Testimony has become central in the exploration and denunciation of human rights abuses throughout the world. Consequently, over the course of the last fifty years, studies, especially academic ones, have sprouted attesting to, and contesting, the power of testimony. The veracity of a life experience is always put into question by the inaccuracy of memory. Questions as to who remembers, why that particular memory, and to whom the memory is addressed seem to consume interpreters of memory and testimony. By extension, an autobiography that reveals abuse for the express purpose of denouncing a human crime and calling for sociopolitical action is a distinctive form of testimony.

16. Jonassaint (*Pouvoir*, 140) notes that Luc Grimard says in his preface to the second edition of Justin Lhérisson's *Zoune chez sa ninnaine* that, according to the dictionary, *coup d'Cadet Jacques* means violation, rape. Freeman and Laguerre's 1998 *Haitian-English Dictionary* has *kadejak* meaning rape.

17. In the foreword to the NCHR report, Edwidge Danticat reminds us "that the *restavèk* system is part of a distressing global phenomenon. Rights belong to the 250 million children worldwide who are exploited for their labor. Thus we cannot, and should not, harbor this practice on cultural grounds. It is an injustice no matter where it happens and it should be stopped" (Archer and McCalla).

18. Cadet chooses to describe himself as a "restavec" and not as a child domestic laborer. It must be noted that Cadet's case is not typical of *restavèk* children. They rarely have contact with their parents and are, to a certain extent, abandoned to the poverty of the city. Cadet can trace his family origins and, with money from his white biological father, manages to travel back to meet his mother's friends. He learns about his mother and finally speaks with his absent father. Although his mother is deceased and his father refuses to acknowledge paternity, Bobby can trace and identify with his family roots. In addition, Blanc Philippe never totally abandons Bobby. Philippe makes sure that he has a home, even if it is not his own. This places Bobby more in the category of *timoun kay moun,* a child at someone's house, or *timoun kay bèlmè,* a child at a stepmother's or mother-in-law's house.

19. In a new, growing tradition of diaspora literature, writers who are emotionally anchored in both Haiti and the United States unravel painful memories of violence and dehumanization to discover their place in the world as citizens and active advocates for human rights. Like Edwidge Danticat, Joanne Hyppolite, Assotto Saint, and Myriam J. A. Chancy, Cadet fights for the potential of Haiti as a great nation and Haitians as a great people. Like his fellow diaspora writers, he is not unaware of the challenge this represents.

Chapter 5. Mapping Home: Inaccessible Memories

1. In October 2004, the National Archive welcomed new directors Roberto Cassá Bernaldo de Quirús and Raymundo Manuel González de Peña. They are embarking on a carefully crafted long-term plan to fix the archive and save its collection

2. What happened to the bodies that disappeared during Trujillo's reign of terror? What became of Trujillo's cast-off lovers? What really happened to the money the Trujillo family had stashed away? How was Balaguer's rule crueler than his predecessor's?

3. Viriato Sención describes this in his novel *Los que falsificaron la firma de Dios.* Even though all of the names have been changed, everyone knows who the protagonists are.

4. "New York City hosts the largest concentration of Dominicans outside of their home island of Hispaniola. In 1990, a total of 332,713 were reported to be living in New York City, comprising 65 percent of the total Dominican population in the U.S." (Hernández, quoted in Pessar, *A Visa for a Dream: Dominicans in the United States,* 22). Dominican leaders argue that the number is actually twice that number, if not three times, since many Dominicans are illegal and have avoided census reports (ibid.).

5. In theory, this is the way it should be. However, if we look at the number of households led by single mothers, both in the Dominican Republic and in the United States' Dominican communities, we learn quickly that women are much more independent in action. In a report archived by PROFAMILIA, Octavio Estrella writes that every thirty-five minutes a woman breaks her relations with, and dependency on, the father of her children (10). Another report states that up to 75 percent of

Dominican households are supported solely by women (Caram de Álvarez 2). Many women do not go to the judicial system to get alimony. In some cases, this makes sense, because the fathers have no money. In other cases, the women feel too hurt by their ex-partners or simply do not trust the court system. In the United States, women also gain independence from abusive or unsupportive relationships. Aurelia exemplifies the traditional role a woman can take, and Iliana serves as a contrasting example.

6. This is a stereotype that also responds to a reality. Julia Alvarez in *How the García Girls Lost Their Accents* points to the different ways women dress in the United States and in the Dominican Republic. Angie Cruz in *Soledad* describes the way girls in Washington Heights dress differently to defy their cultural codes of attire. Carmelita Tropicana has played with gender oppression through clothing in her performance pieces, cross-dressing and overdressing. These clearly are all responses to a gender stereotypical expectation placed on women in the Caribbean and its diaspora. Many Caribbean women defy this stereotype.

7. There is a long history of Dominican denial of African traits. Ernesto Sagás traces this, arguing that the Trujillo regime, with the intellectual, ideological savvy of his advisors Manuel A. Peña Batlle and Joaquín Balaguer, turned African rejection in Dominican history into a state-sponsored ideology (46). Even before that, the Dominican Republic engaged in conscious whitening. Julia Alvarez points to this in her novel *In the Name of Salomé*, in which she describes a painting of the poet Salomé Henríquez Ureña. A woman whose original features included a wide nose and full lips was portrayed as a sophisticated nineteenth-century European woman with long limbs and delicate features. In particular, her color was lightened exponentially for posterity. Salomé, one of the Dominican Republic's greatest female poets, is "cleansed" of her African heritage.

Chapter 6. Conclusion: Present Memories

1. This piece was circulated via Michele Wucker's list serve group, Dominican@yahoogroups.com. Other pieces referring to the same matter also were reported via Bob Corbett's list serve group, corbetre@webster.edu.

2. For example, in the city of Fonds Verrettes about three thousand have been reported hurt.

Bibliography

Audiovisual Sources

Fortunato, René. *El poder del jefe*. Santo Domingo: Videocine Palau, 1991. Videocassette.

Jacobson, Mandy, and Karmen Jelincić. *Calling the Ghosts: A Story about Rape, War, and Women*. New York: Bowery Productions, Women Make Movies, 1996. Videocassette.

Kramer, Karen, dir. *Children of Shadows*. Haiti and New York, 2001. Videocassette.

Magloire, Rachele, dir. *Les Enfants du coup d'état*. Pétionville, Haiti: Productions FANAL, 2001. Videocassette.

Muñiz, Ángel. *Nueba Yol*. New York: Ideal Enterprises, 1996. Videocassette.

Peck, Raoul. *L'Homme sur les quais*. New York: KJM3 Entertainment Group, 1993.

Pederson, Frode Højer, dir. *They Call Me Dog: A Film about the Cinderellas of Haiti*. Danmark Radio/UNICEF, 1995. Videocassette.

Sixto, Maurice, dir. *Ti Saintanise*. 1971. Audiotape.

Print Sources

Abbott, Elizabeth. *Haiti: An Insider's History of the Rise and Fall of the Duvaliers*. New York: Simon and Schuster, 1988.

Abréu, Dió-genes. *Perejil: el ocaso de la "hispanidad" dominicana, celebración de la multiplicidad cultural desde New York*. Dominican Republic: Mediabyte, S.A., 2004.

Aggleton, Peter, ed. *Bisexualities and AIDS: International Perspectives*. London: Taylor and Francis, 1996.

Agosín, Marjorie. *At the Threshold of Memory: A Bilingual Critical Anthology of New and Selected Poems*, edited by Celeste Kostopulos-Cooperman. Buffalo, N.Y.: White Pine, 2003.

Alcántara Almánzar, José, ed. *Antología mayor de la literatura dominicana, siglos XIX y XX: Prosa*. 2 vols. Santo Domingo: Ediciones de la Fundación Corripio, 2001.

Alexis, Jacques Stephen. *General Sun, My Brother*. Translated by Carrol F. Coates. Charlottesville: University Press of Virginia, 1999. Originally published as *Compère Général Soleil* (Paris: Gallimard, 1955).

Alvarez, Julia. *How the García Girls Lost Their Accents*. Chapel Hill, N.C.: Algonquin, 1991.

———. *In the Name of Salomé*. Chapel Hill, N.C.: Algonquin, 2000.

———. *In the Time of the Butterflies*. Chapel Hill, N.C.: Algonquin, 1994.

———. *¡Yo!* Chapel Hill, N.C.: Algonquin, 1997.

American Psychiatric Association. *Diagnostic and Statistical Manual of Mental Disorders*. 4th ed. Washington, D.C.: American Psychiatric Association, 1994.

Archer, Merrie, and Jocelyn McCalla. *Restavèk No More: Eliminating Child Slavery in Haiti*. New York: National Coalition for Haitian Rights, 2002.

Arenas, Reinaldo. *Antes que anochezca*. Barcelona: Tusquets, 1992. Translated by Dolores M. Koch as *Before Night Falls* (New York: Viking, 1993).

Arias, Arturo, ed. *The Rigoberta Menchú Controversy*. Minneapolis: University of Minnesota Press, 2001.

Balaguer, Joaquín. *Memorias de un cortesano de la "Era de Trujillo."* 1988. Santo Domingo: Editora Corripio, 2002.

———. *El pensamiento vivo de Trujillo*. Ciudad Trujillo: Impresora Dominicana, 1955.

Barnhizer, David, ed. *Effective Strategies for Protecting Human Rights*. Aldershot: Ashgate, 2001.

Baud, Michel. "'Constitutionally White': The Forging of a National Identity in the Dominican Republic." In *Ethnicity in the Caribbean: Essays in Honor of Harry Hoetink*, edited by Gert Oostindie, 121–51. London: Macmillan Caribbean, 1996.

Behar, Ruth, ed. *Bridges to Cuba*. Ann Arbor: University of Michigan Press, 1995.

———. *The Vulnerable Observer: Anthropology That Breaks Your Heart*. Boston: Beacon, 1996.

Bell, Beverly. *Walking on Fire: Haitian Women's Stories of Survival and Resistance*. Ithaca, N.Y.: Cornell University Press, 2001.

Bellande-Robertson, Florence. *The Marassa Concept in Lilas Desquiron's "Reflections of Loko Miwa": A Socio-Literary Analysis of the Haitian Race/Color and Gender Problematic*. Dubuque, Iowa: Kendall/Hunt, 1999.

Beverley, John. *Subalternity and Representation: Arguments in Cultural Theory*. Durham, N.C.: Duke University Press, 1999.

Black, Jan Knippers. *The Dominican Republic: Politics and Development in an Unsovereign State*. Boston: Allen and Unwin, 1986.

Blassingame, John W., John R. McKivigan, and Peter P. Hinks, eds. *Narrative of the Life of Frederick Douglass, an American Slave, Written by Himself*. New Haven, Conn.: Yale University Press, 2001.

Brown, Henry Box. *The Narrative of the Life of Henry Box Brown*. 1850. Introduction by Richard Newman. Foreword by Henry Louis Gates Jr. Oxford: Oxford University Press, 2002.

Brown, Norma, ed. Introduction to *A Black Diplomat in Haiti: The Diplomatic Correspondence of U.S. Minister Frederick Douglass from Haiti, 1889–1891*, by Frederick Douglass, edited by Norma Brown. Salisbury, N.C.: Documentary Publications, 1977.

Bruner, Jerome. "The 'Remembered Self.'" In Neisser and Fivush, *The Remembering Self*, 41–54.

Cadet, Jean-Robert. *Restavec: From Haitian Slave Child to Middle-Class American*. Austin: University of Texas Press, 1998.

Caldeira, Teresa P. R. "Crime and Individual Rights: Reframing the Question of Violence in Latin America." In Jelin and Hershberg, *Constructing Democracy*, 197–211.

Caram de Álvarez, Magaly. "Es penosa la situación de la mujer en República Dominicana." Text of an address. Santo Domingo: PROFAMILIA, MUDE, CIPAF, 1987.

Carrithers, Michael, Steven Collins, and Steven Lukes, eds. *The Category of the Person: Anthropology, Philosophy, History*. Cambridge: Cambridge University Press, 1985.

Caruth, Cathy, ed. *Trauma: Explorations in Memory*. Baltimore: Johns Hopkins University Press, 1995.

———. *Unclaimed Experience: Trauma, Narrative, and History*. Baltimore: Johns Hopkins University Press, 1996.

Casas, Bartolomé de las. *Brevísima relación de la destruición de las Indias*. 1552. Edited by André Saint-Lu. Madrid: Cátedra, 1984.

Chancy, Myriam J. A. *Framing Silence: Revolutionary Novels by Haitian Women*. New Brunswick, N.J.: Rutgers University Press, 1997.

———. *Searching for Safe Spaces: Afro-Caribbean Women Writers in Exile*. Philadelphia: Temple University Press, 1997.

———. *The Spirit of Haiti*. London: Mango Publishing, 2003.

Chauvet, Marie. *Amour, Colère et Folie*. Paris: Gallimard, 1968.

CHRPROF. *Violences exercées sur les femmes et les filles en Haïti*. Port-au-Prince: Centre Haïtien de Recherches et d'Actions pour la Promotion Féminine, 1996.

Cocco de Filippis, Daisy, ed. *Documents of Dissidence: Selected Writings by Dominican Women*. Foundational Documents Series. New York: Dominican Studies Institute, CUNY, 2000.

———, ed. *La literatura dominicana al final del siglo: Diálogo entre la tierra natal y la diáspora*. Dominican Studies Working Paper 2. New York: Dominican Studies Institute, CUNY, 1999.

———, ed. *Madres, maestras y militantes dominicanas (fundadoras): Ensayos selectos*. Santo Domingo: Editora Búho, 2001.

Le Code Noir; ou, Recueil des réglemens rendus jusqu'à present. . . . Paris, 1788.

Cohen, Stanley. *States of Denial: Knowing about Atrocities and Suffering*. Cambridge: Polity, 2001.

Concannon, Brian, Jr. "Justice for Haiti: The Raboteau Trial." *International Lawyer* 35.2 (2001): 641–47.

Cruz, Angie. *Soledad*. New York: Simon and Schuster, 2001.

Cuello, José Israel. *Documentos del Conflicto Dominico Haitiano de 1937*. Santo Domingo: Taller C, 1985.

Danticat, Edwidge. *Breath, Eyes, Memory*. New York: Soho, 1994.

———, ed. *The Butterfly's Way: Voices from the Haitian Dyaspora in the United States*. New York: Soho, 2001.

———. Foreword. *A Community of Equals: The Constitutional Protection of New Americans*, by Owen Fiss. Boston: Beacon, 1999.

———. *The Farming of Bones.* 1998. New York: Soho, 1998.

———. *Krik? Krak!* New York: Soho, 1995.

Dauphin, Marcel. *Coeurs en écharpes: Nouvelles.* Port-au-Prince: Éditions du Soleil, 1979.

Dávila-Mendoza, Dora. *Un concierto de voces: Mujer, familia y sociedad en Santo Domingo colonial.* Dominican Studies Working Paper 3. New York: Dominican Studies Institute, CUNY, 1999.

Dayan, Joan. *Haiti, History, and the Gods.* Berkeley and Los Angeles: University of California Press, 1995.

De Filippis, Daisy Cocco. *Desde la diáspora/A Diaspora Position.* New York: Ediciones Alcance, 2003.

Den Tandt, Catherine. "'El masacre se pasa a pie': Haitian and Dominican Border Talk." In *Marginal Migrations: The Circulation of Cultures Within the Caribbean*, edited by Shalini Puri, 253–86. London: Macmillan Caribbean, 2003.

Dépestre, René. *Ainsi parle le fleuve noir.* Grigny: Paroles d'aube, 1998.

———. *Encore une mer à traverser.* Paris: CD Gallimard, 1998.

———. *Le métier à métisser.* Paris: Stock, 1998.

Derby, Lauren. "Haitians, Magic and Money: Raza and Society in the Haitian-Dominican Borderlands, 1900 to 1937." *Comparative Studies in Society and History* 36.3 (1994): 488–526.

Deren, Maya. *Divine Horsemen: The Voodoo Gods of Haiti.* New York: Chelsea House, 1970.

Desmangles, Leslie G. *The Faces of the Gods: Vodou and Roman Catholicism in Haiti.* Chapel Hill: University of North Carolina Press, 1992.

Díaz, Junot. *Drown.* New York: Riverhead, 1996.

Díaz-Quiñones, Arcadio. *La memoria rota.* 2nd ed. San Juan: Huracán, 1996.

Dieng, Adama. "Intervention on the Situation of Human Rights in Haiti by the Independent Expert." Report to the 55th Session of the United Nations Commission on Human Rights, Geneva, 22 April 1999.

Dominican Studies Institute. www.ccny.cuny.edu/dsi/about.htm.

Donnelly, Jack. *International Human Rights.* 2nd ed. Boulder, Colo.: Westview, 1997.

———. *Universal Human Rights in Theory and Practice.* Ithaca, N.Y.: Cornell University Press, 1989.

Duarte, Isis, Clara Báez, Carmen Julia Gómez, and Marina Ariza. *Población y condición de la mujer en República Dominicana: Estudio No. 6.* Santo Domingo: Instituto de Estudios de Población y Desarrollo, PROFAMILIA, 2001.

Dubois, Laurent. *A Colony of Citizens: Revolution and Slave Emancipation in the French Caribbean, 1787–1804.* Chapel Hill and London: University Press of North Carolina, 2004.

Dumas, Pierre-Raymond. *Panorama de la littérature haïtienne de la diaspora.* Port-au-Prince: L'Imprimeur II, 2000.

Eakin, Paul John. *How Our Lives Become Stories: Making Selves.* Ithaca, N.Y.: Cornell University Press, 1999.

Edmondson, Belinda. *Making Men: Gender, Literary Authority, and Women's Writing in Caribbean Narrative.* Durham, N.C.: Duke University Press, 1999.

Eisenstein, Zillah R., ed. *Capitalist Patriarchy and the Case for Socialist Feminism.* New York: Monthly Review Press, 1978.

Ellison, Ralph. *Invisible Man.* 1952. 2nd ed. New York: Vintage International, 1995.

Elsass, Peter. *Strategies for Survival: The Psychology of Cultural Resilience in Ethnic Minorities.* Translated by Fran Hopenwasser. New York: New York University Press, 1992.

———. *Treating Victims of Torture and Violence: Theoretical, Cross-Cultural, and Clinical Implications.* New York and London: New York University Press, 1997.

Emeterio Rondón, Pura. *Estudios críticos de la literatura dominicana contemporánea.* Santo Domingo: Librería la Trinitaria, 2005.

Estrella, Octavio. "Cada 35 minutos una madre se querella contra el padre de sus hijos: La ley 2404." Archival documentation, PROFAMILIA, 1987.

Étienne, Gérard. *Cri pour ne pas crever de honte, chant littéraire.* Montréal: Nouvelle Optique, 1983.

Felman, Shoshana, and Dori Laub. *Testimony: Crises of Witnessing in Literature, Psychoanalysis, and History.* New York and London: Routledge, 1992.

Fischkin, Barbara. *Muddy Cup: A Dominican Family Comes of Age in a New America.* New York: Scribner, 1987.

Flores, Juan. "Broken English Memories: Languages of the Trans-Colony." In *Postcolonial Theory and the United States: Race, Ethnicity, and Literature,* ed. Amritjit Singh and Peter Schmidt, 338–48. Jackson: University Press of Mississippi, 2000.

———. *Divided Borders: Essays on Puerto Rican Identity.* Houston: Arte Público Press, 1993.

Fornerín, Miguel Ángel. *La Dominicanidad Viajera: Ensayos sobre la diáspora, cultura, sociedad, política y literatura en el Santo Domingo de fin de siglo.* San Juan/Santo Domingo: Editora Imago Mundi, 2001.

Freud, Sigmund. "The 'Uncanny.'" 1919. In *The Standard Edition of the Complete Psychological Works of Sigmund Freud,* edited by James Strachey, 17:219–52. London: Hogarth, 1955.

Fuller, Ann. "Challenging Violence: Haitian Women Unite Women's Rights and Human Rights." *Association of Concerned Africa Scholars Bulletin,* spring/summer 1999.

Galeano, Eduardo H. *Las venas abiertas de América Latina.* Montevideo: Universidad de la República, 1971.

Galván, Manuel de J. *Enriquillo: Leyenda Histórica Dominicana (1503–1533).* 1882. Madrid: Ediciones de Cultura Hispánica, 1996.

García, Cristina. *Dreaming in Cuban.* New York: Knopf, 1992.

García, Mélida, and Miguel de Camps Jiménez, compilers. *Antología de la literatura Gay en la República Dominicana.* Santo Domingo: Editora Manatí, 2004.

Geggus, David Patrick. *Haitian Revolutionary Studies*. Bloomington and India-napolis: Indiana University Press, 2002.

————, ed. *The Impact of the Haitian Revolution in the Atlantic World*. Columbia: University of South Carolina Press, 2001.

Gergen, Kenneth J. "Mind, Text, and Society: Self-Memory in Social Context." In Neisser and Fivush, *The Remembering Self*, 78–104.

Gil, Rosa María, and Carmen Inoa Vázquez. *The Maria Paradox: How Latinas Can Merge Old World Traditions with New World Self-Esteem*. New York: Putnam, 1996.

Gingras, Jean-Pierre O. *Duvalier, Caribbean Cyclone: The History of Haiti and Its Present Government*. New York: Exposition, 1967.

González, Raymundo, Michiel Baud, Pedro L. San Miguel, and Roberto Cassá, eds. *Política, identidad y pensamiento social en la República Dominicana (Siglos XIX y XX)*. Santo Domingo: Doce Calles, 1999.

Grann, David. "Giving 'The Devil' His Due." *Atlantic Monthly*, June 2001, 55–75.

Grasmuck, Sherri, and Patricia R. Pessar. *Between Two Islands: Dominican Interna-tional Migration*. Berkeley and Los Angeles: University of California Press, 1991.

Green, Mary Jean, Karen Gould, Micheline Rice-Maximin, Keith L. Walker, and Jack A. Yeager, eds. *Postcolonial Subjects: Francophone Women Writers*. Minneapolis: University of Minnesota Press, 1996.

Gutiérrez, Franklin. *Evas terrenales: Biobibliografías de 150 autores dominicanas*. Santo Domingo: Comisión Permanente de la Feria del Libro, 2000.

Haïti, la voie de nos silences: 117 femmes haïtiennes écrivent. 4 vols. Pétionville, Haiti: Pressmax, 1998.

Haïti Solidarité Internationale. *Les Fondements de la pratique de la domesticité des enfants en Haïti*. Port-au-Prince: HSI, 2002.

Hayner, Priscilla B. *Unspeakable Truths: Confronting State Terror and Atrocity*. New York and London: Routledge, 2001.

Herman, Judith Lewis. *Trauma and Recovery*. New York: Basic Books, 1992.

Hernández, Ramona. *The Mobility of Workers under Advanced Capitalism: Do-minican Migration to the United States*. New York: Columbia University Press, 2002.

Hesford, Wendy S., and Wendy Kozol, eds. *Haunting Violations: Feminist Criticism and the Crisis of the "Real."* Urbana: University of Illinois Press, 2001.

Hibbert, Fernand. *Masques et Visages*. 1910. Port-au-Prince: Henri Deschamps, 1988.

Hicks, Albert C. *Blood in the Streets: The Life and Rule of Trujillo*. New York: Cre-ative Age, 1946.

Holloway, Karla F. C. *Passed On: African American Mourning Stories: A Memorial Collection*. Durham, N.C.: Duke University Press, 2002.

Howard, David. *Dominican Republic: A Guide to the People, Politics, and Culture*. New York: Interlink, 2000.

Human Rights Watch and National Coalition for Haitian Refugees. "Rape in Haiti: A Weapon of Terror." *Human Rights Watch and National Coalition for Haitian Refugees* 6.8 (1994): 1–29.

Hurbon, Laënnec. *Voodoo: Search for the Spirit.* Translated by Lory Frankel. New York: Abrams, 1995.

Huyssen, Andreas. *Present Pasts: Urban Palimpsests and the Politics of Memory.* Stanford: Stanford University Press, 2003.

James, William. *Pragmatism; The Meaning of Truth.* 1907–9. Cambridge, Mass.: Harvard University Press, 1978.

Jay, Martin. *Refractions of Violence.* New York: Routledge, 2003.

Jelin, Elizabeth. "Citizenship Revisited: Solidarity, Responsibility, and Rights." In Jelin and Hershberg, *Constructing Democracy*, 101–20.

———. "The Minefields of Memory." *NACLA Report on the Americas* 32.2 (1998): 23–29.

———. "The Politics of Memory: The Human Rights Movement and the Construction of Democracy in Argentina." *Latin American Perspectives* 21.2 (1994): 38–58.

Jelin, Elizabeth, and Eric Hershberg. *Constructing Democracy: Human Rights, Citizenship, and Society in Latin America.* Boulder, Colo.: Westview, 1996.

Jiménez Sabater, Max A. *Más datos sobre el español de la República Dominicana.* Santo Domingo: INTEC, 1975.

Jonassaint, Jean. *Des romans de tradition haïtienne: Sur un récit tragique.* Montreal: CIDIHCA; Paris: L'Harmattan, 2002.

———. "Haitian Literature in the United States, 1948–1986." In *American Babel: Literatures of the United States from Abnaki to Zuni*, edited by Marc Shell, 431–49. Cambridge, Mass.: Harvard University Press, 2002.

———. *Le Pouvoir des mots, les maux du pouvoir: Des romanciers haïtiens de l'exil.* Montréal: Presses de l'Université de Montréal; Paris: Arcantère, 1986.

Jones, Vanessa E. "A Loss for Words. Junot Díaz Was a Wunderkind When His First Book of Fiction Came Out. Seven Years Later, He's Still Working on a Follow-Up." *Boston Globe*, 4 March 2003.

Krohn-Hansen, Christian. "Masculinity and the Political among Dominicans: 'The Dominican Tiger.'" In Melhuus and Stølen, *Machos, Mistresses, Madonnas*, 108–33.

Laguerre, Michel S. *American Odyssey: Haitians in New York City.* Ithaca, N.Y.: Cornell University Press, 1984.

———. *Diasporic Citizenship: Haitian Americans in Transnational America.* New York: St. Martin's Press, 1998.

Lawless, Elaine J. *Women Escaping Violence: Empowerment through Narrative.* Columbia: University of Missouri Press, 2001.

Levi, Primo. *Survival in Auschwitz.* Translated by Stuart Woolf. New York: Touchstone, 1996.

Leys, Ruth. *Trauma: A Genealogy.* Chicago: University of Chicago Press, 2000.

Lhérisson, Justin. *La Famille des Pietite-Caille; Zoune chez sa Ninnaine*. 1905. Paris: Éditions Caribéennes, 1978.

Loftus, Geoffrey R., and Elizabeth F. Loftus. *Human Memory: The Processing of Information*. Hillsdale, N.J.: Lawrence Erlbaum Associates, 1976.

Lorey, David E., and William H. Beezley, eds. *Genocide, Collective Violence, and Popular Memory: The Politics of Remembrance in the Twentieth Century*. Wilmington, Del.: Scholarly Resources, 2002.

Mack-Kit, Samuel. *Le Problème des noirs et la Révolution de 1789*. Paris: OKEM, 1989.

Magloire, Eddy. *Regards sur la minorité éthnique Haïtienne aux États-Unis*. Sherbrooke, Que.: Naaman, 1984.

Magloire, Jean. *Su excelencia el presidente Sténio Vincent*. Port-au-Prince, 1937.

Marrero Aristy, Ramón. *Over*. 1939. Santo Domingo: Librería Dominicana, 1963.

Mateo, Andrés L. *Al filo de la dominicanidad*. Santo Domingo: Libreria la Trinitaria, 1996.

———. *Mito y cultura en la era de Trujillo*. Santo Domingo: Editora de Colores, 1993.

Matibag, Eugenio. *Haitian-Dominican Counterpoint: Nation, State, and Race on Hispaniola*. New York: Palgrave Macmillan, 2003.

Mauss, Marcel. "A Category of the Human Mind: The Notion of the Person; The Notion of Self." Translated by W. D. Halls. In Carrithers, Collins, and Lukes, *Category of the Person*, 1–25.

Melhuus, Marit, and Kristi Anne Stølen, eds. *Machos, Mistresses, Madonnas: Contesting the Power of Latin American Gender Imagery*. London and New York: Verso, 1996.

Menchú, Rigoberta. *Me llamo Rigoberta Menchú y así me nació la conciencia*. Edited by Elisabeth Burgos. Barcelona: Argos Vergara, 1983.

Méndez, Juan, Dinah PoKempner, Norris Pascale, and Joanna Weschler. *Putting Human Rights Back into the Habitat Agenda: An Update*. New York: Human Rights Watch, vol. 8, no. 3, 1996.

Métraux, Alfred. *Voodoo in Haiti*. Translated by Hugo Charteris. New York: Schocken, 1972.

Michel, Claudine. *Human Rights and Community Development through Low-Income Women's Leadership: The Voice of an African-American Organizer*. Boston: William Monroe Trotter Institute, 1996.

Moreiras Menor, Cristina. *Cultura Herida: Literatura y cine en la España democrática*. Madrid: Ediciones Libertarias, 2002.

Moya, E. Antonio de, and Rafael García. "AIDS and the Enigma of Bisexuality in the Dominican Republic." In Aggleton, ed., *Bisexualities and AIDS: International Perspectives*, 121–136.

Moya Pons, Frank. *The Dominican Republic: A National History*. 1995. Princeton, N.J.: Markus Wiener, 1998.

Nacidit-Perdomo, Ylonka. *Contrapunto: Desconciertos y Territorios Afectivos de*

Mujeres. Montreal: CCLEH (Crítica Canadiense Literaria sobre Escritoras Hispanoamericanas), 2001.

———. *Sobreaviso: Escritura de mujeres*. Montreal: CCLEH, 1998.

El Nacional (Santo Domingo). "Ratifican llamada a marcha de gays." 30 June 2001.

National Coalition for Haitian Rights. "Haitian Rights Coalition Urges Haiti President to Fulfill Promises on Children's Rights." News release, 12 June 2001. www.nchr.org/hrp/restavek/childrens_rights.htm.

———. "Restavèk No More." Restavèk Project page, updated regularly. www.nchr.org/hrp/restavek/report_pr.htm.

Neisser, Ulric, and Robyn Fivush, eds. *The Remembering Self: Construction and Accuracy in the Self-Narrative*. Cambridge: Cambridge University Press, 1994.

Nesbitt, Nick. *Voicing Memory: History and Subjectivity in French Caribbean Literature*. Charlottesville: University of Virginia Press, 2003.

Nora, Pierre. "Between Memory and History: Les Lieux de Mémoire." In *Realms of Memory: Rethinking the French Past*, edited by Pierre Nora and Lawrence D. Kritzman, translated by Arthur Goldhammer, 1–20. New York: Columbia University Press, 1996.

Nunca más: Informe de la Comisión Nacional sobre la Desaparición de Personas. Buenas Aires: EUDEBA, 1984.

Olney, James. "Some Versions of Memory/Some Versions of Bios: The Ontology of Autobiography." In *Autobiography: Essays Theoretical and Critical*, 236–67. Princeton: Princeton University Press, 1980.

Padgett, Tim. "Of Haitian Bondage." *Time*, 5 March 2001.

Pérez, Loida Maritza. *Geographies of Home*. New York: Viking, 1999.

Pessar, Patricia R., ed. *Caribbean Circuits: New Directions in the Study of Caribbean Migration*. New York: Center for Migration Studies, 1997.

———. *A Visa for a Dream: Dominicans in the United States*. Boston: Allyn and Bacon, 1995.

Pichardo, Tony. www.ciir.org. Accessed 7 June 2004.

Prestol Castillo, Freddy. *El masacre se pasa a pie*. Santo Domingo: Taller, 1973.

———. *Paisajes y meditaciones de una frontera (era de Trujillo)*. Ciudad Trujillo: Cosmopolita, 1943.

Price-Mars, Jean. *La République de Haïti et la République dominicaine: Les aspects divers d'un problème d'histoire, de géographie et d'ethnologie*. 2 vols. 1953.

Racine, Marie, and Kathy Ogle. *Like the Dew That Waters the Grass: Words from Haitian Women*. Washington, D.C.: EPICA (Ecumenical Program in Central America and the Caribbean), 1999.

Rigaud, Milo. *Sténio Vincent, révélé par la justice et par l'opinion publique*. Port-au-Prince: H. Deschamps, 1957.

Rosario, Nelly. *Song of the Water Saints*. New York: Pantheon, 2002.

Safa, Helen I. *The Myth of the Male Breadwinner: Women and Industrialization in the Caribbean*. Boulder, San Francisco, and Oxford: Westview Press, 1995.

Sagás, Ernesto. *Race and Politics in the Dominican Republic.* Gainesville: University Press of Florida, 2000.

Sagás, Ernesto, and Sintia E. Molina, eds. *Dominican Migration: Transnational Perspectives.* Gainesville: University Press of Florida, 2004.

Salazar, Carolyn. "One in Ten Children in Haiti Is Enslaved." *Miami Herald,* 12 April 2002.

San Miguel, Pedro L. *La isla imaginada: Historia, identidad, y utopía en La Española.* San Juan: Isla Negra; Santo Domingo: La Trinitaria, 1997.

Scarry, Elaine. *The Body in Pain: The Making and Unmaking of the World.* New York and Oxford: Oxford University Press, 1985.

Schaffer, Kay, and Sidonie Smith. *Human Rights and Narrated Lives: The Ethics of Recognition.* New York: Palgrave Macmillan, 2004.

Scharfman, Ronnie. "Theorizing Terror: The Discourse of Violence in Marie Chauvet's *Amour Colère Folie.*" In Green et al., *Postcolonial Subjects,* 229–45.

Scott, Joan. "Experience." In Smith and Watson, *Women, Autobiography, Theory,* 57–71.

Seed, Patricia. "'Failing to Marvel': Atahualpa's Encounter with the Word." *Latin American Research Review* 26 (1991): 7–32.

Sención, Viriato. *Los que falsificaron la firma de Dios.* Santo Domingo: Editora de Colores, 1992.

Shea, Renée H. "The Hunger to Tell: Edwidge Danticat and *The Farming of Bones.*" *MaComère: Journal of the Association of Caribbean Women Writers and Scholars* 2 (1999): 12–22.

Shemak, April. "Re-membering Hispaniola: Edwidge Danticat's *The Farming of Bones.*" *Modern Fiction Studies* 48.1 (2002): 83–112.

Simonson, Peter Grant. "Masculinity and Femininity in the Dominican Republic: Historical Change and Contradiction in Notions of Self." Ph.D. diss., University of Michigan, 1994.

Slavin, J. P. "Restavèk: Four-year-old Servants in Haiti." www.nchr.org/hrp/restavek/haiti_insight1.htm.

Smith, Hawthorne E. "Despair, Resilience, and the Meaning of Family: Group Therapy with French-Speaking African Survivors of Torture." In *Understanding and Dealing with Violence: A Multicultural Approach,* edited by Barbara C. Wallace and Robert T. Carter, 291–316. Thousand Oaks, Calif.: Sage, 2003.

Smith, Sidonie, and Julia Watson, eds. *Women, Autobiography, Theory: A Reader.* Madison: University of Wisconsin Press, 1998.

Sommer, Doris. *One Master for Another: Populism as Patriarchal Rhetoric in Dominican Novels.* Lanham, Md.: University Press of America, 1983.

Sorabji, Richard. *Aristotle on Memory.* Providence: Brown University Press, 1972.

Stoll, David. *Rigoberta Menchú and the Story of All Poor Guatemalans.* Boulder, Colo.: Westview, 1999.

Suárez-Orozco, Carola, and Marcelo M. Suárez-Orozco. "Rethinking Immigration." In *Children of Immigration*, 16–35. Cambridge, Mass.: Harvard University Press, 2001.

Suárez-Orozco, Marcelo M., and Mariela M. Páez, eds. *Latinos: Remaking America*. Berkeley and Los Angeles: University of California Press, 2002.

Tal, Kalí. *Worlds of Hurt: Reading the Literatures of Trauma*. Cambridge: Cambridge University Press, 1996.

Taylor, Charles. "The Person." In Carrithers, Collins, and Lukes, *Category of the Person*, 257–81.

Torres-Saillant, Silvio. *Caribbean Poetics: Toward an Aesthetic of West Indian Literature*. Cambridge: Cambridge University Press, 1997.

———. "Dominican Literature and Its Criticism: Anatomy of a Troubled Identity." In *A History of Literature in the Caribbean*, edited by A. James Arnold. Amsterdam: J. Menjamins, 1994–2001.

Torres-Saillant, Silvio, and Diógenes Céspedes. "Fiction Is the Poor Man's Cinema: An Interview with Junot Díaz." *Callaloo* 23.3 (2000): 892–907.

Torres-Saillant, Silvio, and Ramona Hernández. *The Dominican Americans*. Westport, Conn.: Greenwood, 1998.

Torres-Saillant, Silvio, Ramona Hernández, and Blas Jiménez. *Desde la Orilla: hacia una nacionalidad sin desalojos*. Santo Domingo: Editora Manatí, 2004.

Trescott, Jacqueline. "Edwidge Danticat. Personal History. In a 1937 Massacre, the Writer Found a Fable for Our Time." *Washington Post*, 11 October 1999, sec. C.

Trouillot, Évelyne. *État de Droit et Enfance en Haïti: Restituer L'Enfance*. Port-au-Prince: Haïti Solidarité Internationale, with CCFD (Comité Catholique contre la Faim et pour le Développement), 2001.

Trouillot, Hénock. *La Condition des nègres domestiques à Saint-Domingue*. 1995.

Trouillot, Michel-Rolph. *Silencing the Past: Power and the Production of History*. Boston: Beacon, 1995.

Turits, Richard. "A World Destroyed, a Nation Imposed: The 1937 Haitian Massacre in the Dominican Republic." *Hispanic American Historical Review* 82.3 (2002): 589–635.

Ugalde, Antonio, Frank Bean, and Gilbert Cardenas. "International Return Migration: Findings from a National Survey." *International Migration Review* 13.2 (1979): 235–54.

Última hora del día. "Desfile de gays en la Avenida del Puerto." 30 June 2001.

UNICEF Haïti. *Les enfants d'Haïti en situation particulèrement difficile: Un État de la question*. 1996.

United Nations. UNICEF and IDGPM (Dirección general de promoción de la mujer). *Informe general del Seminario: Situación socioeconómico de la mujer Dominicana*. Santo Domingo: UNICEF, IDGPM, 1988.

Urbina, Nora. "Del armario al mundo." *Rumbo* (Santo Domingo), 30 October 2000.

U.S. Census Bureau. Current Population Reports: Voting and Registration in the

Election of November 2000. Compiled by Amie Jamieson, Hyon B. Shin, and Jennifer Day. Series P20-542. Washington, D.C.: GPO, 2002.

U.S. Citizenship and Immigration Services. *2000 Statistical Yearbook of the Immigration and Naturalization Service.* uscis.gov/graphics/shared/statistics/yearbook/2000/Yearbook2000.pdf.

U.S. Department of State. Bureau of Democracy, Human Rights, and Labor. *Country Reports on Human Rights Practices, Dominican Republic.* 4 March 2002.

———. *Dominican Republic: Country Reports on Human Rights Practices.* 2001.

Vargas Llosa, Mario. *La Fiesta del Chivo.* Madrid: Alfaguara, 2000.

Vásquez, Jaime Lucero. *Anónimos contra el jefe.* Santo Domingo: Taller, 1987.

Vega, Ana Lydia. *Falsas crónicas del sur.* Río Piedras: Editorial Universidad de Puerto Rico, 1991.

———. *Pasión de historia, y otras historias de pasión.* 3rd ed. Buenos Aires: Ediciones de la Flor, 1990.

Vega, Bernardo, ed. *Trujillo ante una corte marcial por violación y extorsión en 1920.* Santo Domingo: Fundación Cultural Dominicana, 1995.

———. *Trujillo y Haiti.* Vol. 1. Santo Domingo: Fundaciòn Cultural Dominicana, 1988.

Veloz Maggiolo, Marcio. *Uña y carne: Memorias de la virilidad.* 2nd ed. Santo Domingo: Cole, 1999.

Vernet, E. Louis. *La domesticité chez nous.* [Port-au-Prince?], 1935.

Wolf, Eric R. "Aspects of Group Relations in a Complex Society: Mexico." *American Anthropologist* 58 (1956): 1065–78.

Wright, Richard. *Black Boy (American Hunger): A Record of Childhood and Youth.* Introduction by Jerry W. Ward Jr. New York: HarperCollins, Perennial Classics, 1998.

Wucker, Michele. *Why the Cocks Fight: Dominicans, Haitians, and the Struggle for Hispaniola.* New York: Hill and Wang, 1999.

Yelvington, Kevin. "The Anthropology of Afro-Latin America and the Caribbean: Diasporic Dimensions." *Annual Review of Anthropology* 30 (2001): 227–60.

———. "Patterns of 'Race,' Ethnicity, Class, and Nationalism." In *Understanding Contemporary Latin America,* edited by Richard S. Hillman, 229–61. Boulder: Lynne Rienner, 2001.

Zentella, Ana Celia. *Growing Up Bilingual: Puerto Rican Children in New York.* Malden, Mass.: Blackwell, 1997.

Index

Lucía M. Suárez, assistant professor in the Department of Romance Languages and Literatures at the University of Michigan, Ann Arbor, is a cultural and literary studies scholar. Suárez has published articles on comparative Caribbean diaspora writings, with a particular focus on women's experiences. She is now working on her second book, *Dance and Citizenship in Brazil.*